KATHERINE HALL PAGE

The BODY in the IVY

A FAITH FAIRCHILD MYSTERY

AVON
An Imprint of HarperCollinsPublishers

AVON BOOKS
An Imprint of HarperCollins*Publishers*
10 East 53rd Street
New York, New York 10022-5299

Copyright © 2006 by Katherine Hall Page
Excerpt from *The Body in the Gallery* copyright © 2008 by Katherine
Hall Page
ISBN: 978-0-06-076366-4
ISBN-10: 0-06-076366-3
www.avonmystery.com

First Avon Books paperback printing: November 2007
First William Morrow hardcover printing: November 2006

Avon Trademark Reg. U.S. Pat. Off. and in Other Countries, Marca
Registrada, Hecho en U.S.A.
HarperCollins® is a registered trademark of HarperCollins Publishers.

Printed in the U.S.A.

10 9 8 7 6 5 4 3 2 1

For Faith Hamlin, without whom...

*Every murderer is probably
somebody's old friend.*

—AGATHA CHRISTIE,
The Murder of Roger Ackroyd

Acknowledgments

As always, many thanks to my agent, Faith Hamlin; my editor, Sarah Durand; Jeanne Bracken, Lincoln Library reference librarian; Ethel Clifford; and David Fine for culinary expertise.

The BODY in the IVY

TRAGEDY AT
PELHAM COLLEGE

Senior Plunges to Death from Tower

Pelham, Ma, May 17 —

The body of Hélène Prince of New York City, a senior at Pelham College, was found early yesterday morning at the base of the 182-foot Gothic tower that dominates the campus, by Professor Robert LaFleur of the Math Department. LaFleur, who was passing the spot on his way to his office, told reporters that at first he thought someone had left a white garment of some kind in the abundant bed of ivy that grows beneath the tower. Upon closer inspection, he determined it was the lifeless body of a young woman and sought help. Upon arrival, campus police pronounced Miss Prince dead, an apparent suicide.

An art history major, Miss Prince had planned to leave for a job in Paris, France, immediately after graduation. Friends and family have said that she did not appear depressed, but was looking forward to graduation and her new job. She leaves her mother and father, Mr. and Mrs. Theodore Reynolds Prince, and her twin sister, Elaine, also a Pelham senior. The Pelham police have not released any further details pending their investigation. Expressing deep regret and in consultation with the Prince family,

Pelham President Virginia Franklin said commencement ceremonies would proceed as planned and that she was sure this was what "Prin," as she was known, would have wanted. "She was a campus leader and beloved by all. She will be missed," Franklin said. In lieu of flowers, the family requests contributions to the Hélène Prince Scholarship Fund at Pelham College.

From the May 17, 1970, issue of
The Pelham Town News

One

Faith Sibley Fairchild stared out the train window, the book she had brought to while away the trip resting unopened in her lap. The scenery wasn't particularly engrossing—yards backing up to the tracks, some with fences or hedges in an attempt to block the view and every so often a town center, a glimpse of a bandstand in the middle of a green or a white clapboard church with a spire, followed by a row of pines. A New England flip book. The churches reminded Faith of First Parish in Aleford, Massachusetts, where her husband, the Reverend Thomas Fairchild, tended the spiritual needs of the community while Faith quite literally catered to its physical well-being, continuing the business she had started in her native New York City in the late 1980s. Her clientele looked different—if a man was in a tux and a woman in a gown it was either the opening night of the Boston

Symphony or a wedding—but the food was of the same quality. It wasn't a question of serving no boiled dinners before their time, but never serving them at all.

June had finally arrived and the flickering shades of green outside were deeply comforting after a winter of record snowfall that had stretched well into April. The cold had clung to May, and Faith found herself placing her palm on the window to feel the warmth of the day's bright sunshine. She was alone in the row of seats that stretched to both sides of the aisle. Later trains would be packed as Bostonians headed north for weekends by the shore.

Alone. This was such an unusual state of affairs that she wasn't quite sure what she was feeling. When she wasn't involved with Tom and their two children, eleven-year-old Ben and eight-year-old Amy, she was at work with her staff or active in other Aleford pursuits that mostly revolved around the church and the kids' school. Technology meant she was always within reach. She slipped her cell out of her purse. No service. She smiled. What she was feeling snapped into focus as fast as the TGV, the swift French train they had taken last summer from Paris to Lyon. Faith felt absolutely wonderful, suspended for a few brief hours with no responsibilities whatsoever. Wonderful. The book slipped unnoticed to the floor.

The train was making that clickety-clack train noise that never failed to excite her, bringing with it the notion of all those other trains—Trans Siberian, Orient Express, Canadian Pacific—and trips, some imagined; some real. She was back in Grand Central Station with her sister, Hope, one year younger, pulling away from

4

their parents to spot Camp Merrydale's banner, darting toward it squealing excitedly with several dozen other girls, accompanied by counselors who already looked exhausted.

Another journey. One of her camp friends lived outside Philadelphia, and twice a year Faith would be placed on the train in Penn Station and be met at the 30th Street Station in Philly. She could still remember the names of the stops on the way and her disappointment when she discovered that Cherry Hill, New Jersey, bore little resemblance to what she had been envisioning—a town filled with acres of delicate blossoms ripening into sweet ruby-red fruit.

She'd missed the glory days of train travel, Faith thought regretfully. The Twentieth Century from New York to Chicago. Nick and Nora Charles traveling coast to coast in style with Vuitton steamer trunks and martinis in the club car. And her favorite, Hitchcock's *North by Northwest;* Cary Grant and Eva Marie Saint in a compartment larger than most NYC studio apartments. Faith thought wistfully of the meal they had consumed— brook trout—with a Gibson first for Grant. Fine linens, cutlery, china, and glassware—fresh flowers on the table. The only sustenance offered on this train consisted of prepackaged sandwiches with expiration dates so far in the future they were ready-made time capsules, and a machine that offered the ubiquitous snacks that Americans seemed unable to exist without, despite the absence of either nourishment or flavor. Faith had packed her own lunch—smoked turkey, watercress, and a dollop of mango chutney on buckwheat-walnut bread, one of her assistant Niki's delectable blondies, some muscat grapes,

5

and a bottle of Voss water. She wasn't hungry yet, and besides, having the food was like having a few hefty deposits in the bank—or a number of dinners in the freezer. You were tempted to use them, but it felt equally good just to know they were there.

The train swayed slightly from side to side, the motion keeping time with the sound of the tracks. Another movie, *Silver Streak*. Gene Wilder is in the bar with Ned Beatty, supposedly a vitamins salesman, who is telling Wilder he's in "for the ride of your life." Pick a woman, any woman. "It's something about the movement of the train that does it." Faith *did* find herself thinking about Tom, heading by plane in the opposite direction for the weeklong annual meeting of the denomination in Virginia. Beatty strikes out with Jill Clayburgh, who responds to his obvious come-on by pouring her drink in his lap to "cool" him down. And it's Wilder who gets to eat dinner with her—another well-appointed table and menu: macédoine of fruit, beef oriental with rice and carrots, apple pie à la mode, a bottle of Mouton Cadet 1961, and several bottles of Korbel in an elegant champagne bucket back in another spacious compartment. *Ah, for those days.* Faith sighed to herself and resolved to watch all three movies upon her return. Plus Agatha Christie's *Murder on the Orient Express*.

Another train going in the opposite direction hurtled by and for a moment the sensation of motion was suspended as her car traveled parallel to the next. Then the passing train built up speed. Faith looked at the people in the cars. The train was as empty as the one she was traveling on. There were only two people in the car moving rapidly by her now. Her cinematic musings took hold again. More Hitchcock—Uncle Charlie, Joseph Cotton, trying to push his niece off the train to her death. And more Christie—Margaret Rutherford as Miss Marple views a murder in the train next to hers in *Murder She Said*. Faith continued to gaze into the passing compartments. It would be so easy. A blunt instrument or a sharp knife, the victim shoved under the seat, not to be discovered until North Station in Boston, the murderer having stepped off in Exeter, New Hampshire—or stayed on. Tomorrow's headline nonchalantly reading today's paper wherever the trip ended.

The rattle of the two trains subsided and once more she stared at the landscape. She laughed at herself and realized her own book had fallen to the floor. She retrieved it. There was no body beneath the seat.

Midnight's Mirror by Barbara Bailey Bishop. Faith had never read anything by the bestselling author and thought she'd better at least skim the book. Barbara Bailey Bishop was her employer and her house on Bishop's Island was Faith's final destination.

"Of course I'm flattered that she wants me, but it's impossible. You understand, don't you? I can't leave Tom and the kids to fend for themselves for a whole week."

"Don't you ever think about what might be best for you and your business? An endorsement from Barbara Bailey Bishop would be priceless." Faith's sister, Hope, had sounded more than a little exasperated.

"I know that, but I simply can't take that much time off. If her island were within commuting distance of Aleford that would be different, but it isn't from what you're saying."

"No, it isn't. It's not commuting distance from any-where and that's why she likes it. You know how it is, the richer you are, the more remote you can be. But back to my point. Everything can certainly be worked out. In fact, I *have* worked it out and there's nothing to stop you from taking the job."

Faith had been surprised her sister hadn't started with her plan, including transportation instructions and a list of what to pack. Motherhood—Hope's little Quentin was almost a year and a half old—hadn't cramped either Hope's or her husband's style. They still prided them-selves on their workaholic lifestyle—could Quentin the father really be billing ninety hours a week? Doable with the aid of a nanny and a housekeeper, both absolute treasures, and the BlackBerry chip that seemed to be implanted in Hope's brain. The only change had been to move from a choice apartment on Manhattan's West Side to a choice town house on Manhattan's East Side.

Her sister's call had come just as Faith was leaving for her own place of employment, the Have Faith catering kitchen on the outskirts of Aleford. Hope had been so excited that it had taken a few moments for Faith to understand what this "once-in-a-lifetime" job entailed. Apparently the author, Barbara Bailey Bishop, was host-ing a mini-reunion of her Pelham College chums on her own private island and wanted Faith to cater it. There would be ten people in all, counting Faith. When she wasn't feeding them, Faith was to consider herself one of the guests, a novel approach to help and a first for her.

"The house sounds fantastic—ten bedrooms all with private baths, a spa, indoor and outdoor pools, tennis courts, gardens. Your dream kitchen, I'm sure," Hope had gushed. Faith's first cynical thought had been to wonder about the septic system, knowing from the Fairchilds' own small vacation abode on an island off the coast of Maine—sans spa—what a strain multiple baths could mean, but apparently "BeBe," as her fans called her, had this all figured out.

Hope had pressed on. "It's only January, so you have plenty of time to work things out with Niki and the rest of your staff for any dates you've already committed to for that week in June. Ben will be out of school and in camp by then and Amy can come with me to the house in Amagansett. You know how much she adores being with the baby, and I'm planning to work from there a lot this summer, just like last year."

"And Tom?" Faith had asked ruefully.

"You know very well that once his groupies hear you're out of town they'll be falling all over themselves to bring him horrid casseroles and loaves of disgustingly healthy bread. Plus, your friends will invite him to dinner," Hope had said dismissively.

Faith knew it was true. Those dedicated handmaidens of the Lord's representative here on earth, privately referred to by Faith and Hope as "Tom's groupies," would make sure that he wanteth for naught. The same with the Fairchilds' circle of friends. It might be the twenty-first century, but a woman alone while her mate is away contents herself with Lean Cuisine and *Desperate Housewives* reruns while a man alone is the toast of the town.

"If for no other reason, think about the money, Faith!"

Faith *had* been thinking about the money ever since Hope had mentioned the fee, an astronomical amount that was easily double what she had ever made on any prior job.

"Why does she want me in particular? Did her secretary say anything about that?"

Hope had made little tsk-tsking noises. "If you undervalue yourself, everyone else will, too."

"That's not what I mean. I know I'm good, but how does she know? It's been years since I worked in the city."

"According to her secretary, Owen, that's exactly why she does want you. She was at the Stansteads' Christmas party and a number of other events you handled, including the ones at Gracie Mansion. He said something about her never having forgotten the fennel soup you did and some kind of special New York chocolate dessert bars."

" 'Manhattan Morsels' I called them. They *were* good. I used to add a little applesauce, as in the Big Apple, to keep them moist. Hmmm, I should do those again."

"And you can. In June for Barbara and her Pelham friends. It will be fun. You know how much I love getting together with my Pelham buds. These women are older—I think they graduated in sixty-nine or seventy—but—"

Faith had interrupted her sister. "I know, I know. Pelham women are special." Pelham was one of the nation's oldest and most prestigious women's colleges and Hope's loyalty bordered on fanaticism. Yet it was true that an inordinate number of the college's graduates had made names for themselves—and Pelham—in everything from politics to the silver screen. Having attended single-sex schools from kindergarten on, Faith had opted for a coed university, but when she was with Hope and her Pelham friends, she often thought she might have made a mistake.

"She saw you in the alumnae magazine. I sent in a picture of little Quentin's christening, the one with my classmates, and since you're his godmother, you were in the middle holding him, next to me, 'sister, Faith Sibley Fairchild.' You should thank Pelham and me!"

Her sister had figured it all out. It was *the* job of Faith's career. Barbara Bailey Bishop was notoriously reclusive. No one, except presumably her agent and publisher, knew what her real name was, not even her alma mater, Hope had revealed. The author was very generous to the college, but with the proviso that she not appear and not be known. Virtually anonymous donations. Fans guessed at the year she had graduated, but no one knew which Pelham "girl" she had been. She made J. D. Salinger look like Paris Hilton.

Interviews with Barbara Walters and others were conducted in the manner of Mafia informants. Ms. Bailey appeared completely in the shadows. The author photos on her book jackets were dark silhouettes, changing little over the years, which suggested the classic profile and tumbling tresses might now owe more to art than nature. She didn't tour or attend conventions. Print interviews, when granted, were conducted by phone or through her longtime secretary. Her oft-stated reason for all this was that she wanted to have a life of her own, and if easily identified she would never be able to walk around in public. Although Faith thought the Garbo act a bit extreme, there was no doubt that the author would be mobbed wherever she went in virtually every corner of the world. Her books, a combination of romance and suspense, were hugely popular with both men and women. She'd won enough awards for a bank of trophy cases in the U.S. and started at the top of every bestseller list, staying there for months, yet it was the Europeans who treated her as a *femme sérieuse* on a par with Proust. She had been awarded every French and Italian literary prize. Every year the literati bemoaned the shortsightedness of the Nobel committee. Symposia abroad, with scholars debating the meaning of the color of the heroine's Capri pants and the like, were held in increasing numbers each year.

"Millions, no make that billions, of people would kill for the chance to meet her. I can't believe you're hesitating!"

Faith couldn't believe she was, either. "Okay, I'll do it."

"Good," Hope had said. "I already told them you would."

The whistle blew. The train was approaching a crossing. Faith looked at the gates and cars lined up behind them. The whistle blew again. Funny how the scene outside changed as she altered her gaze. Looking off into the distance, objects were easily identifiable; next to the tracks, everything was a blur. The opposite of life, she thought. You could tell what things were when they were in front of you, but not when they were far away. Or could you?

The drone of the jet engines had not lulled Roberta Dolan to sleep. Even if she had not been so excited, she wouldn't have wanted to miss a moment of the flight. She had never flown first class before and the experience of having an attendant respond to her slightest need was exhilarating. The instant her glass was empty more deliciously cold Pellegrino water appeared; champagne had been offered, but Roberta tried to keep her body free from such toxins. She did accept another helping of the smoked Scottish salmon appetizer, though, with a slight pang of vegan guilt.

The call had come in late February when the weather in Calistoga had been bleak for paradise—rain and more rain. She had been surprised when the owner of the spa where she had been working for the last few years summoned her to the phone. No one ever called her at work. In fact, no one called her much at all. A man's voice had asked her if she was Roberta Dolan, and of course she was. That is, she was now, back where she started from, after two marriages, the second worse than the first if that was possible—and it was. "Yes?" she'd responded, and he'd introduced himself as Owen, the writer Barbara Bailey Bishop's personal assistant. Ms. Bishop was hosting a small gathering of female friends in June on her private island and wanted to provide massages in the spa. Would Ms. Dolan be willing to be the on-site masseuse? All expenses paid and a fee that was equal to what Roberta made in a year. She had gasped and accepted immediately. She had been so stunned that it wasn't until after she'd hung up that she'd thought to wonder why world-famous Barbara Bailey Bishop wanted her in particular. Yes, she was very good and the spa's star masseuse—highly skilled in Swedish, Shiatsu, Reiki, and reflexology—but how would Bishop on the East Coast know that? Unless she had come to the spa incognito! Roberta had spent many happy hours during the intervening weeks thinking back over her clientele, choosing first one sheeted and turbaned figure then another as her benefactress. She'd also spent many hours preparing herself for her task. She did not know how old the women were or what conditions they might present, so she had prepared herself for all possibilities, meditating and centering, connecting the energy of her *hara* chakra, her lower abdomen, with her hands—letting the breath of her body transform itself into touch. She did this briefly at work before each massage, but engaged in the practice at length when she was home. She tried to visualize the island, the women, meditating in silence without her rain forest music so her mind could hear the sound of the ocean and the wind. At times she thought she could hear the low murmur of the women's voices—the receivers of her gift of touch.

The tickets and instructions had arrived shortly after the conversation, and the intervening months had passed quickly as she made her preparations. She shipped the stones she had collected over the years for hot rock massage, perfect for bringing gentle, soothing heat to each chakra and the area around it. Roberta treasured her stones. Then there were her oils for massage and aromatherapy. As a world-famous author, Barbara Bailey Bishop was bound to be stressed by the constant pressure to produce her books. Everyone has stress, of course; it's one of the life forces. So Roberta had packed her special chamomile oil, and tea. She gathered the flowers herself and prided herself on her clients' reactions, stress reduction the natural way. And lavender. It was calming as well and wonderful for hair and skin. Skin. She'd mixed some oregano oil for cellulite. The smell sometimes made her clients hungry, but there was no doubt about its effect. Finally, she'd included hypoallergenic oils and creams, even plain vegetable oil infused with some extracts of orange, vanilla, and ginger from the grocery store for anyone severely allergic. If you can eat something without a reaction, it can be used on your skin. She sipped some more water. Hydrate, always hydrate—especially on a plane. She hoped she had thought of everything. There wouldn't be any way to replace something she'd forgotten to pack. Owen had assured her that Ms. Bailey's personal spa was fully equipped with a massage couch and chair, plus an abundance of linens, including robes. Everything she would or could need had been shipped several weeks ago, so that all Roberta had had to do was wait. And now, she thought, looking out the window at the piles of fluffy white clouds, the wait was over.

Hartford at rush hour. Hartford *always* seemed to be at rush hour, Lucy Stapleton fumed. She was listening to Anne Tyler's *Ladder of Years*. It was about a mother who runs away from home. A mother who actually does it, acts on that impulse all mothers have at some point. You're on the way to pick up milk and the thought that you could just keep driving becomes so tantalizing you have to pull over, get your bearings—and eventually your milk. Well, Lucy had left her home behind, but she would be back in a week. Ned would miss her, but not that much. Would enjoy the solitude with the girls gone, too. Young women did such extraordinary things these days. At their age, she'd spent the summer playing tennis, sailing, flirting. Callie was building houses in Nicaragua, or at least Lucy thought that was the right country. One of those places. And not because it would look good on her college applications; she was done with all that, starting at NYU in the fall, much to Ned's annoyance. Now that his alma mater was taking girls, he figured that's where his daughters should be going—even if he wasn't comfortable with the change, an opinion he voiced vociferously. When Lucy pointed out this might be what was discouraging the girls from considering Yale, he tempered his remarks. When they still weren't interested, he'd said, "Let them go to Pelham," and couldn't understand why his wife wasn't pushing her old school. NYU! What kind of people went there? Certainly not his kind, and he was damned sure he wasn't going to pay for it—until Lucy quietly told him she would if he didn't. Then there was the house-building project in Central America. "Dad!" Callie had exclaimed when he'd objected—she'd stopped calling him "Daddy" last summer, Lucy noticed. "I want to do this. It's important work. The world is not just Connecticut and a very small part of New York City, you know!" He'd freshened his drink, and Lucy's. "Talk to me in five years, or less, when you've gotten this out of your system, my little bleeding heart." Their older daughter was at Stanford and spending the summer as a PA on an independent film that she had assured them would take Sundance by storm. Ned had wanted to know if it was X-rated, and had elicited a "Daddy!"—Becky hadn't followed her sister's example. Both of them called Lucy "Mom" and, except as toddlers, always had.

16

The traffic started to move. Lucy looked at the outside temperature gauge on the dash. It was hot for June, which made sense since it had been excruciatingly cold until late May.

When Barbara's assistant, Owen, had phoned in February to invite her for a week on Bishop's Island, she had hesitated. She hadn't seen the author in many years. She had told him she'd get back to him, then discussed it with Ned when she picked him up at the train.

"Go. Be indulged. It sounds like quite a place."

The decision was obviously of little interest to him.

So she had called back and accepted. "A small, fun group of ladies," Owen had said. "Barbara is sorry you two haven't stayed in touch and wants you to join them."

A fun group of ladies. She'd been with groups of ladies her entire life, some a whole lot more fun than others. It remained to be seen where these ladies would fall.

It wasn't that she minded using Barbara Bailey Bishop's private plane. In fact, it was a kick, but Gwen Mansfield would have preferred to use her own. She had no trouble admitting to herself that it was all about control. Her whole life, her whole career, was based on taking control and maintaining it. She'd been divorced and then widowed, admittedly a loss of control on that one. The investment counseling she'd started to do after business school had been targeted on women, and after the thousandth time she'd heard herself deliver the same lines about female financial empowerment, she wrote them down. Right time, right audience—women in the eighties. The first book became a financial bible; she became a regular on every show from Oprah to Louis Rukeyser, and her firm, the Mansfield Group, was still a wildly successful alternative to mostly men in suits at Smith Barney. She employed men, of course, and they dressed in suits, even on Fridays, but Armani not Brooks Brothers. Some of her female employees favored the same haute business couture, but many opted for a softer Eileen Fisher look. In sum, the Mansfield Group was *not* your father's brokerage house.

The attendant offered her a glass of champagne. "Dom Pérignon 1990."

Gwen barely looked up from her laptop. "Laphroaig, a few rocks, and something to eat."

"We have some nice smoked salmon. Ms. Bishop has it sent over from Scotland—"

"Spare me the details. I'm sure it's a fisherman who catches the fish in the morning, races to his smokehouse, and has it on the plane the next day or whenever. Whole grain bread, no crusts, cut in triangles, and unsalted butter and capers on the side."

The drink, in a Baccarat tumbler naturally, arrived, followed swiftly by a refill in a new glass and the food. Gwen put her laptop on sleep and set it aside. The scotch had given her a pleasant buzz and the Scottish salmon looked good. When Bishop's assistant, Owen, had called in February asking her to provide a weeklong seminar in money management for a group of his employer's friends on the author's private island, Gwen had said no. She hadn't done groups for years. He mentioned the fee, more than she expected, but at this point in her life, she could afford to turn it down. She'd thanked him for the offer, said something about being honored or similar bullshit, and hung up. That afternoon flowers arrived, nothing hokey like roses or orchids, but winter whites: peonies, lisianthus, ranunculus, lilacs, tiny dahlias, and snowberry branches in a large blue and white Ming ginger jar, the top nestled in a cushioned scarlet silk box that accompanied the arrangement. Gwen collected Chinese porcelain. The piece was exquisite, breathtaking with the flowers, each petal perfect, each scent heady but not cloying. It was like Gwen's perfume, a mixture made only for her. She had searched for a card, the name of the florist. Her housekeeper had said that it had been left with the doorman. They were at Gwen's duplex in New York's San Remo, a business pied-à-terre. She also had a house in Palm Beach and one in L.A., plus a suite at Claridge's in London.

"Ms. Bishop hopes you are enjoying the flowers." The call had come the next day. Nothing crass, no "She hopes you will reconsider." Just "Ms. Bishop hopes you are enjoying the flowers." It was all about control and Gwen took charge. "I think I'll be able to work that week into my schedule after all," she'd said. She'd always admired a good seduction.

The prospect was exciting. A week filled with music, her music and that of other dedicated musicians. Rachel Gold had had no idea the famous author Barbara Bailey Bishop was a music lover. She was turning her home on her own private island over to a select group, which she'd asked Rachel to lead. Even before Bishop's assistant,

Owen, had mentioned the fee for Rachel's services, she had decided to accept the offer. When he mentioned how much money was involved, Rachel felt dizzy and had to sit down. Her reputation as a classical guitarist was international, but limited. She was known as a "musician's musician" and her following veered toward the cultlike. Her recordings were not about to go gold. An old joke, but as true now as when Ms. Gold had started her career in the early seventies. The call had come in February, and thinking about the gathering in June had taken Rachel through the bitter winter days—days that sapped her spirit. It would be her own mini-Marlboro, mini-Tanglewood. Her mother had rejoiced with her and begged her to use some of the money to buy decent clothes. "If only the real Loehmann's was still around!" Mrs. Gold had spent wisely and well under the guidance of Mrs. Loehmann herself, making pilgrimages to Brooklyn each season for bargain known and unknown designer originals. When she was a child, Rachel had loved to watch her mother get dressed for the Met or Carnegie Hall. The swish of taffeta, glitter of tiny jet beads on filmy silk, the smell of Arpège—the Lanvin atomizer reverently lifted from the clutter on her mother's dressing table to deliver the final touch. Daytime wear was as ritualistic. Her mother would no more have left the apartment without matching hat, gloves, and purse than ride naked down Fifth Avenue in one of those touristy horse-drawn carriages.

Rachel was a regular on Amtrak, shuttling to Boston, D.C., Providence, but she'd never traveled on the Acela first class. Owen—or was it Mr. Owen?—had apologized for the inconvenience of changing trains and had offered to send a car or Ms. Bishop's private plane. Rachel had gently but firmly rejected his suggestions. Things like that, rock star accoutrements, made her nervous. A train ticket was all she required.

The motion of the train was lulling her to sleep. She felt her eyelids grow heavy and flutter. She gave in, smiling to herself. This week will be a dream come true, she thought.

"You'd better take my car, since you'll be dropping the dogs off."

"No can do. No time."

Phoebe James looked at her husband. Wes had been sitting in the kitchen leisurely reading both the *Times* and *Wall Street Journal* for over an hour while he ate his weekly three-minute boiled egg, accompanied by one unbuttered slice of wheat toast, half a grapefruit, and one cup of black coffee. Now he was slinging the strap of his laptop case over one shoulder and sprinting for the door.

"But if I have to take the dogs, I'll miss my plane! And the kennel is on your way!"

"Not on my way, Phebes, at least a mile *out* of my way. Have the twins do it."

"You know the twins left for work at eight!" Phoebe felt the familiar rush of anger that seemed to accompany most of the conversations she had with her family these days. It mounted as she thought about what missing the plane would mean. All the arrangements had been made, the connections. It would mean missing the whole thing. Her week!

A week off. A week alone. Well, with some other

women, but she was sure she'd have plenty of time to herself. And she'd be out of the house. Away from everything—and everyone. She took a deep breath, a yoga cleansing breath learned during a brief try at salutations to the sun as a way to combat insomnia. It didn't work. Or rather, she didn't. Wait, "No judging"—that was what the teacher intoned several times a class. "Yoga is not about judging." Phoebe was judging now. Judging the extremely well-preserved fifty-five-year-old corporate lawyer standing in front of her, poised in mid-flight, with a slight smile on his face. She wanted to smack it right off.

"You don't have to board the dogs. You can leave them here." He turned away from her and put his hand on the doorknob.

"You know I can't do that. Molly and Piper would die of starvation, and poop all over the house because no one would walk them, and even if you did, they'd get away from you like that time last year. I thought we'd never see them again."

He opened the door and stepped out into the garage. "Well, they're your dogs; do what you want."

And he was gone.

She thought about calling the town recreation department and getting a message to the twins. They couldn't carry their cells at work. One was lifeguarding at the pool and the other coaching tennis in the day camp. Imagining the call that would follow—the reluctance displayed by whichever daughter had decided to respond—took Phoebe out of the house with the two Irish terriers and into her car. She certainly wouldn't have a good time if she had to spend it worrying about the only creatures in her Short Hills, New Jersey, home who seemed to respond to her. Wait, her son, Josh, responded, but it wasn't the way a mother prays for, or a father, either, and that's why her son was at some wilderness camp in Colorado where they apparently had to hollow out logs, make their canoes, and carve their paddles before they could set off on a trip that cost as much as a year's tuition at college. Plus they had to cook all their meals, wash their clothes in streams while doing push-ups, and so forth. It was intended to make some kind of man out of him, but Phoebe's secret fear was that Josh would return angrier than before. Wes had arranged the whole thing and Josh was westward-bound before Phoebe had sewn one nametag on or seriously studied the brochure.

When the dogs saw where they were going, they weren't happy. Phoebe had to drag them in from the parking lot, and they complained vociferously as she left the kennel. It all took forever. She was several blocks from home when she faced the fact that there was no way she would make her flight. She was tempted to pull over and sob, but decided to wait until she reached the comfort of her own home before breaking down. She'd seen a woman crying alone in her car in the Short Hills Mall parking lot a few years ago and the image still haunted her, as well as the fact that Phoebe hadn't knocked on the window to offer help.

Pulling into her street, she was surprised to see a very shiny Lincoln Town Car parked in front of the house. Turning into the driveway, she was even more surprised to see a pleasant-looking young man in a chauffeur's uniform get out and walk toward her. She stopped the car and rolled down the window, but didn't get out of her Mercedes wagon. He seemed an unlikely mugger or rapist, but you couldn't be too careful in this neighborhood, as the prominently displayed alarm system signs on every lawn—symbolic of the inhabitants' every worst nightmare—attested.

"Mrs. James?"

Phoebe nodded. That seemed safe enough.

"Ms. Bishop sent me. She thought it might be more convenient for you to fly from Morristown. A small plane is waiting. And she didn't want you to have to try to figure out how to get there on your own. I'll wait in the car while you finish your preparations." He smiled.

A very pleasant face.

Phoebe got out of the car.

"I don't know what to say. You see, I'm running late and—"

"You're not running late now. Take your time. You have all the time in the world."

She walked into the house, dazed. Her suitcases were by the door and the light raincoat she thought she'd better bring was draped across them. She'd been ready for days. Ready as soon as she got the phone call in February from a man named Owen who worked for Barbara Bailey Bishop. Phoebe was being invited to some kind of reader's focus group on the author's private island for a whole week. She didn't take in all the details, but assumed it must be because she'd graduated from Pelham. Although he hadn't mentioned Pelham. But how else would BeBe have gotten her name? Ms. Bishop was an alum, although Phoebe didn't know which class. In the last reunion class record book—she'd never attended a reunion, but conscientiously wrote for the book every five years—Phoebe had listed the author as her favorite. Someone must have seen it and told Bishop about it. So what if it would have been more in keeping with Pelham English Department standards to list Joyce Carol Oates? Bishop might never win a National Book Award, but her words completely transported this reader from her own existence to another world, a much more interesting and ultimately satisfying one, with a frisson of danger along the way.

Phoebe picked up her bags, punched in the alarm code, and strode down the front steps. The driver immediately got out of the car and came to help her. Was this the mysterious Owen? Phoebe felt as if she were stepping into the pages of a Barbara Bailey Bishop novel, and as she leaned into the soft leather of the back seat of the car, a thought crossed her mind: how had Owen, BeBe, or whoever else was involved known Phoebe was going to miss her plane? As quickly as it came, she chased it away. Of course they would know. She was going to be taken care of this week, *her* needs anticipated and met. She sighed happily. She wouldn't need her yoga breathing—or her Zoloft—at all.

Christine Barker pressed the icy glass of ginger ale against her forehead. She thought these bouts were over. The first time she was sure it was some kind of food poisoning and let it go, happy to have survived. Then came the next—and the next. Then the doctors. No sign of an ulcer, no allergies, nothing. Perhaps Ms. Barker might want to consult a different kind of doctor? Ms. Barker did not. If it were all in her head, she'd deal with it. Then the nausea, the relentless vomiting—never at the same time of day or night—stopped. Sometimes for years. Now it was back after one of those long hiatuses. Today was the third day. The day she was supposed to leave. She'd kept a few dry saltines down and this was her second glass of ginger ale. Oddly enough, she wasn't tired, although she'd slept little these last days. She felt light, cleansed—no, wrong word. Just light. "Cleansed" suggested what the doctors had intimated.

She really didn't see how she could go and was glad now she hadn't accepted all the arrangements the man Owen had proposed. She'd make her own way; she'd told him and let him know which flight she'd be on. So far she hadn't made the call. Not one way or the other.

The air inside her house was humid, heavy with the threat of summer. Although she was on the water here in the Chesapeake, it could still be brutally hot.

She stepped out onto the back porch. There was a slight breeze. She sat down in a wicker chair she'd rescued from the town dump, repaired, and painted bright blue. A soft cushion covered with a remnant of William Morris chintz from one of the fancy Georgetown decorating stores protected the backs of her legs from the uncomfortable and unattractive fretwork these chairs invariably produced.

Everything was packed. Her tools, slides, books, note cards—and a few clothes and toiletries. She *could* go if she decided to. She sipped her drink slowly, carefully. She closed her eyes and played her favorite game, "What can I smell?" Over the years she had perfected her olfactory acumen and could sit for an hour or more isolating the fragrance of her flowers, the smell of her vegetables, herbs, the scent of the grass, the trees, the shrubs, the soil, even—occasionally—an animal. She'd turned over one of the raised beds before she got sick, and it beckoned like Odysseus' sirens with their irresistible song, "We know all things which shall be hereafter on the earth." So apt. But the money beckoned with another chant that would have melted any wax.

She was stunned when the author Barbara Bailey Bishop's assistant had called in February and asked her to present a weeklong series of lectures on topics of her own choosing to a group of dedicated gardeners on Bishop's private island, noted for both its cultivated and wild landscapes. She had not known that Bishop, an avid gardener, was a fan of the column Christine wrote for a small gardening magazine. Yes, she'd had articles in *H&G* and some other publications, but was best known by the cognoscenti for this column, "Young Herbaceous" (no longer as appropriate as it was when she'd started it). Bishop's assistant had named a fee that instantly became a new greenhouse with all the bells and whistles. She'd said yes right away and had spent the intervening months planning the greenhouse and the talks, happily going through her slides. One would focus on Lady Salisbury, Britain's preeminent historic garden designer, who had labored for over thirty years on those of her former home, Hatfield House, a Jacobean palace. Christine had corresponded with the Dowager Marchioness for many years, and whenever Chris was in England they chatted in person, spending many golden hours lauding organic insect control, despising pesticides, and above all, extolling the importance of talking to one's plants—*really* talking to them. Another session would focus on dirt, a marvelously complex topic dear to every true gardener's heart. Another, a full day of walking around the island, a kind of "what would you do if you were head gardener/landscaper?" day. A challenging, fun day.

The panic hadn't set in until last week when she realized that she was actually going to have to do it all. Go to a new place. Be with strangers. Talk to them. It was one thing to give a single lecture to a garden club. That was bad enough. Quite another to be the captive star attraction for an entire week.

Besides, she wasn't used to talking to that many people. Plants, yes, people, no. She took a deep breath. Her mouth and nose were filled with the scent of the garden. She picked Perdita to concentrate on, a fragrant apricot-colored rose from the British rosarian David Austin. It would continue to bloom all summer. "Rosarian," a funny word—was Austin a Rotarian, as well? Her glass was almost empty. She stood up and stretched. Her friend Emily would keep a close eye on the garden. There, she did, too, have people to talk to besides plants.

As quickly as it came, her mysterious illness would leave her. She could feel it ebbing away now as she drained the glass of ginger ale. She would be tired for several days, but she'd be able to control the nausea by eating lightly, virtually not at all. She could pass the whole thing off as a new diet she was trying. It was a group of women. They'd understand. Probably too well.

It was almost eight o'clock. She'd be able to make the noon flight. Christine went into the house to make her call. She *had* to have that greenhouse.

Margaret Howard was ecstatic. At last, one of her major goals as Pelham's president was about to be fulfilled: she was going to meet Barbara Bailey Bishop and she was going to accept the author's most generous donation to date—an endowed chair plus funds for the renovation of the library's writing center, a place students went for both help and enrichment. The new center would publish a journal of student writings, accepting submissions from sister schools, as well. She glanced down at the speedometer. Whoa! She hadn't realized her little Mini-Cooper could go this fast. A meeting with the Art History Department chair, who was leaving with a group of students for a tour of Tuscany, had taken more time than Margaret had planned. She couldn't wait to get to the island. "A small house party," Bishop's assistant, Owen, had said when he called with the news in February. He also asked that the president not make the announcement public until June, when Ms. Bishop would join her in releasing it to the press. Margaret had not even told Charles, her husband, which had not been that difficult since they tended to be like ships in the night, a commuter marriage since the beginning.

When she thought back, it seemed as if she had wanted to be president of Pelham from the moment she had stepped on campus for her admissions interview in 1964. Subconsciously at first, then with each passing year, the goal emerged from hiding until it dominated her thoughts. Margaret had used her Pelham time as training: class president for three years, student body president her fourth, and a visibly active presence on campus continuously. Then came the period of exile as she earned her credentials and polished her C.V., each job a step higher, a step closer to the prize. When the call had come seven years ago, she was more than ready. Charles was used to being "Mr. Howard" at the various campuses along the way, showing up for photo op events and holidays. They owned a small town house near Dupont Circle; D.C. had been the base of Charles's operations since law school. Governments came and went, but both parties relied on his nonpartisan expertise in the area of international trade agreements. It wasn't a loveless marriage. They cared about each other, enjoying each spouse's successes. It was a marriage of equal partners—at least that was how Margaret viewed it—and if she sometimes smelled perfume that she knew wasn't hers in their D.C. bedroom, she never mentioned it. The arrangement suited her. She needed a consort and it wouldn't do to rock the boat.

Boat! Owen had offered to send a car to bring her to the Bishop's Island boat, but Margaret would be driving to Ohio to see her mother after the week on the island, and if there was a place she could leave the Mini, that would be easier. There was, he assured her, and she wasn't to worry about time. Someone would meet her whenever she arrived.

Margaret wondered who the other guests might be. Luminaries from the literary world? Bishop's identity had become a campus tease over the years, with some asserting that she didn't exist at all, but was a group of

30

several writers working together. Was this what Margaret would find? That the nom de plume was a feather boa?

The assistant had mentioned that the house had a spa, plus indoor and outdoor pools. Accordingly she'd packed her workout clothes and a bathing suit, but she wouldn't be wearing it in public. She'd struggled with her weight all her life, "big bones" her mother had said disapprovingly when Margaret reached puberty. The big bones had grown bigger; she'd grown taller—and even looking at a piece of cake added a pound. Academic robes covered a multitude of sins, but she had decided long before her Pelham graduation that she wasn't going to rely on clothing to camouflage her girth. She'd stay thin, or at least thinnish, and she had. But she still wouldn't wear a bathing suit in front of what she was sure would be a gathering of the beautiful people. Ecstasy filled her again. It would be a fabulous week. When would Barbara make the announcement? In her mind, Margaret was on a first-name basis with the author ever since the call came. There would be many pleasant hours discussing plans with Barbara; Maggie had brought photos and drawings of the existing library space. And as a hostess gift she'd had a Pelham chair shipped to Barbara's New York address, the one the assistant had given for correspondence. She hoped the writer would appreciate the double entendre.

Almost there. Almost there. What a triumph for Pelham. What a triumph for her.

The train was slowing to a crawl as it pulled into the station. Faith had finished every morsel she'd brought with her and read several chapters of *Midnight's Mirror*. No doubt about it, Bishop could spin a page-turning tale. The late morning light flattened the scene outside the window, casting shadows that turned ordinary objects into dramatic images. The one cast by a signal post looked exactly like a turreted tower.

Two

"Mrs. Fairchild?" A man dressed in Dickies, work clothes Faith had come to associate with New England workmen, reached for her bags as she stepped onto the platform. His trousers' knife-point creases and shirt's total lack of wrinkles set him apart from those familiar to her, though. The clothes weren't new—no sheen on the fabric—but they had been ironed to a fare-thee-well.

"Yes?"

"Barbara Bailey Bishop asked me to meet your train and drive you to the dock." He looked middle-aged, which meant he could be anywhere from forty to seventy in these parts, and lifted her bags easily, even the one loaded with her knives and other special kitchen equipment. They walked along the platform toward the terminal, and he paused at the door before going outside.

"Are you hungry? There's plenty of time. Or do you need—"

Noting the start of a faint blush, Faith interrupted him before he had to say whatever euphemism he employed.

"I'm fine. We can get going now if you like."

He nodded and she followed him out to an old woody parked at the curb. The station wagon, in mint condition, was attracting a lot of attention. He opened the door for Faith to sit in the rear. She would have preferred the front—after all, she was part of the help, too—but she followed his slight nod and got in. He closed the door firmly behind her, put her bags in the back, and got behind the wheel. She had the feeling there wouldn't be much conversation on this trip. He wasn't Owen, or Mr. Owen—whether it was a first or last name had never been established. Their voices were completely different. Both Yankees, but one from above and the other from below the salt. She wondered how long the trip would be and was about to ask, then decided to let herself be surprised. Long or short, there wasn't anything she could do about it.

The train ride had been relaxing. Now she felt her calm ebb as she mentally went over her checklists of supplies, menus, possible catastrophes. There was a caretaker/gardener who would help her clean up, she'd been told. Was he also her chauffeur? If so, he'd make an unusual sous chef. Not that she needed one for such a small group, but it was always good to have an extra pair of hands around. She didn't know any Pelham grads except for Hope's friends, and like Faith's sister they had only a nodding, or dialing, acquaintance with food preparation. Perhaps in this older Pelham group, she'd find a kindred spirit, or at least a foodie or two.

They were well away from the station and into the country before Faith turned her attention from her thoughts to the views through the side window. The road soon narrowed, and after a turn at a large salt marsh, it disappeared altogether, becoming a dirt strip running parallel to the shore. A great blue heron watched them pass, briefly looking up from the mud flats. The tide was out. Then suddenly they were in the woods, the pines so dense, only a few rays of sunshine managed to struggle through. After several murky minutes, they were in the open again. But now it really *was* the coast. Faith could see a long dock ahead and moorings, white and bright pink mooring balls of all sizes bobbing in the water. The fishermen's spots were empty, awaiting their return with the day's catch, which would be soon. When you started as early as they did, 2:00 P.M. was getting close to supper and bed. The other moorings were filled with pleasure boats, sail and motor, waiting for weekenders or their summer owners. This was deep water, unaffected by the tide and no place for herons. A single dark line of cormorants was perched on the roof of a long, low wooden building. An ornithological Greek chorus. Screeching gulls and terns wheeled about overhead.

"This is it. You're the first." Her driver pulled the woody into a spot beside the building and stopped.

He got out and retrieved her bags. As she walked toward him and he toward her, they almost ran into each other. She supposed she should have waited to be fetched.

"I can run you over to the island now. No point in hanging around here. Could be hours."

"Thank you."

"Might want a sweater. Cool on the water."

She had thought of that and pulled a fleece L.L. Bean jacket from the oversized handbag she'd kept with her. Her companion waited for her to put it on, then walked off toward the dock. She quickened her pace to keep up with him, looking about. Save for the two of them, she didn't see another human being. Plenty of birds, but no people.

Ms. Bishop must be into vintage accoutrements, Faith thought as she stepped into a large mahogany Chris-Craft runabout that was waiting at the bottom of the ramp moored at a float marked PRIVATE. There were no other places to tie onto, except for the one currently in use. She wished Tom were with her. The car would have been a treat, but the boat would have provided a major life experience. She could hear him now: "Do you know how rare these are? And this one looks as if it's never been in the water!" Like the skipper, the boat seemed to date from the 1940s.

She sat in front before she could be waved anywhere else and put on the life jacket draped across the seat. The sky was blue, not a cloud to be seen, and the smell of the salt water was as intoxicating as any French perfume or brandy. Faith took a deep breath and smiled at the man next to her, who had effortlessly started the boat, no sputtering false chokes. He favored her with one in return.

"Like being on the water?"

"Very much," Faith answered.

"Good thing. We've got a ways."

Thirty minutes later Faith began to think the description "a ways" was not mere New England understatement, but actual fact. Before too long, they'd hit Nova Scotia. At this point, she had no idea whether the island was off Maine, New Hampshire, or, considering the distance, Massachusetts.

Lobster boats returning home had passed by them earlier, the one-handed wave from the figures in oilskins a greeting, but more important, a signal that all was well. She hadn't seen another boat for fifteen minutes or more.

Faith was glad she had her jacket. There was only a slight breeze, but the speed of the boat increased its effect, and she was almost cold.

They were in open water, far away from the mainland. No more points of land with clusters of small and, in some cases, obscenely large houses—McMansions even here. Islands like green pincushions dotted the horizon and Faith began to speculate on which one might be the author's private retreat.

"Is Ms. Bishop's island one of those?" she asked, pointing starboard.

"Nope, Indian Island is further out."

"Indian Island?"

"Bishop's Island now. Folks around here still call it by the original name."

Maybe there was a shell heap on the island. Last summer Ben had become interested in the Abenaki, who had summered on Sanpere Island long ago, as did the Fairchilds now. They left traces, which were mostly in museums off island, although a few artifacts remained on display at the Sanpere Historical Society in one of the old schoolhouses, open from 1 to 4 on Wednesdays and Saturdays in season and otherwise by chance.

Almost an hour now. Perhaps there was a helipad. She couldn't imagine Bishop doing this trip often—to have a meal with friends on the mainland, say, or to see a movie.

A tiny, lone speck directly in front of them was getting larger.

"That's the island."

When the boat came close to the dock, Faith could see a figure waiting. Her employer? But upon closer view, she saw it was another man, looking much the same as the one beside her, except he was wearing well-pressed denim overalls.

He grabbed the line and made the boat fast. Suddenly the air was warm again, and sweet. A gentle breeze was carrying a smell like lilacs or some other old-fashioned flower past the rockweed and kelp swept up by the tides, lining the long rocky beach in front of her. Her bags were handed out, and after carefully placing the life jacket as she'd found it, Faith followed. The two men nodded to each other and moments later the line was back in the boat and the Chris-Craft was headed back the way it had just come.

"Good-bye!" Faith called. "Thank you!"

The skipper raised one hand and gunned the engine.

She turned to the man next to her.

"Hello, I'm Faith Fairchild. I'll be doing the cooking this week."

"Name's Justice—Brent Justice. She left a note for you up at the house."

Apparently that was going to be the extent of the present conversation, and in light of it, Faith's expectations for the future were low. Once again she fell into step. They walked down the long dock and around a good-sized boathouse. Faith stopped. She had to take a moment. Justice looked at her quizzically, but she didn't say anything. She was too busy staring at the house. It was absolutely beautiful—and absolutely perfect.

It sat in understated splendor on a rise above the beach. A long screened-in porch stretched across the front of the dwelling, a simple white farmhouse with gables in its mansard roof, a slightly elegant touch that did not seem out of place. It graced the structure like a becoming hat on a beautiful woman. A simple, almost geometric, gingerbread railing on each side of the porch added some further embellishment. Rough granite steps led up to the door in the center. Pale pink, white, and deeper pink *Rosa rugosa* bushes—beach roses—had been planted several deep, the source of that ineffable smell.

She realized her companion was still looking at her. She laughed.

"I'm sorry. It's just that the house is so wonderful. I've never seen one like it—and in such a fantastic setting." She knew she was gushing. When she'd thought about the house at all with its multitude of bedrooms, baths, a spa, pool, she'd pictured something more like the monstrosities they'd passed on the way out.

"Yup. Nice place. Cost a pretty penny and took a while to build what with everything having to come from the mainland. Wasn't much on the island before, but she wouldn't hear of getting rid of even one shingle.

Amos Hardy kept sheep out here in the forties and fifties. We even remade his old boathouse."

Perhaps she had been wrong about Brent Justice's laconic nature. He was a veritable font of information. They started walking again.

"When did Ms. Bishop build her house?"

"Let me see. Must have been eighty-three or eighty-four."

"So she's been here a long time."

Justice didn't seem to think the statement required an answer. Faith quickened her pace. She couldn't wait to see more of the place.

The porch was filled with Bar Harbor rockers and wicker made comfortable with plenty of soft cushions. There were planters at either end, overflowing with flourishing patriotic red geraniums, white nicotiana, and blue lobelia. Passing through the house's front door, Faith entered a room that reminded her a little of the all-purpose living rooms turn-of-the-twentieth-century rusticators from Boston and New York had scattered in their "cottages" along the coast. Windows for "the view," lots of furniture—sofas, chairs, bookcases, tables, tables for meals and always tables for jigsaw puzzles. The difference between those rooms and this one, aside from the absence of the smell of mold, was that the furniture wasn't a motley assortment of Great-aunt Martha's things too good for the Salvation Army, and the couch Cousin Alec's second wife replaced with a new one, even though that one was just fine. This furniture matched. Not in a complete set from Ethan Allen way, but as in all in perfect shape and all eclectically expressing the same theme—comfort. Form might follow function, but here in Barbara Bailey Bishop's home, comfort added three letters to form. There was grouped seating large enough for a dinner party's postprandial coffee and liqueurs— and nooks with small window seats flanked by bookcases for a cozy solo read on a foggy day. The ceiling was high and the room was wide. Faith could see an adjoining dining room, a table large enough for twelve set next to a bay window overlooking the view to the side of the house. The floors in both rooms were oak, covered in part by Orientals, a rainbow of color. The far end of the living room was completely taken up by a granite-faced fireplace with a gray driftwood mantel.

"Note's over there, kitchen's through that door, and your room's up the back stairs. She's working. Be back later."

Faith came down to earth with a thud. She'd almost forgotten why she was here. The kitchen, then the back stairs—a back bedroom. Not a scullery maid's airless box room in an attic, but not one of the front rooms facing the water.

She picked up the note, set in plain view on what she was sure was a Nakashima coffee table from the 1950s, a free-form slab of exquisite black walnut, and went through the door Brent Justice had left open into the kitchen.

It was like her first glimpse of the house. She stopped dead in her tracks. Hope had been right. It *was* her dream kitchen. But there would be time to gloat over the Wolf stove later. And what kind of stone could the counters be made of? She'd seen plenty of black granite, but never any with threads of gold and flecks of cerulean blue.

"Propane, gas generators, some solar."

"Excuse me?" Brent's words interrupted her thoughts, and it took a moment for her to grasp the context. "Oh, how it's powered, because of course there isn't any electrical service out here."

He nodded, and they continued on.

The house seemed to go on forever. Faith glimpsed what looked like a solarium, as she walked down the hall off the kitchen, then followed her guide up a broad staircase that had been carpeted—for comfort and safety, she supposed. It ended at another hallway, this one with a series of closed doors. It could almost have been a hotel—or dormitory. The landing was big enough for more comfy chairs, which were set next to a window. An old chest was covered with an assortment of the latest magazines and today's newspapers—Faith had the same copy of the *Times* in her bag. An arrangement of wildflowers in a beautiful blue and white Ming vase had been placed off to one side on the deep windowsill. Faith looked at the handyman with renewed respect. Who else could have been responsible for the flowers? These and all those in the living room downstairs. And more in the kitchen on the center island, calendulas in a bright yellow Provençal pottery pitcher. Or were there elves like the shoemaker's who did the flowers, fetched the papers, arranging everything before dawn? Then again could it, in fact, be the hand of Bishop herself?

Brent Justice had said the writer was working and would be "back later." Did that mean she wasn't here in the house? He stopped by one of the doors. It had a little brass slot into which a card with "Faith Fairchild," written in exquisite calligraphy, had been placed. Just like an English country house; but Faith didn't think there would be any changing cards or tiptoeing in at midnight and out at dawn shenanigans.

"Doesn't Ms. Bishop write here in the house? You said she'd be back later."

"She has a cabin in the woods. Claims she has to be in a place where she can't be distracted."

Faith could understand the logic, although it surely must seem ridiculous to a New Englander like Justice that someone would build an enormous house, then have to escape to a cabin to do whatever it was writing people did. Bishop would certainly be distracted, what with looking out the windows and being tempted by the comforts of home. Which reminded Faith, where were the spa and the pool?

"I understand there's a pool and a spa. Not that I'll have time to use them," she added hastily. She'd be feeding him, too, and didn't want him to think he was in for a week of microwave macaroni and cheese while she was lounging about.

"House is kind of built like steps. Two floors in front, then three in the back. All that stuff and a place to watch movies is on the first floor all the way in the back. Starts under the kitchen."

He opened the door to her room, and all of Faith's thoughts of upstairs/downstairs disappeared. It was spacious with a view of a different beach in the distance. As you faced the house, this room was on the right side overlooking a meadow, a sea of wildflowers and grasses, and finally the sea itself. She should have known better. It *was* an island after all. They were surrounded by water and none of the rooms would have a bad view.

"I'll leave you to it." He set her bags down. She'd been

so muddled by everything that she hadn't thought to have him leave the one with her culinary equipment in the kitchen. It didn't matter. She'd bring it down herself.

"Thank you so much." There was an awkward moment. She didn't know whether he was supposed to help her in the kitchen before dinner or was strictly on cleanup detail. She decided to go with a simple, "See you later."

He nodded. "All your stuff is here and put away. There's a pantry with another fridge and a freezer on the first floor next to where she keeps her wine."

Faith nodded back. It was catching. She'd read the note, change, and take a quick tour.

Justice stopped at the door. "Garden's out back. Strawberries are coming in—a few kinds—chard, lettuce, peas."

And he was gone.

Faith took the note and sat down on the bed. Not too soft, not too hard. She'd sleep well here. The envelope wasn't sealed. The writing was the same as that on the room card. Surely the woman didn't write her books in longhand!

Dear Mrs. Fairchild,

   Welcome to Bishop's Island. I trust that you had a pleasant journey and that Brent has shown you where everything is. Actually, I am sure he hasn't, but he will at least have settled you into your room. Please feel free to acquaint yourself with the house. Your orders arrived and I have added a treat or two myself, as you will discover.

44

*My guests will all be here by seven o'clock,
and should I be delayed by a fit of inspiration, I
would like you to act as hostess and offer cocktails and hors d'oeuvres before dinner at eight.*

*I am so glad you were able to take all this on
and am looking forward to meeting you. It should
be a most illuminating week.*

Sincerely,

Faith frowned. After all that fine, no doubt laborious
calligraphy, Bishop's signature was a mess, indecipher-
able. Faith knew that this was not uncommon among
authors who had to sign thousands of copies of books.
Some, and obviously Ms. Bishop was one, had developed a scrawl. She recalled a story a bookseller had
told her about an elderly gentleman who, upon being
handed the book he had asked a famous mystery author
to sign, handed it back and said sternly, "Now, young
man, sign it so I can read it. The way your teacher
taught you to!" The author, not known for complai-
sance, instantly complied.

She changed into her work clothes, not bothering to
unpack. Ms. Bishop had asked that tonight's dinner be a
buffet. Faith had supposed it was to accommodate late
arrivals, but now she was assuming it was to create an
informal ambience for the group's first night together.
That long boat trip would be difficult in the dark even
with the fancy GPS and other devices Faith had noticed.
The women would surely all be here at sundown. There
would be no late arrivals. She'd have the cocktail hour
on the front porch, which by chance or design faced

west. As the sun set, everyone could move indoors. The living room had numerous tables besides the Nakashima gem and Faith decided to make it a movable feast. She didn't know how often these alums got together, but if they were anything like Hope's friends, it wouldn't matter. They'd pick up where they left off. Having to graze would facilitate conversations.

She wished she could call Tom—or her neighbor and closest friend, Pix Miller, and of course Hope! Her cell certainly wouldn't get service out here. She turned it on, and the total lack of those annoying little bars confirmed her fear. How did the writer communicate with the outside world? She must have satellite service.

As she was leaving her room, she noticed a small white box tied with sheer silver ribbon on a table that served as a desk beneath the window. She opened it, and inside there was an exquisite necklace. A card from the author, her name engraved on the top, read, "This is the work of my favorite jewelry designer, Sharon Adams, who is based in the Boston area. You may be familiar with her name. A little thank-you for what I know will be a week of culinary delights." Faith did indeed know of Ms. Adams's work and this was no little thank-you, but a *very* generous gesture. She had always wanted a piece of the jeweler's work, and this choker was a treasure. An insert from Ms. Adams described the piece's materials as chalcedony with almandine garnets. The chalcedony was translucent, and the beveled pieces looked as if they had been carved from moonlight; the tiny garnets flashed red, bits of Mars. She put it away, resolving to wear it tonight.

Back in the kitchen, Faith began the delightful task

of exploring. Few women, and an equal number of men, no doubt, could resist the opportunity to open cupboards, closets, and other doors in someone else's house. Faith's mother-in-law, Marian, was a show-house junkie, and with a husband and daughter in the real estate business, an open house one, as well. "I can give them tips," she'd told Faith once. "Tell them how to make places more salable." Possibly, Faith had thought. Her mother-in-law did have good taste and a good eye, but it was really Marian's insatiable curiosity about the way other people lived that motivated her. Faith could recognize the trait, because she had it herself in abundance. Taking a stroll at night and looking into lighted rooms was almost as good as a Broadway show.

Two sinks, one deep for washing vegetables, were placed beneath a window that overlooked the garden. A door leading outside was to the left. The pale green of new leaves and other colors that gleamed against the rich, dark earth drew Faith, but she resisted. She'd go once all the food for this evening was in order. Brent—after reading Bishop's note, this was how Faith thought of him—had said there were strawberries. If she had time, she'd pick some to garnish the individual lemon tarts she'd made for one of tonight's desserts, and see if there were enough for breakfast. Now she needed to locate the wine cellar and the downstairs pantry. Feeling a bit like Alice, she opened doors, discovering a broom closet, a pantry/china closet, a door to the dining room, and finally a door that led to some stairs.

She was going to have to learn that nothing about this house would fit any preconceived notion, as in the present case, "basement." At the bottom of the stairs, there was a short hallway to the right. Directly in front of her was the pool. A wall of French doors opened onto a fieldstone patio with the meadow beyond. The pool itself was lined with pale blue tiles, some with the titles of Bishop's books emblazoned in darker blue; others decorated with fanciful sea creatures. Mermaids, Mermen, Kingsley's Water Babies. The water was celadon green, the walls and ceiling sky blue. Instead of chlorine, the air smelled of roses, the beach roses. Faith walked the length of the pool. A large Jacuzzi, its waters a deep aquamarine, was set near the windows. She was beginning to feel like a character in a fairy tale. She was alone in this magnificent house, but she could hear echoes. Someone splashed about in the water, someone else laughed, ice clinked in tall glasses, someone whispered in another's ear. They were all waiting for the prince to come and break the spell.

The spa was through two double doors at the end, and it was as well equipped as the day spa where Faith occasionally treated herself to a facial, manicure, and pedicure. She closed the doors behind her and went in search of the pantry Brent had mentioned, finding it down the short hallway at the bottom of the stairs. The refrigerator was stocked with the author's "treats": beluga caviar; foie gras; several varieties of smoked fish, including what Faith assumed were local mussels; at least five kinds of mushrooms—from portobellos as large as butter plates to tiny shiitakes. Two of the vegetable drawers were filled with artisanal cheeses. The wine cellar had a glass door. Faith didn't need to open it. Any sommelier worth his or her tastevin would swoon. She went back upstairs to the kitchen to get ready for the opening party. She understood now why the distance to the mainland didn't matter. Barbara Bailey Bishop had everything you could possibly desire here on the island; you never had to leave, nor would you want to for a long time. Suddenly the week seemed very short . . .

Faith was in the kitchen assembling the last salad, a simple one of field greens. She had a tray of *crottins de Chavignol* ready for the oven if anyone wanted warm goat cheese on top. Inevitably there would be at least one woman, if not more, who was on the Atkins, the South Beach, or a just plain low-calorie diet. She'd done one dish—adapted from the famous version at San Francisco's fabulous Slanted Door restaurant—of cellophane noodles and crab, in this case the East Coast's peeky toe variety, not West Coast's Dungeness (see recipe, p. 317). This was a supplement to the baskets of various kinds of foccacia and other breads she'd prepared. Just as there were the dieters, there was bound to be a carb craver. She'd be better able to plan the rest of the week's meals after meeting the women tonight.

It was time to head out to the garden. There were several trugs conveniently stored near the door and a series of different-sized scissors and clippers, labeled FLOWERS, HERBS, and VEGETABLES. Someone was extremely well organized.

She had barely had a chance to take in the herb garden when she heard the boat arriving. She briefly regretted the intrusion. It had been a lovely fantasy while it lasted— a deserted island with the perfect house stocked with her favorite food and drink. Yet there was nothing she liked better than cooking for a receptive audience, and Bishop, at least, would be one. After all, the woman had remembered Faith's fennel soup roughly thirteen years later. She watched Brent go down to the dock. He was alone and pushing one of those large, two-wheeled garden carts in front of him, presumably for the luggage. The boat's arrival and departure was almost as swift as hers had been. Should she greet the party? The note had asked her to act as hostess for cocktails, but hadn't mentioned filling in to welcome the guests. Faith decided to leave it to the caretaker/gardener/all-purpose factotum that Brent appeared to be. There was still a great deal to do for tonight and she wanted to bake two kinds of muffins for breakfast—something relatively healthy and something like doughnut muffins that decidedly were not.

She filled the trug with a variety of herbs, nasturtiums for the salad, then headed for what she could see were strawberry beds. A quick glance told her that she would need a larger container and that there were an abundance of tiny, ruby-red *fraises des bois* and what looked like Earliglows, the succulent variety of bigger berries that had stood the test of time. She popped one in her mouth. It was warm and delicious. Like the smell of the pines that towered in the distance, essence of strawberry should be bottled, but neither could ever be reproduced. She ate some of the small berries, a completely different taste—sweet as well, but with the underlying flavor of wild berries, truly berries from the *bois,* the forest. She would have to make a coulis for panna cotta or some other dessert. The color of the sauce would complement a number of dishes. Strawberries! Maybe fruit soup; maybe jam. There must be a greenhouse tucked away someplace; even elves couldn't produce fruit like this before July.

As she walked back to the kitchen, she heard voices and saw the group approaching the front of the house along the same path she had taken a few hours before. Brent was in the lead and three women were following him, one clutching a guitar case. Faith smiled as a mental image leapt to mind, of the old friends gathered in front of the fire listening to their own Joni Mitchell/Joan Baez. She could almost hear them joining in: "I've looked at life from both sides now." This was going to be fun. They were too far away for her to make them out clearly, but their silhouettes were sleek, and judging from the pile of suitcases in the cart, their wardrobes extensive. She ducked behind a spirea bush in full bloom and turned to go in the door. One of the women had raised her voice and her words were clearly audible, slicing through the late afternoon air with the same kind of precision Faith used to dice onions: "What on earth are we all doing here?"

Two hours later Faith heard voices in the front room. Brent was leading another group of guests to the stairs that curved up from the dining room. She realized he'd taken her the back way, so she could see the kitchen. She'd noticed that there was another staircase joining the kitchen stairs, but hadn't thought about where it started. Both ended at the same landing.

It was a little after six. She hoped this new group was the rest of the women; she hated to think of the boat having to make another long round trip—but then the skipper must be used to it. How else would the papers get here, unless Bishop arranged a helicopter drop for such essentials? Three in the first group, four in this one, their hostess, Faith, and Brent—she ticked them off on her fingers. Just as Owen had said, ten in all. Ten little Indians. She shook her head and mentally replaced the old nursery rhyme with the one her children had loved instead: "Ten little monkeys jumping on the bed . . ." The one where mama calls the doctor, who makes everything okay, but "No more monkeys jumping on the bed!" She could hear Amy and Ben chanting the last line and smiled to herself.

At a quarter to seven Faith stood in the middle of the porch. The weather had cooperated beautifully and the early evening air was almost balmy. It was so still an unseen hand seemed to have brought the landscape into sharp focus. Several bottles of champagne were chilling in the ice buckets Faith had discovered in the china closet; each one was a different style, a different period. She'd put out the caviar, also on ice, with a mother-of-pearl spoon, toast points, lemon, chopped hard-boiled egg whites and yolks, and minced shallots, although she preferred hers au naturel when it was of this quality. There were smoked mussels and shrimp, a seafood pâté, as well as a multilayered vegetable one. She'd scattered brightly colored dishes of olives about, with receptacles nearby for the pits. A token platter of crudités—she found that while these looked wonderful, people usually only picked at them conscientiously before heading for the good stuff—sat on a glass-topped table next to the caviar. There was a small brass gong near the stairs in the dining room. She'd sound it at seven.

With her attention to detail, Bishop had, no doubt, outlined the night's schedule in a letter of welcome to each alum, but with the hostess still absent, Faith thought it wouldn't hurt to gather the guests promptly. They must be hungry after their respective journeys. Her sandwich seemed days away; she knew *she* was starving. She wasn't the kind of cook who ate while she worked. A taste here and there to correct seasonings was all she took. She eyed the Dom Pérignon and the crystal flutes with anticipation. She hoped the ladies would come down soon—and also that they wouldn't want pink drinks. She could mix up whatever anyone desired, but the champagne was both festive and perfect for the evening's menu, starting with these appetizers through the desserts. What had they drunk in the sixties? She laughed to herself—perhaps these Pelham girls hadn't been drinkers but smokers.

She sounded the gong; the pleasant tone was loud enough to be heard upstairs, but not too loud, not too intrusive. She noticed something she had missed before—a series of small glass cylinders in a row across the mantel. Each held a single, perfect rose. Not beach roses, but hybrids. She recognized Peace. Were they all French Meilland roses? Her eyes swept across the weathered wood. Ten, there were ten vases, ten roses.

The dining room stairs weren't carpeted, and she turned swiftly at the sound of footsteps.

"Hello," she said. "My name is Faith Fairchild. I'll be cooking for you this week."

The woman looked as if she was in her forties, even late thirties, not fifties. She was slim and dressed in a simple coral linen sheath. Her dark hair was free of gray whether from luck or design, Faith couldn't tell. She couldn't read the woman's expression, either. The good cheer Faith would have expected at a reunion like this was eclipsed by what could only be described as wariness. Poised on the bottom stair, the woman was looking toward the living room as if trying to decide if she should enter it. She took the last step.

"I must be the first," she murmured almost to herself, then seemed to remember Faith and said, "Oh, sorry, I'm Rachel Gold. The note said cocktails would be served on the porch. Is that where Barbara Bishop is?"

"Ms. Bishop is finishing up some work and has asked me to act as hostess until she gets here. I'm sure it won't be long."

Rachel nodded and looked somewhat relieved. "Good. I need to find out what the schedule is. Her assistant wasn't very clear. Have the other musicians arrived? There was a masseuse on the boat out with me; I gather there is a spa. I'm not sure who the other person was. I think she said something about finance, and she wasn't carrying an instrument of any kind, unless it was shipped ahead. I didn't catch either of their names."

"Musicians?" Faith said, then realized who was standing next to her—Rachel Gold, the famous classical guitarist. Tom, who had worked his way up from "If I Had a Hammer" to Villa-Lobos, would be thrilled to hear Faith had met her. She put out her hand. "My husband and I are great fans of yours. It's an honor to meet you."

Rachel blushed. "Thank you. If you are a music

lover, then this week should be a treat for you. I had no idea Ms. Bishop was so interested. I've been thinking of it as a kind of very small Tanglewood or Marlboro, playing all day in this magnificent setting."

A musical Pelham group. They must have come together through their shared interest back during their undergraduate years.

"I know Pelham has a fine music department. How special for you all to get together. My sister is an alum, a later class."

"Pelham?" Rachel said, and seemed about to add more, but her attention, and Faith's, was directed to the stairs where a group of four women was descending in silence.

This is not the party I imagined, Faith said to herself as she welcomed the group and steered everybody out to the porch. They were followed almost immediately by two more. Seven, Faith counted. They were all here— except for the hostess, and Brent, of course. It wasn't his cup of tea, or Moxie, or whatever his preferred beverage was. Knowing the ungodly hour at which most New Englanders ate, Faith had left dinner for him in the kitchen. Now she eased the cork out of one of the champagne bottles and started pouring.

"Please, everyone, help yourselves. Ms. Bishop should be here shortly and I'm pinch-hitting until then." The women's uneasiness was contagious. Faith never used sports metaphors. She wasn't sure she even knew what pinch-hitting was.

She continued nervously, "I'm Faith Fairchild and I'll be your caterer for the week." She had launched herself into flight attendant mode and could barely keep herself from saying, "Fasten your seat belts, it's going to be a bumpy night."

A tall woman in a bright Lilly Pulitzer took one of the flutes and drained it. Faith promptly refilled it, and watched as she strode to the center of the porch and addressed the group.

"All right, let's go around the room. I'm Gwen and"— she pointed to a slight woman, who looked tired, as if she'd been ill, with long hair pulled carelessly into a scrunchie—"you're Chris Barker, a little grayer, but amazingly the same. You too, Lucy, except your hair is shorter."

"You too, Gwen, except yours is blonder," Lucy— Talbots from head to toe—shot back.

"And we know you from your pictures in the *Times*, Rachel. Would know you anyway."

"But you were supposed to be musicians," Rachel said, taking a glass from the tray Faith was passing, since no one was moving. "I was hired to lead a musical retreat."

"And I was hired to conduct a financial seminar," Gwen said. "Ms. Bishop, whoever she is, has been very clever." Faith noted that anger and admiration seemed to be vying for first place.

"It's all of us, isn't it," said a woman who was waging a possibly hopeless battle with the years. She needed to drop twenty pounds and get rid of her dated Jane Fonda shag cut. After two cherry tomatoes, she'd gone straight for the sesame breadsticks. "I'm sure we all recognize Maggie, or I should say, Madam President—we've seen your picture often enough in the alumnae magazine. Congratulations, by the way. And I'm Phoebe. Phoebe

56

James now. I live in New Jersey with my adoring hus-band, perfect sixteen-year-old twin daughters, an ador-able thirteen-year-old son, and two darling Irish terriers." How many glasses of champagne had the woman gulped down? Faith wondered. The irony was obvious—and very sad. "I thought I was coming to some sort of fancy book group retreat," she finished in a softer tone of voice and sat down abruptly.

"And that leaves?" Gwen said.

"Me. Or I? Bobbi Dolan—and I know I look differ-ent. I headed straight for California after graduation, literally got in my car that afternoon and turned left. After a few summers of love, I made two bad marriages, studied massage working my way up and down the coast. It was in L.A., of course, that I got the lenses, the work, and the hair. Clients don't want you to look better than they do, but they do want you to look good."

"So what the hell are we all doing here?"

Faith recognized the voice and the question posed earlier when some of the women had been walking from the boat to the house; the speaker had been Gwen. She was apparently a very take-charge lady. Faith won-dered what her last name was. A financial seminar? Could she be Gwen Mansfield, her own sister Hope's personal idol? Faith knew that Mansfield had gone to Pelham—Hope had mentioned it often enough. And the age was right. But surely she was far above giving financial seminars no matter how much money Bishop may have offered. There must be another reason for Mansfield's presence.

"Please," Faith said, thinking she should take charge herself. "Enjoy the sunset and have something more to eat. Dinner will be a buffet in the next room at eight and I'm sure Ms. Bishop will be here by then."

Her words were brave. At this point, she was as confused as they were and not sure about anything.

"I was told she was endowing a chair and going to fund a renovation of our writing center," Maggie said. She sounded mournful.

"Don't worry, Prez," Gwen assured her. "You'll get your money. If not, you can always sue. Probably we all can."

Bobbi spoke up. "Do you mean we might not be getting paid? That is, I was supposed to give massages; I'm really very skilled."

"I'm sure you are, pumpkin," Gwen said. "And you can start with me. There should be time before we leave in the morning."

"Leave?" Chris said in a puzzled voice. The thought of retracing her steps so soon was exhausting.

"What were you told?" Phoebe asked.

"That I was to prepare a series of lectures for garden devotees."

"Of course! I've seen your byline. And you write that wonderful column. Stupid of me. I never thought Christine Barker was our Chris," Phoebe enthused.

Chris brightened. "Then you're a gardener?"

"A vicarious one. That is, I read about other people's gardens. My husband likes lawns and shrubs; he's not much for flowers. When I suggested patio tomatoes in tubs, he told me that Jersey might be the Garden State, but he for one didn't want a truck farm in his backyard."

The adoring husband, Faith reminded herself.

One woman had remained silent during the discussion. The one Gwen had pointed out as "Lucy." She had refused the champagne and gone to the drinks table and made a stiff scotch rocks, Faith had noticed.

The food and drink were helping, but the air of unease that was so palpable from the onset had not lifted much. Everyone had been lured here under false pretenses, except for her, Faith realized. She was a cook and she was cooking. But then she wasn't a Pelham grad. It was a reunion, just as Owen had described, but apparently she was the only one who knew it ahead of time. Judging from the lack of recognition in most cases, and the lack of knowledge about what had been going on with each other's lives since college, this was not a group that had stayed in touch. So why had Bishop gathered them together and in such a devious way? If she had told them it was going to be a Pelham reunion, would they have turned her down? Certainly not the president—Margaret Howard, another of Hope's role models.

Gwen's glass was empty. Faith opened the second bottle and filled it. Gwen sat down and looked at her watch—very thin and very expensive.

"It's a quarter to eight. What do you say we help Faith—sorry, your last name escaped me—move the food and drink into the other room while we wait for our hostess to make an appearance. And answer a few questions."

"Faith is fine, and if you'll all go inside, I really can handle this myself."

Gwen nodded—she was obviously more used to being waited on, than helping the help—and the group

59

moved toward the door. Faith was interested to see that several were finally talking among themselves. There was a smile here and there. Perhaps it would be all right, after all. It was clear they had all known each other, what, almost forty years ago? A surprise party. A surprise reunion, engineered by Bishop.

Faith brought some of the food into the kitchen and some into the living room where they'd be joined by the warm entrees. There was a buzz of conversation now and she was about to announce that dinner was served, when a noise at the fireplace end of the living room cut sentences off midair. All eyes were trained toward a slowly opening door. The woman coming into view was beautiful, startlingly beautiful, Faith thought, and certainly couldn't be the same age as those gathered below, even the ones who looked great. This woman belonged in an entirely different category. A deep purple silk caftan did not hide her body's curves, but flowed against them, accentuating each asset. Faith recognized the thick, shoulder-length curling dark hair from the author's book jackets, but now she could see her face. Violet eyes and high cheekbones. Flawless skin. Her lips, turned upward in a smile of welcome, were deep crimson. One small dimple deepened as the smile broadened.

For an instant, the room was completely still, then all at once someone dropped a glass—it shattered on the floor—and someone screamed while someone else cried out, "Prin! But you're supposed to be dead!"

Lucy got up and walked over to the door, confronting the figure poised there.

"I don't know what you're up to, Elaine Prince, but you'd better tell us and tell us quickly." She faced the group. "Pull yourselves together, ladies. It's Elaine, not Prin. We all know that Prin died the day before graduation, and dead is dead."

Three

FRESHMAN YEAR

How was she ever going to get her mother to leave? Maggie Howard wondered dismally. At this rate, the woman would still be at Pelham four years from now—which was no doubt exactly what she wanted.

"Six o'clock, Big Sister, Little Sister picnic. Meet at the Bell Desk at five-forty-five. You know where that is; we passed it coming in. Every girl takes a turn sitting Bells." She smiled coyly at her daughter. "Don't forget that if she says you have a 'caller,' it's a young man and a 'visitor' is female or over the hill."

Her mother knew more about Pelham than she did, Maggie reflected, not for the first time. It wasn't that she wasn't happy to be here. She was ecstatic. From the moment she'd opened her acceptance letter, a fat, not thin, envelope, she'd felt as if she were living in a dream come true. Except it was a dream she'd been forced to share with her mother.

Starting in second grade, Mrs. Howard had started grooming her only child for what she firmly believed was the crème de la crème of the female counterparts to the all-male Ivies. If a chromosomal prerequisite meant her little girl couldn't go to Harvard, Princeton, or Yale, then Pelham it would be. The first step was putting Maggie in private school, even though it meant that Mrs. Howard had to give up her secretarial job in their small town and take a higher paying one in Cleveland, commuting an hour each way, to pay the tuition. Then she'd honed in on Pelham alums at church, the League of Women Voters, town committees, the PTA, and cultivated them. Sometimes she would spot the discreet, tasteful school ring, but more often than not she had nothing more to go on than her own uncanny intuition. When the time came for an alumnae interview, the number of women who offered to sponsor her application had embarrassed Maggie. Meanwhile her mother had absorbed every aspect of Pelham's history and traditions, from the sublime—all those notable graduates—to the ridiculous—"visitors" and "callers." Gentlemen callers—it sounded like something straight out of Tennessee Williams. But there would be no depending on the kindness of strangers for Maggie. Despite the fact that she had used women hardly known to her, Mrs. Howard had never relied on anyone but herself, and she'd brought Maggie up the same way. "Hoe your own row" was her maxim, probably even before Maggie's father died when Maggie was an infant.

One out-of-focus picture of her father holding her in his arms was all she had. A wallet-sized graduation shot of a serious-looking young man with a crew cut—holding his mortarboard in front of him like a shield, as if he already knew the outrageous misfortune that would be his—was the only keepsake her mother seemed to possess. Maggie wasn't sure whether her mother never mentioned him because she was angry at that most ultimate of desertions or unbearably sad at losing him. Both sets of grandparents were dead by the time Maggie could toddle, and aside from a cousin, there didn't seem to be any other kin on either of her parents' sides.

And so Maggie's little Buster Brown–clad feet were set firmly on their path toward Pelham and Weejuns. Pelham girls were well rounded, so Maggie took piano lessons, learned to play tennis, and excelled at other sports, particularly field hockey. She was a natural athlete and much happier in gym than in the classroom. The only subject that didn't require tremendous effort was math, and everybody knew that girls weren't supposed to be good at it. As for the rest, the essays, the dates of the kings and queens of England, *i* before *e,* except after *c*—she sweated away at home in private. "You don't want them to call you a 'greasy grind,'" her mother admonished. But Maggie had to bring home *A*'s. When she didn't, her mother wouldn't speak to her for days on end. If it was something that could be done over and handed back in, not for a grade increase, just for the practice, then that was what Maggie did. She hoed her own row, and it wasn't easy. She envied her classmates who seemed to be able to waltz through classes while Maggie doggedly repeated the box step, over and over again.

Why wasn't she leaving? How could Maggie start her new life—this new life of freedom—if her mother continued to sit on her bed reading every inch of type in the orientation materials she'd already read ten times at least at home? All the other parents were gone, and Maggie was sure the reason her roommate had stuck her head in, introduced herself, then ducked out was that she assumed Maggie wanted private time with her mother. Maggie had had eighteen years of private time with her mother and that had been more than enough.

"Well, I guess I'd better get ready for the picnic," Maggie said.

She was wearing a Villager shirtwaist with tiny flowers, almost a twin of the one her mother had on. Her circle pin was on the appropriate side of her collar. There were a bunch more shirtwaists hanging in the closet, along with a John Meyer suit for church, John Meyer skirts, several round-collared oxford-cloth blouses—the female equivalent of Ivy League button-down shirts, and, in the chest of drawers, matching sweaters. It had strained their budget, but Mrs. Howard had pored over *The American Girl* and *Seventeen* to get it all just right. Never mind that "big-boned" Maggie—a sharp contrast to her whippet-thin, petite mother—looked far better in slacks and other casual clothes than in these that emphasized her thick waist, muscular calves, and broad shoulders.

At last Mrs. Howard stood up. "Wear the new madras Bermudas with your yellow blouse—and tie the blue Pelham sweatshirt around your neck. I'll see you downstairs; I want to have a last word with your housemother."

Maggie started to protest. Her mother had already had many words with Mrs. MacIntyre, the housemother. But it wouldn't do any good; if Maggie had learned one thing, it was to keep her mouth shut and let her mother do what she intended.

She'll be gone soon. She'll be gone soon. Maggie had been repeating the words as a mantra to keep herself calm for the last hour.

"Sure, that will be fine," she said.

Maybe she could run back upstairs and change into jeans after her mother left and before the picnic. No, she thought ruefully, she'd be streaming out the door with the rest of the freshmen and their Big Sisters from the junior class, with Mrs. Howard waving a cheery good-bye to them all. The picture of devotion. Devotion to herself. Maggie had never been fooled into thinking that her achievements had anything to do with her. It was all for the glory of the Howard name, the Florence Howard name.

"You know the 'Mrs.' is not a courtesy title, like British cooks. Pelham housemothers have to have been married—and widowed, not divorced," Mrs. Howard said, nodding in satisfaction. She expected no less of Pelham.

Maggie didn't bother to reply. She'd heard it all before, and besides, her mother wasn't listening. She was rehearsing what she planned to say to the housemother. Maggie knew what that was, too. No, Mrs. Howard would not give her daughter *blanket permission*— Pelham's term for the permission slip that had to be signed if a freshman was to be allowed to stay overnight anywhere but at the house of a Pelham student, alum, or designated relative. Even with the signed form, students had to notify the housemother forty-eight hours in advance. Mrs. Howard thought all freshmen should be restricted, and that the form—just look at the name the students had coined—was an open invitation to licentiousness.

The door closed. Maggie stood in the center of the room. It was good-sized, much larger than the one she had at home. One bed was near the window, the other by the door. There were two plain oak chests of drawers, similar desks, bookcases, and desk chairs. Unbleached muslin curtains hung at the diamond-paned window. The dorm, Felton, was one of the original ones, and the bricks were covered with enough ivy to please even Mrs. Howard. Maggie closed her eyes and spun around, her arms outstretched. When her roommate, Roberta Dolan, walked in seconds later, she was speechless for a moment, then the two girls started to giggle and fell on the beds laughing. It was going to be a wonderful four years.

Would she ever get used to the sound of so many female voices? Rachel Gold wondered. Her head was pounding after the picnic and soon she had to go to a meeting in the housemother's living room—a discussion of the Bluebook, Pelham's rulebook. There would be another one tomorrow night. What rules could possibly be so complicated as to require two meetings? Her Big Sister had warned her to pay attention. That they would be tested on their sign-outs and other regulations.

At least she had a single. If she didn't want to talk to

anyone, she could shut the door. Thank God for that—and she could, Yahweh, more specifically. Another Jewish girl at the school she'd attended in Manhattan had told her Jews always got singles at schools like Pelham. There were thirty-four freshmen in this dorm and she was the only one in a single, so it appeared the information was correct. Someplace, they'd put three girls in together. There was no Hillel chapter listed among Pelham's clubs, so she'd have to rely on chance to identify her lansmen, or rather, -women. What was the college nervous about? It wasn't contagious and far more likely that a Jehovah's Witness or fundamentalist would try to proselytize than a Jew. But then there wouldn't be too many of them, either, if any. Too extreme. Too "not one of us."

Required morning chapel had only been discontinued last year; two semesters of Biblical Studies had not. She'd seen several black girls at the picnic. Presumably they'd be in singles, too. And any Asian girls. Anyone different. The Chinese Civilization course was called "Chink Civ." Her Big Sister was taking it and had rattled the course nickname off without hesitation.

Rachel was willing to bet that the majority of those girls at the picnic happily consuming burgers with their straight teeth, tossing their shiny hair, showing off their smooth, not too dark, tanned skin in sleeveless oxford-cloth blouses, believed firmly that God was an Episcopalian and the Jews, clever as they were, had messed up forever and ever, world without end, when they killed Christ. Amen.

Depression settled over her like a sour washcloth. She missed her room in the Golds' Upper West Side apartment with its view of tall buildings, sidewalks, streets, rooftops, and water towers. At night, she always pulled her shade up when she turned out her light so she could see the White Way outside—a sight that never failed to enchant her. She still couldn't understand why her parents had refused to let her go to Juilliard—or any other music school. Her teacher had pleaded with them, but they had been firm. Her mother had gone to Pelham and her best friends were still her Pelham buddies. They wanted Rachel to have what they called a "normal college experience." There would be plenty of time for her music later, and besides, Pelham had an excellent music department, although you couldn't major in it. "Normal!" Rachel had shouted at them. What was normal about a place that didn't let you major in music? And what was normal about being in a school without men? And what was normal about living on a campus in the middle of nowhere? Sure, there was a bus to Boston and Cambridge from the center of town, but it took an hour. Students couldn't have cars until second semester senior year, not that Rachel cared. She didn't even have a driver's license. You didn't need to have one in the city. Her brother, Max, didn't have one, either. Kids from the suburbs had licenses and cars. She would never live in the suburbs. *Again,* she amended bitterly, gazing out the window at the walls of foliage that bordered the grassy quadrangle below.

Max. He was the only one who understood. Her eyes filled with tears as she thought back to last night. He'd known she wouldn't be able to sleep and had slipped in to talk to her. He didn't try to reassure her with any bullshit, just said he knew how she must be feeling. He'd be feeling the same way in a year. Max was even more talented than Rachel. From an early age, he had demonstrated extraordinary gifts—a perfect ear and the ability to pick up virtually any instrument in no time. For a while, he'd stayed mainly with the violin, but by age ten, it was clear that his real talent was the piano. His hands were the hands of a born pianist, long tapered fingers, strong. When he played, they flew across the keys in a kind of dance, an extension of his swaying body. He was a traditionally romantic-looking musician—dark, curling hair, always a little too long.

But if, in fact, Max was a prodigy, he never acted like it, nor did his parents treat him like one. He played sports, excelling at basketball, much to the chagrin of a string of music teachers. He broke a leg—stepping off a curb on Amsterdam Avenue directly into a pothole—but never injured his hands. Like his sister, he explored the city with friends, hanging out in the Village, heading to Chinatown for Sunday-morning dim sum breakfasts, and attending as many performances of as many different kinds of music as possible. Both Rachel and Max attended one of New York's special public schools, the High School of Music and Art. Even though they were a year and a class apart, they shared the same group of friends, all aspiring performers. They were like twins, everyone commented. They had had a special language growing up that had been reduced to a few words and phrases now. Their fights were bitter, passionate, and brief. Their apologies profuse.

When Max had said he would be going through the same thing in a year, Rachel had been tempted to wake her parents up and tell them she would only go to Pelham if they didn't make Max try for an Ivy. She felt her anger bubble up all over again. It was four years! A waste of four years! Max was already being hailed as one of the most promising musicians of his generation. The *Times* had done a story on him last year after a school concert at Carnegie Hall. The headline had read, YOUNG MAX GOLD DOESN'T NEED TO PRACTICE TO GET TO CARNEGIE HALL, a reference to the old "How do you get to Carnegie Hall? Practice" joke.

Her parents had repeated the same arguments for Max they had used with Rachel. "You need a quality, well-rounded liberal arts education. Education is for life. You want to be ignorant?" Rachel had proposed she and Max take classes at NYU or the New School, but her parents wanted them to "have a taste of campus life." "The city will still be here when you come back," her father had said. "Campus life"—it sounded like porkpie hats and raccoon coats, the Harvard-Yale game, undergraduates drinking too much, and panty raids. No, thank you.

Yet here she was and Max would be following. Not Pelham, of course. He was applying early decision to Harvard. She was sure he'd get in. He'd scored two 800s on his SATs; had a 4.5 GPA, because of his AP courses; tutored at a settlement house—and then there was his music. She figured she was at Pelham as a legacy; her grades hadn't been so hot, although she had decent scores. It never seemed to matter. Only the music mattered. She'd get through the year, and then Max would be at Harvard or someplace else in the Boston area. They'd worked it out. Maybe Brandeis. This was her only consolation: Max close by, especially if he had a car. Maybe she could say she wouldn't stay at Pelham unless her parents gave Max a car. He'd have to get a license, but that couldn't be hard. Look at all the idiots who passed the test. A car would mean freedom. They could get rid of it when he graduated and moved back to the city.

She took her guitar out of its case. The dorm rooms didn't have locks—in case of fire, supposedly. More likely for random bed checks. Men were allowed in your room on Sundays from 2:00 to 4:00 P.M., with the door ajar ten inches, and three feet on the floor at all times. When she'd read that to Max and their friends from the rulebook, they'd had a great time thinking of all the things you could do and still obey the letter of the law. "Better bring 'Twister,'" advised her friend Sally, who was off to the Curtis School of Music in Philadelphia.

Rachel had composed a piece for high school graduation and found herself playing it softly. What would happen if she skipped the meeting? Her Big Sister, a girl from Scarsdale who was engaged to someone at Dartmouth, would come looking for her. She couldn't feign illness. Not this early. She'd save it for something worse. She put the Martin guitar back in its case. Tomorrow she'd walk into town. There was bound to be a hardware store or maybe a bicycle shop where she could get some kind of lock to attach to the bar in the closet. It wouldn't discourage a serious thief, but would keep away anyone who might think her precious instrument was available for a few rounds of "Michael Row the Boat Ashore."

There was a knock at the door. Rachel glanced in the

mirror. Her oval face looked paler than usual. She swept her straight, black hair into a clip at the nape of her neck.

"Coming," she said with all the enthusiasm of Marie Antoinette stepping into the tumbrel.

The living room of the housemother's suite at Felton was furnished with an eclectic mix of Chippendale and Gothic Revival custom furniture, supplemented by Mrs. MacIntyre's own penchant for chintz-covered, overstuffed armchairs, appropriate receptacles for her ample frame. Ensconced in one, she greeted the girls as they filed in, the Big Sisters from the junior class chatting noisily, the freshmen quiet as mice, clutching their Bluebooks, pens, and notepads. Appropriate to the periods represented, the lighting was poor, casting shadows on the wood-paneled walls. The diamond-paned windows were partially obscured by heavy, maroon velvet drapes. Little of the brilliant sunset outside penetrated the Pelham sanctum.

"Now, ladies, I believe we are all here, so let's begin, shall we? Oh, wait, here's one more." Mrs. MacIntyre had seen the doorknob turn. Not much got past her.

Maggie Howard was sitting on the floor by the fireplace facing the door. She had her notepad open and her Bluebook turned to the first page. She'd underlined what she thought were the most important points throughout the book. "Honor Code" on page 1 was underlined twice. She looked up at the late arrival and gave a start. She was the most beautiful girl Maggie had ever seen off a movie screen, and apparently the rest of the room felt the same way. Everyone was staring as hard as she was.

The girl had dark brown hair that fell in soft curls to her shoulders. She was as tall as Maggie, about five eight, but the physical similarity ended there. A white polo shirt that might have been her brother's or a boyfriend's was tucked into navy linen Bermuda shorts, emphasizing her tiny waist. Slender, but not skinny. Maggie instantly felt ten pounds heavier and wished she hadn't indulged in that second slice of Pelham Fudge Cake (see recipe, p. 322) at dinner. But what was most striking about the girl was the color of her eyes. They were violet. Contact lenses? Somehow Maggie didn't think so. Long dark lashes emphasized the color. Not even the hint of a zit on her glowing face—and when she smiled, as she did now, a small dimple appeared.

"You must be Mrs. MacIntyre. I am so sorry. Daddy was being tiresome and insisted we stop in New Haven to meet some old classmates of his who were dropping their sons off. Mother, Elaine—that's my sister, she's in Crandall—and I begged him not to, but he said it would just take a minute; of course it didn't. Then no one seemed to be able to find a phone, and rather than take even more time, we simply came on along. Please forgive me." She smiled again. "Oh, how silly, I almost forgot. I'm Hélène Prince, but call me Prin—everybody does."

She waited, bowing her head ever so slightly for the housemother's reaction. The Pelham Bluebook had two pages devoted to penalties for being late: late returns from vacations, late returns from absences, to name two categories. Being late to Freshman Orientation wasn't named specifically. Perhaps it had never occurred before. Mrs. MacIntyre took a moment or two before saying, "A Pelham student should always have a dime in her shoe to make an emergency phone call. Public telephones are readily available. However, the only person you have hurt so far is yourself, by missing the opportunity to meet your fellow freshmen. I will check with your sister's housemother at Crandall to be sure she feels as I do that we can excuse your lateness this time." She paused, then softened the tone of her remarks. "Sometimes it's difficult to keep Elis in line."

A few of the juniors laughed and one said, "Did I hear correctly? Mrs. M. casting aspersions on a Yale, not Harvard, man?"

"I'll be sure to get that dime," Prin said, glancing down at her soft shocking-pink Pappagallo flats. A dime would have to go below the sole of her foot or make an indentation in the leather.

She walked across the room and sat down in an empty space on the floor next to Maggie. She smelled faintly of cigarettes and something else, something minty. Maggie, who could only reliably identify her own Jean Naté and her mother's precious Chanel No. 5, wasn't sure whether it was perfume or Life Savers. The question was solved when Prin took out a roll and offered one to Maggie. Not sure whether it counted as food—not allowed in the common rooms, unless at tea on Friday afternoons or some other college-sponsored event, and surely the housemother's living room would be included in the prohibition—Maggie shook her head, but tried to look pleasant so as not to offend the goddess next to her. Maggie had become good at looking pleasant over the years. Girls liked her and at her prep school she had been awarded all sorts of posts by her peers, attaining the status of head girl—the school had mimicked its British counterparts since its inception—during her last term. It suddenly became very important that this girl, her *sister,* like her, too, and Maggie stuck her hand out for the roll as soon as Mrs. MacIntyre was looking the other way. Prin seemed about to laugh, and Maggie wondered why, but as she sucked on the candy, the housemother's words soon drove the thought from her mind.

"You've all read the book. Why do we need to go over it? Anyone?"

"So we won't disgrace you, Mrs. M.," a tall redheaded Big Sister said.

"Don't be so smart, Cynthia." Obviously the redhead was a favorite. "But you're not far off. Replace disgracing me with each of you and there's your reason. The sign-outs, the hours, in short, the rules, may seem old-fashioned, but you're here to learn. And not just academics, but how to make your families proud—how to contribute to society."

Rachel Gold knew if she didn't tune this woman out, she'd have to leave. In loco parentis—that's what the rules were really for. To keep Pelham parents' precious daughters safe, and virgins if possible. That's what they wanted, even her own, supposedly more liberal, parents. The parents who had gone nuts when they discovered she'd let a male friend from school sleep on the floor of her room when he was locked out of his apartment by accident. His parents had been away and he'd been at a concert with Rachel and Max. He could have slept on Max's floor, but her room was much larger. It never occurred to Rachel that her parents would be upset. It wasn't as if she'd been having wild, passionate sex with him. Now she was sorry she hadn't. If Pelham was the punishment, then the crime should have been worthwhile.

"Our house president, Sarah Stevens, will pass out blank sign-out sheets and we'll go over it together, then tomorrow night you'll do one on your own to hand in."

And so it began. After covering every possible contingency—"What if your date doesn't tell you ahead of time where you're going?" to "What happens if I put the wrong time, say we've switched off daylight savings?"—the group adjourned to the dining room for vanilla ice cream with butterscotch sauce and toasted almonds, the "Pelham College Special" at Bailey's Ice Cream Parlor in the center of the village.

Classes didn't start until Thursday and the next three days were filled with appointments and events. The freshman class was addressed by their dean, the dean of the college, the dean of students, and finally the college president herself. Maggie's head was in a whirl. She'd passed her posture picture—a strange experience where she stripped to her underpants, had marks made on her spine with some kind of fluorescent adhesive patches, then entered a dark cubicle after which there was a flash of light and a photo produced, all to check for any curvature that might require a special phys ed class. Similarly, she passed the speech test, although one of her new friends, Sandy Shaw, a pretty girl from West Virginia with a charming lilt to her voice that Maggie envied, failed. The New England accent that always brought President Kennedy to mind was apparently not considered a handicap, nor was the British accent of several classmates—but the South, New Jersey, and certain sections of New York were beyond the pale. Florence Howard had erased any trace of the Midwest from Maggie's speech, until she could have qualified for an anchor position on the nightly news anywhere in the country.

Sandy was enrolled in the speech class, but told Maggie that the moment she was home, her accent would be back—or else. It had been hard enough to convince her family to let her come North to Pelham, and surprisingly hard to leave them when the time came, but "If I come home talking like y'all—'all of you,' " she'd added pointedly—"that will be the end of it."

Then there were tryouts for the choir, various other smaller vocal groups, including Pelham's answer to the Whiffenpoofs, the Pelham Pearls; team tryouts, clubs to join. Maggie felt as if she were at a banquet table, and she always had trouble resisting a tempting dish.

Tuesday morning, Prin tapped her on the shoulder as she was finishing her breakfast. She wished it had been the day before when she'd limited herself to coffee and half a grapefruit, but the popovers this morning had been more than she could resist. Each dorm had its own kitchen and Felton was known for its baked goods—and yearly contribution to the freshman ton.

"We're all meeting in the laundry room tonight at nine after the sing-along or whatever it is."

Freshmen were meeting in the auditorium to learn the traditional college songs. They had until Sunday to create their own class song, which would be performed at the all-college chapel service.

"What for? And why the laundry room?" Maggie asked.

"We have to talk about the class elections and it's the only place big enough for all thirty-four of us."

"Okay. I'll tell Bobbi."

Maggie and her roommate were getting along fine. Roberta—"Bobbi"—Dolan was from Pennsylvania, bluntly explaining that her parents were working-class people who'd struck it rich when her father, who had never been to college, invented and patented a type of truck suspension that apparently all trucks had to have. Bobbi didn't know too much about it. All she knew was that one minute she was sharing a bathroom with five other people and the next she had her own. Like Mrs. Howard, Mrs. Dolan had decided on Pelham for her only daughter and enrolled Bobbi in private school. She confessed she had liked her public school better and that it had been really hard to leave her friends; she was thirteen at the time and never stopped feeling like the new girl. She was very happy to be at Pelham, where everyone was a new girl. Bobbi had no prior connection to Pelham, like Maggie. When she'd heard this, Maggie had thought about all the legacies. There had been a special tea at the college president's house on Sunday afternoon for alums and their daughters. Florence Howard told Maggie, "Someday you'll be bringing your own daughter, *my* granddaughter, to that tea." It was a rare moment of mother-daughter bonding. Maggie vowed to be at the tea, and felt just as excluded as her mother did.

The laundry room was cozy—warm and filled with the scent of Ivory Snow. Prin and her roommate, Phoebe Hamilton, a shy girl from Bedford Hills, New

York, who was rumored to be as smart as she was rich—and she was very rich—were sitting side by side on one of the washing machines. Prin was braiding Phoebe's rather lifeless, mousy brown hair into one long braid down her back. It didn't improve Phoebe's looks much but was obviously making her feel good. Two spots of color had appeared in her normally wan cheeks and her pale gray eyes were shining. Girls who hadn't claimed seats on the appliances were leaning against the walls or sitting on the floor. Someone was passing around a big bag of chips. The noise was loud, but not deafening. There was a lot of laughter. Four girls Maggie didn't recognize as being in Felton entered and were warmly greeted by Prin.

"Hey, everybody, this is my twin, Elaine; her roommate, Chris; our friend from home, Lucy; and *her* roommate, Gwen."

It was immediately obvious that Elaine and Prin were not identical twins, although they were the same size and body type. Not that Elaine Prince was unattractive. It was just in comparison to her sister that she looked plain. Virtually anyone did.

"Okay, okay, you may be wondering why I called you all here together," Prin said.

"I know, it was Colonel Mustard in the Conservatory with the candlestick," someone said, and everybody laughed.

"Very funny. Anyway, tomorrow at our class meeting we're going to nominate our officers—"

"And you want us to put you up for president. Sure, now can we go back to our own dorm?" Lucy said.

"Again, very funny. You know perfectly well that I'd

be terrible. I'd forget to go to meetings. It's all I can do to learn the damn song. No, I'm going to nominate Maggie Howard. Felton hasn't had a president since World War One or maybe even the Civil War—"

"Pelham didn't exist then," Phoebe said softly.

Prin patted her on the head. "To continue, I think it's time for a Felton prez and Maggie would be great. There are thirty-four of us plus my sister and you other three from Crandall, so if we all vote for Maggie, she'll get it. Is anyone at Crandall organizing like this?"

Elaine shook her head. "Not to my knowledge. I mean, no one's dragged us into any suds-filled rooms." She looked at her sister with admiration. "I don't think anyone in our class has given it the thought you have, Prin."

Prin shot her sister a pleased look and tossed her hair back.

"Anyway, I've been talking to a few girls in other dorms, telling them how great Maggie would be, and if we all do vote for her it should go off without a hitch. Any discussion?"

"I'm assuming you've asked Miss Howard if she wants the job and have checked to see whether anyone else had a burning desire for it?" Lucy said. She obviously enjoyed needling Prin, and it seemed to be an old, and friendly, routine.

"Of course Maggie wants it. Just look at the girl's posture. She was born to lead. Any other discussion?" Prin ignored the second part of Lucy's question.

Maggie had been sitting straight as a ramrod on the concrete floor, but it was as much from shock as innate leadership ability. Prin was picking her! Why?

"Gwen is really good at math; let's put her up for treasurer," Elaine suggested. "Everyone at Crandall would vote for her, too."

There was general agreement and soon the girls were exiting into the basement hallway. Maggie tried to catch Prin's eye, and when that didn't work, she wiggled her way forward, finally getting close enough to tap Prin's shoulder.

"Um, I need to talk to you."

Prin turned around. "Sure, what's on your mind?"

Maggie glanced around. She didn't want to air her misgivings in front of everyone.

Prin said quietly, "Cold feet? I meant it when I said you were a natural and don't tell me you haven't been doing this kind of thing forever. I'll bet you had Robert's Rules memorized backward and forward by the time you were ten. Besides, I'll be around to help you. The power behind the throne." Maggie felt relieved. Yes, she *had* been doing this kind of thing forever and Pelham was just another school, after all. No, that wasn't true, it was Pelham! But Prin would be there for her. They were a team.

She woke up at dawn the next morning, too excited to sleep. She didn't want to wake Bobbi, so she lay in bed savoring the moment. "The power behind the throne." Prin's phrase leaped to mind. Quickly, Maggie replaced it with another one, "She was born to lead."

And so she would.

That afternoon Pelham's Class of 1970 elected Margaret Howard as their president, and Gwen Mansfield, the other laundry backroom choice, as treasurer. The races had been close—Prin was obviously not the only king-maker on campus, but she prevailed. Maggie's speech had been well received, especially her ironic promise to make it her top priority to get the "three feet on the floor" rule reduced to two feet.

When the meeting was over, Prin grabbed Maggie's hand and pulled her out of the building, ignoring Maggie's well-wishers.

"Let's go up to the tower. This is a special occasion."

"But won't it be locked? It's after four o'clock," Maggie said.

Pelham's Gothic tower atop the main administration building was a landmark for miles around, dominating the gentle suburban landscape that surrounded the campus. Students were allowed to go to the top in pairs from 10:00 A.M. to 4:00 P.M. every day except Sunday. An elevator went to the top floor, then behind a door reminiscent of a medieval manor house, a series of winding stairs led upward. A similar door opened outward to the top, revealing what was, indeed, a magnificent view. The city of Boston, the City on the Hill, lay shimmering far off on one side, distant mountains on another, and on the two sides in between, the microscopic daily lives of Pelham, Massachusetts, and the town next to it, South Pelham.

"I know where the key is—it's a secret passed down from mother to daughter; at least my mother passed it down. Before students were allowed to smoke on campus, she and her friends used to go up to the tower to satisfy their cravings. Come on!"

Maggie followed Prin inside and up, reluctantly at first—she didn't like heights—then, infected by Prin's wild mood, with mounting anticipation. By the time she stepped out onto the roof, any hesitation was long forgotten. She spun around again, as she had in her room, her eyes widening. But she didn't laugh this time.

"It's like being on top of the world," she had said solemnly.

"No," Prin corrected her. "Not *like*. We *are* on top of the world." And she laughed.

Dear Max,

As I told you at Thanksgiving, if I don't think too hard, it's not that bad here. Some of the girls still make me want to throw up—the ones in their cashmere twin sets with pearls only on weekends for dates; everybody looks like a slob during the week. These are the girls who also knit during lectures, sweaters and scarves for their Princeton, Dartmouth, Yale, or maybe Harvard honey. Outside of class they spend a lot of time in the common room on our floor playing bridge and smoking. They have to have some brains or they wouldn't be here, but so far I haven't seen much evidence. I know I sound like a bitch, but they get to me sometimes. I see their future lives in Westchester or Connecticut, or wherever, going to the Club for bridge, but essentially doing what they did before Pelham and what they're doing here. On weekends, they get a little tight, enough to let their boyfriends get to second base, but not third until there's an engagement ring and a date set.

I'm sorry, I didn't mean to go into all that. Maybe I'll end up a sour old spinster, a fate worse than death according to most of the women here, but it would be better than the lives they'll have. Ending up like the women in that Salinger short story, "Uncle Wiggly in Connecticut." I'd have my music and that's really why I'm writing. I couldn't wait to tell you! I've finally found a teacher. You know I kept asking around in the music department and it paid off. I could have found someone in Cambridge or Boston, but it would have been expensive. This woman, Ruth Hamilton, lives in Pelham and teaches at the Berklee College of Music. We've worked out a deal where I babysit in exchange for the lessons. She has two kids, boys, one six and one eight. I hate babysitting, but these kids seemed great. Not whiners (or needing their diapers changed, ugh!). Mrs. Hamilton thinks I could get a scholarship for Berklee's summer program, but I want to come home. I miss the city so much it hurts. Ditto you, brother dear!

The friends I told you about are still okay, even fun. Sledding down the hill outside the dorm on trays we stole from the dining room on the night of the Great Blackout (still can't believe that you were actually on the Staten Island Ferry coming back and saw the whole city disappear!) is still the most fun I've had here. Sure, the blackout was a once-in-a-lifetime thing and everybody went a little crazy, but I wish the girls here were looser. Now get your mind out of the gutter. You know what I mean. None of them is what I would call a kindred spirit. Maybe Prin, the gorgeous one. She and her twin live in *the city and actually like music other than the Fab Four (although there's something about George that gets to me!). The family must be richer than God—town house on the East Side and a big pile out in the Hamptons, but the girls don't flaunt it—not like the snob at the end of the hall who keeps talking about "Pater's private plane." We're going to get together over Christmas vacation—yes, that's what it's called. No other religion exists here, remember—and Prin's roommate, Phoebe from Bedford Hills, will come in and join us. I haven't figured her out. She worships Prin, which is a little weird, but she's absolutely brilliant. She's in my English class and comes up with things that never would have occurred to me in a million years. I think she's immature, in the crush stage. Remember when I was in 7th grade and in love with Wanda Landowska? Prin isn't famous, but she will be someday at something incredible. It has to be hard for her sister, Elaine. She's nice enough and smart, but Prin takes up all the air in the room. She can't help it.*

Please don't tell Mother and Dad that I'm not hating Pelham. I'd leave in a heartbeat if I could go to Juilliard, but then they'd make you go to Harvard (congratulations, by the way! I knew you'd get in) and we'd be apart, so I'll stick it out and next year we'll have fun.

Love,
Rachel

"What are you doing in Phoebe's dresser?" Prin shut the door to her room behind her. Bobbi Dolan tried to put something back in the open drawer, but Prin stopped her, grabbing her hand.

"Show me what you've taken," she said firmly.

Bobbi started to cry and tried to push Prin away.

"Show me," Prin said, tightening her grasp on the girl and pushing her toward the bed. "Sit down and show me what you've taken!"

Sobbing noisily, Bobbi sat down and slowly opened her hand. A pair of Phoebe's earrings lay in her palm.

Prin stood over her, looking down with contempt. "So you're our little sneak thief."

Early in November, girls started missing things from their rooms: scarves, cosmetics, things without much value, then money, and finally, jewelry. There had been enumerable house meetings with stern injunctions from Mrs. MacIntyre for the girl to come forward, confessing either to the housemother or the house president.

Prin strode over to the drawer. "Those aren't her best. Sure you don't want the diamond studs? You could get more for them?" Her voice dripped with sarcasm. "And why have you been ignoring my humble possessions? There's the watch I got for graduation that I never wear. Piaget. Surely you'd want that?"

Bobbi had buried her face in Phoebe's spread. Her whole body was shaking, her cries muffled but piteous. She lifted her head.

"I'll stop. And I haven't sold anything. It's all in one of my suitcases in the storage room."

Prin looked incredulous. "Omigod, you're a klepto!" Instantly she grinned as if meeting a real live kleptomaniac was just what she had been hoping to experience. It was that or the kind of grin a hunter makes when he finds a trap full. Maybe both.

"You can't tell Mrs. M.! Please, I'll give everything back and never do it again. *Please!*"

"Are you asking me to break the honor code? Remember, that makes me as guilty as you. Maybe not *as* guilty, but I'd still be in a lot of trouble for not revealing the harm a member of the Pelham community is inflicting on the rest of the community. I think that's a direct quote." Prin was clearly enjoying herself. "Now, let me see—first I'm supposed to encourage you to turn yourself in. How about it?"

Her mocking suggestion was met with silence.

"If that doesn't work, I'm supposed to turn you in myself. Should I do that, my sticky-fingered friend?"

"No one will know except for the two of us!" Bobbi sat up, pleading.

Prin regarded her for a moment, then said, "Go wash your face with some cold water and come back here. I'll decide what I'm going to do while you're gone."

It didn't take long. Bobbi didn't look much better. Her eyes were swollen and her lips trembled. She was clearly terrified. Whether she would be able to stay at Pelham or not was up to the girl sitting at her desk with her typewriter open in front of her.

"Here it is. You're going to tell me all about what you've taken and from whom and I'll write it down.

88

When, if you can remember. Then you're going to sign it and date it. After we finish, you're going to put everything you took in a bag—I've got a big one from the bookstore—and leave it under a carrel in the library. Campus police will do the rest. Be sure to put something of yours in. Now start talking."

"But what are you going to do with the paper, papers?" Bobbi saw that Prin was making a carbon copy.

"Nothing—for now. And it's always a good idea to have a copy of an important document. Maybe I'll take that one home with me over vacation. One here; one there. Just in case the dorm burns down."

Bobbi didn't feel like crying. She was filled with panic. Why did Prin have to come in at just that moment? Why hadn't she been at lunch with everyone else? Could she have suspected Bobbi? She'd stop; she'd have to stop. But it had been so many years. Starting with the move. She'd go to the mall by herself, telling her mother she was meeting friends. But she didn't have any friends. Gum, nail polish, that kind of thing, then stuff from the gym lockers at school. They were warned not to leave valuables in them, but girls did. Just like at Pelham. The housemother had a small wall safe. You were supposed to put your good jewelry there, but no one ever did. Prin was waiting for her to start. Bobbi couldn't speak. She wouldn't speak.

"I'll write it myself," she whispered hoarsely.

"Suit yourself," Prin said, getting out of the chair, "but get going. You wouldn't want Phoebe to walk in and read over your shoulder now, would you?"

Bobbi started typing. Prin had looked at her with such contempt, as if Bobbi weren't a person but something unpleasant to be avoided on a sidewalk. During orientation, Bobbi had been in one of the stalls in the bathroom and overheard Prin and an upperclassman talking. It was a conversation she had promptly forced out of her mind, but it came back now. "Bobbi Dolan, you mean? Her father is a truck driver or something like that who found a golden goose," Prin had said. The other girl had commented, "I'm surprised at the admissions department. Next thing you know they'll be letting in garbage collectors' daughters." Prin had joined in her laughter, saying, "Tacky, very tacky." Bobbi had waited until they left before emerging and then washed her hands several times.

When she finished typing the confession, it was all she could do to keep her fingers from the keys, adding the words screaming in her head: "I hate you, Prin. I hate you, Prin. I hate you, Prin, I hate you and I wish you were dead."

Four

"Has everyone been getting something to eat and drink? Mrs. Fairchild is famous. I'm sure you've heard of her Have Faith products. I'm quite addicted to the spiced green tomato chutney myself."

Elaine Prince was playing the role of perfect hostess.

"So lovely to see you all. Do sit down and get comfortable. And please don't start again, Lucy." The lady in question had opened her mouth to speak. "I'll explain everything. You're here to have fun and relax. Starting now. Mrs. Fairchild, be a dear, won't you, and pour me some champagne?"

Faith had been cleaning up the shards from the flute that Margaret Howard had dropped. She finished quickly, replaced and refilled the college president's glass, handing another to the author.

"Would you like me to prepare a plate of food for you?"

"How kind, but I'll wait a bit, thank you."

Bishop sat in one of the large armchairs with her back to the fireplace, commanding a view of the room and its occupants.

"Do admit, if I had told you that this was going to be a reunion, most of you probably wouldn't have come. And it's high time we had one—our little group, that is."

Still apparently fixated on the possible loss of income, Bobbi Dolan said, "So, what that man said—your assistant, Owen—none of that was true?"

"Oh no, Bobbi—and gracious, you have changed, love the hair—I would never ask him to lie for me. We'll have massages, listen to Rachel play, glean some advice from Gwen, and learn about some fabulous gardens from Chris—I do want her to tell me what to do with mine. Who else? Well, Phoebe, you, Lucy, Maggie, and I will be the audience. And Mrs. Fairchild, of course, when she's not whipping up something in the kitchen to tempt us from our diets. The island is enchanting; we can take walks in the woods, have a picnic on a different beach each day."

She looked about the room with the satisfied air of a veteran camp director. Faith half expected her to announce water sports at two o'clock; bonfire and group sing at nine.

"Maybe everyone else has a week's time to spare, but I don't," Gwen said angrily. "If it's all the same to you, I'll be leaving in the morning."

Faith had been watching the women's faces and

Gwen's was the easiest to read. The others looked bewildered and in some cases, oddly enough, frightened. As soon as Barbara, no wait, she was Elaine, announced that all the promises would be fulfilled, Bobbi Dolan had visibly relaxed.

Elaine leaned back in the chair. "I'm afraid that won't be possible. I thought you might react this way and I wanted us all to have at least *one* day together, so I told Tony Marston, the man who runs the boat, not to come tomorrow. And the boat is the only way off the island. If you still want to leave on the day after tomorrow, then fine."

"No, not fine!" Gwen exploded. She was extremely angry. "Get on the phone or whatever you have here and get in touch with him immediately. *I'm* leaving in the morning."

Obviously a woman who was used to being in control of situations, Faith thought.

"I'd like to leave, as well," Rachel Gold said. "And you can keep the fee. You're right. I wouldn't have come if I had known what you intended, and now that I do know, I'm not comfortable staying."

Before anyone else could speak, Elaine stood up. In her flowing robe, she looked like a deity—or a 1940s movie star.

"You're going to have to make the best of it. This is where I do most of my work and I have intentionally made it impossible for anyone to reach me. No phone, not even a satellite one; no radio, nothing. The boat comes twice a day and that is how I communicate with the outside world."

Gwen's jaw dropped, then she snapped it shut.

"I don't believe you. Someone in your position wouldn't be here without any means of communication. What about emergencies?"

"Brent flies the flag upside down; it's only happened once. A guest broke an ankle after the boat left for the day and we didn't want the poor woman to suffer through the night. A fisherman picked her up. And as for not believing me, you're welcome to search the premises, but can't you simply accept the situation and get to know your friends again? Wall Street isn't going anywhere."

Before Gwen could respond, Lucy spoke up. "I've been around boats all my life; I'll take anyone who wants to leave to the mainland tomorrow. You must have a flotilla in that huge boathouse."

"A relic from the island's former owner, which I restored for purely aesthetic reasons. We had a rowboat of some sort, but I believe it sank. You can ask Brent. Boats don't interest me. I haven't even sailed since our days together at the club, Luce, and you may remember how bad I was at it."

Lucy opened her mouth to say something, then abruptly closed it.

No matter how competent the sailor, a trip by canoe or rowboat back to the mainland would be impossible even if there were one, Faith thought, remembering how long it had taken to get out to the island.

"Now, please, let's not waste this lovely food, and I'm sure there's something special for dessert," Elaine urged.

Rachel Gold got up and quietly left the room. Gwen followed her—not so quietly.

"If you get hungry later, come down and raid the refrigerator. There's also bottled water, other drinks, and snacks on the landing," their hostess called after them as if their departure was nothing out of the ordinary.

Lucy Stapleton sighed audibly. "Well, you may have changed your appearance, Elaine, but not your personality. You never would admit there was anything wrong in the garden and you still don't. I'm going to have more to eat, go to bed, and yes, tomorrow I'd love a massage and maybe Chris can tell me how to grow Asiatic lilies without red bug."

Before long, the others followed suit, and Faith was kept busy serving, but not too busy to watch Phoebe James. She had moved next to Elaine, wordless at first, gazing at her hostess.

"You *do* look exactly like her," she said.

She reached out and lightly touched the purple silk caftan, then drew her hand back, but Elaine caught it, holding it in hers for an instant before releasing it.

"You're so beautiful, just like she would have been," Phoebe said.

"Oh no, Prin would have been much prettier. She always was. But we'll never know, will we?"

The plates of food Faith had left for Brent Justice— dinner plus two desserts—had disappeared. When she went to fill the dishwasher, she'd found his plates rinsed and stacked. Maybe in the future he would give her a hand with cleaning up. She didn't feel like tracking him down now. He'd left several quarts of strawberries and some rhubarb on the counter.

She pushed the button to start the dishwasher, marveling at how you could still have all the modern conveniences far away from a power company—not to mention luxuries like the pool—if you had enough money. And there was no question that Barbara Bailey Bishop/ Elaine Prince had enough money.

Before she'd gone up to bed herself, the last one, Prince had told Faith that she should have coffee, fruit, and some baked goods ready in the kitchen at 7:00 A.M. for any early risers, then take orders for full breakfasts at 9:00 A.M. "Let's keep it all casual. Oh, and think about a nice picnic lunch. There are hampers in one of the storage closets next to the wine cellar. Brent will load the cart and leave it at the spot I've picked. Could you have it ready at noon for him?" she'd said.

Faith went to check and the hampers were, as she suspected, the British type fitted with china, glassware, cutlery, thermoses, boxes for sandwiches and other fare. They would have been more at home at Ascot than on this rocky island. There were insulated bags for wine and other drinks. Cucumber sandwiches? Chutney and cheese? She felt as if she'd stepped into a Merchant-Ivory film.

At last she turned out the kitchen lights and went upstairs. It was only 11:00 P.M. but it felt much later. It had been a long day. There were voices on the landing. Faith stopped and devoted herself to unabashed eavesdropping. It was Christine Barker and Phoebe James.

"I'm sorry I didn't stay in touch, but well—you know," Phoebe said.

"We couldn't get away from Pelham and each other fast enough," Chris said.

"Oh no, not you. I always liked you, Chris. It was just that everything was so confused, so horrible. I don't even really remember it all. I know my mother was mad at me for moping around that summer. That's what she called it—'moping'—and then I met my husband. I mean, he wasn't my husband then, but we got married the following June, so I didn't go to Columbia. My parents didn't see the point and my mother said we needed the time to plan the wedding."

"But Phoebe, wasn't your senior thesis published in some journal? I always pictured you teaching at some university and getting one of those genius awards."

Phoebe laughed. It ended in what sounded like a sob to Faith.

"Wesley didn't—doesn't—want to be married to a bluestocking. Then there were the kids."

"Aren't your daughters only sixteen and your son thirteen? What did you do all those years before they were born? Forget that. It's really none of my business. I'm sorry."

"No, it's nice to talk. I don't have friends the way a lot of women do. Maybe if I did, I wouldn't need a shrink." There was that laugh again. "We lived in the city, New York, on the East Side. I gave the right kind of parties for Wes's career and tried to get pregnant. It took a while. Wes was so sure it was me—never any problems in that department on the James side—that he didn't get tested until one of the specialists said he wouldn't work with us unless he did. It turned out that his swimmers weren't quite the champions he thought they were."

The two women laughed together. It was hard for Faith to keep herself from joining in. Ah, men.

"I should never have given in so easily; I desperately wanted to go to Columbia." Phoebe's tone of voice switched abruptly to deep regret. "I *was* smart, wasn't I? But girls weren't supposed to be in those days. Maybe not now, either. My daughters are smart, but it's the old 'Never let them see you sweat.' All those *A*'s look effortless. And looks! They're gorgeous. Wes is so proud of them. When we go out to eat, he has one of them on each arm. Trophy daughters. Josh and I bring up the rear. My girls gave up on my appearance long ago. They used to make suggestions; now they don't bother. Just stare right through me. I'm furniture. For Wes, too. At least Josh notices me—even if it's in a negative way, it's something. I'm the enforcer. The giver of curfews. He tries to fight with his father, but Wes doesn't fight. It's one of his least endearing qualities. He's provided me with everything a woman could want—a big house in a select suburb, trips all over the world, jewelry I never wear . . ." Her voice trailed off. "I do have two darling dogs—Irish terriers— Molly and Piper. Molly and Piper don't care what I look like and they like to hear what I have to say." She stopped abruptly. "I've been talking too much. What about you, Chris? You never filled out anything for the reunion record books, but you're married, right? Kids?"

"No, I'm not married and I never, that is, I don't have any kids."

That odd pause after *never* jumped out at Faith. She wondered whether Phoebe picked up on it, too.

"That's too bad," Phoebe said in what seemed to Faith a slightly envious voice. Her next words confirmed it. "So, you've always been free to do whatever you wanted, go wherever you wished." It wasn't a question, but a statement of fact.

Chris said, "Not exactly. I've had to make my living and for a while I was supporting my mother, too. When my father died, his pension died with him and Social Security wasn't enough. My mother didn't want to lose the house. I moved in and helped out. My brother has a large family, and well, I was, as you said, free."

There was a moment of silence.

"I meant it when I said I love your columns. I have that book, the collection of them. I'm looking forward to tomorrow—and the rest of the week. I want to stay," Phoebe said.

"I'm not sure I will," Chris said slowly. "Phoebe, why do you think Elaine gathered us here?"

"For a reunion. We *did* use to be close. We lived together all those years. It can't be anything else. I mean, what else could it be?"

"A trial?" Chris said, but before she could add anything to her words, Elaine's voice came from one end of the hall.

"See, I knew it would work out. Here you are having the same kind of girl-talk gabfest we used to have back at Pelham! Don't let me interrupt you. I want to leave a note for my handyman on the kitchen table. You can't imagine how early he gets up in the morning."

Before her employer could discover her on the stairs, Faith thought it prudent to ascend.

"Everything was delicious, Mrs. Fairchild," Phoebe said. She had stood up and Chris was following her; apparently the gabfest was at an end. "And I do know your products. They have them at the Williams So-noma in the mall near my home. I like the chutneys too, but your Peach Melba jam is my favorite."

"Thank you," said Faith. "I'm glad I tucked that into the selection I brought—and please, everyone, do call me Faith. See you in the morning. Good night."

The group split up with more *good nights*. Faith closed her door.

A trial?

Faith was up early, but when she went into the kitchen it was apparent that Brent Justice had come and gone. Bless the man, he'd made coffee. The large urn was sending a fragrant message her way—"drink me"—and she got herself a cup. Perhaps he was in the garden. She wanted to pick lettuce for salad and see what else was coming in. The strawberries he had left glistened in the early morning light. It was impossible to overdose on straw-berries in season and she'd make them a running culi-nary theme throughout the week. Freshly picked ones as a breakfast choice each day. And the rhubarb was beg-ging to be made into strawberry-rhubarb pie. She'd also do an old-fashioned rhubarb crumble with some straw-berries to balance the tartness (see recipe, p. 321). She set her cup in the sink and picked up two of the trugs and a small basket. There should be enough wild strawber-ries to make the coulis she'd envisioned yesterday for tonight's panna cotta with some saved for a liberal gar-nish. As she went out the door, the clear morning air with the smell of the sea and growing things intoxicated her. She'd toss strawberries with fig vinegar, a change from balsamic, roast them with a smidgeon of butter, make shortcake—the real kind with biscuits, not sponge cake—offer sorbets of the various varieties, do cold fruit soup—the list was endless.

Faith was alone in the garden, but Brent's hard work was in evidence everywhere. She didn't see a single weed in the raised vegetable beds, in the rows of flowers in the cutting garden, among the herbs, or in the borders surrounding the house that mixed sedums, lupine, ferns, daisies, and other native plants with their cultivated cousins—mallow, astilbes, hostas, lilies, peonies, delphinium. There was plenty of lettuce, some rainbow chard, and spinach. Too soon for much else, but plenty of promise. The peas were doing nicely, twining gracefully up the strings Brent had rigged up, and runner beans were beginning their ascent on rustic twig tepees. Several of the beds had arched twig trellises. One lone lush purple clematis was already in bloom, more buds ready to burst, in abundance.

Putting the laden trugs down, she went to the strawberry beds and soon filled her basket with the *fraises des bois*, a process that might have taken less time if she hadn't eaten so many as she picked. They were irresistible. The day was filled with promise. Already the sun had warmed the fruit and the top of Faith's head. She'd have to remember to unpack the squishable straw hat she'd brought and leave it in the kitchen by the door. The sky had changed from watercolor blue to deep robin's egg, with plenty of cumulus clouds that looked as if a child had cut them out of construction paper and pasted them in the sky.

It was quiet. Only an occasional seagull's cry or the screech of a tern interrupted the stillness. Faith had come to relish any time alone, a rare commodity in her always too busy life. She'd heard an echo of that in Phoebe's voice last night as she spoke of wanting to stay for the whole week. To have time alone, time just for herself.

The captive reunion, as Faith had come to think of it, might work, after all. Gorgeous weather, good food, and this extraordinarily beautiful place might smooth over any initial annoyance at having been tricked into coming. Chris and Phoebe had reconnected. Perhaps the rest would, too. Maybe not Gwen, but everyone else.

Mint, thyme, rosemary, chives—she snipped some herbs and reluctantly went back inside the kitchen to set up the early risers' buffet. It was going to be hard to stay inside on a day like this.

Rachel Gold was sitting on a stool at the counter.

"I'm so sorry," Faith said. "I got carried away in the garden. There's coffee and I was just about to set out juice and muffins. Or I can make you a nice omelet with the fresh herbs I just picked."

"That sounds wonderful. I was too upset to eat last night and I'm starving."

"Then let me get you some coffee and a muffin right now. Or there's tea—English Breakfast, Earl Grey, Lapsang souchong, Darjeeling, chai, herbal, you get the idea."

"I do—Elaine has provided for every possible taste. She was always very thorough. Coffee is fine. Black."

As she placed the food in front of the musician, Faith was struck again by how much younger some of the women looked than others. Rachel was in the first group.

Her dark hair showed only a few strands of gray and was cut short, fitting her head like a sleek cap of feathers—like a cormorant's. Her oval face was unlined; she wasn't wearing any makeup and still her skin glowed. Faith tried to remember what she knew about Ms. Gold. The covers of Tom's treasured early albums pictured her with a serious expression on her face, her long hair spilling over her shoulders as she held her guitar, poised to play. The liner notes on these or the CDs that replaced them never mentioned a husband—or a lover. Rachel Gold was apparently totally devoted to her music. Faith also recalled that Rachel, like herself, had been born and raised in Manhattan. Unlike Faith, Rachel still lived there.

As she whisked the eggs, Faith said, "My husband and I have always loved listening to you—several times in concert and over and over again at home."

"Thank you," Rachel said, smiling. Faith hadn't wanted to sound like a sycophant, but did want to convey their appreciation of the woman's extraordinary talent.

"I grew up in the city, too, but I live outside Boston now, lured away by my husband who still can't quite believe that people are born and raised in the Big Apple. He thinks of it as a stopover, not a point of arrival—let alone the end of the journey." She placed the fragrant omelet on the counter, accompanied by brioche toast and a mound of the fresh strawberries. "Jam, jelly—or perhaps chèvre? I have some from Sunset Acres farm that's sweetened with a little honey, cranberries, and a hint of orange."

"This is fine, thank you. I never have more than

coffee, yogurt, and fruit normally." She began to eat with obvious relish.

"You made a great sacrifice for your husband—am I wrong or was there a bit of longing in your voice?"

"There's *always* a bit of longing in my voice when I talk to a fellow New Yorker, especially one who's probably living in a great apartment—West Side, pre-war, and don't tell me rent-controlled."

"Okay, I won't tell you. Suffice it to say you're three for three."

Relaxed by the food, Rachel stretched, got up, and poured herself another cup of coffee.

"Is this your cup? Would you like some?" she asked.

"Sure," said Faith, "but I should be waiting on you."

Rachel resumed her perch by the counter. "I'm not good at being waited on. I didn't grow up with servants, unlike some of the ladies upstairs asleep. Not that we were poor. Not by any means. My mother didn't clean and still hasn't plugged in an iron in her life. But she loved to cook. That particular gene missed me, much to her chagrin. She's sure it's why I never married."

"We should trade. My mother is still mystified by my profession, although she would never call it that. A profession is what she and my sister do—things for which you need briefcases."

"What did Elaine tell you about this week?"

The question was an abrupt change of topic, and tone.

Faith sat down. "I never spoke to her. Her assistant called and said Ms. Bishop was having a small reunion of Pelham classmates. I had a company in the city before I was married and she remembered attending some of the events I catered. My sister is a Pelham alum and I was in a photo with her in the alumnae magazine that Ms. Bishop saw. That's how she tracked me down. I was flattered, and curious to meet her, of course, although the first time I ever read anything by her was on the train coming here."

"So you're the only one of us who knew what was going on, or rather, that we would all be here." Rachel seemed to be talking to herself.

"But it's okay now, isn't it?" Faith said, trying to keep the end of the conversation she overheard last night from her mind. "You were friends at Pelham and now you have time to reconnect in this beautiful spot. My sister's closest friends are her Pelham classmates. They see each other often; even the ones who have scattered come to the city when there's something going on." There must have been at least ten Pelham friends at the christening, Faith remembered, and more at Hope's wedding.

Rachel pushed her empty cup away. "I haven't seen any of these women since graduation. And I don't have fond memories of Pelham. The opposite. I couldn't wait to leave."

"Then you won't be staying on here," Faith said.

"No, I won't be staying."

The words hung in the air, stale smoke after a party.

Faith picked up the dishes and moved toward the sink.

"I think I'll take a walk," Rachel said.

"The gardens are lovely and there seems to be a path into the woods back by the greenhouse."

Out the window the sun was shining brightly.

"I probably won't need this, but I'll take it anyway—more quotations from Chairman Mom: 'Take a sweater just in case.'" Rachel was obviously trying to lighten the mood.

Faith wasn't playing; Rachel had dropped a bomb, so she could, too.

"Who was Prin? And do *you* know what's going on here?"

Rachel stood still and took her hand from the doorknob. She looked straight at Faith.

"Prin was Elaine's twin sister. She took a swan dive off Foster Tower in the center of campus into the ivy many, many feet below just before graduation. She was beautiful—for whatever reason, Elaine has made herself over to look a lot like her sister. Prin's eyes were the first feature anyone noticed. Violet, and without lenses, which must be how Elaine is achieving the effect. Besides being beautiful, Prin was, well, clever, very clever. Everyone here knew her." She paused and seemed to be deep in thought. "As to what's going on, I think Elaine has convinced herself that Prin's death wasn't an accident or suicide, but murder."

"Murder!"

Rachel nodded. "Yes, murder—and one of us the murderer."

Before Faith could ask her what could possibly have led her to this startling, even bizarre, supposition, Rachel Gold opened the door and left.

Faith watched the group emerge from the woods and stand still, struck by the view as she had been earlier when she'd come out with Brent and the cart. The path through the woods was lovely, winding past stately pines and the occasional hardwood, a large black oak that begged for a child's tree house, birch groves, swaying poplars. Rocky ledges were covered with various carpets—deep green velvet moss, grizzled gray lichens like old men's beards, mountain cranberries, the fruit still pale and small, low junipers, and bunchberries. The path was studded with granite outcroppings and gnarled roots. The cart bounced along. Brent, who had obviously been this way many times before, had cushioned the hampers with the picnic spreads they'd be sitting on.

The view had stopped her in her tracks, too. It wasn't the change from the scant, filtered sunlight to the brilliant day, although that was arresting. It was the view—straight out to sea from the top of a high bluff. Faith had crossed the small meadow, and looked over the edge. Far below, the surf surged up over the rocks. There was a thunder hole, and the echo from the pounding waves reached all the way to the top of the cliff. This was not a sandy beach, a beach to stroll upon, peering into tide pools, but one composed of rocky slabs tossed up by an angry sea. It was wild—and very beautiful.

Now the group was moving toward the edge, the way she had. Elaine was in the lead. Faith had set out the picnic at the start of the meadow where there was some shade. The writer strode over. Faith, adept at reading the body language of employers, tried to prepare herself for what was sure to be a complaint. But what? The spread could be photographed for *Gourmet* or *H&G* without a single addition or alteration. Besides the colorful Pierre Deux Provençal spreads, there were cushions upon which one might sit or recline against. Low folding tables held the food and drink. Faith had set out a salad of roasted vegetables in a rosemary vinaigrette, another of field greens. She'd grouped bowls of red and yellow grape tomatoes, tiny new carrots, and sugar snap peas around a lemon dill hummus dip, light on the garlic. There were tea sandwiches: cucumber, watercress, smoked salmon, crab, and egg salad with caviar. She'd also provided heartier fare—focaccia with layers of provolone, slivered marinated artichoke hearts, and prosciutto; another with smoked turkey, farmhouse cheddar, and chutney. There were old-fashioned brownies, oatmeal-raisin cookies, and lemon squares to go with a fruit salad—nectarines, melon, grapes, fresh mint, and of course strawberries—for dessert. A quick trip to the garden yielded a bouquet of lady's mantle, delphinium, Shasta daisies, and lilacs, which Faith had placed in a galvanized metal watering can she'd found in one of the kitchen closets. The watering can—that must be it! Too plebeian?

"Mrs. Fairchild, why have you set up so far back from the cliff? Surely you must have seen that the view out to sea and to the shore below is magnificent."

So this was it.

"Yes, it's absolutely gorgeous, but I thought some of your guests could want a bit of shade and it's better for the food, too. Plus you might have some acrophobiacs." Faith smiled as she offered the last, lighthearted, she hoped, remark.

"None of my guests have phobias of any sort."

Now what to say? Faith wondered. Hasten to assure

her that Faith had not meant to imply anything, that of course her classmates had all their marbles and then some. But before she could say anything, inane or otherwise, Ms. Bishop continued.

"Impossible to move all this now. We'll just have to make do. Tonight we'll dine at the house, and then gather at the shore for a bonfire. Brent will see to that. All you have to do is provide some sort of refreshments."

Something told Faith that s'mores would be out, although they were being featured in some of New York City's trendy restaurants, along with milk 'n' cookies.

Margaret Howard, the college president, was the first to arrive at the picnic table.

"Thank God you didn't set up any closer to the edge of the cliff," she said, piling her plate with food. "I can't stand heights. Just looking at it from here gives me vertigo."

So much for phobia-free guests, Ms. Bishop, Faith thought with more than a touch of smugness. With the thought came another—working for the famous author wasn't going to be the piece of cake Hope had promised and Faith herself envisioned.

All the women, even Gwen Mansfield, had trekked out to the picnic. Faith had been surprised to see her. She'd appeared in the kitchen at nine o'clock and asked that a carafe of coffee, pitcher of skim milk, and some fruit be brought to her room. Faith made up a tray, adding a basket of muffins, scones, and whole-grain toast plus jam and butter. When she checked an hour later, the tray was in the hall—the carbs, even the toast, untouched. A picnic didn't seem to be Ms. Mansfield's thing, but perhaps she didn't want to be left alone in the house. Although, given the increasingly tense atmosphere, Faith wouldn't have blamed her. The mood was at great odds with the weather and the setting, but it was there. The women had divided into three groups, physically close but conversationally separate. Chris, Phoebe, Rachel, and Bobbi made up one; Gwen and Lucy another; Elaine and Margaret the third. The college president had mentioned Barbara Bailey Bishop's generous offer to the college when she'd come down for breakfast, and Faith was sure the administrator wouldn't let her patron out of her sight until the deal was signed, sealed, and delivered. From the snippets of conversation coming her way, Margaret Howard seemed to be laying it on thick, enumerating the benefits that would accrue to generations of Pelham women from the writer's gifts. The writer herself was looking extremely bored, not even bothering to reply. She had been picking at some salad and put her plate to one side. Glancing at her companion, she said, "Care to take a stroll, Maggie?"

"I'd be delighted," she said. "There were so many lovely-looking trails in the woods. Beckoning, like the road less traveled by." She beamed at her hostess, obviously pleased at the opportunity to work in a literary allusion.

"No, I want to go over by the cliff. It's such fun to sit on the top and look down."

Margaret Howard blanched. "Well, I'm not . . ."

"I'll come." Gwen hadn't taken anything to eat, but was drinking some Pellegrino water. She finished the glass and handed it to Faith, who happened to be close by. Faith had the feeling that it was not mere chance, but some kind of ordering of earth's molecules that she happened to be where she was. The Gwen Mansfields of the world always had people in position to provide whatever service they might need.

Everyone watched as the two women walked across the meadow, filled with splashes of color from hawkweed, crown vetch, clover, and Indian paintbrush. They were the same height and walked with the loose grace of people with personal trainers. At the edge they sat down, their legs out of sight over the cliff.

The group had watched silently, and taken a collective audible breath as the two assumed their precarious perch—then let it out as Lucy spoke.

"Like sister, like sister. The tower, cliffs, the highest possible place, where you can look down at everyone else, although in Elaine's case, it's only some seagulls and a whole lot of marine life." Faith noted the bitterness in the woman's voice. She wished she knew more about Prin, the dead woman. The murdered woman?

No one said anything, unlike the two figures in the distance who appeared to be in deep conversation. The wind had picked up and blew Elaine's hair about. Gwen's was pulled back in a tight knot, not a single strand escaping.

"How about some dessert, ladies?" Faith asked brightly. She was beginning to feel like a camp director, or counselor, herself.

"Sure," Phoebe said. "It's a vacation. Those brownies are calling my name."

"Brownies have always been calling your name," Bobbi said, standing up and offering a hand to Phoebe. "Remember how we used to break into the kitchen for leftover desserts when it was something good like Pelham Pudding or Fudge Cake?"

Her words triggered a flood of food reminiscences, and suddenly the reunion was the way Faith imagined it would be, the way her sister's were.

"Garbage salad!" shrieked Rachel. "I'd completely forgotten about it! And we actually loved it. What was in it anyway?"

Lucy ticked off the ingredients on her fingers, "Lettuce, iceberg, no arugula or mâche, but they don't get that even now at Pelham, I'm sure; cucumbers, Velveeta cheese cut into matchsticks, hard-boiled eggs, cucumbers, more matchsticks of some kind of processed meat, tomatoes carved from wood, and tons and tons of French dressing."

"And sit-down dinner every night—in skirts or a dress. I told my daughters about it recently and you would have thought I was describing life in Victorian times," Lucy said.

"It *was* life in Victorian times. That's when all the rules were first made up. 'Gracious living,' I believe it was called. Then all hell broke loose the fall after we left." Chris sounded regretful.

"Maybe we were an anachronism, but I liked being forced to stop working and eat with all of you every night. I think kids now are missing out; no conversations, just grabbing whatever—and that's exactly what they say—before rushing back to their dorm rooms to instant-message each other," Phoebe said.

Faith found herself laughing in appreciation. It was the perfect description of her friend and neighbor in Aleford, Pix Miller's daughter's campus life.

She bent down to gather up the empty plates, straightened up, and looked toward the figures on the edge of the cliff interrupting the horizon.

It was empty.

The light from a bonfire transforms even the most ordinary-looking face into something exotic and primitive. Conjuring up images of tribal rites, urgent signals, and secret summer nights—don't tell the grown-ups—a bonfire binds a group close with its flickering, mesmerizing flames, its fragrant smoke enveloping all impartially. Faith stood in the shadows watching. There were no stars in the ink-black sky and beyond the light cast by the fire the woods—the entire island—was devoured by the darkness.

All eight women sat on rustic stumps artfully arranged around the fire ring. Brent had laid the fire and placed more wood within reach. Elaine had been feeding it steadily, never letting the flames die down to embers. She and Gwen had not slipped off the edge of the island but had walked into the woods unnoticed, emerging just as the startled group was running toward the cliff—some with greater alacrity than others.

During the afternoon, Bobbi had given some massages and Chris had led a tour of Elaine's gardens, as well as talked about her own, showing photographs that illustrated her special gift for growing things. It wasn't clear whether she would continue with more of her planned programs. Only Rachel and Gwen had said they were leaving, and only Maggie, Phoebe, and Bobbi had said they were staying. And Faith.

Why had Bishop hired her? Faith wondered, staring

into the flames for an answer. She saw faces, goblinlike, and shapes—ancient walled cities with towers. But these were the images she always saw in bonfires on the beach at Sanpere or those by the pond where they skated in Aleford. There was nothing in the fire to guide her. The story that Elaine—Faith alternated between the nom de plume and the writer's real name—recalled Faith's culinary expertise from fifteen years ago now seemed a bit far-fetched. Faith knew she was good, but that good? Had the writer heard something else about Faith? That Ms. Fairchild had had more than her share of murderous encounters? Had solved more than her share? Rachel's words hadn't been far from Faith's mind all day.

"So, who's going first?" The night was chilly away from the fire. Elaine Prince had wrapped a deep red pashmina scarf over her head for the walk to the beach. It was draped around her shoulders now, as fiery as the flames. "With our life stories, that is. Mine is an open book, no pun intended. You all know much more about me than I do about you."

"That's not true," Phoebe said. "You seldom give interviews. And to start, I would never have dreamed that you were who you are. That is, you didn't write when you were in college. And you weren't even an English major."

Elaine laughed. "Our Phebes, always out for the truth. Yes, I was a history major, but what could I do with that? Teach? I can't imagine anything more boring. Lucy knows how it all started. We were sharing an apartment in the city and both of us working for publishers. Luce, you were trying your hand at a novel and I suppose that's what gave me the idea. I went off to

Europe where my parents were living and then drifted from here to there, writing all the time. I know people thought I'd done something disgraceful, like join a cult or marry one of the help. My parents thought it was rather amusing—the way no one ever asked where I was or what I was doing, too well bred to come right out and say something. I suppose that's when I first began to enjoy being anonymous. In fact, I was writing, just like Lucy."

Lucy, intent on the fire, didn't say anything.

"By the way, whatever happened to your book?" Elaine asked.

"You know very well what happened," Lucy snapped.

Bobbi jumped into the conversation, steering it away from the shoals. "I for one would like to hear whatever somebody wants to share. I've often wondered what happened to all of you. Last night I told you about me. It isn't a long or very interesting story. Having no skills whatsoever and not wanting to go back home, I headed to California after graduation, as I said. My parents weren't pleased. In fact, we became almost completely estranged. Their 'hippie' daughter wasn't going to give them bragging rights—or, as my marriages failed, grandchildren. My sister called me when my father was dying and I flew home, but he didn't want to see me, and my mother was upset that I'd come—and angry with my sister, who totally caved. I wasn't even there twenty-four hours. To them, I was nothing more than a prostitute. They didn't understand the philosophies behind massage at all."

Chris reached over and took Bobbi's hand. "I'm sure

you have wonderful friends in California who do, and remember that old saying, 'Friends are God's excuse for family.'"

Bobbi looked grateful. "I *do* have a great group of friends. And Calistoga is a very special place. The mineral pools and volcanic-ash mud baths are famous, but there's so much more—great places to eat, galleries . . ."

"You should work for the chamber of commerce," Gwen said sarcastically, but then took some of the sting away from her words. "Calistoga is fun. I've been there several times."

"And what about you, Gwen? Married? Kids? I know you're a financial wizard—bought the book—but what else?" Lucy asked.

"You may recall my first husband, Geoff Weaver. We got engaged senior year and married at the end of our first year in business school. Finances got tight and of course I was the one who dropped out to shore up the family fortunes. He decided after the B School that he wanted a law degree. By then, we had one child and another on the way. The summer I spent between our junior and senior years at Katie Gibbs proved fortuitous, and I got a secretarial job at Goldman Sachs, plus a new focus. It's such a cliché, but as soon as my husband passed the bar, he passed on us, too. Oh, he paid child support, but I decided I'd never be dependent on a man, or anyone other than myself, again—and I haven't. My second marriage was for love, and a little bit for money. David was older and we had ten very happy years together before he died. Since then, I've preferred to remain a merry widow, enjoying my career and alternating coasts."

"Where do your kids live and what do they do?"

"My sons went to live with their father when they were teenagers and we have not stayed in touch." Gwen's tone of voice made it very clear that the subject was off-limits. "It's getting rather windy, Elaine. How long do you intend for this little gathering to last?"

The wind *was* picking up and the fire was swirling higher, producing arcs like Fourth of July sparklers. Faith had brought various hot drinks ranging from cocoa to Irish coffee and had been refilling the women's mugs. Phoebe and Maggie were the only ones who ate full portions at lunch and dinner, so Faith had only brought cookies and fruit, which no one had touched. She thought of the groaning larders and wondered what she would do with all the leftover food at the end of her stint on Bishop's Island, although Indian Island, the original name, seemed more appropriate tonight. The bonfire suggested other, earlier incarnations.

"It's not up to me when we head back, it's up to you. But we haven't heard from everybody yet. Rachel?"

The musician had been lost in thought, and her head jerked up at the sound of her name.

"What? Oh, the story of my life? No, thank you. I'll pass. Give Maggie my turn."

"Checkbooks out, everyone," Gwen said dryly. "Sorry, Mags, but you know that's what your job is all about. I admire what you've done."

"Thank you—and anyone who wants to make out a check to Pelham is more than welcome. I have no qualms about asking for donations anywhere, any time," she said in an upbeat manner. "But you're not completely right, Gwen. Fund-raising is a major part of my job, but not the most important part. The most important part is maintaining the excellence and integrity of the college. Fortunately, I have extraordinary faculty, staff, and students to help me."

"Tell about your husband. He's in government, right?" Phoebe said.

"Yes, we met when I was working at Georgetown. And he's been in several governments. Equal opportunity opinion giver on international relations and very careful to keep his party affiliation secret."

"A Deep Throat who speaks many tongues?" Lucy said mockingly. Faith had noticed she'd had more Irish coffee refills than the others.

"He *is* fluent in a number of languages, yes, but his connection to Bernstein and Woodward has always been purely social," Maggie said.

Was it Faith's imagination or did Maggie's quick response seem a bit too defensive? What exactly did her husband do? She wished one of the women would ask for specifics. It wasn't her place to intrude.

Rachel spoke up. "You got exactly what you wanted, Maggie. I meant to send you a note when you were inaugurated. President of our class all those years, then student body head, and a whole bunch of other things. Your being Pelham's president was meant to be."

"Just as being a world-famous guitarist was meant to be for you," Maggie said, obviously pleased.

Elaine interrupted the exchange of kudos.

"And how about you, Mrs. Fairchild? Do you have anything to say? What do you think of us? You've had twenty-four hours to form some opinions. Don't be shy."

"What she means is do you think any of us is a murderer?" The tide was coming in. The sound of the waves, the wind in the trees, and the crackling of the fire almost, but not quite, drowned out Lucy's question, an echo of Rachel's, earlier.

Unanswered, it reverberated in the dark night as they walked silently back to the house single file.

"Why are you so sure I did it?"

"I couldn't sleep—jazzed about graduating, I guess—and decided to take a walk. The fire door was propped open, so I knew I wasn't the only restless one. I saw you and Prin. I tried to catch up, but you were walking too fast, running almost. You were both laughing. I figured you were heading for the tower. It was her favorite place. You went in the back door—the one that she always unlocked. But when I got there, it didn't open. You or Prin had locked it behind you. That seemed odd, so I decided to stick around. I'm not sure why; maybe I wanted to try one last time to really be a part of your group—the inner circle, Prin's inner circle. She never liked me."

"Poor Bobbi. It still bothers you, doesn't it? Surely you had a better reason for getting rid of her than I might have? The green-eyed monster. And then there was your little peccadillo freshman year."

"She told you about that?"

"She told me everything."

"Later you came out the door; she didn't. I thought she might have stayed behind, but the next day I knew she hadn't. I don't know why you did it, but you did. Maybe it was an accident."

"Why didn't you say something then—or later? Discretion? Or simply biding your time, perhaps. Waiting for the right moment? Waiting until you needed the money? That is what this is all about, isn't it?"

"Yes. It's always seemed like a kind of cushion for my old age. Knowing I could ask you for it. And now I need to buy my little house. I don't want to live anywhere else. The owner is giving me first refusal. It's not that much, but I don't have it, even with the money from this week."

"After your little house, won't you want a little car or a little something else? Isn't that what blackmailers do?"

"I'm not a blackmailer! How could you think such a thing! This is a one-time business arrangement."

"Don't get upset, dear. You won't have to live somewhere else. Now let's relax in the Jacuzzi and then you can give me one of your famous massages. I'll get some bubbly and glasses. We'll drink a toast to the future."

"You're being wonderful about this. I can't thank you enough. Just a glass for you, though. I don't drink alcohol often and never before I give a massage. The toxins interfere with my centering."

"Whatever you say. Now take off your nightgown and slip into a suit or nothing at all. I'll start the Jacuzzi and get myself some wine. Toxins have never bothered me."

"It was an accident, wasn't it? I mean, Prin fell somehow."

"Of course."

The jets started pulsating, and Bobbi lowered her

nude body into the steamy, bubbling water. She was in very good shape and looked with approval at her flat abdomen. People often mistook her for a woman in her early forties, not fifties. She closed her eyes and sank down up to her neck, stretching her arms out to either side on the surface, enjoying the sensation as they bobbed about. She felt the water, her favorite element, wash away the last traces of the guilt she had about what she was doing, guilt that had almost prevented her from setting up this middle-of-the-night rendezvous. But it had worked out, worked out perfectly. The journey takes us on many roads, each in its own time. This was the right road and the right time.

She didn't hear the woman come up behind her, but she felt the blow. It wasn't a sharp pain, but it stunned her.

"Oh!"

Then there was the water—hot, foaming—in her nose, her mouth, stinging her eyes. She tried to lift her head up, but something was holding her down. She kicked her legs and flexed her arms, struggling to get out, get away. The tiles were slippery, and she was sinking farther into the froth. The sound of the pulsating jets mixed with the sound of her own blood pulsating in her ears. She gave in to the water and let it take her. It was the end of the journey.

Faith looked at her travel clock. It was five o'clock. Not time to get up, but she was wide awake. The wind had increased during the night and now it wailed outside her window. She got up and pulled the heavy drapes aside.

It was pitch-dark. Not even a hint of dawn's rosy fingers, unlike yesterday. She walked back and switched on the light next to her bed. The generators were still going strong. Brent would be up and was probably in the kitchen. It looked like they were in for some weather, as people around here said. She'd better talk to him about it.

She put on jeans and a heavy sweatshirt. Out in the hall, she had to switch on a light to make her way to the landing, and the view out those windows was no clearer than that from her room. It hadn't started to rain yet, but it would. No one was going to be leaving the island today—or most likely tomorrow, either.

Brent wasn't in the kitchen and hadn't been. The baked goods she'd left out for him, covered in Saran Wrap, were untouched. The coffeemaker wasn't on. She felt the kettle on the stove. It was cold. It occurred to her that she didn't know where he slept. Not in the part of the house where the women were; all but one of those rooms were filled. There was no name on that door and, in any case, she didn't see Brent, a lone male, feeling comfortable bunking down in the midst of this group. Maybe he had a room on the ground floor somewhere or in a place of his own on the island, an outbuilding like the writing cabin. It was not a day for getting up early. She didn't blame him for sleeping in. She went to the pantry for the coffee grinder and noticed that the door leading downstairs was ajar and that lights were on. He must be seeing to the generator and whatever else supplied the power for all these amenities. It was something she ought to know about, and she went down to ask him to show her what to do in case of an emergency.

Faith walked into the pool room. The wind was rattling the French doors, but otherwise the room was silent. There was no sign of the handyman. She walked past the long pool, its still, deep celadon water a sharp contrast to the raging weather outside. The pool lights were on, illuminating the tiles, but nothing else. The surface of the Jacuzzi, at the far end, was also still, but one of its lights wasn't shining. There was something in the way. Bobbi Dolan was lying at the bottom, an empty champagne bottle floating above her motionless body. Faith went into the water to try to pull the woman out, but couldn't. She stepped into the warm water to check for a pulse and immediately realized there was no hope of resuscitating the masseuse. Bobbi had been having her own private party, and the party was over.

Five

SOPHOMORE YEAR

Lucy Stratton was sitting on the front porch of her family's Long Island summer house waiting for her friends Prin and Elaine Prince to arrive. It was August and she'd be heading back to school before too long. Freshman year hadn't been as bad as she'd thought it would be. After being in school with girls her whole life, a women's college was the last thing she wanted, but it wasn't her decision, her mother had said firmly. If Lucy wanted to pay her own way, fine. She could go to the University of Chicago, and why that was her daughter's choice was completely beyond her. Jews and hippies. No, Pelham had been where the Stratton women had always gone; Lucy was a Stratton woman, ergo . . .

At Pelham, it had been wonderful to be out from under her mother's control—only to be manacled once again this summer. Lucy's plan to go to Kentucky as a Vista volunteer barely saw the light of day. "You'll come home with lice—or worse." The race riots sweeping the country had put an end to her twice-weekly trips into the city to tutor in Harlem. She'd felt completely safe and the program director had even called Mrs. Stratton to reassure her, but "Burn, Baby, Burn" had etched itself in Lucy's mother's consciousness. She'd been uneasy about having her daughter associate with those people anyway and now she had an excuse to call a halt to the fraternization that might have led to something too unspeakable to utter. Lucy wished she *had* met a handsome black man, someone with an Afro and a dashiki who would take her away from her little white-bread world. They'd have beautiful café au lait children and work together, side by side, correcting centuries of oppression. At night while everyone slept, she'd write wonderful stories, weaving themes of racial injustice into a rich tapestry of timeless literature. Family sagas, tales of men and women whose love conquers the prejudice surrounding them . . . she could do it. If there was one thing she knew about herself, it was that she was born to be a writer, flinging the words that filled her imagination onto blank paper like seeds onto a furrowed field. Her creative-writing professor had been encouraging. Told her to spend the summer roughing out a novel. He'd especially liked a short story she'd written about a girl so different from her parents and brother that she believes she has been adopted, only to discover it's true. Lucy had been lucky to get into the class as a freshman, and she planned to take the advanced seminar with the same professor next semester. She didn't mention the course to her parents. They weren't interested in what she was taking anyway—or how she was doing. She was there and would graduate. That was all that mattered.

Elaine and Prin were late. She hoped Daddy wouldn't be annoyed. This whole tennis thing was his idea. Last month he'd suddenly decided they had to enter the father/daughter doubles at the club and that the Prince sisters were the perfect practice partners. Their father didn't play tennis—or golf. Too busy having to make money, her father had said smugly. He'd inherited his, going into his office at the firm only a few days a week, but in the summer he didn't even do that. Instead he "devoted himself to his family." His phrase. Until July that had meant sailing and golfing with Lucy's older brother and his friend Ned Stapleton. They both had one more year at Yale. Lucy's brother would enter the firm, as had his father, grandfather, and great-grandfather before him. Thank God she was female, Lucy thought. The notion of following all those footsteps made her feel as if she were about to walk into quicksand.

She'd given in to her mother on college, and on her summers, but as soon as she graduated, Lucy would be her own woman. Twenty-one and free to do as she pleased. An apartment in the Village, a job of some sort while she wrote. She wouldn't take a nickel from her parents. Waitressing. She'd had enough practice last year at Pelham. Freshmen waited on tables weeknights and Sunday dinners. The kitchen manager, a formidable lady in a white uniform with so much starch that it crackled when she moved, conducted a mandatory training session for them during orientation week—"Raise right, lower left." It had seemed sublimely stupid at the time, but now she realized, it might come in handy.

Where could the Prince sisters be? Daddy was down at the courts already. She picked up the book she had been reading. Zora Neale Hurston's *Their Eyes Were Watching God.* The short story Lucy had written for her seminar had been her perfect fantasy. Of course she loved her family, but she didn't really belong. Take reading, for example. She was the only one who read. The *Times* was delivered every day and the Strattons subscribed to *Life, Time,* and *Vogue.* Not *The New Yorker.* She had to buy that herself. Communists, her mother had said when Lucy had asked for a subscription. She had to keep her copies in her closet. Her brother's *Playboys* were strewn all over his room. *It* was acceptable—a magazine devoted to women as mindless sex objects. But nobody except Lucy read the *Times* or even the magazines. They were carefully arranged on the coffee table and that was that. There were books in her father's den, his old law books and some on sailing. At some point someone had filled the bookcase in the living room with the Harvard Classics, all one needed to know, "Dr. Eliot's Five Foot Shelf and Fifteen Minutes a Day." No real books in the house, cherished volumes to be read and reread—except for the ones in her room. She'd have so many books in her apartment that people would have to clear them from the chairs before they could sit.

She put the Hurston down. She couldn't concentrate.

Where were they? Daddy was sure to be more than annoyed by now.

She'd roomed with Gwen Mansfield freshman year and they'd decided to stay together. Gwen was pretty high-powered—a class officer and headed for business school. She wasn't around a lot, which was fine with Lucy. It gave her the solitude she craved—to write and dream. The library was less conducive for such activities. There were always some girls whispering loudly in a nearby carrel or someone with a stuffy nose sniffing continuously. Elaine and Chris Barker were rooming together again, too. Chris was a bit quiet, but nice enough. She was majoring in botany and pretty much lived in the greenhouses. Their bio professor had practically had an orgasm over Chris's project on orchids. Everyone else had stuck with less exotic plants with noticeably less exotic results. All four were staying put in Crandall House, moving one floor higher.

At last! She could hear a car coming down the drive. Prin would be driving, as usual. Lucy wasn't even sure Elaine had a license. She'd never seen her at the wheel of the little sky-blue Karmann Ghia that seemed to be for their use only. Prin. She'd be in Crandall next year, along with a bunch of her friends from Felton. She'd grouped people with high numbers in the housing lottery with people who had low numbers, so they could all move together. She wanted to be in one of the new dorms, she'd told Lucy, wanted to hear traffic. There wasn't a whole lot of traffic to hear, but Lucy sympathized. At Felton, you were back in the horse-and-buggy era with only the lake nearby. At least at Crandall there were reminders that it was the twentieth century outside Pelham's gates. Besides the occasional passing cars, the dorm was modern, built in the fifties—the 1950s—as unlike the ivy-covered brick dorms as, well, Jane Fonda was to Rebecca of Sunnybrook Farm. Lucy laughed inwardly at the images her thoughts conjured up.

I'll bet Prin has her eye on Crandall's penthouse, the one reserved for juniors or seniors, Lucy thought. When the leaves were off the trees you could see Boston's skyline from its windows. Prin liked to be up high. She was always dragging someone up to the tower in the middle of the campus. Lucy had gone with her a few times and the view was pretty spectacular. The penthouses in the new dorms were an architectural feature that had somehow slipped by the powers that be, and were. No one had considered what having four bedrooms, a common room, and bath—a private apartment far from a housemother's eyes—might mean. Yes, you took the same elevator, but there were also stairs from the fire door. Someone was always propping it open for a late-night return after a friend had faked a sign-in. Lucy had heard that a draft evader boyfriend of a girl in one of the other new dorm penthouses had lived there for a month before going to Canada.

The car kicked up some of the gravel on the drive as Prin braked. Mother won't like that, Lucy thought automatically.

"Sorry we're late. Is your father pissed off?" Prin said, getting out of the car.

"Don't know. He's down at the courts."

"He's such a sweetie. I'm sure it will be okay. Prin

was taking her time getting dressed, as usual," Elaine said. She was carrying both racquets.

Lucy had never thought to apply such a term to her father, but Elaine was probably right. Her father liked the Prince twins and, besides, he needed them to help practice for the tournament. He'd already cleared a space on the mantel for the trophy. Even without the twins to help get them in shape, Lucy knew they'd win. She had always been good at sports, especially tennis, and her father regularly swept the club's men's singles tournaments. She led the way around the house to the back, past the pool and cabana to the courts.

The house had been built on a spit of land, so there were views of the water from the front and back. It was warm, but a strong breeze kept it from being too hot. She should feel happy, she thought. A beautiful day, friends, tennis—good exercise and something to alleviate the boredom that filled her waking hours here. But she wasn't happy. With a writer's instinct she tried to find the correct word to describe how she *was* feeling. To describe the sameness of her life. Even her tennis whites never varied. Her mother simply ordered larger sizes until Lucy had stopped growing.

All three tall and slender with smooth skin lightly tanned by the summer's sun, Lucy and her friends made an attractive picture strolling together. Up close, Prin drew the most attention, as usual. She'd wound a bright purple scarf around her waist—a nonregulation act that would be forbidden at the club. The scarf intensified the color of her eyes. A light wind was blowing, arranging her hair into loose curls that swept across her face. She didn't bother to push them away. It was as if she knew that their disarray made her look even more attractive. Elaine was pretty, too, but not like Prin. Prin had been born first and Lucy always imagined that God or genetics had used up all the coloring on the elder twin, producing a pastel version in Elaine. Same-shaped body, very similar facial features, but pale gray eyes and light brown hair that hung straight to her shoulders. It was blowing about, too—into Elaine's mouth, across her nose. She seemed to be battling it, using both hands to push the strands back in place.

Did they hate their lives, the lives that were virtual duplicates of hers, the way she did? Lucy wondered. They were close to the courts. Her father was smiling and waving. Not angry at all. He looked relieved. Had he thought they wouldn't show up? Why was this so important to him? He'd never entered this tournament before, even when the tennis pro had suggested it last summer. He'd never done anything with Lucy. She was her mother's department. As they drew closer, she blurted out, "I can't believe that when my children—if I have any—ask me what I was doing during the Summer of Love, I'll have to say 'Nothing.' Why don't we go out to San Francisco for a week? We have time before school starts."

"What about the tournament?" Elaine seemed bewildered at the radical suggestion. "And where would we stay? What would we do?"

"We'd put flowers in our hair, sleep in Golden Gate Park, get stoned in the Haight. That what you have in mind?" Prin said.

131

"Kind of, but I was thinking North Beach and Ferlinghetti. The flower part's okay and maybe the Mary Jane."

"Who's Mary Jane?" Elaine asked.

Prin and Lucy laughed. "Mary Jane is marijuana, you wanna?" Prin said, giving her sister a hug.

"What's going on?" Mr. Stratton asked. "I thought we were going to play some tennis, not spend all day gabbing."

"We are," Prin answered, "but we had to explain some of the facts of life in the sixties to my wonderfully naïve sister."

William Stratton was striding away from them. "You play with me, Prin, and we'll beat the pants off Lucy and Elaine. There's your facts of life in the sixties."

"So are we going?" Lucy asked, walking to her side of the net.

"Sure, just as soon as your mother says you can," Prin said.

"Guess that means the tournament for you, Luce," Elaine said.

"Shut up and serve."

The maid brought a pitcher of iced tea down an hour later. Mr. Stratton was crowing over his victory, although it had been a close match.

Suddenly Prin looked at her watch. "Omigod, I've got a dentist's appointment in ten minutes! Could you take Elaine home, Lucy? Check out that new boutique in East Hampton on the way. They're carrying Mary Quant, so maybe you'll find something for your trip to San Francisco."

"What trip to San Francisco?" Mr. Stratton had been mopping his face with a towel and suddenly tuned in.

"A joke, just a joke. Don't worry," Lucy said. She shot a look at her friend; sometimes Prin went too far.

"I'm sorry to be a bother," Elaine said.

"Don't be silly. Give me a minute to change and we'll go. The new store sounds like fun, and we can get some ice cream afterward. We've burned up enough calories for at least a kiddie cone."

"I'm for the showers, too. Good game, girls. Want to try to get even tomorrow?" Mr. Stratton asked.

"Sure." Prin grinned, getting into her car. Then she was off, Sergeant Pepper blaring from the radio.

It didn't take Lucy long to shower and change. Elaine was on the porch. They walked toward the garage and Lucy realized the last thing she wanted to do was go shopping, even at this trendy new place. She'd been having one of those out-of-body experiences for the last hour, the kind where people's voices sounded as if they were coming from the end of a tunnel, the kind where she felt as if she might come to and be someplace else. Or come to and be dead. She shook her head, trying to clear away these thoughts.

"Would you mind very much if I took you straight home? I'm feeling a little tired. Must be the heat."

Elaine looked anxious. "Are you okay to drive? I can always call Jackson." Jackson was the Princes' butler/chauffeur/jack-of-all-trades.

"No, I'm fine. Just kind of beat."

The round trip to the Princes' house only took twenty minutes. Lucy retrieved her book, went into the kitchen for a cold can of TaB, and climbed the stairs. She *was* exhausted, exhausted by a lot of things, and all she wanted to do was curl up in bed with her book. She was surprised to hear voices from the end of the hall where her parents' master bedroom suite was. Her mother's car hadn't been in the garage, and besides, it was her bridge club afternoon. She'd never come home early from that—more likely late and smelling ever so slightly of a few too many gin and tonics. Her brother and Ned Stapleton were sailing with some other Elis in Newport.

She walked up the last few stairs and froze at the top. It was her father and Prin. His back was toward Lucy. He was naked. Their clothes made a trail on the hall carpet. Prin was arched against him, her eyes closed. Lucy had not made a sound, but Prin opened her eyes, looking over William Stratton's shoulder at his daughter. She slid one hand down her lover's back and grasped his buttock hard. He moaned. Still Lucy couldn't move. Prin smiled at her, a taunting triumphant smile, the smile of a winner. She moved her other hand to the back of Lucy's father's neck and pulled his face toward hers.

And Lucy fled. Noiselessly, rapidly, not stopping until she was down by the shore, where she retched in the bushes before kicking off her shoes and plunging into the cold water to try to wash away the image of Prin and her father, to try to wash away the poison that was coating her skin, seeping into her body through every pore.

As she crashed through the waves, she thought, "She's evil. Evil, evil—and I wish she was dead!" Her tears were mixing with the salt spray and she cried out loud, "Hélène Prince, I want to kill you!"

Max Gold finished the Chopin mazurka he was playing on the baby grand piano in the living room of his sister's dorm at Pelham College. There was a smattering of applause. It was Friday afternoon, teatime at Pelham. He'd laughed at the quaint custom at first, but had come to appreciate it. Teatime. The frantic pace of whatever you'd been doing during the week slowed and you could relax for a few hours. At the moment, he was so relaxed, he felt limp. It was usually this way when he played. His body became an extension of the instrument—the piano, the violin—and the separation, the transition back to not playing, always took a moment or two. He focused on the keyboard. His hands were still resting lightly on the ivory keys. Steinway—the piano was a good one, kept in tune, Rachel had told him, by a little man who appeared regularly and checked it out by playing Gershwin and Brahms.

He turned his head and looked about the room. Rachel was smiling at her brother. Until last fall, he'd thought there would never be another smile he'd search for at the end of a performance, but that had changed. *She* was sitting next to Rachel. He didn't have to move his gaze. She was smiling, too, and he felt a twinge of guilt at how much more her expression meant to him than Rachel's. Prin's expression. Hélène's—he preferred her given name to her nickname. He had never seen anyone so beautiful—not in person, hanging on the walls of a gallery or museum, up on the screen or on the stage. And there were many extremely beautiful women in New York City. He'd been approached by some of them for years now, the combination of his talent and good looks apparently irresistible. Rachel teased him about his groupies and told him he was encouraging them by mimicking the appearance of the romantic composers he was interpreting—Chopin incarnate. Max's dark curls were a little long for Mr. Gold's approval, but they were ardently defended by Mrs. Gold, who also bought fitted velvet jackets and ivory silk shirts for winter concerts, a departure from the tuxedos Max wore the rest of the year.

Hélène. A musical name, although she claimed not to know Beethoven from Bartók. He'd found her confession of total ignorance endearing; her desire to be educated even more so, even though he knew that she'd been to plenty of concerts and the opera. Her family had season tickets to everything, including a box at the Met. In Boston, Max and Prin went to concerts—often with Rachel—but the evenings spent in his room at Dunster House listening to records alone together were far better. She had a good ear and her enthusiasm worked like a drug on him. Pieces he had listened to hundreds of times sounded new. By Thanksgiving, he was totally, completely in love with her. She'd become a part of him— like the instruments he played—and a fundamental part of his music. The wonder was that she loved him back.

Christmas vacation was a whirl of parties, the city— from the tree at Rockefeller Center to the wreaths around the statues of the lions in front of the public library—decorated just for them. She wanted him to come with her family to their place in Aspen, but he was performing in several concerts. She said she wouldn't go without him, but he insisted, feeling very noble. And now it was February, the month for lovers.

He had booked a table at the Ritz for dinner on the fourteenth and bought her a heart-shaped locket at an antiques store in Harvard Square, exchanging the chain for a thin black satin ribbon back in his room. It was more suitable for his Olympia, his divine mistress, and definitely more romantic.

He walked over and sat between the two women, resolving, as he did so, to spend more time with Rachel. She hadn't said anything, but he knew she had counted on him to get her away from the confines of Pelham more than he had. He wished she would meet somebody, but his attempts to fix her up had been gently, even humorously rebuffed. Rachel did not need her little brother to get a man; she'd let him know. She went out occasionally—someone from MIT—but kept that part of her life separate, whereas he couldn't keep himself from including Hélène in everything they did, and talking about her when they were apart.

An attractive blonde approached them arm in arm with a young man. "Rachel, Prin, I'd like you to meet Andrew Scott. He spent last semester at Oxford and is back at Harvard now."

"Hello," Rachel said. "This is my brother, Max. You've met him, haven't you, Gwen?"

She nodded. "We enjoyed your playing very much. You're at Harvard, too, aren't you? First year?"

"Thank you and yes, I'm a freshman—Dunster House," Max said. He covered Hélène's hand with his, moving closer to her. Andrew was very good-looking in a Nordic-god sort of way. But Hélène wasn't interested in anyone else, she'd told him repeatedly—and she could have anyone she wanted, he'd told himself.

"Well, see you around. I'm in Lowell House. Stop by. Good to meet you all," Andrew said, and they walked off.

"Seems nice," Rachel said. "I think he's the one Gwen met last spring; the one she kept calling 'the hunk.'"

"Hmmm," said Prin, as she pulled Max to his feet. "Let's go to the top of the tower. You can sing to me. Rachel?"

"Maybe another time."

The smell of earth, any kind—it didn't have to be a rich loam—was headier than the most expensive perfume. What was it Prin wore? Joy—that was it. Well, joy was a synonym for dirt as far as she was concerned, Chris Barker told herself.

It was her favorite time of week—Friday afternoon. No one came to the greenhouses to work on their required Bio 101 projects, complaining about the tedium of measuring their plants, never thinking, as she did, what a miracle each millimeter was. Last year, especially in the beginning, the greenhouses were an escape, a refuge. They were the reason why she'd come to Pelham, refusing to look at any more colleges after she'd seen them: fifteen interconnected greenhouses, 7,700 square feet, with over a thousand specimens from all over the world, desert, tropical, and semitropical species as well as the more, well, garden variety. Their guide had told them that the century plant, *Agave americana,* a desert specimen from Mexico, was due to bloom the following year. Chris took it as an omen. She'd go to Pelham and be there for the historic event. There would be others for whom it would mean as much; she'd find kindred spirits. But she hadn't. Even the fact that the plant stalk was shooting up from its spiky celadon fronds like a spear of Brobdingnagian asparagus at the rate of five inches a day didn't draw the crowds she'd assumed would come. The faithful few, mostly professors and greenhouse staff, kept watch as a hole was cut in the greenhouse roof, slowing the growth to two inches per day in the cooler air. When the plant's twelve branches burst into bloom—clusters of hundreds of glorious yellow-green flowers against the blue sky—it was over twenty feet high. At this point, the century was duly photographed for the school paper and made the *Boston Globe,* but still didn't cause the stir on campus among her peers that she'd envisioned. She had dragged her reluctant roommate, Elaine Prince, to witness the phenomenon—"Greenhouses are so moist; my hair will wilt even more"—and tried to explain why it was so special. "It only blooms once in a hundred years. We won't be here next time. It's a living time capsule!" Elaine had been marginally more impressed. She was an easy roommate; no annoying habits and she spent a lot of time at her twin sister's dorm across campus. Nice, but not a kindred spirit.

The fact was that Chris had been overwhelmed by homesickness at Pelham, desperate to leave, and desperate to tough it out. She had never been away from home before, not even to camp. Every summer, she, her brother, and sisters left for their grandparents' farm in central Pennsylvania where they joined their cousins for weeks of total freedom. The adults came and went, but the children were a fixture, building tree houses,

139

swimming in the pond, tending the animals, and producing comic operas on a stage rigged up in the old barn, operas that borrowed considerably from Gilbert and Sullivan, with life in the country as their main inspiration. The Lord High Executioner became the local tax collector and Yum Yum was Chris herself, transformed into a Dorothy Gale orphan. Chris's grandmother was a self-educated horticulturalist, and every grandchild was given a garden plot at the beginning of each summer. Only Chris needed larger and larger ones as the years went by, eventually providing more vegetables for the table than the farm's vegetable garden and so many cutting flowers that the children set up a stand by the side of the road.

It was always a wrench to put on shoes again and return home to school and a mostly indoor life in the Philadelphia suburb where they lived. The Barker children attended a Quaker school, although they were Episcopalians. Chris's mother liked the school's philosophy and high caliber of instruction. Chris's brother went to Haverford, one sister to Bryn Mawr, another—the rebel in the family—to Stanford until only Chris was left at home for several years with her parents all to herself. And as the cousins grew up and scattered, her summers became similarly intimate with her grandparents. She didn't really see why she had to go to college at all; why couldn't she apprentice with a real gardener, someone who got paid for doing what Chris loved? Her parents had been quietly insistent, and when she saw the Pelham greenhouses, it had seemed college would be all right.

But it wasn't. She didn't like sitting in someone's

room—usually filled with smoke—gossiping or playing bridge or knitting. She knew how to knit. Her grandmother had taught her years ago, but Chris didn't have a beau, as some girls archly called their boyfriends, and didn't feel like making a sweater for her brother or anyone else in the family. They all had plenty of sweaters.

She had been the only cousin on the farm for most of the previous summer, and it had been idyllic. Pelham College seemed like something she'd read about in a book or dreamed. The farm was real. She loved to walk in the garden in the early evening cool when the long light that brings everything into sharp focus caught the plants she'd tended during the steamy days. Often her grandmother would come, too, moving more slowly this summer than the previous one, much to Chris's secret concern. Granny would recite the names of the flowers, the old-fashioned ones she'd grown up with and had passed down to her grandchildren: heartsease, hens and chicks, Turk's cap, cranesbill, spurge, and bachelor's buttons. She taught Chris about the herbs in her herb garden, thyme and tarragon for chicken, sweet woodruff in a May wine bowl, mint in new peas. And she'd warned her about the dangers of oxalis, digitalis, and deathly sweet lilies of the valley: "The roots, my dear—and the water. We had a cat once that used to drink from the vases and pitchers of flowers I'd have around. I'd shoo her away, but she would be up on the table the moment my back was turned. I'd put a bunch of lily of the valley in one of the spare bedrooms and she got in. It was very sad."

At the end of August, Chris had begged to stay on

the farm for the year. She wanted to experience the change of seasons in the country, promising to go back to Pelham the following fall. Her grandparents had said no. She had to go back to college, be with young people. It hadn't been good for her to spend the summer alone; they had been selfish. "I'm the selfish one!" Chris had cried. "This is what I want!" But September found her back at Pelham, and it hadn't been as bad as the first year. Elaine's sister, Prin, and her friends had moved into Crandall. They were a fun group—and interesting. Elaine herself seemed to blossom near her sister, becoming more animated, displaying a quick wit that Chris hadn't noted the year before, even though they'd roomed together. They had stayed together and their room became a gathering place. This was what it was like to have a group of friends, Chris realized, although she slipped away to the greenhouses often. Now, looking at her watch, she put away her tools and cleaned up. She was hungry and there were always such good things for tea.

When she entered the dorm living room, with its contemporary furniture that always reminded her of a hotel lobby, Rachel Gold's brother was playing the piano. Rachel was Chris's favorite and she sometimes sat outside Rachel's door listening to her play. She never asked to come in. Rachel's music seemed as private to her as Chris's attachment to the world of growing things.

Max Gold was only eighteen, but he was already a famous musician. Chris watched him as he played. He seemed to go into a trance. Music was supposed to make plants grow better; she had never tried it, although she'd talked to them for as long as she could remember. It would be an interesting experiment. Three plants—she'd talk to one, play music for another—classical—and give the last the silent treatment.

Rachel's brother was in love with Prin. It was hard to imagine any man who wouldn't be, she thought. Prin was gorgeous. Her eyes were the color of Superba clematis, deep, velvety purple. Chris watched as he got up from the piano and went over to the couch to sit between Prin and Rachel. He was smiling at both of them, but his gaze was locked on Prin. Would she ever be in love like this? Chris wondered. She thought about it a great deal. Just before sleep a shadow figure would enter her mind, a silhouette against lush foliage. She could almost feel his hand in hers as they walked off through forests, meadows, fields, and flowers. Max was taking Prin's hand now, covering it. Chris shuddered slightly—a mixture of fear and delight.

Maggie was coming undone, unglued, unhinged. There was no way she could finish her poli sci paper and study for her economics midterm, both tomorrow. She'd managed so far, but this semester was a killer. And she was so tired. How did Prin pull it off? Her roommate never seemed to do any work, but it always got done. She sighed and turned back to her text, but the words kept blurring before her eyes. Maybe a short nap, just a little one. She'd set the alarm to make sure she didn't sleep too long. Her bed beckoned. No, she couldn't take the time. She'd work on the paper instead. Maybe another cup of coffee would do it—and a candy bar. She was wearing her pajamas, no tight waistband to chide her.

She had been elected class president again this year

and also to house council, at Prin's urging. They were in a new house, she said, and needed one of their own to be on it. Maggie was sure to be elected, since the other sophomores knew who she was from her tenure as class president. With these activities and her work on the *Pelham Gazette,* the school paper, it was like having several, additional full-time jobs. Maybe she should drop the paper for the rest of the semester, but it was fun covering faculty meetings, her beat, and interviewing people on various topics for her column, "The Pelham Perspective."

"Maggie, wake up! Don't you have a lot of work to do?"

It was Prin. Her cheeks were flushed and her hand on Maggie's arm had been cool. She must have just come in through the fire door.

"I only dozed off for a moment. Out with Max?"

"Something like that."

"What time is it, anyway?"

"Nearly one o'clock."

"Oh no! I couldn't have slept that long. What am I going to do?"

"First go splash some cold water on your face and we'll figure something out."

Maggie trudged disconsolately down the hallway to the bathroom. Cold water wasn't going to do it, unless there was enough for her to drown herself in. She couldn't flunk out. Her mother had not been thrilled with Maggie's grades last year or first semester, but they'd been respectable, and her mother *was* thrilled at her daughter's growing political power on campus.

Back in the room, Prin had changed into pajamas and was sitting cross-legged on her bed smoking a Gauloise. Maggie had gotten used to the smell of the French cigarettes, but not to the point where she was tempted to try one herself.

"How about an extension on the paper?"

Maggie shook her head. "Already had one. This is it."

"Okay, you'll just have to pull an all-nighter. Start with the paper, then I'll quiz you on the economics in the morning when I get up. Your class isn't until eleven, right?"

"Yes, but I'll never be able to stay awake, let alone produce anything coherent."

"That's why I'm going to give you a little something to help you out," Prin said. She went to her closet and took out her traveling vanity case, unlocking it with a small key. Maggie had wondered why Prin kept it here instead of in the luggage room in the basement, but hadn't really given it much thought. Prin took a vial of what looked like prescription medication and shook a small red pill into her hand, closed the container, put it back, and locked the case.

"Instant energy. Take it with some TaB, the caffeine will help, too."

"What is it?" Maggie asked dubiously. Was this the secret to Prin's seemingly effortless success? She certainly didn't sleep much.

"An upper, something to speed you on your path to success." Prin was laughing. "Come on, would I ever ask you to do something dangerous?"

Maggie popped the pill. It didn't take long. Soon she

was feeling on top of the world—and all her work. She breezed through the paper, and when she took her midterm the next morning it was as if she could see the answers printed in front of her next to the questions. She'd never felt this way before—totally self-confident with energy to burn. When she got back to the room, Prin was stretched out on her bed reading a biography of Mozart.

"Where can *I* get those pills?" Maggie demanded.

"Don't worry." Prin got up and stroked Maggie's hair. "I have plenty. Now, my little dynamo, you'd better get some sleep. Take this one."

Maggie opened her mouth obediently and swallowed.

"Sweet dreams," said Prin.

"It's a complete anachronism and I don't want to be a part of it."

"I can't understand what's gotten into you, Lucy! Your behavior during the holidays was totally unacceptable—staying in your room all the time. We barely saw you, and treating your brother's friend, Ned, so badly. Would it have killed you to go to the cotillion with him?"

"Probably."

"That's not funny, young lady. And your grandmother is terribly upset that you're not going to be coming out. Frankly, I'm happy to be spared the expense. Your father is convinced you're on drugs. He says you were talking about going to San Francisco last summer. Nobody goes to San Francisco except hippies and, well, perverts."

"Gays and lesbians, Mother? Is that what you mean?"

"I will not have you using that language!"

Lucy held the phone away from her ear. She was in the pay phone cubicle in the corridor. Gwen was on their room phone with Andrew, as usual, and so her mother had called the dorm number, furious after reading the note Lucy had sent home. There was no way she was having her father come for Sophomore Father's Weekend. She hadn't been able to stand the sight of him since that afternoon last summer and had not had to fake an illness to get out of the tennis tournament. She'd been sick for the rest of the summer. The doctor had thought it was a severe summer flu. Only Lucy knew what it really was. And Prin. Prin knew. She'd sent flowers, masses of Stargazer lilies. Their cloying scent had lingered long after Lucy had given them to the maid, telling her to keep them for herself or throw them out.

"Lucy, are you there? Answer me!"

"I'm here, Mother," she sighed.

"Your father has already arranged to drive up with Ted Prince. They'll be there in time for the class dinner Friday night and they've made reservations for all of you for Saturday night at Locke Ober's. I'm sure there'll be space for some of your other little friends and their fathers—they've reserved one of the private dining rooms. You'll be back on campus in time for the dance. That weekend with my father is one of my most cherished memories. Someday you'll be glad I insisted. We don't live forever, you know."

Lucy thought quickly. There was no way she was

going to get out of this, so she might as well *get* something out of this.

"I'll do it, but only if you agree to let me spend my junior year abroad. Not San Francisco, Europe. Pelham has several programs and I could also apply to some sponsored by other schools."

"Are you blackmailing me?" Her mother's voice cut like a knife. Lucy winced.

"That's a very ugly term. No, I am not. This is simply something I want to do and have been thinking about for a long time."

The last part, at least, was true.

"Paris?"

"Maybe Paris."

"All right, then. But you'd better behave yourself."

Whenever she found herself feeling sorry for her mother—betrayed who knows how many times?—Mrs. Stratton said or did something that was almost as over the top as her husband's behavior, and Lucy could only long to put as much distance as possible between them.

She said good-bye and hung up the phone. The phone cubicle was dark and cozy. She pulled her knees up on the seat and wrapped her arms around them. Lucy hadn't wanted to come back to Pelham, but she knew she had no choice in the matter. She could try to change dorms, but she'd still see Prin on campus. By the time she'd left for school after Labor Day, she'd determined not to let Prin win. That's what avoiding her would have meant. Instead, for a while she had been pleasant, even friendly, secretly delighting in the occasional confusion she saw on Prin's face. Obviously she'd expected—and wanted—

a different sort of response. But it was too hard to keep up the pretense and Lucy stopped. She began to watch the girl and the way she manipulated those around her. It was all a game, and the higher the stakes, the more Prin enjoyed herself. She had Phoebe as a trained lackey, totally in her thrall, happy to be included in Prin's inner circle. Lucy was sure Phoebe, so brilliant, was doing papers now and then for Prin. Rachel's brother, Max, was probably doing some, too, so they could spend more time together. He was very obviously infatuated. Lucy wasn't sure whether Rachel was on to Prin, and once or twice she almost asked her what she really thought of their classmate, but didn't. Lucy liked keeping her knowledge secret where it could fester, a canker of the soul. And what about Elaine? Did she know what her twin was up to, what she was really like?

Sophomore Father's Weekend. How incestuous could you get? Prin would dance with all the fathers, flattering them, flirting in that way she had, which combined childlike innocence with worldly sophistication. Prin could dance with Lucy's father all she wanted. Lucy wouldn't be dancing with him. As far as she was concerned both of them could rot in hell and the sooner the better. She remembered hearing that one year a girl's father had had a massive stroke on the dance floor and died. Maybe Lucy would get lucky.

"I need a favor, roomie."

"Sure, Prin, anything," Maggie said.

"I forgot to sign in last night and I need you to fill in the time."

Maggie had been filing her nails. She looked up, aghast.

"I can't do that! Last night's sheets are already in the housemother's office. Only the house council member responsible for going over them has access to them. And it's not my week; besides, falsifying a sign-in would be more serious than not signing in. Tell us you forgot and went straight to bed, which you did, and all you'll get is campusing for two or three weekends. I'll recommend mercy," she finished with a smile.

Prin walked over and sat on the arm of the easy chair Maggie was sitting in. It was a comfy one covered in bright blue and white chintz that Mrs. Prince had had delivered from Paine's; a similar one to Elaine.

"I have plans for next weekend and the weekend after. They don't include being restricted to campus. Plus, I don't like the idea of going before house council. Too tacky. It will take you five minutes. Go downstairs, open the file, put in the time—no one will have looked at it yet, it's only Monday and you don't meet until Thursday—close the file, and come back upstairs."

"What if Mrs. Archer catches me?"

"Tell her you have a busy week and you're checking the sign-outs each day instead of having to do them all at once before the meeting."

"But she'll know it's not my week. It's Claudia's turn."

"Honestly, the moment I ask you to do one little thing, when as I recall I've been doing quite a few little things for you . . ." Prin stood up and walked over to her closet.

Maggie began to panic. She had no idea what was in those magic pills, but she'd needed them more and more frequently. If Prin decided to stop giving them to her, what would she do? Filling in Prin's missing time was no big deal, she tried to convince herself. She could go down now and make sure Mrs. Archer was out. It *would* only take a few minutes.

Prin was pulling out a light gold suede miniskirt and a white Victorian-style blouse with a high collar and ruffles.

"Max is taking me to Club 47. Tom Rush is there tonight." She appeared to be totally focused on selecting an outfit, taking out a bright blue satin shirt and holding it up to the skirt. "I'd look like a Sunoco sign. Maybe I'll wear jeans and borrow Elaine's cashmere sweater. I can't think why Aunt Eleanor gave it to her when it's exactly the color of my eyes. Probably mixed up our packages after one too many martinis, or as she calls them, 'martoonis.'"

"All right, all right," exploded Maggie. "I'll do it, but while I'm gone you'd better be praying that I don't get caught. If I do, I'll have to resign from both offices and be on probation for the rest of the semester. Maybe worse. I could be expelled." Her voice quavered with the last words.

"You won't be, sweetie, don't worry. After all, have I ever steered you wrong?"

Six

When Faith opened the door after knocking loudly—barely hearing the "Come in" over the growing storm—she was surprised to see the author sitting at her desk fully dressed. In turn, Barbara Bailey Bishop was clearly surprised to see an employee at such an early hour and in her private space. She quickly covered what she had been writing with a sheet of blank paper.

"Yes?"

"I'm afraid there's been a terrible accident. One of your guests—Bobbi Dolan—has drowned in the Jacuzzi." Faith struggled on, waiting for a reaction—shock, regret, even fear. "There's an empty bottle of champagne in the water . . ."

"We'll have to do something with the body." Bishop stood up, went to the window, and gazed out. "A regular nor'easter; it could go on for days. Gwen will be upset; she's stuck here."

Whatever Faith had expected, this wasn't it. After the abrupt comment about the body, the author seemed to be thinking aloud, musing.

"There's foul-weather gear in the closet between the living room and the kitchen. You'll have to get Brent. His cabin is behind the boathouse, unless he's already down in the kitchen."

"He wasn't there a few minutes ago and there was no sign that he'd been in," Faith said. Going out into a gale in search of a handyman to help deal with a corpse had not been part of her job description, yet she nodded and started back out into the hall. Bishop's tone had left no alternative, yet Faith wanted Brent Justice, too. He'd been through storms like this; she hadn't. With mounting panic, as she looked at the dark sky and the storm clouds that promised torrents of rain, Faith realized that, along with the others, she was stuck here, too.

"Use this way, it's faster." Elaine—it was Elaine Prince, Faith reminded herself—pointed to a doorway, which when opened revealed a staircase. It was the one Elaine had descended the first night, making her grand, and startling, entrance. "We've weathered worse than this. Never had the generators fail, so don't worry about that."

Light, heat, and food had been the farthest things from Faith's mind, but it was a reassuring reminder.

"Tell Brent what's happened. He'll know what to do."

As Faith went down the stairs and passed the fireplace that dominated one end of the living room, she noticed that two of the bud vases on the rough-hewn wooden mantel had fallen over. The roses lay in a puddle of water on the floor. Vibrations from the storm rattling the nearby windowpanes must have caused them to spill on the uneven surface. She'd clean the mess up later. The important thing now was to get Brent and figure out what to do with poor Bobbi Dolan.

The foul-weather gear closet was stocked with enough slickers, rain pants, and boots to outfit any number of Old Salts. She donned the nearest to hand and grabbed a flashlight from the shelf. Stepping outside, she felt the first raindrops splat noisily against the hood of the jacket. She tied it tighter, bent her head down, and walked toward the boathouse, straight into the wind. The gusts were so strong, she seemed to be taking two steps backward for every step forward.

At the boathouse, there was a well-worn path leading into the woods. She hadn't heard any thunder, which meant no lightning at the moment. Corpse or no corpse, she wasn't going into the pine forest—or anywhere except back to the house—if there was a possibility of being struck and ending up as one. Under the canopy of fragrant balsam boughs, she noticed that the light was changing from deep gray to pale yellow—storm light, that pause before total darkness set in. The wind had quieted, too. It was as if she were directly in the eye. She walked quickly. The boots were big and her feet were slipping on the wet, moss-covered trail. She was cold— and she was afraid. She flashed on her conversation with Hope, a dream job. It *was* a dream, a nightmare.

Brent's cabin was constructed from the same weathered pine as the trees surrounding it. Protective coloration. You had to look hard to find it. There were no lights on. Perhaps he was having a good lie-in, as she'd imagined earlier. No picnics today, gardening or other chores. Faith knocked on the door. The eerie quiet that had begun when she entered the woods continued, and the sound was unnaturally loud.

There was no answer.

Where could the man be? Had she missed him? Could he be tending to something in the first floor of the house? He would have had to walk through the pool room. Would have had to walk by the Jacuzzi. Faith closed her eyes at the thought, jerked them open, and knocked again—harder.

"Mr. Justice? Are you there? It's Faith, Faith Fairchild. There's been an accident at the house."

Her voice sounded a few pitches higher than usual.

There was no answer.

She turned the knob, and as she expected, the door was open. The room appeared empty in the low light. She trained the beam of the flashlight against the walls. Clearly Brent Justice was a minimalist; the décor was almost monastic. A small table with one well-worn chair stood before a small window. On the other side of the room was a narrow bed, its dark khaki blanket stretched tight. You could have bounced a quarter off it. Had Justice been in the army? There were two oil lamps, one on the table and one on a shelf built into the wall next to his bed—a bed that had either not been slept in or made up immediately upon rising. A wood stove was his source of heat. She held her hand above it and then touched it, palm flat out. It was stone cold. The iron kettle on it was empty.

A door revealed a closet with work clothes, a heavy winter parka, and a dark suit—for funerals and purchased sometime in the sixties, judging from the lapels. Faith closed the door, not sure why she'd opened it. Her unease at finding the cabin unoccupied had been increasing as she regarded its emptiness—the lack of even one personal possession. Maybe the small chest of drawers contained a cherished photograph. Maybe it just contained underwear and socks.

There was a small sink, a bar of Lava soap next to the tap, and a tiny round window like a porthole above. Peering through it, she could just make out a privy. Surely he didn't stay here through the winter. He must move into the big house or go to the mainland. She pictured him in one of the cozy Capes she had passed coming to the dock, and as she did so realized she was stalling, lingering in this small, empty place to avoid dealing with what awaited in the filled-to-the-brim one next door.

As she left, she decided to check out the boathouse on her way back. He might have a shop there. She retraced her steps, more slippery now than before. He was probably piling the wooden storm shutters into that cart, scolding himself for not having put them in place last night. Faith had noticed the hardware on the outside of the kitchen windows. Yet how would he have known about the storm? If Elaine was to be believed, they had no way of receiving communication from the outside world except by boat.

Of course Brent could have known the storm was coming by some sixth sense, some special New England built-in weather predictor—a shift in the wind, a change in the pattern of the waves—that was as common as baked beans on Saturday night. What was that saying her friend Pix had taught the kids? "Red sky in the morning, sailors take warning; red sky at night, sailor's delight"? Something like that. Yet, innate ability or not, Faith didn't believe a native like Justice would live out here without a marine VHF/FM radio, when so much of his life depended on the weather and tides. He hadn't put up the shutters, so the storm must have been sudden.

She didn't bother knocking at the boathouse. The wind was picking up, and he wouldn't hear her. Besides, a boathouse, unlike a cabin or house, was more public and one could ignore etiquette.

Inside there was no light at all—no windows. Faith waited for her eyes to become accustomed to the dark, and after a moment she was able to make out a light switch on the wall. There hadn't been any wires outside here or at the house. They must be buried underground, carefully hidden so as not to destroy the view. It wouldn't have cost much more to extend a line to Justice's cabin—about as much as Elaine had spent on the caviar for this reunion. It must have been his choice.

She flicked the switch and realized at once that she had been correct. Brent Justice had a full shop here, complete with a circular power saw big enough to handle all but the largest trees brought down by age and the elements. There was a ramp sloping down toward the double doors. The building must have been used for boats at one time. There were also racks on the wall where canoes and other watercraft had hung. The boathouse was devoid of any actual vessels, just as Elaine

157

had said. Could the writer be phobic about water? Perhaps she couldn't even swim? If her sister had drowned rather than fallen, it would make sense. But no, you wouldn't live on an island, especially this island so far out to sea, if being on and near water were a problem for you. There had to be another reason.

Empty of boats, the structure was also empty of human beings; no clues here to the caretaker's whereabouts. She should get back to the house, should already have left. Reaching for the light switch, her hand caught the end of something resting along a low beam. It fell to the floor with a crash. Curious, Faith crouched down and looked. Canoe paddles—brand-new ones, their maker, "Old Town," stenciled in script on the wood. Not something fashioned by Brent Justice. Paddles implied canoes, just as a boathouse implied boats. But where were they? And why had the hostess denied their existence?

By the time Faith arrived back at the kitchen door, she was soaked through, despite her gear. She had stepped out of the boathouse into a raging storm. It had seemed to take forever to reach the house. The kitchen lights were on and she'd headed for them. The door opened in and as she pushed it, she almost fell flat on the floor. The room was toasty warm and smelled like coffee.

"Mrs. Fairchild! Are you all right?" Rachel Gold got up and put her arm out to steady Faith.

They were all there. All except Bobbi Dolan, who was soaked through as well, Faith thought, pulled back into the tragic situation now that she was out of the storm. If the women had been talking, her arrival interrupted their conversation. The room was silent. Their faces were sober, some more strained than others. Faith noticed that Phoebe James looked as if she had been crying. Only their hostess was dressed. The others were in their robes, including a chenille number worn by Maggie Howard that could have dated back to her Pelham days.

Lucy Stapleton put a steaming mug of coffee in Faith's hand. "Take this with you while you get out of those wet things."

Faith took the mug and looked at Elaine Prince. "Brent Justice wasn't in his cabin, or in the boathouse. Has he been here?"

Elaine shook her head. "No, but Brent's a wanderer. He'll turn up. Lucy's right. You go change, then come back and we'll figure out what to do." Her tone was matter-of-fact.

Faith was annoyed. They weren't planning a dinner party, or in Elaine's case, a plot twist.

"This doesn't strike me as wandering weather. Are there any other buildings on the island where he might be? Your writing cabin?" The thought of going out again to search for the man was daunting. Maybe one of the other women would volunteer. They were older, granted, but most of them were in great shape. A little water wouldn't hurt them, and she'd had enough.

The author waved a hand toward the door. "You must be freezing. Go on now."

Faith did as she was told, acutely aware that her question had been neatly sidestepped.

When she returned to the kitchen, there were baskets of muffins and scones on the island, butter and pots of jam. Lucy was making more coffee. No one was eating at the moment, but apparently coffee was in demand.

"The spa rooms are air-conditioned. We can put Bobbi in one for now," Elaine said, addressing her suggestion to Faith. Faith wondered who the *we* was that Ms. Prince had in mind. In any case, she was sure that Elaine intended Faith to be part of it.

"How can you talk about Bobbi in such a callous way? The woman is dead!" Phoebe shouted and covered her face with her hands, her sobs audible. Chris went over and put her arms around Phoebe.

Elaine looked a bit surprised. "I don't mean to sound harsh, but we have to deal with the situation. Poor Bobbi. She was so looking forward to this week. I would have thought, living in California, that she would have been especially careful about drinking too much in a Jacuzzi—it's just like a hot tub, you know."

"You remember she used to get herself into one kind of mess or another at school. Didn't always show the best judgment, I'm afraid." Gwen Mansfield spoke with the assurance of someone whose judgment never faltered. Phoebe lifted her tear-streaked face and seemed about to say something more, then reached for a muffin instead.

"We can't just leave her where she is." Rachel was pale and her voice a whisper.

The room went completely silent again.

Faith sighed. "I'll move her, but someone will have to help me." After all, she'd no doubt seen more dead bodies than anyone else present. For a brief moment, imagining her husband's response to this latest discovery, she was glad there wasn't a phone.

"I'll do it," Lucy said.

Faith was relieved. Lucy would have been her first choice. The woman was strong—and calm.

There was a sudden buzz of talk. "Are you sure?" "Maybe I should help, too?" "Couldn't it wait until we find the handyman?" all overlapped each other, until Lucy said, "Come on, Mrs. Fairchild. Soonest done, soonest over."

As they descended the stairs to the first level, Faith said, "Under the circumstances, I'd rather you call me Faith." She was quite certain this was going to be a bonding experience of some kind and first names appropriate.

Lucy nodded. "And I'm Lucy. Now, how do you propose we move her? She was small, but she's, well, dead weight now, plus being wet."

They were at the end of the room. Faith had turned the lights off earlier and now she turned them on again. She had a sudden thought and wasn't sure why it seemed important.

"Did anyone come down to look at her while I was gone?"

"I didn't. I imagine Elaine would have. No one else said they did, but I wouldn't have known unless I'd seen someone head for the stairs. Elaine woke each of us up with the news—and the news about the storm, which wasn't really news. I'd been awake for hours wondering how serious it was. This isn't hurricane season, but it's behaving like one. Oh dear, I'm rambling. To answer your question: I'd be surprised if anyone other than Elaine came down here. It would have been a pretty ghoulish thing to do."

"But if she'd been a particular friend?"

"None of us have been in touch since college. Bobbi roomed with Maggie freshman year, but they weren't that close. She and Phoebe roomed together sophomore year, and we all had singles junior and senior years. Phoebe was probably her closest friend back then, but there's no one now."

The two women crossed the room and stood by the side of the Jacuzzi. The water was still and the bottle had sunk to the bottom, joining Bobbi Dolan. Her hair streamed out and her eyes were wide open, their blueness intensified by the color of the water. Her naked body looked oddly childlike and Faith was reminded of the Kingsley Water Babies on some of the tiles that lined the large pool. Only in the book those sprites had been alive.

"We'd better get suits on. There's an assortment in the changing room if you didn't bring one." Faith had discovered them when she'd taken inventory the first day, a day that seemed a very long time ago.

"I brought one, but I'll use one of those. It will save time, and besides . . ."

Faith had already decided the same thing. She'd never be able to wear hers again after this gruesome chore.

"Before we change, we should turn up the air-conditioning in the spa room," she said. "And I think we can take the mat from the massage table and use that to move her."

"Good idea. Poor Bobbi. She really was a very good masseuse. I had one yesterday and she managed to get a kink out of my neck that's been bothering me for months. Such an unnecessary death. I'm sorry. That sounds so trite—and I suppose the same can be said of all deaths, most deaths," she added.

"She was in good health, hadn't even made her four-score and ten, and it was an accident—something that shouldn't have happened. You're right: unnecessary," Faith said.

The spa room was quite cool and Faith set the controls at an even lower temperature. The body would be all right here for some time. They dragged the mat next to the Jacuzzi and went to change.

Lucy proved to be as fit as Faith had suspected. She had an athlete's body. Well-toned muscles, lithe. "Do you play a lot of sports? Run?" Faith asked as they changed.

"I used to play sports when I was in school, and yes, I do run. It's my passion."

"Tennis? That's my husband's passion."

Lucy bent over to pick up her robe, which had fallen to the floor. "No. I was never very fond of tennis."

Faith tried very hard to think of Bobbi Dolan's body as if it were an inanimate object—like one of those dummies used for CPR training. It didn't work. As soon as she put her arms under Bobbi's to lift her out, Faith was overwhelmed with sadness—and revulsion. From the look on Lucy's face, it seemed she was having the same response. They worked quickly and soon the body was in the spa, covered by one of the sheets Bobbi would have used for a massage.

In silent accord, Faith and Lucy headed for the showers, then clad themselves in the luxurious terry-cloth robes provided and sat on the chaises by the pool. Faith found herself oddly reluctant to return to the kitchen.

Judging from the way the baked goods were moving, there wouldn't be much meal preparation called for. The storm meant they would all be staying indoors. Bobbi's death canceled anything in the way of entertainment. She wondered what the women would do. Stay in their rooms? Stick together in a group? Safety in numbers?

Safety. It had been there since she'd come upon the body. This thought, not below, but on the surface of her mind. This thought that Lucy was addressing.

"She didn't drink, you know."

Faith did know. The first night, Bobbi had opted for mineral water while the others drank champagne. It had been the same at the other meals.

"Before the massage, she was asking me some life-style questions—purely voluntary, she said, but it helped her to get in touch with my essence, something like that. I drink too much. I told her that. Out of boredom, because that's what people like me do in the places I go— the club, dinner parties, events. She was sorry for me. No, she didn't say so, but I could tell. Anyway, she mentioned that she avoided toxins, which included alcohol. That she'd been tempted to have a glass of champagne on the plane, but knew she'd regret it."

"And yet she drank an entire bottle of it."

Lucy shrugged. "So it would seem."

In the quiet that followed, the sound of the wind and pelting rain filled the room, yet neither woman said anything. Each seemed preoccupied with her own private thoughts. Then Faith spoke, blurting out only a part of what she had been thinking about, impelled by the vivid picture of a life cut off with such finality. Bobbi must have had dreams, plans, dental appointments?

"What would you like to be doing with your life?" Faith asked. "I'm sorry, that's terribly personal. It's just that it can all come to such a sudden end—and you seem . . ."

"Dissatisfied? Bobbi picked up on it, too. Not all that difficult. What would I like to be doing?" She paused for such a long time that Faith started to get up. It was really none of her business.

"I've raised two wonderful daughters. I'm pretty proud of that. The younger one is off to college this fall. Not Pelham, thank God—NYU. She wants to be a social worker, change the world. Her sister is at Stanford. She wants to change the world, too, but in a different way—visually, films. I suppose I felt the same when I was their age. It's hard to remember. Oh, I know you're going to tell me I'm not all that old and I'm not, but you'll find that life gets in the way of a lot of your memories. But what would I like to do with myself? Write books." She smiled a little. "I wrote one once. *That* memory is clear."

"When was this and what was it about?" The day, and perhaps days, stretched far ahead; they were captives of the storm. There was no rush to get back to the others, to do anything now that they had done what they had to do.

"The year after I graduated from Pelham, I was living with Elaine in Manhattan. You may have heard it mentioned last night. Our parents had arranged it all." The bitterness in her words was unmistakable, Faith noted. "We were both working in publishing houses. I read the slush pile—hoping to discover a genius—made coffee, picked up the senior editors' dry cleaning, and loved every minute of it. After a few weeks of reading, I decided to try my hand at it. A coming-of-age novel, like most first novels. Holden Caulfield in a skirt. We all wore skirts in those days. Miniskirts.

"I'd written some fiction at Pelham and my professors were very encouraging. *The New Yorker* sent very polite rejection letters, but *Mademoiselle* published one."

"And then . . . ?"

"And then one day in the early spring, I came home after work to find my mother burning my almost completed manuscript in the bathtub. It was one of those old-fashioned ones with the lion's paw feet—the bathtub, of course. Mother was always very resourceful. She had doused the stack of paper with lighter fluid—everybody smoked then, who knew?—and dropped a match on top. Whoosh—it must have been quite a sight. I came in on the ashes."

"But why?"

"She didn't like it. She'd read enough to convince herself that it was, as she put it, 'filth.' I had planned to use a pen name, but she couldn't have known that."

"How had she known you were writing it at all? Did you tell your family?"

"Not very likely. No, Elaine told her. For my own good, she said. It worried her to think that the book might be published and people would think it was truth disguised as fiction. I believe those were her exact words. You see, some memories don't fade. She said pseudonyms never worked. That people would figure out who the writer was. We moved in a very tightly circumscribed world, it's true. Although I really wouldn't have cared if people knew I had written it."

This was a wound as sharp and deep as it was on that day so many years ago. Faith put her hand on top of Lucy's.

"What did you do? Move out?"

"What I did was accept a dinner invitation from Ned Stapleton, a friend of my brother's, and get extremely drunk. My daughter, Becky, was born nine months later."

"You can't refuse to walk down the aisle with your father! I don't know what's the matter with you! Naturally, we would like to have more time to plan our only daughter's wedding, but you've taken care of that very nicely. Not that we don't simply adore Ned. Marrying him is the first sensible thing you've done in years."

"Can't you just shut up, Mother? I could have had an abortion, but besides the fact that it's very hard to find one that's safe, I find I can't do it. And I could have eloped. In fact, I wanted to, but Ned is insistent on having a real wedding with all his Yale buddies getting drunk and trying to screw my bridesmaids. So, let's just get through it as best we can. You can walk down the aisle with Father and me. Plenty of couples do that now, even in your circle. Then after the bouquet is tossed, we can try to see as little of each other as possible."

It had all happened as she had foreseen, except for the amount of contact. Ned turned out to be a traditionalist when it came to family, and weary with one, then two lively babies, she gave in, watching her father and his father carve turkeys in alternate years and her mother and his mother hand out gifts before Christmas dinner. Her parents were gone now and only Ned had cried at their funerals. She suspected the tears in his eyes were produced by terror, the realization that death was a tier closer, but it was just one of the many things they never discussed. And here she was telling this woman she barely knew, things she hadn't told anyone else. Ever.

"So, what did you do with the copy?"

"How did you know?"

Faith smiled. "Writers are an obsessive bunch. They always keep copies. Was it in the freezer?"

"No, at work, filed under *M* for *mine*."

"There's more, isn't there?"

"Are you sure you're just a caterer? Not a psychic—or a witch?"

"I'm sure, but I can usually tell when someone's keeping something back."

"Handy skill," Lucy said. "Yes, there's more. Elaine's first book was published the year after I was married—under her pen name, but I knew right away who had written it. She had adopted my style, even some of my characters, and a whole lot of the plot."

"Essentially your entire book?"

"Essentially, but not actionably. She'd added suspense, a woman in peril, cutting out all the coming-of-age stuff. And it was sexier, much sexier.

"I had read parts out loud to her when I was working on it and she'd ask me why I had written something a certain way, discuss character, and so forth. I was her Iowa Writers Workshop. She hadn't even majored in

English. History, which came in handy for her historical fiction. Oh, she's talented. Very talented."

"But so were you."

Lucy got up. "Damned straight."

It was time to leave.

"You go on up and let them know that we're done. I'll be along soon. I wonder if anyone will want lunch?" Faith said. She wanted a closer look at something—and she wanted to take it alone.

"I can't imagine ever being hungry again, but that's just me. I'll ask. You don't have to tell me what you're going to do, what you're looking for, but look hard. Bobbi never drank that champagne." And after giving Faith a swift hug, she left.

Faith changed back into the clothes she'd been wearing, leaving her shoes at the door, then returned to the Jacuzzi and got down on her hands and knees. There wasn't much, but it was definitely dirt. A few specks of dark, rich loam at the rim. Carefully she paced the whole room looking for more. There was another bit in the grout of the floor tiles directly in front of one of the French doors that led to the patio. She found the third deposit on the doorsill. Bobbi Dolan hadn't been wearing shoes. Her nightclothes had been tossed onto a low table near the Jacuzzi, her slippers, Chinese brocade like the ones Faith had seen in every Chinatown she'd visited, were neatly placed underneath. The soles were worn, but there was no trace of soil on them. Faith regarded the virtually undetectable dark flecks. The three fell in a straight line to the door. She went and looked out. It was impossible to see anything until she found the switches that controlled the patio lights, instantly bringing the wild scene to life. Some of the furniture had been blown against the house and several planters had toppled. The tall meadow grasses were blowing horizontally. Faith thought of Lucy's words and looked hard. It was as difficult to see as the dirt had been, but there was a section of the grass that appeared more flat than the rest—as if something, or someone, had been dragged along on top of it. She wanted to go out and investigate, but not without the proper gear. And what was she looking for? All she had to go on was a little loam. Loam—the kind favored by gardeners.

Back upstairs only the college president was in the kitchen, washing out the coffeepot.

"Please leave that; I'll do it," Faith said, reminded of her official reason for being on Bishop's Island.

"You've had enough cleaning up to do this morning," Maggie said. "I don't mean to sound callous—Phoebe was right to use the word. Elaine and all of us have been reacting as if Bobbi wasn't a person. A person who was very much alive at this time yesterday." She started wiping the counter with swift, efficient motions. Faith imagined it was the way she dealt with the endless paperwork and other tasks that composed her job, her remarks the other night to the contrary.

"Where is everyone?" Faith said.

"Upstairs getting dressed. Trying to figure out how to make the best of what is a horrible situation." Maggie sounded as if she were trying to do the same.

"Did you know Bobbi Dolan? After college? Was she an active alum?"

Maggie seemed startled by Faith's questions. "No one here has been active save myself, of course, and Elaine, only we didn't know it was Elaine making such generous contributions. I believe Bobbi has been on our class missing list almost since graduation."

"Missing list?"

"No address, no information. Some alums go to great lengths to make the list," she said ruefully.

The deluge of magazines and fund appeals from the institutions that Tom and Faith had attended that regularly flooded their mailbox made the notion attractive, but Faith was astonished that someone could disappear in the current information age when privacy had been virtually clicked away.

"So the last time you'd seen her before this week was at graduation?"

Maggie nodded. "We were roommates freshman year and got along all right, but she was a bit like a puppy dog, trying to get out—or in her case in—always nipping at our heels."

It was a strange simile, and demeaning, Faith thought. "Your group?"

"I suppose you could call it Prin's group. She was the center." Maggie smiled in reminiscence. "I was active on campus. Class president, student body president, lots of activities. Chris lived in the greenhouses, but was still lots of fun. Gwen wasn't a grind, but she was hell-bent on summa and made it. Lucy, Elaine, little Phoebe—we were all friends. Rachel, too, although her music came first always. Then after her brother died, she kept to herself. It was a mistake for her to come back to Pelham—he died the summer after our sophomore year. I don't know why she did. The people she was closest to were in New York."

"How sad. He must have been very young. Was it an illness or an accident? That poor family . . ." Faith thought of Rachel's face, the one in her publicity photos and the one before her as she came through the kitchen door this morning. There was something buried deep in her eyes, something suggestive of perpetual mourning, of loss.

"It was suicide. He'd just finished his freshman year at Harvard."

"Are you talking about Max?" Chris had entered the room. She was wearing a worn navy turtleneck and jeans.

"Yes. It really was very tragic. He was well on his way to being world famous." Maggie addressed Faith. "He was a pianist. Very talented." She was speaking in her public, Madam President voice, as if the room were filled with potential donors.

"It *was* tragic and I'm sure Rachel wouldn't want us to be talking about it. The gardens will be destroyed and the oak outside my window has lost a huge branch." She pointedly changed the subject.

Maggie raised her eyebrows and said, "I certainly didn't intend any disrespect. We all know why—"

"I said we shouldn't mention it," Chris said coldly.

There was a brief moment when the air hung heavy with emptiness, then Maggie said, "Well. I'm off to look for something to read. Everything I brought seems uninteresting and it's going to be a long day."

It already was. Not even noon, Faith noted, looking at her watch.

"I wonder if I might have a piece of fruit? I'm not hungry, but if I don't eat, my system can sometimes go out of whack," Chris said.

"Of course. I'm sorry I didn't make that clearer to everyone, but please feel free to come and eat whatever you want day or night. There are some nice peaches and I picked more strawberries late yesterday. Let me cut some up for you."

Faith's initial impression that Chris had been ill returned. The woman looked exhausted. She thanked Faith and sat down on a stool by the island. Setting the fruit down in front of Chris, Faith was about to start asking about Bobbi Dolan—how well Chris had known her—when she broached the subject herself.

"Pelham was the wrong school for Bobbi. Wrong for others of us, too, but particularly wrong for her. She was bright enough, but never seemed at ease. The cashmere-sweater-and-pearls girls, like those old Breck shampoo ads, were pretty overwhelming for her. Even though she'd gone to a fancy private school. We were both from Pennsylvania. I went to private school, too, but it was run by the Quakers and we were definitely not encouraged to think about material goods."

"But Bobbi had been?"

Chris nodded. "Her father had made a great deal of money quickly, and I gather Bobbi's life changed from running through a sprinkler in someone's backyard to swim meets at the club. But she sounded as if she'd found some kind of peace out in California and she was extremely good at what she did."

"She gave you a massage?"

"Yes, Shiatsu. And it wasn't just the physical well-being I experienced afterward—gardeners have chronic back troubles—but the mental state I found myself in. Almost a kind of euphoria. And she knew it, shared it. It was as if she had given me a gift."

Someone was coming up from the ground floor. It was Elaine.

"We're all gathering in the living room to talk. You, too, Mrs. Fairchild." The peremptory tone of her voice was harsh and in apparent recognition, she added, "Please."

This was possibly the only occasion Faith could recall when offering food seemed out of place. Gwen was sitting in the large chair by the fireplace where Elaine had sat the first night. Phoebe, Chris, and Rachel were spread out on one of the large sofas. Maggie and Elaine were in adjoining easy chairs. Lucy sat in a straight-backed chair near the door. Someone had lighted the fire and the flames were snapping, adding to the noise of the rain slashing against the windows. Glancing at the flowers on the mantel, Faith realized that she had forgotten to clean up the spilled ones and went back into the kitchen for a paper towel. When she returned, Chris was righting the vases. She'd picked up the flowers.

"The roses have been out of water too long, I'm afraid. A shame—Indian Sunset and Carte Noire—two of my favorites. They still smell lovely, though."

Faith wiped up the water and took the roses from Chris. They *were* fragrant, but under the sweet scent, she detected an odor of decay.

Elaine was speaking when Faith entered the room

again, selecting a chair that gave her a view of everyone.

"My hope is that we can join together and turn things around. We can't bring Bobbi back, sadly, or change the weather, but we can get to know each other all over again. Draw on our life experiences since Pelham and share the wisdom we've gleaned."

"You sound like a heroine in one of your books—or that obnoxious poster, 'When life gives you lemons, make lemonade,'" Gwen said sarcastically. "I don't know how much wisdom I've 'gleaned' since Pelham, but one thing I've learned is to trust my own instincts. And my instincts are telling me to go upstairs, do whatever work I can that doesn't require an Internet connection on my laptop, and wait out the storm. With my door locked." She got up and moved toward the door.

"Wait," called Elaine. "What are you suggesting? I won't have my guests upset by anyone, even you, Ms. Moneybags." Her cheeks were scarlet with annoyance.

Gwen sighed audibly. "I don't know what I'm suggesting, but the sooner you tell us why you really invited us all here the better. Bobbi's dead, your handyman has gone walkabout, and if I could figure out a way that you might have engineered it, I'd blame you for the storm, too."

Faith was quick to note the use of the word *too*— apparently so did Elaine. Her face now a fiery red but her voice frosty, she said, "I invited you to try to renew old ties, pure and simple."

Lucy was shaking her head. She had been drinking from a mug. As Faith had passed her, there had been the sound of ice cubes clinking together; it obviously contained something even stronger than the coffee left in the pot. "I'm with Gwen on this one. Why did you wait all these years for a reunion? And why lure most of us here with such specious pretexts? It's all about Prin, isn't it? It was always all about Prin." She spoke with great deliberation, enunciating each word. Faith wondered how much "coffee" she'd had to drink. After the morning they'd had, Faith wasn't surprised that Lucy might want a shot of something, but this seemed more excessive than that.

"Prin? What would this have to do with Prin? Or let me rephrase that, if anyone here thinks that my invitation has something to do with my late sister, speak up."

Gwen opened the door. "Play all the word games, and any other games you may have in your twisted mind, Elaine. I'll be in my room," she said and left.

Elaine attempted a bright smile, taking in the whole room. Her expression was, however, more of a grimace. "Gwen always was a party pooper. 'I have to study,' remember? Now, I don't see why we can't have a good time together. Perhaps Chris could tell us some more about all those wonderful gardens she's visited and her own, of course. Then, Rachel could play later this afternoon."

"Rachel is not playing—at any of this. I'll be in my room, too," Rachel said. As she got up, Chris followed suit. "I don't feel like lecturing just now. I'll be upstairs, as well."

Faith realized she needed to speak. With the flock scattering fast, she had no idea what kinds of meals, if any, she should be preparing. They were bound to get hungry at some point, though.

"Would you like me to bring trays up or will you be coming down for . . ." She hesitated. It was past lunchtime, but nowhere near time for dinner, despite the darkness outside. "Meals?"

"Why don't you ring a bell? There must be one somewhere. Serve the food buffet style like the first night, then each of us can do as we choose. It doesn't seem right to make you cart trays up and down for us." Maggie was moving into her institutional, organizational mode.

"I don't mind doing trays," Faith said.

"No, Maggie's right. That won't do. Use the gong again, the one in the dining room," Elaine said. "It will be like the old days. Our housemother always sounded a gong for dinner," she explained to Faith.

No one seemed to be objecting. "All right, then. In the meantime, there is plenty to eat if anyone is hungry now. Fruit, cheese, crackers, cookies—"

Maggie interrupted her. "I'm sure we can fend for ourselves."

Faith wondered if this was a dismissal. It felt like one, but she wanted to find out what the others were going to be doing.

Phoebe spoke up. "I came because I wanted to meet you, Elaine. I mean you as Barbara. I've read all your books and I'm a huge fan. I'd be happy just to sit right here by the fire and talk with you. Maybe you could do a reading." She sounded wistful.

"Of course I will, just for you, Phebes, and anyone else who cares to join us." She looked at the remaining women. Maggie leaned a fraction of an inch closer to the author from her adjoining chair. "That sounds delightful," she said. Faith had the distinct impression Maggie would sit on the author's lap or at the least perch on the arm of her chair if she could. *Chair* being the operative word. A corpse, a storm—Pelham still came first.

Lucy was definitely more than a little drunk. "Don't worry, Miss Maggie, Elaine isn't about to go back on her promise. Pelham will get the money," she said.

"I haven't been thinking about that at all; I'm a fan, too, and I'd love to hear about the process," Maggie shot back. "How Elaine gets her ideas."

"What about you, Lucy?" Elaine asked.

"Oh, I'll be around. Don't you worry your pretty little head about me. I already know how you get your ideas."

Faith put out some food on the island in the kitchen and made fresh coffee. Then she went into the pantry/china closet to get clean cups and plates. Tucked almost out of sight next to the shelves at the far end, there was a pegboard with hooks, each holding a key. They were the keys to each room, as well as other doors. Each was clearly labeled on the board and with a tag on each key. The bedrooms by their wallpaper patterns, "The Strawberry Thief," "Rosa Mundi," and so forth. There had been a key in the door of each room. These were duplicates. Faith looked at them carefully. One space was labeled "Master." A master key or the key to Elaine's master bedroom suite? She started to leave, then turned around and pocketed the key to her own room, "Ivy."

At the door leading to the living room, she could hear Elaine's voice reading aloud. She did it well; no stammering and her voice had a pleasant pitch. A group of friends listening to a book on tape come to life on a stormy afternoon. There shouldn't have been anything wrong with the picture—but there was.

With that group occupied and the rest sequestered in their rooms, she had a little time. Taking some rain clothes from the closet, she went back to the pool room. This time she didn't switch on the lights. She went to one of the outside doors and pushed it open. The storm had picked up speed; the wind howled. All the patio furniture was now piled in an untidy tangle against the house. Several planters were broken; all of them over-turned. She trained the beam of her flashlight on the place she'd noted earlier, the place where the tall grass looked different. It was harder to detect now, but she could still see it. The wind was behind her and pro-pelled her forward. She followed the track for as long as she could, then the wind changed and the rain began to sting her face like a swarm of hostile bees. She could barely keep her eyes open to see and turned around to head back into the house. She'd try again, and again and again, if necessary.

She knew there was something to find—and she was pretty sure she knew what it was.

Seven

First she stretched her arms up and touched the head-board, then reached for the footboard with her legs. For a moment she lay taut, elongated, with her eyes closed, unwilling to open them, unable to start another day. Max had killed himself in June. Sped off the highway toward a scenic turnout and over a cliff into the ocean without apparently slowing down, looking at the view, or hesitating in any way. "He wouldn't have felt any-thing; there wouldn't have been any pain," the police had reassured the family. Rachel had wanted to scream, "Of course he felt something, you morons! Of course he was in pain! Why do you think he drove over the cliff? For a thrill?" But she'd kept quiet. Very quiet. No tears, even at the funeral. No tears while the family sat

180

shivah and every table in the apartment was covered with offerings of food—deli platters, bagels, lox, cream cheese, stuffed cabbage, chopped liver, kugel, rugelah, crumb cake—that no one ate. She was still keeping quiet and she still hadn't cried. It was the only way she could think of to keep herself from getting in a car and following her brother.

She slept a lot. "Sleep is the sweet escape." She wondered where the phrase came from, but not enough to try to find out. Her parents wanted her to go to a grief counselor. *They* were going to one. Her mother cried every day; her father almost as often. Rachel didn't need a grief counselor, didn't need someone to tell her it wasn't her fault, help her deal with survivor guilt. Because it *was* her fault. She'd introduced him to Prin, even encouraged the relationship, and when she realized what Prin was really like, she should have told Max. He wouldn't have believed her, but she would have prepared him for what was to come. She would have opened his eyes to the possibility that Prin would dump him. Unceremoniously, cruelly; humiliating him, destroying him.

Rachel flicked her eyes open and looked at the clock next to her bed. Eight o'clock. She had a nine o'clock class. She closed her eyes again. If she pictured a blank sheet of paper in her mind, getting larger and larger until it occupied every corner, she might be able to fall back to sleep. It sometimes worked.

Her parents hadn't wanted her to come back to Pelham, but she'd insisted, lulling them with false assurances: "I want to be with my friends." "I won't see Prin; we move in different worlds." This last was true.

They did move in different worlds; Prin in Hades. Rachel had no doubt that the breakup had been calculated from the beginning and that Prin had never loved Max. But why? Was it to hurt Rachel? Except Rachel had been her friend, dazzled by Prin, as they all had been. Had she sensed Rachel's later misgivings? Unlikely, when they weren't that clear to Rachel herself. And so Rachel had freely shared her most precious possession with Prin—Max.

She would never forget the moment when she'd introduced her brother, presenting Prin as if she, too, were a special gift. It was at the beginning of sophomore year. Rachel and Max had been walking to the dorm from Max's car—the car Rachel had urged her parents to buy him, so he could come rescue her, the car that would carry him to his death. Prin was ahead of them and they soon overtook her. The autumn sunlight had blazed through the red swamp maples, the first trees to turn color. Rachel had been stunned at the way the light had caught her friend and her brother, binding them together, two glorious children of nature. As the year had progressed, though, she'd begun to wonder about her classmate, but had never given voice to her uneasiness, had never done anything to make Prin suspect. She had chided herself for being jealous and gone out of her way to support Max's growing attachment, an attachment Rachel believed Prin shared. The three were together a lot; Rachel was seeing more of Prin than she had the year before, and even when they weren't with Max, Rachel found herself watching Prin. Watching the way she led Phoebe around on a leash, the way she used Maggie's various offices, and the way others reacted to Prin. Lucy Stratton hated her. It was subtle, but like a leitmotif that underscored their every encounter. Lucy would move to another table if Prin sat down at hers; walk out of the living room if Prin was there, holding court. Yet they had grown up together, were obviously friends freshman year. What had caused the change? And Bobbi Dolan. At times Rachel caught her looking at Prin with what could only be described as fear in her eyes. Prin made a point of including Bobbi, remarking effusively on a new hairstyle or outfit, yet with an underlying series of notes, a descant of sarcasm. Faint, all so faint that Rachel thought she was looking too hard. Trying to find fault. That no one could be good enough for Max.

But it was there. All of it. She didn't know any of the details, and now she didn't want to.

Chris Barker was the only person Rachel could stand to be around. She was taking two of the same classes as Rachel, including this morning's, and if Rachel wasn't there, she'd slip a sheet of carbon paper in her notebook and drop the notes off afterward. Rachel didn't mind doing the reading for her courses and often stayed up all night, buried in her books. Chris seemed to understand. She was the only girl who hadn't tried to offer condolences. Besides Prin. She'd sent flowers the day of the funeral, or rather the card had read, "Deepest sympathy from the Prince family," but Rachel knew who had ordered them. A massive basket of Stargazer lilies, their heavy scent reminiscent of an expensive whore, which was what Prin was. And Max had paid the price. Rachel had told the doorman to send them back to the florist with the message that delivery had been refused; then she had gone into the bathroom—the one she had shared with Max—and vomited bile, since she had eaten nothing, resting her head finally on the cool white porcelain, spent, empty. She smelled the lilies for days and the nausea didn't go away until the odor did.

Nine o'clock. Too late to go to class. She closed her eyes, willing the sheet of paper to fill every part of her brain.

He had wanted to marry her. "Yes, I know it sounds ridiculous. I'm only a freshman in college, but Rach, I'm sure. Hélène is my soul mate. If I hadn't met her now, we were destined to meet another time. And the miracle of it all is that she loves me as much as I love her." He was solemn. His was not a delirious, head-over-heels passion, but the pledging of his troth for life and ever after. The taking of a vow. In May, he showed his sister the ring he'd bought—a sunburst of diamonds, one large perfect stone surrounded by smaller ones in a platinum setting.

And Prin had said yes. School ended. They were all back in the city, and it started. She had to do something with her sister, her mother. They were going out to the Island. It was hard to get into town. She hated the drive and the train was a bore. Max cut rehearsals and drove out, but there were always so many people around, he complained to Rachel. He almost never saw his fiancée alone. Then she stopped taking his calls. "Miss Hélène is not available," the maid would say. Max grew increasingly despondent, and desperate. "I just don't understand, Rach. What's happening?" He wrote letters—pages long—sent telegrams. There were no replies. One night Rachel overheard her father give Max the old bullshit "plenty of fish in the sea" line and Max left the apartment, slamming the door behind him. They didn't see him for two days. Bleary-eyed, he told Rachel he'd gone out to her house and tried to force his way in to see her. He just wanted to talk to her. Just talk. Her father had come out onto the porch and told him to leave. To stop harassing his daughter. She didn't want to see him. When Max tried to argue—he'd spent what he thought were happy dinners, concert outings with the family—Mr. Prince told him he didn't want to go into it, but Max was a very sick young man. "What have I done? What has she told you?" Max had shouted. He shouted the same questions at Rachel, who could only shake her head. "There's nothing wrong with you. It's Prin." She tried telling him about her suspicions, about the poison Prin spread, but he'd put his hands over his ears and told her to stop. That she wasn't to talk about his beloved that way.

Rachel called the Princes herself, asking for Elaine, but when the maid heard who was on the line, Rachel got the same reply as Max. She debated giving Phoebe's name, or calling Phoebe. Maybe she knew what Prin was up to. But Rachel didn't need to call Phoebe. She knew herself. She tried to talk to Max again. Tried telling him that his beloved was really a monster. She'd pulled his hands away from his head and, panting, struggling, pushed him into a chair and forced him to listen. "She's not worthy of you! You have to let her go! Let the *idea* of her go!" He sat silently, very still, and then looked up at her with those beautiful eyes, eyes that were filled with tears. "It's no use, Rach. Save your breath. I

185

love her." Then he left. It was the last time she saw him. Ever.

No "sweet escape" this time. No blank sheet of paper. No sleep. Just images of those terrible days. The phone call from the state police. Her mother's screams. The questions: "Was your son depressed about anything, Mr. Gold?" "Had he voiced suicidal thoughts, Mrs. Gold?"

She'd come back to Pelham as penance. It was the one place in the world she most did not want to be, so it was the place she had to be.

Rachel hadn't played her guitar since Max's funeral, but she'd brought it to school, mostly to convey an air of normalcy to her parents. She hadn't been in touch with her teacher. Hadn't even kept the instrument in tune. She got out of bed now and went to the closet, removing the guitar from the case. Then she sat on her bed and tuned it. When Chris came by with the notes from class, she heard the music and didn't go in. Rachel was playing the same piece over and over, Ravel's hauntingly beautiful *Pavane pour une infante défunte*— a pavane for a dead princess. Not a princess, Rachel was thinking, a prince. He had been a prince, a prince among men. Her mouth tightened. But his princess was a Prince, too, and Rachel wanted to kill her, wanted her *défunte*.

"This junior class is the worst I've ever had in all the years I've been at Pelham," Mrs. Archer complained to Mrs. MacIntyre, who had come by for a chat, and she wouldn't say no to a touch of something. "You must remember some of them from freshman year."

186

"What seems to be the problem? And who are you talking about?" The two women had come to Pelham the same year, childless widows whose grief was tempered by the fact that neither of the deceased had left a penny—no insurance, no savings, no nothing. Pelham offered the only livelihood for which the women were qualified, and over the years both had come to view the college as a lifeboat. "I don't know what I would have done if this hadn't turned up," they had repeated to each other on innumerable occasions. The housemother's suites were large and attractive with small kitchenettes, although meals were provided, of course. They had health insurance, and a modest pension would come to them when, and if, they retired. More than one colleague had simply stayed until she moved on to that final dormitory. Increasingly white hair and softly folding wrinkled skin added rather than detracted from these Minervas, wise women keeping watch over the Vestal Pelham girls by day and by night, especially night. And it was true that in the case of Mrs. Archer and Mrs. MacIntyre they fulfilled their obligations to the letter—very little got by them, hence Mrs. A.'s complaint about her juniors. She might not be as quick on her feet as she once was, and a pillowy bosom complemented her dowager's hump, but her sharp, china-blue eyes didn't miss a trick.

"Last year during housing, none of the juniors wanted the penthouse—such a foolish idea, wish we could block it off—so the sophomores drew lots and the group that got it, Gwen Mansfield, Phoebe Hamilton, Maggie Howard, and Prin—Hélène Prince—seemed tickled to death."

"I don't know Gwen, but Phoebe, Maggie, and Prin were all in Felton. I'm sure I must have mentioned Prin, such a lamb and makes Elizabeth Taylor look homely! Don't mind if I do." She raised her glass for another drop.

"I thought the very same thing the first time I met her. She used to be here a lot visiting her sister, Elaine," Mrs. Archer said as she topped up their drinks.

"Phoebe is very brainy. I never got to know her well, but she was always pleasant, and Maggie, well, she was our star, the first freshman class president from Felton in twenty-five years. I'm sure she'll end up as student body president and, who knows, president of the college someday!"

Both women smiled at the thought of one of their protégées, their favorites, at the helm of the ship that had carried them so well. So what if they had to scramble about to find a place to stay over vacations and in the summers when the dorms were closed? Early on there had been house-sitting jobs, and for the past number of years, they'd gone in with two other housemothers, renting a small bungalow one of them knew about in New Hampshire. It wasn't as if the college was turning them out.

"Gwen was class treasurer freshman year and a real go-getter," Mrs. Archer said, flying the Crandall flag. "We'll be hearing about that one, too. Wants to go to business school, of all things. Well, the times are changing."

"You can say that again. But what happened to upset you, dear?"

Mrs. Archer made a face. "Miss Gwen announces

on moving-in day that she's not going to live in the penthouse. She called the college the week before and they told her it was impossible to change room assignments at that late date. I told her the same thing. Well, she refused to move her things from the foyer. I took her in here and spoke to her sternly, but she was dead set against going up there. And wouldn't tell me why."

"What a mystery!"

"Not for long. You know how much I rely on my girls to keep me up-to-date on what's happening. I let Gwen go and got ahold of Emily Howie; she's a senior but is tight with that group. She knew all about it. Apparently Gwen's beau, Andrew something, left her for Prin and Gwen was ready to kill Prin."

"And how many times have we had to deal with this sort of thing?" Mrs. M. smiled indulgently. "Little cats!"

"I don't know what part Prin played in it, whether she was poaching or not, but she didn't say no to him when he asked her out. Emily says Prin told her that she thought Gwen had broken up with the young man."

"Hmmm. Go on."

"Under the circumstances, I thought we could bend the rules a little and let someone take Gwen's place. I didn't want to find Prin with a knife in her back," she said, chuckling.

"No, noo." Mrs. MacIntyre laughed back. "That wouldn't do at all. In your place I would have acted the same, and have."

"The problem was that I couldn't find anyone who wanted to switch."

"Now, that's odd. Most girls would jump at the chance to live in the penthouse, especially junior year."

"Exactly. Now picture the scene, everyone has been bustling about moving in all day, Gwen's things are still where they've been, and at dinner, I announce a meeting in here for all juniors at seven-thirty."

"They must have been puzzled."

"No, they weren't. At least not from the looks on their faces. They all seemed to know exactly what was up."

"Then what happened?" This was better than the soaps, Mrs. MacIntyre thought.

"They trooped in, settled themselves, and I said I was looking for someone to trade places with Gwen. She stood just there, by the door, as far from Prin as she could get."

"And how was Prin taking it?"

"She came in with her friends, talking and laughing, as usual. I started by asking the girls I knew were friends of the three: Bobbi Dolan, Lucy Stratton, and Chris Barker. Rachel Gold would have been in the group, too, but—"

"Yes, terrible. And in any case, she would be in a single. More comfortable for everyone all around."

Mrs. Archer nodded vigorously. "I didn't get any takers. In fact, Lucy said she'd move into the utility closet on her floor before she'd move into the penthouse."

"They get so up in arms over the silliest things. Probably upset with one of Maggie's votes or something she wrote in the paper."

"I had to let everyone go. I couldn't force the issue when Gwen was clearly in the wrong. She had signed the housing contract. I told her so. She stayed behind, telling me she'd be sleeping on one of the couches in the living room until I could find a place for her. Well, that got my dander up."

"I don't blame you one bit! Who did she think she was?"

"Gwen Mansfield, that's who. I got an earful from her mother about ten minutes later. A Pelham alum, and daughter of an alum, who between them had given enough money to the college to build several dorms, and she'd be building a new one for her daughter to sleep in if I didn't do something soon, a fact she would be telling the president unless she heard back in an hour."

"Nice of her to give you that long," Mrs. M said sarcastically, yet the name was familiar, and one of the first things a housemother learned was to keep the alums happy, their pocketbooks open.

"I don't mind telling you I was in a quandary. There isn't an inch of space in the dorm and I was going to have to call around to see if anyone else could take her in."

The two women exchanged knowing looks. Best handle situations among themselves and not involve the housing office. Least said . . .

"Then comes a knock at the door and it's Elaine Prince, Prin's twin sister, although they look no more alike than, well, I do to Audrey Hepburn." The two women had seen *My Fair Lady* twice together at a movie theater in Framingham. " 'I'll switch,' she says, and I ask her if she's sure and she says she is and I call Mrs. Mansfield to tell her the problem has been successfully resolved, she says she hopes so, and I was so tired I went to bed before Carson."

"But this isn't what's upsetting you," Mrs. MacIntyre said. "I know you, Dolly, plus this is the kind of thing that comes up from time to time."

"You're right, as usual. No, it wasn't the room change; it's a feeling I get when I'm with the juniors. They're unhappy, on edge. Not the way our girls are normally—papers, exams, boyfriends, pimples on a date night. Something's going on and I intend to find out what before something worse than this happens."

Mrs. MacIntyre raised her glass. "To your undoubted success!"

"Thank you, Mildred. Have another."

One of the great annoyances of dorm life was a fire drill. Roused from sleep and loath to leave their warm beds, especially during the colder months, which in New England meant most of both semesters, the students hated these intrusions. Crandall's fire marshal was senior Liz Applegate, extremely diligent or extremely sadistic, depending on whether you were her friend or not. Most of the juniors fell into the "nonfriend" camp.

"This is the third one this month! We have got to make Mrs. A. keep her in line," grumbled Maggie as she slipped her Weejuns on her bare feet and reached for her duffel coat.

"Don't forget a valuable," Elaine called from the stairwell.

"Damn! Here, my psych notebook, that's priceless."

"You know she'll just make you go back and we'll have to stand there shivering while you get a real one."

Producing a valuable—jewelry, a treasured photo, your purse—was supposed to indicate clearheadedness and was required along with the coat, shoes, and a towel. Maggie grabbed the Italian leather jewelry box Prin had given her for Christmas, which contained her circle pin and a few other modest items. Phoebe threw her a towel and they left together.

"We'd be dead by now, you know, a fat lot of good our valuables and a dry towel to protect us from the smoke would do. If there really ever is a fire I intend to get the hell out as fast as I can from way up here." Maggie was still slightly astonished to find herself in the penthouse when she had a lifelong dislike of heights. "I'll take the demerits."

"But how will you know if it is a real fire or not?" Phoebe asked sensibly. "This could be one now. We won't be sure until we're outside."

"I'll know, trust me." Maggie yawned. She had pulled another all-nighter last night with the help of Dr. Prin, as she referred to herself, and hadn't had time to get some sleep until an hour ago. There had been a class officers' luncheon meeting, a faculty meeting to cover, then house council after dinner, plus reading for tomorrow's classes.

"Oh dear," Phoebe said. "We didn't talk to Elaine about who was going to answer when Prin's name was called. Come on, we'd better hurry up. It was a near miss last time when you and I both started to speak at once. I think Elaine should always do it. Their voices *do* sound alike."

Maggie hastened after Phoebe, who was flying down the stairs. The elevators were verboten during fire drills and in any case the penthouse inhabitants generally used the stairs for their comings and goings, for privacy as much as exercise. The outside door was almost always left unlocked. All that was necessary was some tape on the spring latch to make it appear closed when campus patrol made its rounds.

It was a starry night, but the moon was hiding behind the clouds as if it knew too much light might give Prin away. It was hard to tell one girl from another in the dark as they stood under the old copper beech designated as the gathering place for Crandall. Despite Liz's demands for silence, the students were chattering away. One voice, louder than the others, was reciting a litany of complaints starting with the drill and continuing to her parents' refusal to allow her boyfriend to share her room when he came to visit her at home over break. "They are so square! Can you believe it? I mean they must know about sex—they do have three children!" This produced a laugh. "Anyway, they should count themselves lucky that I'm coming at all."

Maggie stuck close to Phoebe, and they managed to find Elaine. When Prin's name was called just after hers, Elaine moved a few feet to the left and answered, "Present," in her sister's usual fashion, instead of "Here," and Liz put a check next to Prin's name. Elaine had no idea where Prin was. She had made it clear years ago that twin or no twin, her sister wasn't to question her about her whereabouts—or anything else for that matter. Ever.

Gwen Mansfield heard Elaine answer for Prin. Liz, and Mrs. A., might be fooled, but she wasn't. There was a very subtle difference in the two voices. It had to do with tone more than pitch. There would be some momentary satisfaction in exposing the sisters right now, but Gwen was saving her ammunition for something bigger, something that would penetrate Prin's armor and go straight into her heart—if one existed. Despite the cold, Gwen's face was burning. Prin was probably with Andrew. Andrew. *Her* Andrew. They had been perfect together, both ambitious, competitive, smart, good-looking. There had been strong mutual admiration—and equally strong mutual attraction. The sex had been terrific, marathons with neither willing to stop, their hunger for each other never totally satisfied. Always an appetite for the next time.

If she'd known Prin was going to be one of the group on the Vineyard, Gwen would have gone with Andrew. Sailing had never been her thing—and then there was the thought of their reunion, one made spicier by the nature of their parting with the smallest hint of a quarrel, a tease. Her intent had been to shake up his obvious complacency a little. And it had all gone wrong. Very wrong. It wasn't Andrew's fault, though. He was a man, after all. It was Prin's. Gwen had seen her in the city only days earlier, told her about how much she loved Andrew, talked about their plans to attend the same business school before their inevitable walk down the aisle, joked about their GRE study sessions that always ended in bed. No, it wasn't Andrew; it was Prin. All Prin. Looking up into the tree, its limbs devoid of leaves, snaking out over the heads of the girls below, Gwen realized she was enjoying the wait, actually getting off at times when she thought about what she might do to Miss Hélène Prince. Would do.

So Prin was illegally off campus—again—Bobbi Dolan said to herself. She was standing next to Elaine and watched her move over to answer for her sister. She itched to turn both sisters in; Prin would be campused for the rest of the semester, and depending on where she was and when she turned up, she could even be expelled. For a moment, Bobbi allowed herself to think about how wonderful that would be. No more newspaper clippings about women arrested for shoplifting under her door or in her mailbox. Or, what was worse, Xeroxed copies of her statement enclosed in greeting cards and sent through the mail. It had gotten to the point where she put off going to her mailbox, afraid of what she would find. It had been freshman year! They were juniors now. Why couldn't Prin let it go? But she'll never let it go. Bobbi came down to earth with a resounding thud as if she had fallen from someplace very high. She had realized early on that Prin despised her, not for what she had done, but for who she was, someone who didn't belong. Bobbi at Pelham was an affront. Maybe Prin thought Bobbi would crack and leave. Maybe she just got her kicks from having something on someone. Whatever it was, it was sick. Over the years, Bobbi had thought about going to their class dean and telling her everything. She'd be forced to leave, but so would Prin. Except Bobbi couldn't. Her parents would be more than disappointed; they would hate her. She existed as a "Pelham girl" for them. All last summer, they had introduced her at club gatherings—the new club, the one they hadn't been able to get into before—as "our Pelham daughter." Not "Bobbi" or even "Roberta." She didn't exist anymore. They couldn't utter a single sentence without including Pelham. "Did you know that Bobbi's at Pelham? Oh, you too? Which class? Gracious, you certainly don't look it! Must be something about Pelham!" Ha, ha.

It was freezing. How long was Liz going to make them stay out here? Bobbi couldn't wait to get back into Crandall—and couldn't wait to get out, for good.

Some dorms did a head count. Happily, that had not occurred to Liz, more intent apparently on just dragging them all from their beds as often as she dared. She blew her whistle, the signal for everyone to file back inside holding up their towels and valuables as they passed by her, clipboard in hand, their names now neatly checked off. The clouds drifted away from the moon, and moonstruck, the girls rushed the door, laughing in the bright light and waving at Liz, ignoring her frantic cries to slow down, a sea of rebellion.

Lucy Stratton watched. The world outside Pelham's ornamental iron gates was exploding in real dissent. Vietnam, free speech, civil rights. And racing past the fire marshal without showing her your towel and valuable was the extent of it here. She had lied to her mother and gone to the Democratic National Convention in Chicago after working for Gene McCarthy in the spring. Another Pelham student, Sarah Sterling, had been working for him, too, and lived just outside the city in Highland Park. Lucy told her mother she was going to visit Sarah. A Pelham girl. Mother didn't object. "I wonder if she's related to the Boston Sterlings?" They had been teargassed and narrowly escaped arrest. It had been wonderful. She had never felt

so alive, even as she thought of the recent dead—
MLK, RFK. Next semester she would be in Spain. Her
mother had held out for Paris or London, but in the
end, Lucy had simply filed her application and, when
accepted, announced she was going. She had money
from her grandparents in a trust to which she had access, and she'd use that. "At least it's Europe," her
mother had said, and told her to leave the money where
it was earning nice dividends. Lucy didn't argue. She
was owed.

She smiled as she thought of all the things she was
doing that would upset her mother, not the least of
which was her new boyfriend, Isaac, from Brandeis. A
Jew! A red diaper baby! Reader of *The Daily Worker*!
And Lucy had picked *him* up on the T one evening
coming back from Boston's South End, where she tutored at a settlement house twice a week. Yes, she had
asked him for his telephone number. So much for Emily
Post—and so much for Mrs. William Stratton.

Rachel Gold was the last to go in, waiting until she
could safely pass by with her valuable, her guitar. She
chose to believe that every time the bell clattered, pulling her from sleep, it was a real fire. That she would
descend into flames and be devoured. If so, she wanted
her guitar with her. Ashes to ashes. There was a certain
comfort in the thought.

A figure dashed from the parking lot and, breathless,
joined her.

"Whew, I almost didn't make it! She always locks
the fire door after a drill. What's with all these drills,
anyway? I'm beginning to think Liz is compensating
for being a secret pyromaniac."

It was Prin. Rachel turned around, walked straight back out into the darkness, and waited in the chill night until Hélène Prince was gone.

"But it's pouring! Can't you take the bus—or a cab?"

"Phebes, we have an agreement. You get to use my car whenever you want in exchange for picking me up at the T every once in a while."

"But by the time I walk to the village and get the car in this weather, you could be back here if you take the bus or a cab."

"Don't you go getting all logical on me," Prin chided laughingly. "I have a ton of shopping bags and I'm certainly not going to haul them around anymore. It was bad enough on the trolley."

Phoebe tried one more tack.

"I really shouldn't be driving. I'm getting one of my colds and just took a pill."

"No one is asking you to operate a forklift. Just a car. A very small, easy-to-maneuver car. Now, get going. Those cold pills don't kick in for an hour anyway."

Phoebe sighed. "All right. I'll get to you as soon as I can."

Prin's parents had replaced her Karmann Ghia with a sporty silver Mercedes convertible on her last birthday. Elaine hadn't wanted a car and opted for a new sailboat instead. Sailing was her great love. Since only second-semester Pelham seniors were allowed to have cars, Prin kept hers garaged in the village at a body shop owned by a man named Pete. Over the years Pete had been only too happy to make some extra bucks from Pelham students this way, and his back lot was always filled. It wasn't a very well kept secret, but if the college knew about it, they had never let on. Just as they turned a blind eye to the girls who kept their horses at a local stable, also against the rules. The horse rule had been put in place during the Depression to make the haves a bit less obvious. The campus stable was closed and converted to faculty housing. Since the Pelham scholarship program was nascent in those days, virtually every girl *was* a have, so the rule made no sense from the beginning and the act a pointless gesture. The car rule was a pure and simple attempt to keep the young women from leaving campus unless accompanied by a properly vetted companion. Sign-outs with a male companion asked not only destination, but the date's name, address, phone number. "Why not Social Security number and identifying birthmarks?" Rachel had quipped after the Blue-book meeting freshman year.

Pete's shop wasn't far from campus, but as Phoebe slogged her way along—her slicker, rain boots, and umbrella doing little to keep her dry—it felt like forever. She had been flattered by Prin's offer last fall. Another indication of the close bond between the two. She'd never met anyone like Prin before. It wasn't simply her physical appearance, her startling beauty, but her comfort level in her own skin, a basic, animalistic self-confidence that spilled over to those around her. Phoebe's family noticed the change in their shy, highly intelligent daughter that first Thanksgiving freshman year and congratulated themselves on having pushed Pelham, Mrs. Hamilton's alma mater. Phoebe's private high school had been coed and the fact that she had been at the top of her class in every subject isolated her. The boys felt threatened and the girls weren't interested in having a "brain" for a friend. Her mother had tentatively broached the subject of Phoebe's lack of popularity, but her daughter had merely been puzzled. "You mean you want me to deliberately do poorly, so boys will like me better?" Put that way, Mrs. Hamilton demurred and Phoebe graduated number one in her class, the valedictorian, all alone. Her social life had consisted of dancing school first, then the cotillions and tea dances de rigueur among her family's social class. She came out—looked almost pretty in a long white satin gown on her father's arm coming down the staircase at the Waldorf—then went back in again. Prin had taught her to use some makeup and brought her into Boston for a good haircut. She took her shopping. Money was no problem for either girl and soon Phoebe was as well dressed as her friend, but somehow the outfits never looked quite right on her. The trendy Mod look didn't suit her slightly pudgy body. Miniskirts revealed her thighs as slightly too much of a good thing. She looked best in her preferred jeans and turtlenecks, but not wanting to hurt Prin's feelings, she donned her Op Art paper dresses when the occasion called for them, and Prin's other choices. This was usually to accompany Prin on a double date or to a campus mixer. Phoebe was under no illusions that she was being asked out as a favor to whomever Prin was dating. She didn't mind. It was fun to be with these mostly Harvard men in their Brooks Brothers oxford-cloth shirts and their striped ties. Despite the way she dressed herself, Prin liked her men to hold to tradition and once sent her date back to change when he appeared in a Nehru jacket. Men were not something Phoebe had ever thought about much. She assumed she'd marry one of them someday, but in the meantime, she liked being at Pelham with all her friends and not having to think about such things. But most of all, she loved her classes. Here she came into her own. The professors encouraged her, and her classmates often congratulated her on a presentation or asked to meet for coffee to talk more about something she'd said. Girls *did* want to be friends with "brains," at least Pelham girls did. This empowerment was headier than the champagne Prin always insisted their dates order when they went out together.

The rain was coming down steadily. Prin couldn't have known how bad it was out, Phoebe thought. If she had, she'd never have asked Phoebe to pick her up. Prin wasn't like that. Phoebe knew that something had happened between Prin and Lucy Stratton, but she didn't know what. Phoebe would never ask Prin directly, but from the little Prin had said, it was clear that whatever happened had been Lucy's fault. And Gwen! Was it Prin's fault that she happened to be on the Vineyard just after Andrew and Gwen had broken up? Granted, Gwen might not want to be in the penthouse since Prin was seeing Andrew—it would be awkward, but she shouldn't blame Prin. Weren't they all supposed to be sisters? And in any case, why wasn't Gwen mad at Andrew? Phoebe had seen her talking to him when Phoebe had been on the bell desk and Andrew had come to pick Prin up. It was almost as if Gwen was trying to get him back, flirting away like crazy. Andrew didn't seem interested anymore. Phoebe felt sorry for Gwen.

Of course it was terrible about Rachel's brother. Prin *had* talked to Phoebe about that. She'd discovered he was a homosexual. Phoebe had been shocked. Max hadn't seemed like one, but many artists and musicians were. Thank goodness Prin had discovered it *before* they were married. Tragic for Rachel and her family, but tragic, too, for Prin. She had really loved him, loved him still, she had confessed to Phoebe after a double date and a lot of champagne. She'd kept a picture of the two of them tucked in the side of her mirror along with other photos of her family, Andrew, even Phoebe. One day Phoebe had gone into Prin's room to leave her some notes she'd taken for her in a class she couldn't make—Phoebe hadn't had a class that period and Late Nineteenth-century European Art was interesting. Glancing in the mirror, she saw that the picture of Prin and Max was missing. The part that showed Prin was torn to pieces and scattered on the floor; Max's picture was gone. It had to have been Rachel, poor girl.

She was almost at the garage. Prin had been very generous about letting Phoebe use her car, but she'd only used it twice. She really didn't have any use for one, and if she had, she could have brought her own from home. It wasn't a rule she would have had a problem breaking. You could break a rule if by doing so you didn't harm someone else or yourself, she thought. If she broke this rule and got caught, it would cause harm to herself, but not a great deal. You didn't get kicked out for this kind of thing. It was just another symbol of the college's authority, the whole in loco parentis, antediluvian stuff still rampant at Pelham. Phoebe was heavily into symbolism these days and was proposing to write a senior thesis on "Symbolic Discourse as Represented by Madison Avenue in the Twentieth Century." She was an economics major, but had taken an equal number of courses in the English Department. She already had two file boxes filled with three-by-five note cards, and her advisor thought she might be able to get it published in one of the academic journals.

There was no one at the garage. She went around to the back, past the floodlights that showed the downpour was even heavier than she'd realized. She hated going to the lot at night. Pete kept a Doberman chained up and, as usual, it burst into a frenzy of manic barking when Phoebe passed by. She knew the dog was there as a warning—a symbol—and couldn't get loose, but it always terrified her. She loved dogs and missed her own, but this one seemed to be an entirely different sort of animal, some kind of nondog. It was hard to find the car in the rain. They didn't have regular parking places, but she finally located it, unlocked the door and got in, grateful for the refuge from the rain—and the dog. The engine started right up and she drove out onto the side street that led onto Main Street.

The rain was coming down so hard the wipers made little difference. She hunched toward the windshield, peering desperately as it cleared occasionally, following the taillights in front of her, ruby-red pinpoints in the night. It was slow going.

At the T stop, Prin ran toward the car, pulled open

the passenger side door, and tossed her bags behind the seat.

"What took you so long?" she said, obviously annoyed.

"Have you looked out the window?"

"Now, Phebes, it's not like you to be sarcastic, and very unbecoming. Can't wait to show you what I got. Très cool dress for Princeton next weekend. The slip is the same color as my skin and a sort of crocheted dress goes over it, not crochet like your grandmother's doilies, but crochet like Verushka would wear. Very short—it ends at my crotch—and the whole effect if you look quick is of total nudity." She laughed. "Then a great number from Kitty Haas's store, and I had to have shoes, plus—Jesus!!! Look out!!!"

They were on the side street not far from the body shop. A man walking his dog suddenly crossed in front of them. Phoebe cut hard and swerved toward the sidewalk, but there was a sickening thud. She pulled over and stopped, then panicked and sped to the next corner, turning left.

"Stop, you idiot! Stop!" Prin screamed. Phoebe did and Prin got out, sprinting back toward the scene of the accident.

Phoebe felt completely numb. She had no idea why she had sped off. She had intended to get out of the car when she'd stopped the first time, go back, offer help. Find out what happened. She covered her face with her hands. She didn't want to find out what had happened. She kept hearing the sound, the thud as the car connected with—what? HIT AND RUN, read headlines in newspapers. HIT AND RUN. She was a headline.

Prin was back, dripping wet. "Get going. Turn right at the next street. We can get to the garage that way."

Phoebe didn't move.

"Shit! Get out and let me drive. You killed the dog, by the way. Professor Shaw's dog. And you're damned lucky you didn't kill him. All the neighbors are there. No one saw me—I stayed behind some bushes—and what's more important, no one really saw the car. He only remembers it was silver. Do you realize how much trouble you could have gotten me into?" Prin was livid. She started to drive off before Phoebe could get in the passenger's side, then stopped the car and waited.

"Get in, get in! I don't have all night! Pete will have to bring the car to his brother's shop in Medfield right away. That should be far enough away. Damn! I liked this color. And Pete is going to be pissed at having to go out on a night like this. It's going to cost me—or rather, you."

Phoebe was so tired she could barely move. She started to fasten her seat belt reflexively and then let it drop to either side. What was the point? She had killed a dog. She wasn't sure who Professor Shaw was—she thought he taught chemistry—but in that brief moment, she had seen the dog in the headlights, a chocolate-brown Lab who had turned his broad face toward the oncoming car with happy, doggy anticipation. A beloved dog, a trusting dog. His tail had been wagging.

She started to sob. "I'm a murderer," she cried, then repeated it again loudly, "I'm a murderer!"

Eight

During the night, the storm had worsened. Above the howling winds, Faith heard the sound of breaking branches and falling trees. It was hell outside—and something very like it inside. After a blast of thunder followed by a burst of lightning so close that the next must surely hit the house, someone had screamed and several doors had opened. Faith had opened hers as well and heard someone ask, "Is everything all right?" which was answered hysterically by Phoebe, "No! Everything is not all right! One way or another we're all going to be killed!" Two doors closed abruptly, and just as Faith was about to go offer whatever comfort she could to the poor woman, Phoebe slammed her door shut. As Faith was closing her own, more gently, she saw Chris Barker slip out of her room and down the stairs. In search of a cup of cocoa or something stronger to soothe her frayed nerves?

Faith had served dinner early, sounding the brass gong at six o'clock. The food she had left out earlier had hardly been touched and the refrigerator showed no apparent inroads. The women *must* be hungry, she thought, and she went for comfort food, even though it was not particularly seasonal. Beef stew, or boeuf bourguignon (see recipe, p. 318) if she was pressed to give a name to the offering more in keeping with the status of her employer. It had been simmering all afternoon, filling the house with a reassuring fragrance, the smell of onions, garlic, applewood-smoked bacon, fresh thyme, mushrooms, red wine, and the meat, smells to drive away the specters of the storm and Bobbi Dolan's death. There were egg noodles to go with the stew and a large salad with a cheese course to follow. For dessert she'd made an old-fashioned rhubarb crumble (see recipe, p. 321), which those who wished could have with home-made vanilla ice cream. It wasn't the way most of these women usually ate, but it was the way Faith felt they needed to eat now, although she was aware that some of them would only pick at their plates. She was wrong. There was only one noneater, Gwen Mansfield, who remained sequestered in her room. Earlier when Faith had walked by her door, the sound of keyboarding was clearly audible. The woman was obviously devoted to her work—or to avoiding any and all contact with her former classmates.

As they ate—and in Phoebe and Maggie's cases, heartily—the women had been silent. What conversation there was seemed to be devoted to the food and the weather. Safe topics. And even then, not much about them. The silence was not a comfortable one, not the silence of old friends enjoying a meal so much that there was no need to talk. It was a "Let's eat and get it over with" kind of silence. All of them ate rapidly. Under the surface, Faith sensed a frantic kind of energy—and fear. It erupted twice. "Have you ever been out here during a storm this bad?" Chris had asked Elaine, who replied coolly, "No." And Phoebe's immediate follow-up, "There *must* be a way for you to get some help! We could be stranded for days with . . ." She didn't need to finish the sentence. Everyone knew what she was talking about. A corpse. Elaine had explained again that flying the flag upside down was the SOS signal, and that in light of the meteorological conditions, she thought this both impractical and impossible. She'd smiled after answering, and Faith would have been hard put to say whether the expression was meant to be reassuring or patronizing. Faith had offered coffee and after-dinner liqueurs in the living room, but most of the women demurred. Lucy poured herself a large brandy and left without a word. Rachel and Chris had both slipped away as soon as they had finished eating. Only Elaine, Maggie, and Phoebe remained, a band of survivors huddled together before the fire, which Faith had made. It was one of the useful skills Tom had taught her, unable to believe that, like the rules for touch football, this had not been one of the things she'd learned as a child. It reaffirmed his conviction, as Faith had told Rachel, that New York City was an occasional destination, not a final stop in life.

Before she'd cleared the table, Faith had knocked at

Gwen's door and asked her if she'd wanted a tray. Gwen cut her off as she was describing the dinner menu, saying that she would call down to the kitchen when and if she wanted anything. Although the house had no way to communicate with the outside world, it was totally wired within. As in a hotel, you could call any room from your room phone, including the kitchen. Faith had been tempted to say that room service would shut down early due to weather conditions. She wanted to escape to her own room, too. The group in the living room had dispersed and there was no need for her to stick around. No one had wanted a second cup of coffee, although all of them had refreshed their drinks before leaving. Fortunately, Gwen had called just as Faith was finishing the pots. Ms. Mansfield wanted a bottle of Pellegrino, a BLT on white toast, and a brownie. "Just one." She had been very specific. "Crisp bacon" and "not too much lettuce." So, these were her own particular comfort foods, Faith had thought. Childhood favorites? She'd taken the tray up, knocked, and heard, "Just leave it, thank you." On her way back downstairs to finish cleaning up, Elaine had emerged from her end of the hall and asked her to "Spare me a moment." Faith had expected some sort of acknowledgment of the difficult situation they were in and perhaps thanks for the role the caterer-cum-undertaker was playing. She'd been wrong again. "Leave the lights on in the kitchen in case anyone wants a midnight snack and we'll continue to do breakfast as a buffet, lunch, as well." It had been as if nothing was wrong, that this was the Bishop's Island version of an English country house visit and the mistress was instructing the staff. The thought had prompted Faith to bring up Brent's disappearance.

"Isn't it odd that Mr. Justice hasn't shown up? Shouldn't we be worried?" she'd said.

Elaine Prince had looked annoyed. "I told you not to be concerned. He's more than a little eccentric and is riding out the storm in his own way." Dismissed.

But where? Faith had screamed silently.

Now, after another sleepless night, she went to the window. It wasn't as dark as it had been yesterday and she could make out some of the damage. The row of tamaracks on one side of the meadow had been up-rooted; each pushed forward by the force of the wind, but so neatly that they looked as though someone had laid them out for planting, instead of the reverse. It was still raining hard, but the thunder and lightning that had thwarted all her attempts to sleep had abated. The storm was winding down, she hoped, and felt a sudden rush of elation. Soon they could fly the flag; a boat would come and take them off the island. She had been trying not to think of Tom and the children. When she wasn't able to help herself and did, she had felt a sense of total despair. Would she ever see them again? Bishop's Island had come to feel like a place totally removed from the earth, a place so far away from all that was near and dear to her that she might never be able to get back. It wasn't just the storm that had robbed her of sleep, but panic. Now with the promise of an end to this nightmare, she dressed quickly. The flag was probably in the boathouse. She'd ask Elaine and get it wherever it was, ready to hoist as soon as possible. Should she pack? No, there would be time for that later. She wanted a cup of coffee, and even more, the familiar routine that went with it—grinding the beans, measuring the water, and the smell. She imagined it drifting up here and seeping under each door, carrying its message of normalcy. Nothing bad could happen when coffee was brewing.

The corridor was empty and she couldn't detect even the slightest rustle as she passed each door. Gwen's tray had been left outside hers and Faith picked it up. Not even a crumb remained.

"Thank you for coming so promptly. I'll call the others in a moment."

"Others? I thought you said you had something you wanted to discuss with me in private."

"Oh, I do, but it won't take long . . ." Gwen Mansfield was enjoying herself. She was experiencing the same high that she got when she made a killing on the Street—or when firing one of her employees for cheating her, for ineptitude, or worst of all, for timidity. She let the pause hang in the air knowing that if she waited long enough the other person would fill it. She sat down at the desk; she'd gotten up to answer the door. Her laptop was open, but all her files were closed. The room was pleasantly warm. Gwen had lighted the fire. With its rose-colored carpeting and floral striped wallpaper in similar tones, the setting was cozy, especially in contrast to the storm that raged outside. Gwen glanced out the window. The heavy damask drapes, lined to further block any morning light that could disturb a guest's slumbers, were still pulled back, resting on bright brass rosettes.

"Hideous weather," she said.

"I'm sure you didn't call me in the middle of the night to come and talk about the weather. What is it? I'd like to get back to bed."

"All in good time." She paused again and smiled. It wasn't cat and mouse so much as cougar and mouse.

"I'm really too tired to play games."

"Then don't." It was fun to watch the confusion, even alarm, her words produced. She toyed with the idea of continuing in the same vein. But there was a chance her quarry would leave, and that wouldn't do.

"I wanted to tell you first, before the others."

"Tell me what?"

"That I know Prin was killed—and who killed her."

Gwen heard the sharp intake of breath and continued. "That's why we're here—because one of us killed her."

"You must be insane! It was an accident. The police investigated, and the college! There wasn't anyone at the top of the tower with her!"

"Not by the time the police looked. Or the college," she added ruefully and stood up.

"I'm going to bed. Good night!"

"Oh, I don't think so. Not yet. You see, it's been terribly boring here. Without an Internet connection, there wasn't a great deal that I could do, so I started writing a little story. A little story about a group of young women, and as I wrote, it all became clear. And I knew. Call it process of elimination, intuition, what you will." Her smile was triumphant. "Perhaps I always knew.

"What I don't know is whether you planned it or not.

213

Not, I think. A question of being in the right place at the right time. Any one of us might have acted on the same impulse and I believe that's why we're here. We each had a reason. But I could be wrong. You may have planned it all in advance. It wouldn't have been hard to get Prin to go to the tower." A falling branch crashed against the window. Gwen looked out briefly, then continued. *"Saying it out loud does rather make 'premeditated' seem the likelier possibility. After all, you had the strongest motive."* Her tone was congratulatory, almost as if she was praising someone for a job well done.

She stopped speaking. This time the silence remained unbroken for longer and this time Gwen was the one who broke it.

"Well, I think it's time I called the others."

Gwen walked over to the phone by the bed, opening the lid of the elaborate decoupage box that echoed the wallpaper, to lift the mundane instrument out. She turned away as she did, preparing to sit down on the bed for her task. That was all it took. A few unguarded seconds. The blow was sharp and swift. She gave a startled cry and fell across the duvet. She'd turned the bedspread back earlier when she'd taken a short nap. A power nap—to be sure she'd be at her best.

The log from the pile tidily arranged in a gleaming copper carrier had done the job and was tossed into the flames, causing the fire to leap up. It had served its purpose, but something else was needed to finish the job. Something like the dagger-shaped paper knife from the desk.

It was perfect. Right place, right time.

Gwen's dinner tray had been left on the desk next to her laptop. There was still half a sandwich left.

Chris Barker was sitting at the kitchen counter when Faith entered. Had she been there all night? There was nothing to eat or drink in front of her and she was dressed in jeans and a heavy sweatshirt. When she heard Faith step into the kitchen, she wheeled around so suddenly that the stool she'd been sitting on crashed to the floor. She put her hand to her chest and stated the obvious, "You startled me!" then as an afterthought, "Sorry." She bent down and righted the stool, not so much sitting back on it as collapsing.

"No, I'm sorry. I shouldn't have come up behind you like that. I should have said something."

Now that she was closer, Faith could see that Chris's bangs were wet and she'd taken her boots off, Wellies. The kind serious gardeners wear, the kind in the Smith and Hawken catalogue. She could also see what was in front of Chris. It was an eight-by-ten black-and-white photograph.

Chris looked up at Faith. "I couldn't stand to be inside this house a moment more, storm or no storm. I waited all night, then at five it seemed as if it was letting up, so I went outside and sat on the boathouse dock. I was afraid I'd lose my way if I went into the woods. And a tree has fallen across the greenhouse. I thought at first I'd go there. Elaine will have to replace the glass—I'm rambling, aren't I?"

"Let me make you some coffee, or tea—and something to eat," Faith said by way of a reply.

"Tea, not too strong, and just some crackers—saltines if there are any."

Faith used crushed saltines as a binder in her crab cake recipe instead of potato. She'd requested a box in her food order and had put them in the pantry. As she retrieved them, she thought about Chris's request. This wasn't comfort food so much as it was invalid food. The kind of food Faith's mother gave them when they were sick, moving from ginger ale to weak tea to bouillon. Her first impression of Chris had been that the woman looked ill and this confirmed it. What was wrong?

"I have some ginger ale if you'd rather have something cold," she said, opening the box of saltines and arranging them on a plate.

"How did you know . . . ? Oh, of course, you're a caterer, you deal with food. And in any case, it wasn't exactly a breakfast order. I'll stick with the tea for now, but I'm glad you have ginger ale. I get, I mean, sometimes . . ."

"That's all you can manage. I am just a caterer, but I do know that the mind and the body are connected as surely as the mouth and the stomach."

Chris smiled at her. It was a lovely smile with a lingering sweetness, and a hint of sorrow. Faith had noticed it the first night. Of all the women, Chris was the one with whom she'd had the least contact, or who had made the least impression. Rachel had been equally quiet when the whole group was together, but Faith had talked with her alone and had a sense of who she was. Although there had been Chris's conversation with Phoebe James, the one that Faith had overheard on the first night, the one in which Chris described the caretaking role she'd played for her mother, and then had made the odd suggestion that the week's reunion was actually some sort of trial. And another view of Chris had emerged when she'd forcefully cut off Maggie's discussion of Rachel's brother's suicide. Chris's tone of voice had made it clear that Maggie was to keep her mouth shut. Why? Protective of Rachel? Of Max Gold? She must have known him. Or of herself? What had she felt when he died? Had she been in love with him?

The kettle whistled and Faith made tea for them both. It was barely six o'clock and the rest of her preparations could wait. Chris might not. Faith sat down next to her, hoping to keep her from bringing the food to her room.

Chris was holding the mug in both hands, taking small sips. The photograph was directly in front of her, and it seemed to pull her gaze back whenever she glanced at Faith or around the room.

Faith reached for it. "May I?"

"Feel free. It was lying here on the counter when I came in."

Nine young women were posed in front of an ivy-covered brick wall. They were wearing graduation robes and some had their caps on, not mortarboards, but the soft kind.

Faith pointed to one of the girls, tall and slender, her long hair parted in the middle, streaming over the gown. She was smiling. It was almost the same smile, even the sorrow. The smile in the old photograph was a tremulous one and her eyes shone with unshed tears. Sad to be leaving Pelham? Her friends? Fearful of what would come next? Which had it been for Chris? Or was it something entirely different? Amazing how much she looked the same, except her hair was in a single braid at the moment, but still parted in the middle. It must have been ash blond all those years ago; it was still, but more ash than blond.

"You?"

Chris nodded and reached for a saltine, which she proceeded to nibble the way a child does, starting at one corner.

"And all the others, even Prin?"

She nodded again.

Hélène Prince dominated the picture, not merely because she was in the center of the group, but because of her charisma, her beauty. Faith understood now why the women were so upset at Elaine's appearance the first night. Superficially, she *had* looked like an older version of her twin's face in the photo. A Helen of Troy face, and Faith found herself wondering how much damage that modern version had done. How many ships had she launched? How many lives destroyed? And what about Prin herself, her tragic end, so young? Rachel Gold had said that Elaine was convinced Prin had been murdered and one of her guests was the murderer. Gwen's outburst that it was always about Prin and the suggestion that none of them were safe after Bobbi Dolan's death didn't contradict the notion. A trial, as Chris herself had said that first night on the landing upstairs? Is that what this was? If so, it meant that everyone had had a good reason for wanting Hélène Prince dead. Faith looked at the faces in the picture. They looked barely out of their teens, and in Phoebe's case, barely out of childhood. One of them a murderer? It seemed unlikely. Yet only Prin's face glowed. Only her smile looked genuine. Lucy and Gwen weren't smiling at all, and the others were forced or ambiguous. Perhaps it was simply a case of not liking to have your picture taken. Faith knew she never felt comfortable when the lens was aimed at her.

"I remember the day as clearly as if it had been yesterday. No, more clearly. Mr. Prince, Prin and Elaine's father, took the picture. He sent these large copies to all of us. This must be Elaine's." Chris's voice trailed off, and she picked the photo up, scrutinizing it for a moment before setting it back down. Faith was about to try to prod her to continue when she spoke. "They were on campus staying at the Pelham Inn for the week before graduation. Mrs. Prince was a big deal in the alumnae association and she was involved in all sorts of meetings, luncheons, college things. There were a lot of alums around, especially toward the end of the week, because reunion started the day before graduation. Pelham grads line up by class on either side of the graduating seniors when they march into the ceremony—some sort of passing-the-torch notion. And they were all in white—what a different time that was. We even had to wear white dresses under our black gowns. Purity, virginity, dominant culture—pick one, any one." She stopped again, once more lost in thought, but not for very long. "As we marched, we joked about seeing ourselves in five years, ten years, twenty . . . they all seemed so old, so wrinkled, and now *we* are those wrinkled old ladies. It doesn't seem possible.

"No one wanted the picture taken except Prin and her parents. It was before the actual day. We had just come back from one of the graduation rehearsals. It was very silly, all those rehearsals, but this was a turbulent time, remember, and I think the college was worried that some of us might suddenly unfurl a Vietcong flag, stencil red fists on the backs of our gowns, or take them off and streak—all very real possibilities even at Pelham. At the rehearsals, it was drummed into our heads what would happen if we did, how we would embarrass our families—and be refused a diploma. They couldn't expel us at that late date, but they could bar us from the ceremony at any point during it."

"Were you and your friends involved in any of the protest movements?"

"I was in D.C. for the big march, the Moratorium. Lucy was there, too. She was the most radical of all of us, starting with civil rights. I doubt the others were involved in much. Maybe they lit candles and sang a chorus or two of 'Where Have All the Flowers Gone?' at a campus event, but nothing that would have put them on the Nixon list. Not that I did anything, either. But I don't really know. By graduation, I had other friends. So did Gwen and Lucy. That's what was so awkward about the picture. Prin was adamant about getting one with what she called 'the original group.' I hadn't been in her dorm freshman year, nor had Lucy. But Lucy had gone to prep school with the Princes, so I suppose that qualified her. We were all passing by the Princes on our way back into the dorm and Prin made her father stop each of us. She got *him* to ask us to pose, and of course it would have been rude not to agree. And Pelham girls were *never* rude. He'd do anything she wanted. It was very useful. Her mother, too. They thought Prin hung the moon."

"It must have been devastating for them when she died."

Chris nodded. "But stiff upper lip. They watched Elaine get her diploma a day later and sat through the moment of silence when Prin's name was announced. I think they went to Europe for a while after that. They had an apartment in Paris. Graduation is kind of a blur for me. Maggie was our student speaker and a girl named Lois Russell was class poet." Chris smiled at this recollection.

"What did she do?" Faith asked. "It seems to be a pleasant memory."

"Oh, it is. She'd had to submit her poem to the administration, of course, and they checked to make sure that the scroll she was carrying was the same, but she'd memorized a different one. Not simply an indictment of the war, but a call to arms against injustice and complacency. The last line was something like 'Hurl teacups against false façades, fling Max Factor mud at authority.' It was very funny, very sardonic, and very courageous. We all stood up and cheered. She became a journalist, I think. I wonder where she is now?"

Faith pointed to another face. "That's Gwen, right? And Lucy's next to her?"

Chris nodded.

All of them had had long hair, except Maggie, whose tight curls were cut short. Anything long would have suggested a pot scrubber, not a Pre-Raphaelite. Her hair was even shorter now, clipped close to her head. Phoebe had put on the most weight, but her face had also remained the most like the one in the photograph, no wrinkles, and Faith doubted that someone who didn't bother with makeup or an updated haircut would have had work done. Not so for Gwen—and big time for Elaine. Elaine. That was the greatest transformation. Chris was still sipping her tea and had picked up another saltine. Faith sensed she wanted to keep talking about those long-ago days.

"Why didn't you all want to have your picture taken? Aside from not wanting to have your picture taken, I mean."

"No, you're right, it wasn't that, although most of the women I know do hate to be photographed. More of the baggage we carry around about the way we look and the way we're supposed to look, but this was different. Gwen, Lucy, and Rachel hadn't spoken to Prin for a year or more. The last thing they would have wanted was to pose with her and say cheese."

Faith added hot water to the teapot.

"Rachel blamed Prin for Max's death. She'd dumped him for the guy Gwen was dating. Or maybe that came later. But she had been engaged to Max. It was all so avoidable—I say this from the vantage point of age. Max was a complete romantic, very intense, very talented. But to Prin he was just another boy, just another conquest. I wish now I had said something to Rachel, or Max—but he wouldn't have listened and I didn't really know him that well. Or Prin, but then she wouldn't have listened, either. But Rachel . . . I wish I had talked to Rachel. We might have been able to stop Prin some way or another."

Faith was surprised at the intensity in Chris's voice, the vehemence.

"So you didn't like Prin, either?" she said without pausing to choose her words more tactfully.

"Like her? No, I hated her. Just like Rachel and Gwen—that particular beau had been the love of her life, she said, and perhaps he was. We all thought the men we were involved with were our one-and-onlies."

"And did she steal someone from Lucy, too?" And you, Faith wanted to ask, but she'd gone far enough as it was.

"No, I don't think so. I don't know what happened between them. It must have been something that happened during the summer following freshman year. Lucy came back in the fall and so far as I know never said a word to Prin again. If they were in the same room, Lucy would always move to the opposite side. Rachel and I talked about it, but neither of us felt comfortable asking Lucy for the details."

"And the others—Maggie, Bobbi, and Phoebe? Her sister?"

"Elaine, Maggie, Phoebe, and Prin lived in what was called the penthouse on the top of the dorm. Crandall was one of the new dorms built in the fifties and I suppose the architect was thinking of some way to make a rectangular brick block look more interesting from the outside. There were four singles, a common room, and a bath. They lived there together for two years and they should have been in the picture by themselves. They were the ones who were tight. Phoebe was Prin's special pet. Maggie held every office she possibly could and was editor of the paper. Prin was like her campaign manager. And Elaine? Well, they were twins and twins are usually very close, although I was surprised when Elaine took Gwen's place in the penthouse. Elaine had been so happy to have a room to herself, she'd said during housing week the previous spring. Oh, now I remember about Prin and Gwen's boyfriend. It would have been the summer before junior year that Prin scooped up what was his name, Andrew something, because Gwen wouldn't live in the penthouse when we came back in the fall. Elaine finally stepped in and changed places with Gwen. Rachel had a theory about Elaine, that she resented Prin, but I never saw it. Of course, you never did see Elaine when Prin was around, even if she was sitting next to her. Maybe Rachel was right."

"And Bobbi?"

"Bobbi was the proverbial moth to the flame. Something had happened between them. She'd say terrible things about Prin behind her back, but when Prin would invite her to the penthouse for 'mocktails'—V-8 juice and Ritz crackers—off she'd go."

"And you?" Faith asked softly.

"I went occasionally. Until Prin killed my baby."

Faith gasped and put out her hand to cover Chris's, which still held an uneaten cracker, but before she could touch her, Chris stood up and stumbled to the door, covering her face.

"Forget you heard that," she said as she left. "Forget *everything* I said."

Outside, a curtain of fog had descended. Faith pushed open the kitchen door, walked into the living room, then out onto the porch, which faced the water. Chris's words had been so monstrous that Faith almost thought she could see them suspended against the fog, dark and ugly. "Until Prin killed my baby."

It was still raining, but the winds had quieted. The drops fell straight down, as if some unseen hand had drawn uniform lines with a ruler. She couldn't see what effect the storm was having on the ocean now, but she could hear the muffled sound of the waves on the rocks, not a crashing surf, but one that—with the fog—would keep all boats in port. There would be no escape. Not yet.

She went back into the house, and as she passed through the living room, she noticed that a third small vase had toppled to the floor. Its water and the single rose lay on the rug that had cushioned the fall, preventing the glass vial from breaking. When she'd arrived three days ago, there had been ten roses—and now there were seven.

The kitchen was empty. She crossed the room to get some paper towels. There might not be anyone here now, but someone *had* been here. The photograph that Chris had left on the counter was gone.

Faith wandered upstairs and went into her room. She'd made her bed earlier, and the only book she'd brought with her was Barbara Bailey Bishop's. It might be a page-turner, but Faith didn't feel much like turning its pages. She had only brought the one, assuming she'd be too busy and subsequently too tired, to do much reading. There was a bookcase on the landing and a floor-to-ceiling one in the living room. She could look in both places, but she felt too agitated to sit. She thought about going outside and searching for Brent Justice. At the least, she should check out his cabin again.

She assumed everyone was sleeping in, aside from Chris. It was still very early and there had been no sounds, save faint snoring from Maggie's room. Gwen wasn't typing. Elaine might be up and working, but Faith didn't go to that end of the hall. What had the author covered up so hastily when Faith came to tell her about Bobbi Dolan? It could have been nothing more than a new chapter, but why shield it? It wouldn't have meant anything to Faith.

She sighed heavily. The combination of boredom and anxiety was crippling. She almost crawled back into bed herself and would have if it hadn't been made. She was annoyed with herself. Inaction had never been a problem before and it wouldn't be now. She'd been hired to cook and cook she would. So what if no one was eating? She'd make chocolate chip cookies—big, chewy ones—and fill the house with their seductive smell. Then she'd bake some bread and make soup, chowder or perhaps the fennel soup Elaine had remembered. She went into the luxuriously appointed bathroom and splashed water from the brass, surely not gold-plated, taps on her face. So far, she'd taken showers, but after her labors today, she'd indulge herself with a long soak in the deep tub, using one of the bath oils from the veritable cornucopia of products laid out on the vanity table.

She left the bathroom and grabbed a sweatshirt and heavy socks before leaving. The first thing she had to do was try to locate Brent.

Downstairs she noticed that in her absence, the kitchen had had several visitors. Two mugs were in the sink and the basket of baked goods visibly diminished.

Someone appeared partial to Faith's maple walnut scones. She'd make some more.

She put on rain gear from the closet, struck anew by the assortment, and left the house. It wasn't pea soup, but cotton wool—a white fog that threatened to suffocate her. After walking a few steps and seeing the house disappear behind her, she turned back. Fog was a tricky thing, and without a ball of string, she would surely lose her way in the labyrinthine mist.

Instead she soon became lost in her labors. The time passed quickly once she filled it with the familiar motions of sifting flour, breaking eggs, creaming butter, and beating batter.

Phoebe James walked into the kitchen just as Faith was taking the last batch of cookies from one of the ovens. The scones were baking in the other and she had bread rising on the counter.

"It smells heavenly in here. I couldn't resist, although I should."

"I was just going to take a break and have some cookies. I can't resist, either, especially when they're still warm. Join me?"

"Why not? Have you got skim milk? That will ease my conscience and drown out my girls' voices."

Faith poured two glasses of milk and suggested they take a plate of cookies into the living room where they could be more comfortable. In truth, it was the image of Chris Barker on the same stool and her horrible words that she wanted to distance herself from.

"I'll take the timer with me. There are scones in the oven."

"You devil, you! But I could always push my plate away."

"If you don't mind my saying so, you are certainly not—"

"Obese? No, I don't mind. But I *am* overweight."

"Okay, a little, but you, all of you, are very attractive women. I would never have guessed that it's been what, forty years, since you were in college."

"Thank you." Phoebe sat down on one of the couches facing the water, the view still totally shrouded in fog. Faith sat next to her and put the cookies on the low table in front of them. She took one and bit into it, the chocolate still soft. It was delectable. Phoebe seemed to think so, too.

"Mmmm, yummy. Food didn't start to matter to me that much until after I was married. In college, it was always Maggie who was fretting about calories. Of course, I'm small so every ounce has always shown. But food as solace, as reward, came later for me. At this point, it doesn't seem worth it, dieting, I mean. Every day I look at two gorgeous, skinny females who could walk into any ad you could name."

"Your daughters?"

"Yup, the twins. Apples of their father's eye. Mine, too, until 'Mommy' changed to 'Mother!' and became a pejorative."

"Hang in there. The teen years have been rocky for every mother and daughter I know. I fully expect my eight-year-old to reject me completely when she hits adolescence, which starts at eleven, if my son is anything to go by."

Phoebe took another cookie and curled up on the couch.

"One can but hope. Anyway, they'll be off to college soon and after that you never really come home again."

"Will they go to Pelham?" Faith was steadily steering her course.

"Oh no, well, I doubt it very much. They would never choose a women's college."

"Did you like Pelham?"

"It was a wonderful education. I hadn't thought about that part much, how great the classes would be. I was used to good teachers, but not to being in a community of learners, people who were excited about what they were studying, people who were excited to teach you what they knew and get you to think, really think."

"It does sound wonderful," Faith said. "That's what Pelham was like for my sister, too. She's a more recent grad. And besides the classes, it's the friendships she treasures. You seem to have picked up again with the women here, your old friends."

"It's been good to see them, some of them." She stopped, seemingly unsure how to qualify her statement.

"What was your major?" Faith asked quickly.

"Economics. It was an unusual choice for women at that time, but Pelham encouraged its students to take risks and it was a wonderful department. I also loved my English courses and my thesis bridged both subjects—an analysis of the symbolic discourse of Madison Avenue."

"And what about Prin? She was an art history major, someone said. Did she do a thesis, too?"

A shadow crossed Phoebe's face. "She did and she didn't. It was an exploration of the relationship between the Museum of Modern Art's Good Design shows and the retailing of those products, specifically furniture by Eames and other pioneers."

"Sounds interesting. Both of them," she said. "You all lived together, right, in the penthouse of the dorm?"

"We all had single rooms. We were really very separate those two years. Everyone was very independent." Phoebe set her empty glass on the table, but didn't reach for a cookie. She uncurled her legs and sat up straight.

"Your thesis was published in a journal, I understand. What about the one you wrote for Prin?" It wasn't a very wild guess, just a daring move.

"It wasn't, wait . . . I didn't, that is, maybe I . . ." Phoebe's face was flushed with confusion.

"But why? Why would you write a whole thesis for her?"

The Prince sisters seemed markedly adept at plagiarism.

Phoebe's face shut down completely.

"I don't want to talk about it. It's none of your business."

She got up and started to leave the room, pausing at the door to say politely, "Thank you for the cookies. They were delicious."

Old habits die hard.

Faith put out various things for lunch and all the women except Phoebe and Gwen came, some overlapping. Elaine commented on the fennel soup (see recipe, p. 320), liberally sprinkling hers with the pomegranate seeds Faith suggested as a garnish, saying it was better than she had remembered. Besides the soup, Faith offered to make sandwiches, and there was fruit, plus the chocolate chip cookies to fill in any cracks. For a moment, when Lucy, Chris, and Rachel were sitting companionably at the dining room table, talking about their inability to duplicate Pelham's famous fudge cake, it seemed just like any other fog-bound vacation afternoon—warm and relaxed. Faith resolved to try the recipe she'd concocted after she'd been hired. She knew about the cake from Hope and decided to make it for the group, since Hope had declared her effort a reasonable facsimile. It would serve as tonight's dessert.

She knew Phoebe wasn't suffering any hunger pangs, but she thought she should check to see whether Gwen wanted another tray. She may have come down at some point in the morning, but she hadn't appeared for lunch. Faith went upstairs and knocked on the door.

"Ms. Mansfield? It's Faith. Would you like me to make up a tray for you?"

She knocked again. There was no reply. No sound at all. She put her ear against the door. They weren't hollow—thick oak or pine that had been painted—but she had been able to hear the sound of Gwen's typing yesterday and she could hear Rachel's guitar from her room. She turned the door handle, and as she expected, the door was locked.

She knocked once more, harder. Perhaps the woman was running a bath, or using the whirlpool feature. Faith decided to wait, make the cake, and try again, calling on the room phone. She should have done that in the first place, she realized, but the sense of being cut off from everything was so absolute that she had almost forgotten about the internal communication system.

An hour later she was feeling distinctly uneasy. Gwen Mansfield hadn't answered the phone—a bath that long would leave her looking like one of the Dancing Raisins. Faith went into the pantry and back to the pegboard with all the keys. She thought about taking the one to Gwen's room, but as she reached for it, the image of the woman's reaction if she *was* there forced Faith to pull her hand back. Unlike Chris, Gwen didn't strike her as the outdoors type, claustrophobic after any extended time within four walls, yet she could be outside, sitting in the fog on the patio or porch now that the wind had died down and the rain become a drizzle. Faith went to the porch, but no one was there. She walked down the stairs, circling around to the patio, which was on the same side of the house as her room, and Gwen Mansfield's. It was empty, too. A portico for shade covered part of it during the summer months. The sides of the portico were latticed, and until the storm blew them away, there had been vestiges of wisteria vines that would have been in full bloom by the end of July. Faith eyed the construction. It did not appear to have been damaged and presented itself as a sturdy ladder to the flat roof above. Gwen's room overlooked it. Glancing around for she knew not what, Faith climbed up and pulled herself onto the roof. The window was set above it so as not to impede the view, but Faith could still see in. The curtains had not been drawn and the desk lamp, as well as the lamp next to the bed, were both on. She'd claim eccentricity if Gwen caught her Peeping Tom act.

It wasn't going to be necessary.

Faith couldn't see the entire bed, but what she could see caused her to turn around and rush down the latticework. Gwen Mansfield was lying across the foot of the bed facedown and motionless.

Faith entered one of the French doors, ran past the pool, and upstairs into the kitchen. She pulled open the pantry door and grabbed the key to Gwen's room from the pegboard. As an afterthought, she scooped up all the keys from the board, put them in a Baggie, and tucked that into a flour canister. Then she put the canister behind a phalanx of cleaning products and pails on the floor under the bottom shelf.

No one was in the kitchen and no one was upstairs in the hall. She opened the door and stepped inside, closing it behind her.

There was no question that Gwen was dead. The air had that empty feel to it, the feel that's produced when no living creature has been breathing for a long time. The knife in her back, which Faith recognized as coming from the desk set that was a duplicate of the one in her own room, and probably every other room, was an unnecessary confirmation. The woman had been dead all day, killed sometime after eating the dinner Faith had prepared for her.

Bobbi Dolan. Gwen Mansfield. What had they done? What did they know?

Gwen's computer was on sleep, the tiny light blinking softly. Trying to avoid seeing the owner, awkwardly sprawled in the indignity of violent death, her blood dyeing the bed linens a grotesque red, Faith opened the laptop's lid and pressed a key. She knew she was contaminating a crime scene, but it would be a long time before any investigators made their way to Bishop's Island, and she needed some answers now.

A line of icons indicating various programs and files stretched across the bottom and left-hand side of the screen. One read *Personal*. Faith clicked on it and it opened, displaying a request for a password. Of course. Gwen would never have left her life open to the casual, or not-so-casual, onlooker. Faith tried various combinations of Gwen's name, realizing that it would not be that simple. Ms. Mansfield was much too savvy. Even if Faith knew Gwen's birthday or Social Security number, it wouldn't be those. And then it hit her, and she typed in "PELHAM." The file opened immediately: *Correspondence, Addresses, Birthdays, etc., China Inventory,* and *Misc*. She started with *Misc.;* it was empty. Then each of the others. They were all empty. Gwen, or more likely her murderer, had erased them.

Nothing was out of place in the bedroom or the bathroom. There was no sign of a struggle. Ashes were in the fireplace grate. She must have had a fire last night or at another time. Faith left the room, locking the door behind her, and thought of the vibrant, bold, successful woman lying there, snuffed out as completely as the flames in the fireplace.

There was only one thing to do. She went downstairs and sounded the gong, not pausing until all six women had arrived.

Nine

SENIOR YEAR

At first death meant a visceral, physical longing—
wanting one last embrace, kiss, or simply to be in the
same room, breathing the same air. As time went by,
Chris realized that this kind of missing wasn't the worst
part, the worst part was not being able to tell her grandmother things, talk to her. Her grief became distilled
into three words, "She'll never know."

They had all come to the farm during the summer,
aunts, uncles, cousins, her siblings, her parents. It was
like the old days, except for the reason. The reason was
in bed, the big four-poster she had been born in and
would now die in. They had promised her that. No extraordinary measures. And they weren't needed. She
didn't seem to be in any pain, although a private nurse

came each day, and Chris presumed the clear liquid she saw her mother or one of her aunts add to Granny's juice on occasion must be morphine.

She stayed outside in the garden when she wasn't sitting by her grandmother's bed, holding her hand, talking about everything she could possibly think of, grasping desperately at this last chance to get questions answered, reminiscences straight—"Tell me again how you and Grandpa met"—but never too much at one time. Never tiring her grandmother out, although it was clear that she *was* tired and that this was what was killing her. Chris devoted her energies to the soil as never before, bringing fragrant bouquets to the sickroom and all the rest of the house, fresh fruits and vegetables to the table, consumed as a kind of communion by those who had come to say good-bye. It was never mentioned, but few would see the farm again. They ate Chris's string beans, tomatoes, and corn, the fruits of this small plot of earth made flesh in them. When the raspberries arrived, there were so many that the group visiting at the time made jam and carried those jars away as a mnemonic; some were never opened. Raspberries were her grandmother's favorite fruit and Chris mashed and strained some, still warm from the sun, which her grandmother ate, smiling, and eagerly opening her mouth for the next spoonful like the baby swallows that nested in the barn. It was the last food she would eat. For the next day and a half she lay with her eyes closed until she turned her head on the pillow, grasped her daughter's hand, and stopped breathing. It was so uneventful—no death rattle, nothing they had prepared themselves for—that Chris's aunt wasn't sure her mother was dead at first. Chris had gone in and stroked that soft cheek. She knew there were others in the room, but afterward could not remember who they were. She knelt by the bed and said a prayer, thanking God and asking him to take care of Granny, although it would probably be the other way around, she thought irreverently, picturing the God in her Sunday school texts being urged to try some homemade rose hip jelly—"So good for warding off colds." She got up, stumbled across the room and out into the garden, where she flung herself facedown, letting her tears soak into the ground beneath her.

Yes, she missed hugging her grandmother, holding her arm as they walked in the fields, missed her smell—a soapy, fresh smell and the smell of Pond's, which she swore by and urged on her female relatives instead of all those "fancy, department store lotions" they used. But most of all Chris wanted her grandmother back so she could keep on talking to her. She was the one who grounded her, helped her make sense of her life. After the funeral, it soon became apparent that this was the role she had played for her husband also. Grandpa's detachment, his withdrawal during the summer, even his absentmindedness—potholders in the refrigerator, pajamas still on under his overalls—were ascribed to the grief he must be feeling, the incipient sense of loss. But it was more than that, and less. Taking him to the doctor for the summer cold he'd picked up after the funeral that threatened to become bronchitis, Chris's mother returned to the farm in tears. Her father had Alzheimer's and they would have to find a place for him. He couldn't stay on the farm, not even with help. "How could we know?" she'd cried to Chris, the only one there at the time. "We don't ask him things like who's the president of the United States and what year it is." Grandpa had been pleasant, polite, and answered each question wrong.

Everything had gone so quickly—her grandparents, the farm sold to a neighbor's son and his young family. It terrified Chris. That life could do this, change overnight. She came back to Pelham feeling as if she had lost her bearings. The farm had always been more home than home had been. Then life had changed again and this was what she wanted to share with Granny, the only person who could possibly understand the wonder of it all. Chris was in love and the most amazing part was that she was loved in return. She'd never said those words to a man, never heard them. "I love you." She was so happy that she found herself running not walking, smiling at nothing, and loath to go to sleep, except perchance to dream. Yes, she'd dated, but never seriously. At best they had been funny, at worst boring and sometimes nasty: "What did you expect? I took you to dinner and a movie, didn't I?" She knew what she wanted, someone tender, someone who would take his time and watch the fragile shoot she knew herself to be open up and bloom. And she had found him here, at Pelham of all places. The old Chinese proverb that her grandmother had written out and framed for her so long ago—"A garden cannot be made in a day, or a week . . . It must be planned for, waited for, and loved into being"—had come to life.

She'd put off the math requirement until senior year, hoping that it might be abolished as students at Pelham finally began to imitate their more radical sisters and brothers across the nation's campuses and argue for more say in their curricular choices, urging a total revamping of Pelham's courses. The administration was not budging, however, and stuck to the old "We know what's best for you" line. The line didn't hold for long—the year after Chris graduated, a new president came in, a new broom, but it would be too late for Chris. She went to her first class seething with anger at having to take it and more than a little afraid she would fail the course. Math had always been her worst subject and it was only because her verbal SAT had been in the high 700s that she'd been accepted at Pelham, she was sure. Her mother had gotten her through high school math courses: "It's so logical, dear. You're making it all much too hard." For whatever reason, when Chris saw equations or word problems, they might as well have been in cuneiform.

The class seemed to be all freshmen, methodical girls wisely crossing their required courses off their lists. Chris had taken what she was interested in, assuming that this was why she was in college, and not worrying about the future. It had been a good strategy in a way. She loved her courses and did well, while watching her fellow classmates struggle. She understood why people talked about how much they enjoyed their college years—there was so much to learn. It was fun to be a sponge. But not to wipe out unappetizing sinks, and here she was in the most loathsome one of all. The professor smiled at her and asked her to move forward—"My voice isn't that loud," he apologized. She had taken a seat at the rear of the class by herself, not knowing anyone. "I'm sorry," she said, moving forward. His voice *wasn't* loud. It was low and there was the slightest trace of an accent, Southern, she thought. Wherever he'd gone to college, they must not have had speech tests, she thought, and was grateful. She liked the sound of his voice. If only it had been a different subject. But soon she was grateful for that, too. Her inability to grasp even the simplest concept became apparent that first class and he'd asked her to come see him during his office hours so he could try to clear some things up for her. Instead of being mortified, she felt special, singled out. He *cared*. He wouldn't let her fail. He'd tend to her.

Robert Alexander LaFleur was indeed from the South, if New Orleans, a place that is unique unto itself, can be considered part of the South. He had been an assistant professor at Pelham for three years—"Oh, why did I wait so long to take math?" Chris had cried out to herself when she heard. They'd been on the same campus, passing each other in the library, no doubt, and she hadn't known it. He was thirty years old, a Harvard graduate—"Daddy married a Yankee and we could come back to live in New Orleans so long as we went to college in the North to give it a try." The try had apparently lengthened into an accomplished fact for Sandy, as he was known to his friends and family.

Her first appointment with Professor LaFleur—thinking about his name, she knew they were meant to be—developed into regular tutoring sessions. Chris had never had trouble in any other course, so it wouldn't have occurred to her to wonder why the professor was serving as tutor rather than arranging for one of his advanced students to help her. Chris was taking the supposed gut, the most basic math course offered by the college, the one where students cut out paper and made Möbius strips, the one where the professor brought in doughnuts to explain what a torus was. She soon found that the sessions in his office were the high points of her week. After the fourth one, they took a walk around the lake. It had seemed natural. They were both leaving at the same time, and emerging into the early autumn sunshine had simultaneously exclaimed, "What a beautiful day!" "Hook pinkies and make a wish. I'm very superstitious," he'd said and she'd replied, "A superstitious mathematician—sounds like the answer to a riddle. You know, something like 'who only counts to twelve?'" It was pretty stupid, but Chris didn't mind being pretty stupid in front of Professor LaFleur. He was actually making the murky realms of math make sense. They reached the point at which he would need to head for the parking lot and she would turn off toward the dorm, but without saying anything they kept walking down toward the lake and the path that went all the way around it— through wooded patches and past the manicured lawns of several large estates that faced the college from the opposite shore.

It had also seemed natural that they would drop their books, his in one of those green canvas book bags, hers clutched to her breast, and sit beside the water in a grove of birches. And finally, it had seemed *very* natural that he would kiss her, softly at first, then with a growing intensity to match her own. "You're so beautiful," he murmured, pressing her down upon the soft yellow carpet the fallen birch leaves made. "You're just the most beautiful little thing, cher."

Soon Chris was meeting him at his Cambridge apartment for her "tutoring." Sometimes they'd go out, to the Brattle Theater for the Bogart festival, stopping off at the Bick, the Hayes Bickford, for a bite to eat afterward.

But mostly they stayed in his small apartment cooking for themselves—Sandy couldn't believe Chris had never had gumbo—and spending hours in bed. She loved to hear stories about his family, the generations on his father's side who had always lived in New Orleans, his Boston Brahmin mother who had flouted convention by marrying a Southerner, moving to what her relatives considered a place more foreign than any country in Europe. When he talked about the Garden District houses, elegant meals at Antoine's, beignets and chicory coffee at Cafe du Monde, lazy days on the river, Chris felt as if she was actually there by his side. And someday she would be.

His endearments were soft—"cher" and "shug"—his accent became more pronounced during their lovemaking, and she was seduced by his words, along with his touch, his obvious pleasure—her own, a revelation.

In turn Chris told him all about the farm and her love of growing things—and how devastated she continued to be by her grandmother's death. Sandy wanted to bring her to New Orleans for Mardi Gras, that joyful city ritual, a gorgeous chaos, which would coincide with Pelham's spring break. She secretly got in touch with the new owners of the farm—fantasizing about a long weekend—and was assured that she was welcome to visit any time she wanted and could bring any guests she liked. Aside from that, she didn't talk to anyone about Sandy. Not her parents, who had never been what Granny had been to her. Not even Rachel. She wanted to keep Robert Alexander La-Fleur all for herself, she acknowledged. This wasn't like the kinds of relationships her classmates had with their beaux, getting pinned, even getting engaged. This was much more real, far removed from their trite conventions. This was love unto death.

"I've decided I want to graduate cum laude, maybe even summa," Prin announced as she walked into Phoebe's room without knocking. It had only recently annoyed Phoebe. Last year she'd been pleased that Prin felt so close to her that she didn't bother.

"That's wonderful. But you need to get your thesis proposal in right away. I think the deadline is Friday."

"It is and that's what reminded me. A bunch of Latin words won't matter years from now, but they might make the difference in getting a job in a gallery." Prin had set her sights on working in a trendy gallery in London, Paris, or New York. "They'll think I'm beautiful *and* brainy."

"Well, you are," Phoebe said loyally. "Any place would be lucky to have you."

"I was thinking something like twentieth-century design. That way you wouldn't have to research a whole different subject."

"What!" Phoebe had been going over her notes for a psych quiz the next day and now she turned all the way around to face Prin. "Oh no, not this time, Prin. If you want to do a thesis, you are going to have to do it yourself. Aside from the ethics involved, I simply don't have the time. I started my thesis last spring. Most people do. It's a huge amount of work."

Prin didn't say anything, but sat down on Phoebe's bed and leaned back against the armed cushion Phoebe used when she read late at night.

"I mean it," Phoebe said. "This isn't like a paper. This is big. We'd both get kicked out if we got caught."

Her words hung unanswered. Prin lit a cigarette and blew a few smoke rings.

"Look, I'll help you get the proposal done and organize it. But that's all. Maybe a few Bailey's fudge sundae runs," she said, trying to lighten Prin's mood. The smoke rings and the total absence of any facial expression were never good signs.

"I think you're forgetting something," Prin said quietly.

"What?" Phoebe said boldly, knowing full well what Prin was talking about.

"A certain little accident?"

Three plus years at Pelham suddenly came crashing down on Phoebe. She felt like someone had sucked all the breath from her body, leaving her lungs limp balloons. The friendship, this supposed friendship, had all been leading up to this moment, the moment when Prin would ask her to do something unspeakable, a moment Prin had planned from the start. Not necessarily this very request, but something like it. All the other ones had been a rehearsal, and Phoebe had played her part to perfection to the point where she herself had disappeared into her character. Now she was left without one.

"Take a deep breath," she heard from far away. "Oh shit, here, breathe into this."

Prin had grabbed the paper bag Phoebe used to line her wastebasket and was putting it over Phoebe's mouth and nose. It worked.

Phoebe pulled the bag from her face and stood up.

"No, I'm sorry. I'm not going to do it." She felt totally calm and in control now. The new Phoebe, she thought. A phoenix Phoebe rising from the ashes of the old Phoebe. Prin couldn't tell anyone about the car accident without revealing her illegal car, and besides, it would be her word against Phoebe's. Prin would never take that kind of chance, Phoebe realized. Prin always had to be in control, always had to be the winner.

And so she was.

Prin tapped the ash from her cigarette onto Phoebe's windowsill. "I took the precaution of having Pete take pictures of the front of the car before his brother came, and samples from the dog hair on the bumper. I wrote an account of the accident. He has it all in his safe."

Phoebe was not about to give up. This was blackmail pure and simple. She felt an abhorrence for the person in front of her creep into every part of her being, replacing every molecule of adoration.

"There's no way you can prove I was driving."

"You don't remember what you said to Pete at the garage? I'm afraid you were acting a little crazy, sweetie. 'I'm a murderer! Oh God, I killed the dog' are the words I recall and the words Pete recalls, too. We were just reminiscing about it the other day. I've never liked the new color—didn't really like the silver, either—and Pete's brother is going to redo it for me in candy apple red before graduation. My graduation, that is. I'd hate for Professor Shaw to find out that the hit-and-run driver who was responsible for his dog's death is a Pelham senior."

Phoebe had replayed the scene in the garage that rainy night, along with the rest of it, over and over. All summer, she had tried not to think about it, working extra hours tutoring underprivileged kids and refusing the trip to Europe her parents offered. Penance. And she'd be paying for that night for the rest of her life starting now, once more. She knew she was beaten.

"What's your topic?"

Gwen Mansfield had always liked Pelham's custom of Friday afternoon tea. The food was sufficiently substantial to lure a date out and show him off in turn. After Andrew, she was into trophies, dumping each conquest as soon as he was securely nailed to the wall. Harvard, Yale, Princeton, Dartmouth—not MIT, though. What was the phrase? "The odds are good, but the goods are odd"? The year had gone by swiftly. It was March and she would be graduating cum laude, hopefully summa, in May. Her applications to business schools had been filed well before the deadlines and she was fairly confident. This afternoon her date was a Harvard senior, Geoff Weaver, who was also prebusiness. They'd been seeing each other for a few weeks now. She'd been planning to break it off for a while, but there was something about him—his drive, a single-mindedness she shared—that kept causing her to postpone it. Besides, he was very good in bed and more than passably good-looking, with toffee-colored hair and bright blue eyes. He hadn't fallen prey to the current fashions, sticking to the Brooks button-downs and chinos he'd worn as soon as he was out of short pants. Tonight he was taking her to a party at the Harvard B School given by someone from his house who'd been a year ahead of him.

Gwen saw Andrew before he saw her. He was standing with Prin, his back to one of the large plate-glass windows that lined one wall of Crandall's living room. The sun created an aura surrounding the two figures. Prin had looped her arm through his elbow and had pulled him close. Gwen didn't know whether she hated Prin more for taking Andrew away—Andrew, who had truly loved Gwen, as she had him—or for what Prin was doing to Andrew, stringing him along the way she had poor Max Gold and all the others. Andrew had a slightly silly grin on his face. Gwen pictured a huge cartoonlike ten-ton weight suspended above his head, a thread holding it just waiting for Prin to snip it.

"I know that guy," Geoff said. "He's a Porcellian, too. Andrew Scott. Come on." Harvard didn't have fraternities, but the clubs functioned in an even more exclusive way.

Gwen followed Geoff over to where Prin and Andrew were standing. Andrew stepped forward to shake Geoff's hand, and they immediately started talking about friends in common and what they were doing. Prin tolerated it all for a minute, then broke in. "I think you're forgetting something, Andrew."

He blushed and looked a bit uncomfortable, glancing at Gwen, whom he had greeted hastily, then he stood up a bit straighter.

Prin stretched her left hand out and wiggled her ring finger.

"Yeah," Andrew said, any awkwardness suppressed,

the pride in his voice unmistakable. "I *was* forgetting something. Prin's agreed to marry me."

"Well, great, man. Congratulations. The old ball and chain!" Geoff gave Andrew a playful punch on the shoulder; Andrew pretended to be hurt, rubbing the spot, saying, "Don't knock it, buddy. You should try it yourself. Gwen's a terrific girl."

Geoff looked at the girl by his side appraisingly. "Gwen *is* a terrific girl and I'd be lucky to have her say yes."

"Then why don't you ask her?" Prin challenged. The sun on her diamond was making rainbows on the carpet.

"What do you say, Gwen? I think we'd make a pretty good team." He got down on one knee. "So, do you think you could marry a poor slob like me?"

Gwen looked at Geoff. The whole thing was ridiculous and she was embarrassed at the picture they made in front of the whole dorm. The room had gone quiet; there was an air of expectation.

"Yes," she said. A year ago Gwen's father had informed her that due to some ill-advised investments on his part, the family would be doing some rather drastic belt tightening. There was enough to see her through senior year, but that was about it. Geoff was going to go places and they'd go there together. "Yes, I'll marry you, you poor slob."

He kissed her hand and jumped up. The room erupted in applause. Gwen had just added an M.R.S. to her B.A., supposedly every Pelham graduate's dream.

"We need some champagne," Prin said. "Let's get out of here. I'm thinking the Ritz."

And Gwen was thinking that she had never hated anyone as much as she hated Hélène Prince and never would. She told Geoff she had to go change and made her way through the throngs of well-wishers, including the housemother, who said, "That makes ten of my seniors so far! Thank you, dear."

But one of those seniors wouldn't get her man, Gwen thought. She didn't know how she was going to do it, but there was no way Prin was going to end up in the *Times* bridal section as Mrs. Andrew Scott. Gwen held back her tears of anger and grief until she was in her room, then allowed herself a moment of release, pushing her face into her pillow, and wishing she could be pushing Prin's.

When Chris missed her period, she wasn't concerned. She had always had an irregular cycle and Sandy was very careful about using condoms. He'd been amazed she wasn't on the pill and she'd been just as amazed that he would think she was. He knew she was a virgin and had repeatedly talked about the gift she had given him. The Pill. Everybody talked about it, but you couldn't get it unless you were married and even then it wasn't easy in Massachusetts. Chris had never taken part in the free-wheeling sex discussions that took place in the common room on her floor. She had preferred to think of the act in plant terms—until she met Sandy, and then it was too precious to be vulgarized by the laughter and innuendo she occasionally overheard from other students. Her mother had given her a thorough, straightforward facts-of-life talk when she'd been about eleven, and that was that. The college had what was called "The Marriage

Lecture" for engaged seniors before graduation. Pelham allowed girls who got married before graduating to finish their degrees, but they couldn't live in the dorms. "Don't want us to know what we're missing," Rachel had said freshman year when they'd first heard about the rule.

Yet, as the weeks went by and still nothing happened, Chris began to wonder. She couldn't very well go to the infirmary and ask for a pregnancy test, and she had only a vague notion of what one was, something about a rabbit dying. She certainly didn't want that, but she had to find out. She looked in the Yellow Pages and made an appointment with a gynecologist in Cambridge, using her grandmother's maiden name, "Tolliver," and wearing a ring Granny had left her that at a glance looked like a wedding band. The doctor was very kind, asking her if this was her first internal exam and explaining what he was doing as he went along. His nurse seemed to be about Chris's own age. It was all a bit scary and definitely humiliating. Surely medical science could come up with a better way to examine a woman, but then there wasn't much incentive, Chris thought, picturing a man in her position and how quickly a new device would make its way onto the market.

"Everything looks fine. I'll send this out to the lab, but I don't really need to. From the looks of it, you and Mr. Tolliver are going to have a new addition to the family in about seven and a half months. Why don't you get dressed and come into my office. We can talk a bit about prenatal care and then you'll need to schedule another appointment with my secretary. Congratulations."

Even before the doctor and nurse left, Chris was filled with such joy that she could scarcely keep herself from whooping out loud. Sandy would make a perfect father, so kind, so attentive. April. That meant the baby was due sometime in December. Oh, she hoped it would be before Christmas! This year they'd bought a tree in Porter Square, bringing it back to Sandy's apartment and trimming it with garlands of popcorn and cranberries plus six exquisite blown-glass ornaments filled with colored liquid that Chris had splurged on at Design Research in Harvard Square. They'd used real candles, with a bucket of water nearby, and Chris had thought she had never seen a more beautiful tree. After Christmas, she bought peanut butter and birdseed, to make pinecone treats for the birds the way they always had at the farm. They took the tree and set it up deep in the woods surrounding Walden Pond, then made love on the space blanket Sandy had brought to spread on the snow. She hadn't been a bit cold. Just the opposite. Feeling his body melt into hers, she felt as if she was burning up.

There were babies everywhere when she left the doctor's office—in strollers, on their mothers' laps in the bus. Beautiful babies, but none as beautiful as the precious one inside her. She marveled at the thought of it all. This tiny life, this *seed* growing inside *her*. Nature arranged everything so beautifully. She realized that she had known she was pregnant for quite some time. She'd had a feeling of intense well-being and had noticed a new glow in her eyes, her skin. She laughed and covered her mouth, turning it into a cough. People on the bus would think she was crazy. She'd asked the doctor when her morning sickness would start and he'd told her it varied with the individual: "You might be one of the very lucky ones and never have it." With or without it, Chris knew she was one of the lucky ones. For example, Sandy was home. She'd called him on the chance that he would be. He didn't have a class this afternoon, but he'd had one this morning and might have stayed on campus. When she'd told him she was in town, he had sounded delighted, but said to give him a half hour or so. "The place is a mess, cher." She'd told him she didn't care about dirty dishes in the sink, but was pleased that he thought it was important to clean up for her. Maybe he'd be the type of father who'd change diapers. "I have some good news," she'd said. "Can't wait to tell you."

He flung the door open. "You aced your poetry paper!" Prodded by Sandy, who believed that mathematics was poetry and vice versa, Chris was taking Modern British and American Poetry.

"Yes, I got an *A,* but that's not my surprise."

"You look like the proverbial cat that got that poor little canary. Come here and tell me all about it."

Sandy had an oversized, overstuffed armchair by the window in his bedroom that Chris was sure they had shaped to their bodies over the course of the year. It fit them perfectly and she settled in, her legs over his and her arms around his neck.

"Something smells good." She sniffed the air. Sandy was into incense. "Is it new?"

"You didn't come here to talk about patchouli, now don't be a tease. What's going on?"

252

Chris moved her arms and took his face in her hands.

"You're going to be a father. We're going to have a baby!"

He wrenched her hands away.

"You're pregnant!" He stood up, spilling her out onto the floor.

"Yes, I thought you'd be—"

"I'd be what! Thrilled at the idea of a screaming kid to take care of on no money. Thrilled to be trapped by— Wait a minute. We have never done it without protection. This can't be my kid."

Chris wasn't sure who the person was who was talking to her this way. Sandy had gone someplace, but just for the moment. It was the shock. As soon as whoever this was left and Sandy came back, it would all be okay.

"The doctor said sometimes they can leak. I guess you have very strong guys or maybe I'm extremely fertile." She liked that thought. Fertile, like the soil at the farm that she enriched with mulch, the black soil that gave life to everything she sowed.

"I shouldn't have sprung it on you like this. You'll be a wonderful dad." She placed her hand over her abdomen. "This is one very fortunate baby."

He walked out of the room and she heard the kitchen door close behind him. Should she follow him? She got up and went through the room that served as his study to the kitchen door. He was on the phone, but she couldn't hear what he was saying.

It would be all right. It *had* to be all right. Suddenly she felt very alone—and very frightened.

He came out, and she backed across the room.

"Cher." He held out his hand. "You were right. It was a shock. We'll talk about it tomorrow. Can you come after your last class? You know I have to leave soon."

Thursday nights Sandy volunteered as a tutor at a settlement house in Roxbury. He worked there on Tuesday nights, too.

Chris felt the life—literally—come back into her body. *Her* Sandy was back, her beloved, her lover. They would talk tomorrow. She was finished at one o'clock on Fridays.

"Can you pick me up?" He had a vintage MG. She adored his car. They wouldn't need a bigger one for a while. Babies didn't take up much room.

He pulled her to him and held her close. "I wish I could, but it's in the shop."

Chris thought she'd seen it outside, but that must have been someone else's car.

"It's all right. I can take the T. I should be here by two or two-thirty at the latest." His arms felt wonderful, and she tucked her head under his chin, enjoying the sense of the two, no three, of them standing together as if they were carved from one block of stone.

"I do have to go."

"Of course." She turned her face up for a kiss. Their mouths met.

"I have a little time yet, though," he said, lifting her into his arms and carrying her to the bed.

Senior year was going by too fast, Bobbi Dolan thought as she walked back to the dorm from the libe. Why did it have to close at ten? It was the only place she could really concentrate, and she had a test tomorrow. She'd tried to get locked in overnight during exams a couple of times by going to the ladies' room and standing on the seat in one of the cubicles, but the custodians knew all the tricks and she was always chased out.

It wasn't that she wanted to stay at Pelham. Hell, she couldn't wait to get out. Prin had stepped up her campaign, after leaving her mostly alone for the year. It was as if she wanted to get her final kicks and hardly a day went by when Bobbi didn't get a clipping under the door or in her mailbox. Less than a month left. Her parents had made reservations for the entire family, including both sets of grandparents, at the Pelham Inn when they'd dropped her off freshman year. They'd watch Bobbi get her diploma, the first to graduate from college, not that they would mention that to anyone. They would dress the right way, just as they did at the country club, but people would still know. The brass buttons on her dad's navy blazer were too bright, her mom's Peck & Peck outfits too perfect, everything matched too well. Prin and Elaine's mother had appeared last fall in a hat that looked like it had been *her* mother's, but it had complemented her designer suit perfectly. You were supposed to look comfortable, not rich, if you were really rich, Bobbi had learned. What else had she learned at Pelham? She was majoring in English, because that seemed the easiest thing to do, although now that her college career was almost over, she wished she had been bolder and majored in political science. She'd mentioned the possibility to her mother early sophomore year and she had been shocked. "That's not something women are supposed to do, don't tell me you're turning into one of those radicals!"

Bobbi wasn't, didn't. But she had a plan. A guy she knew at MIT—she had no problem dating MIT men; they were quirky and grateful, too—was driving to California to start a job. He'd offered her a ride and a place to crash, telling her how great the weather was and how easy it would be to get a job. If she'd majored in electrical engineering, maybe, but still the idea was attractive. No winter—and very, very far away from the East Coast. She planned on telling her parents that she'd been accepted for graduate work at Stanford and was waiting to hear about a scholarship. If she made up a scholarship, too, they were likely to brag at graduation and someone, probably Prin, would correct them. She was waiting until the last minute to tell them anything and, oddly, they hadn't asked. It was enough she was graduating from Pelham. Maybe they thought she would get married right away. Maybe that had been their plan all along. That would explain their lack of interest in anything she wanted to do.

She trudged up the stairs to her floor. If she wasn't careful, she put on weight; so walking up the stairs was part of her regimen, as was the way she counted every calorie. The group in the common room greeted her as she entered, and she walked down the hall to her own room. Even with the door closed, she could hear them and the music someone was playing, despite Quiet Hours. It was the Stones—maybe she'd get some satisfaction in California.

Yesterday had been a brilliant, sunny day; today it was raining, but Chris didn't care. If she had a favorite season, it would be spring, with its promise of rebirth, and she would always remember this spring in particular. They had been reading T. S. Eliot in her poetry class, and try as she might, she couldn't agree that "April is the cruellest month."

The T had been slow due to the weather and it was past 2:30 by the time she got to the apartment building. The lock on the front door to Sandy's building was broken. As Chris went in she made a mental note to tell him to have the landlord fix it before the baby came. They'd live here for a while, she supposed, and she didn't like the idea of an unsecured door. Upstairs outside Sandy's apartment a familiar figure was opening his door. But it wasn't Sandy. It was Prin, and much to Chris's further surprise, Prin had her own key. It was on the key chain Andrew had given her, one with a gold crown engraved with her initials. "He had it made to order," she'd told them. She was wearing her buttercup-yellow suede jacket, the one that set off her dark hair so well, and she was carrying a small suitcase. She looked over her shoulder at Chris.

"You idiot! Well, just don't stand there, come in."

Chris stepped automatically across the threshold and Prin shut the door.

"I should have guessed. You've been mooning around all year and lately you've looked like Mona Lisa."

Chris was having trouble getting any words out. Finally she said, "Where's Sandy? And why do you have a key to his apartment?" The last question had almost lodged in her throat, like food about to go down the wrong way.

"He's not here." Prin walked down the short hall and

sat in the big chair by the window. She was obviously very much at home. She lit one of her cigarettes and for the first time Chris felt nauseous.

"Haven't you heard people talking about Sandy? They call him 'LaFleur the deflowerer'? He's humped more Pelham students than the entire Harvard senior class. Make that Yale, too. He was tutoring you, right?" She laughed. "We had a brief fling freshman year—I didn't fall for the tutoring business, though, and that impressed him. We stayed friends and friends help friends. I've been signing out to his apartment and using it at times ever since. A convenient location, and if anyone checked up, which they haven't, he's my uncle with my highly respectable aunt on my mother's side conveniently at Symphony or shopping when the phone might ring. Yesterday he called in his marker and asked me to take care of this."

Chris had stopped listening after the word *humped*. That wasn't what they did, what she did. They were in love.

"He wants to marry me. He loves me."

"Has he asked you?" Prin shoved her ring in Chris's face. It looked sharp and dangerous.

Chris didn't say anything. Her whole body felt numb and heavy. She wanted to go to bed—to sleep, to sleep for a very long time. Yet thoughts like brutal bumper cars kept crashing into her brain. Those Tuesdays and Thursdays—what kind of social work was Sandy doing? The incense yesterday—what was it masking? And yes, it *had* been his car in front of the apartment.

Prin put out her cigarette in an ashtray that Chris

had never seen on the table next to the chair, and stood up.

"Now, we've got to get going or we'll miss the shuttle."

"Shuttle?"

"As in airplane." Prin sounded exasperated. "Look." Her tone softened slightly. "It's early, right? Well, never mind. They'll figure it all out. But we have to get going. I told Mrs. Archer that my parents are taking us to a charity event and that Jackie O. will be at our table. I knew that would do it, Mrs. A. is such a celeb whore. I said I just found out and sent you into town to buy a dress. In the rush, you forgot to sign out. Not to worry, she said. When we get back, I'll tell her there was a bomb threat or something, so the Secret Service of course wouldn't allow Jackie anywhere near the place."

The part of Chris that was listening was amazed at Prin's inventiveness.

"Come on, I called a cab ages ago and it should be waiting."

Prin was taking her home, to New York. Chris had absorbed that much. To cheer her up?

In the plane before she settled down with the new issue of *Vogue,* Prin had said, "He gave you that bullshit Southern line, 'Cher this' and 'Shug that.' Right? Maybe he is from a Big Easy, but I wouldn't be surprised if it was on the banks of the Hudson, as in Hoboken, rather than the Mississippi."

Chris closed her eyes and made herself sleep. She crossed her arms low over her belly.

At La Guardia, Prin pushed Chris into another cab. It was rush hour and the drive into the city took forever.

Prin fumed. Chris felt dazed, as if she was still partly asleep and wasn't taking any notice of how much time was passing.

"We'll miss our appointment!"

"What appointment?"

"Don't worry about it. Before you know it your problem will be taken care of and you can go back to your flowerpots."

Chris was not familiar with New York City. Growing up, she'd made trips with her family for Broadway shows, special exhibits at the museums, and a few, carefully selected sights. Looking out the cab window, she didn't see anything remotely resembling the Empire State Building or Bonwit Teller. And the neighborhood they were in didn't resemble East Seventy-first Street where her mother's college roommate had a town house, the place they always had stayed. Prin told the cab to stop, and when they got out, she said, "Wait here, keep the meter running; we could be a while. There'll be a good tip, I promise."

This couldn't be where the Princes lived, Chris thought. They were extremely wealthy, and the reason Mrs. Archer had bought Prin's story was because they did travel in the same circles as the former first lady. And why did Prin tell the cab driver to wait?

Prin pressed the button next to the door, and they were buzzed in. Chris immediately turned around. The entry smelled of urine and something else, something worse. She was very, very frightened and grabbed Prin's arm.

"Where are we? What's going on!"

"Don't worry. I'm here. I'm going to make sure

you're all right. I could have just sent you alone. Now come on. It's only one flight up."

· On the next floor, Prin pushed open a door. It was glass, but the kind you couldn't see through. There was no name on it. Inside was what looked like a doctor's waiting room, but a doctor who had picked up his furniture from the curb. Nothing matched and the seats on several of the chairs were split. A woman who appeared to be in her late thirties was sitting at a desk, smoking, and reading a newspaper. Prin walked over to her, holding tightly to Chris's hand, as she'd been doing since they left the cab.

"She's next and I'll be keeping her company," she said, handing a manila envelope to the woman.

"Take a number and sit down." She barely looked up.

Chris hadn't been looking at the people in the room, and now she realized they were all women, about ten or more. Some were young, two even younger than she was, others older. One woman seemed to be her mother's age.

"No, now," Prin said. Her voice was the voice of someone who always got her own way. She put a fifty-dollar bill on the newspaper. The woman looked up.

"Okay, now." She pointed to one of two doors behind her.

Prin pulled Chris along. Chris's feet felt like lead. She mustn't go through the door. She mustn't! The door closed behind her and from very far away she heard Prin saying, "You're going to have to knock her out." Chris braced for a blow, but a man lifted her roughly onto an examining table. He was wearing a white coat like a doctor, but it wasn't clean. There were some red stains on it. She tried to get off the table, but Prin was holding her down on one side and someone else on the other.

"It's for your own good," Prin said. "Relax."

Chris saw the stirrups just as the ether cone descended. The last thing she remembered was someone screaming, "Don't kill my baby," and that someone was her.

Hélène Prince was looking forward to graduation and life thereafter. She would be cum laude—it would have been summa if she hadn't stumbled a bit during her oral defense, much to the surprise of her advisor, who had been so pleased with her written work. A family friend had arranged a job for her at one of the top galleries in Paris for the summer, then she'd return to the city and another plummy position there. She'd been offered modeling contracts in both cities and hadn't decided yet whether to go that route. She'd been featured in *Town and Country* when she'd come out and had had offers ever since, but she wasn't sure she wanted to be a model with all that implied—a mannequin. Just another face and body. There was so very much more to her than that. Andrew was transferring from Harvard Law to Columbia. She was waiting until the fall to break the engagement. He'd begun to bore her, but she didn't want to make waves just yet. Her parents adored him, but it was Andrew who would be the ball and chain in the circles she'd be traveling in, circles where he wouldn't fit in at all.

Pelham, however, had been the right choice. She would never regret it, she thought. There were a few things she still had to do, though. She ticked them off on her long fingers. They were as pure white as the rest of her body. She stayed out of the sun, knowing the dramatic effect her skin made with her dark hair and those deep purple eyes. Poor Elaine. No one would ever believe they were twins. She tapped her ring finger, "Maggie," and then her middle finger, "Bobbi." The others had all been taken care of—at least for now, for the Pelham years.

The most recent letter she'd slipped under Bobbi's door informed her that her original signed confession would be on the president's desk tomorrow. Prin had watched the Dolans arrive, swarming around their pathetic daughter, as pathetic as she was. They had driven up to the dorm in a brand-new Rolls. Tacky *and* pathetic. They deserved what she was about to do to their darling daughter.

There was a letter for Maggie, too, with photos. Little Margaret had graduated early from popping pills to other highs, and Prin had been there to record it all. Mrs. Howard had entered the dorm in the Dolans' wake. She went to the bell desk and asked that her daughter, Margaret Howard, be "summoned." Then she walked off toward the housemother's suite, teetering on heels too high, wearing a violently-colored silk print cocktail sheath. Totally, totally wrong. Poor thing. She was no doubt looking forward to Student Body President Margaret's speech at the graduation ceremonies. Something that was not going to happen. It had been hard to mask her inherent dislike of Maggie lately—so big, so awkward, always wanting something. Well, she'd served her purpose. As had the others.

Thank God her mother had such exquisite taste, Prin thought. She'd had identical ivory silk dresses made for her daughters to wear beneath their robes. She'd never dressed them as twins; what suited one didn't suit the other and it was the other who was always suited. But she'd told them that for this one ceremony, she wanted them to dress alike, and even though the style, a slightly Grecian draped bodice with a short, straight skirt, looked as if it had been designed for Prin alone, it didn't look bad on Elaine.

Today, tonight, another day, another night, and then it would all be over.

The dog's leash was tangled in the low branches of one of the rhododendrons that grew in one glorious swath in the low valley next to the library. Phoebe had been reluctantly saying good-bye to the librarians, who had been such a help to her these four years, also bidding farewell to her favorite carrel, down in the basement, next to some heating pipes. No one else ever wanted it, and for that reason alone, Phoebe had remained faithful.

As she freed the dog, she murmured, "Don't worry, boy. That's a good doggie. What a handsome doggie." She was rewarded by a slurpy lick of his tongue. As she unwound the last part of the leash, the dog leaped up, barking and wagging his tail happily. The object of his affection was a tall, gray-haired man approaching rapidly. "There you are, Connor!" he said in obvious relief before turning to Phoebe, taking the dog's leash from her hand.

"I can't thank you enough. For an old man—and I

mean both of us—he can sometimes put on quite a burst of speed. I'm Professor Shaw and you must be graduating, or a very recent alumna. Don't think I've had you in class, though. I teach chemistry."

He put out his hand, and Phoebe shook it. The dog did the same. It was obviously a well-rehearsed routine, and she started to laugh until the name struck her.

"Shaw? Chemistry? I mean, no, I haven't had you and I'm afraid I must be going—"

"I don't mean to keep you. It's just that I'm so grateful. Connor and I have been together for a long time."

He must have had two dogs, Phoebe thought in despair, trying to think how to get away without being rude, yet resolving not to introduce herself in return.

"Is something wrong?"

Her face had always been an open book. She took a deep breath. This was meant to happen. Some kind of cosmic coincidence. That she should rescue one of Professor Shaw's dogs so close to graduation. She had to tell him about how she had been responsible for his other dog's death. But how? She eased into it.

"You, and Connor, must miss your other dog. Were they mates?"

"What other dog? My sister, interfering soul, decided I needed company after I lost my wife many years ago and gave me Connor, a tiny bundle of chocolate-colored fur. We've been together ever since, and I bless my sister daily."

"But what about the accident? I thought your dog was hit by a car last year."

"A car grazed him one rainy night, but he got right up, not a scratch on him. It was my fault for taking him out in such miserable weather, then not paying attention when I crossed the street." He was looking at her curiously and asked again, "Is everything all right?"

"Yes, it is," Phoebe said firmly. "By the way, my name is Phoebe Hamilton and I *am* a graduating senior." She leaned over and scratched Connor between his ears. "I'll look for you in the academic procession, sir," she said to the professor as they left.

She watched them stroll off toward the lake and imagined throwing a stick for Connor. Someday she'd have a dog like that. No, make that two dogs.

She'd been so relieved that she hadn't thought about Prin. About what Prin had done. Now the enormity of it hit her—a hit-and-run. It was evil, pure evil. And with the clarity that truth sometimes brings, Phoebe realized that Lucy, Gwen, Chris, and Bobbi were Prin's victims, too. The whisperings, the rumors she had loyally refused to believe were all true. And Rachel. Max! Her legs started to give way beneath her and Phoebe sat down hard on the grass. Max had loved Prin with all his heart. How could Phoebe ever have thought otherwise? And Prin had not just broken her lover's heart, but killed it. Prin didn't deserve to live.

There was no moon. No stars, but the twinkling lights of the surrounding towns and Boston, far off on the horizon, were like a necklace against black velvet, emeralds, rubies, and diamonds surrounding the tower. The May night air was cool. Prin had put on her graduation dress and said she wanted to come up here one last time. She felt as if she was saying good-bye not just to Pelham, but to her girlhood. Graduation was a rite of passage into adulthood. Her fingers caressed the perfectly matched pearls her father had given the twins, hers slightly pinker than Elaine's, more striking against the milky smoothness of her neck. She lit the joint she had brought with her and inhaled deeply, holding her breath as long as possible until her lungs burned and she let the smoke out with a gasp. She kicked her shoes off and walked barefoot toward the low parapet that surrounded the top of the tower. Between the decorative Gothic spires, there was just room enough to sit, or stand. She stepped up onto the brick ledge, holding tightly to one spire with her left hand while she took another hit. And then she was flying. Flying out into the soft black night, her hair streaming behind her, becoming a part of it.

Flying—and falling.

Ten

"Gwen Mansfield's been murdered," Faith said.

The room was quiet for only an instant. It was hard to tell where the screams were coming from, but soon Rachel's voice rose above the rest, reducing them to moans and whimpers.

"That was the plan, wasn't it!" she cried. "Somehow or other you were going to keep us here and pick us off one by one. You sent that man away after the first day. The first day that was meant to make us believe that this was going to be a pleasant reunion, not a blood-bath. I don't care if you think one of us killed your sister. Your *sister* was a killer and you're one, too!"

Elaine tried to speak. "Shut up!" Rachel had lowered her voice, but the impact was the same. "Just shut up! We're not safe in our rooms! You've got keys, I'm sure. That's how you killed Gwen. And poor Bobbi . . . she probably thought you wanted a massage. We're not safe anywhere in this house." She appeared to be about to attack Elaine, taking several steps toward her, arms raised, then abruptly wheeled about and ran toward the door into the kitchen. Faith stepped to the side as Rachel pushed the door open. Before it closed, Faith could see Rachel racing up the back stairs to the second floor.

Once again, the group was stunned, but not for long. Chris looked around wildly like a caged animal and, without a word, ran onto the porch and down the stairs. Elaine cried, "Stop. Chris, you don't know your way! Stop!" then turned to the rest and said, "She's insane, Rachel, that is. Please, believe me, I had nothing to do with these deaths." She brought her hands together in a dramatic pleading gesture.

"But someone here did, and by saying this, I'm not excluding you, by the way," Lucy said. Her voice had trembled at first, but was getting stronger. "Now what we have to figure out is whether we should follow Chris and Rachel's examples or all stay together where we can keep an eye on each other."

"Together," Maggie, Madam President, said decisively. "I vote we all stay right here in this room until we can get off this cursed island." She pronounced both syllables in the adjective like a thespian. "I propose that Mrs. Fairchild accompany each of us to our rooms to get whatever we need—reading material, handwork, clothing perhaps—and we stay right here until help arrives. How long can this fog continue, after all? We should be able to raise the flag in the morning."

"What happens tonight? When we're sleeping?" Phoebe shuddered.

Maggie had it all figured out. "We sit up in shifts of two, except for Mrs. Fairchild, whom none of us can possibly suspect. She can take one of the watches alone."

Stifling the urge to ask why she couldn't be an extremely clever serial killer, Faith nodded. It was a plan and at the moment a plan was what they needed.

"I need to go to my room first. I need the bathroom," Phoebe said.

Elaine did not offer her private stairs, so they went through the dining room. Phoebe seemed to be having trouble getting her breath, and by the time they reached her room, she was hyperventilating. Faith pushed the woman's head down between her knees and looked around for a bag of some sort. Remembering the brown paper bag the book she'd bought at the newsstand had come in, she dashed across the hall to her room. Phoebe was soon breathing normally, but Faith folded the bag and put it into her pocket for undoubted future episodes. These were not mere anxiety attacks; the woman was terrified. All the women were terrified. While Phoebe was in the bathroom, Faith reflected on this fact and its corollary. Either someone was a consummate actor or the murderer was not one of them. But it had to be. There was no one else on the island—or was there?

She had to get out of the house and look around before it got too dark. The fog wasn't as heavy as it had been earlier and she needed an immediate answer to the question that had loomed for days. Where was Brent Justice? Was he alive? Could he literally be an instrument of Justice, acting for his employer, who did indeed intend to pick them off one by one—including Mrs. Fairchild, her cook, witness to it all? She added herself to the list of terrified women.

After Phoebe, Faith escorted each woman to her room. Passing by Rachel's door as she followed Elaine down the long hall, Faith noticed that it was open and ducked her head inside to take a quick look around. There was no sign of the woman, or her guitar and case. Rachel was trusting herself and her most treasured possession to the elements.

Later, following Lucy to her room, Faith tried Chris's door. It was locked, as she'd expected. Unlike Rachel, Chris had gone straight outside, where she would be spending a very cold night, Faith feared, unless she could find her and bring her some warm clothing. Telling Chris about the watches of the night would not convince the woman to return to the house. Faith was sure of that. "Watches of the night"? Where was that from? Tom would know. Tom—a longing for him pierced her so sharply that she almost cried out. And then the words of Watts's hymn, "O God, Our Help in Ages Past," from Psalm 90, filled her whole being:

> *A thousand ages in Thy sight*
> *Are like an evening gone;*
> *Short as the watch that ends the night*
> *Before the rising sun.*

She followed Lucy into her room and watched her gather a few magazines and books, a sweater, a bathrobe—nothing remotely lethal, the robe didn't even have a belt. They would all see this night out together and the dawn would bring hope and help. Repeating the words to the hymn silently again, Faith felt less alone and hope flickered.

No one was hungry and no one wanted anything to drink, not even Lucy. It was obvious that each woman intended to keep all her faculties about her and was remaining on high alert. Faith doubted that even those not on the official watch would dare to sleep. It was Phoebe, in fact, who had made the notion of sleep impossible. "What if it isn't one murderer, but two? Two of us acting together, most likely Elaine and someone else. You knew who she really was, Lucy. The two of you have been in touch. You and Elaine, sisters in crime." She gave a slightly hysterical laugh.

"I haven't seen Elaine since 1972 and she knows why. The idea of teaming up with her makes my skin crawl, but you have a point. No volunteers. We'll put our names in a basket and Mrs. Fairchild can draw out the shifts," she suggested.

The late afternoon sun was struggling to find its way through the fog, and Faith took advantage of the moment, telling the group that she was going to the boathouse for the flag—she assumed it was stored there—so she could fly it upside down as soon as dawn broke. There would be boats about, she was sure. The fishermen would be eager to haul their traps, and check for any storm damage, after these days of forced inactivity.

"The flag *is* in the boathouse. If not on the shelf by the door, then in the drawer beneath it," Elaine said.

Faith left the room, got warm outerwear from the

downstairs closet in case she found Chris, outfitted herself, and went through the kitchen door. The relief was immediate and enormous. She understood why the two women had opted for the comparative safety of the outdoors rather than remain in the house. The storm had left the air clean and cool. As she walked through the misty fog, she could see that branches were down everywhere, yet already the flattened grasses were springing back up. She took a deep breath, tasting the sea so near—the sea that would provide escape.

First she got the flag, and started down the path to Justice's cabin. It was so washed out in places that the water threatened to spill over into her high rubber boots. When she reached the cabin she saw that aside from a few shingles on the ground, it seemed to have weathered the storm well. Inside, it was as she had left it earlier. If he had been back, he'd left no trace. She was about to leave, when she noticed something under the bed, something wrapped in a blanket. She closed her eyes and leaned against the wall. Was it Brent Justice, a shrouded corpse? She forced herself to walk over and look underneath. Whoever or whatever it was, it wasn't Justice. It was much smaller. Not wanting to touch the cloth, she took a broom that stood at the side of the door and used it to edge the bulky mass out into the center of the room. She noted with relief that whatever it was, it was too light to be a body. Still using the broom, the handle this time, she teased a bit of the blanket back. A guitar case. Brent Justice may not have been here, but Rachel had, wrapping her precious instrument to guard against the moist air and hiding it away.

Faith decided to keep following the path on this side of the island. Perhaps the writing cabin was farther along and Justice might possibly be holed up there. On that first day, Faith had gotten some sense of the island and this was the most wooded portion, the ideal location for a sequestered retreat. The rest of the island consisted of meadows, originally kept mown by sheep but now mechanically; a bog; some rocky beaches; and at the very end the steep bluffs. The light was fading fast. She couldn't stay away too long. Were the women back at the house even now wondering what might have happened to her? But no one had any reason to kill Faith. She hadn't been a part of their deadly history. She didn't know anything—or did she?

An animal was scurrying along on one side of the path, making a slapping noise against the carpet of wet leaves. A large animal. A deer?

The more likely, and more deadly, alternative was just entering her mind when the attack came. She heard herself make a noise that was intended to be a scream, but as she began to lose consciousness she could sense it was barely a gasp. Then there was another sound— sounds. Someone was speaking to her.

"I didn't know it was you! I thought it was one of them! I'm so sorry!" Christine Barker was bending over Faith. "I didn't hit you very hard. The wood was wet and slipped out of my hand, thank God. Are you all right?"

Faith sat up and rubbed the back of her head. She'd have a lump, but that was all. The few milliseconds she'd been out had been as much from shock as from the blow.

"Come with me, off the path. It isn't safe to be where they can find us." Chris seemed to be assuming that Faith, too, was seeking sanctuary in the woods. At the moment, it didn't seem like such a bad idea and she allowed herself to be led deeper into the pine forest. The trees obscured what little light there was, and Faith turned on the flashlight she'd brought.

"I'm afraid I acted too impulsively. I should have gone back to my room," Chris said, glancing at Faith's flashlight.

"I have a jacket for you and some other things," Faith said. "I'm hoping that it will be clear enough tomorrow to raise the distress signal, and once we do, there will be fishing boats that will come and rescue us."

"Whoever's left of us," Chris said, paused, and remembered her manners. She might be hiding from a killer in the middle of a drenched forest, but certain amenities must not be forgotten. "Thank you for the clothes. It was very kind of you to think of me."

Behind a large boulder, the kind dropped by the last glacier that studded this part of New England like nonpareils, she'd made an impressive lean-to from pine boughs. She took Faith's hand, and they ducked inside. It was snug and almost warm, especially with the two of them. The boughs gave off a wonderful fragrance. Under any other circumstances, Faith would have been delighted.

"They're all in the living room, taking turns in twos, to keep watch. It's going to be a long night," she said.

"I don't want to go back," Chris said with an echo of childish stubbornness in her voice.

"I didn't think you would, but I have to. Rachel is out

here somewhere, too, but she did go back to her room, so she'll be able to keep warm." Faith didn't mention the guitar. She'd replaced it exactly as she'd found it. It was Rachel's secret. And what else was Rachel keeping secret?

Chris seemed to be thinking something over.

"Why do you have to go? You can't imagine that I'm the killer. If I were, I'd have finished you off on the path just now." She pulled out an elaborate Swiss Army knife. "I always carry it. It's the one especially for gardeners. A friend gave it to me." This explained the woodcraft. Faith had been wondering how Chris had managed.

"No, I don't think you're the killer and I'm not sure why I have to go back. Because I have the flag? Because I said I would?" Or, she said to herself, because she had to know what was going on, her insatiable curiosity oft regretted by her husband.

Chris sighed, and then said, "I did want to kill Prin, though. When I heard she was dead, I was glad. Glad I didn't have to and glad she was dead. I never believed the suicide story. At first I thought it was an accident. She liked to go to the top of the tower and she was probably stoned. Over the years, I've thought someone got to her first—that someone went up with her."

"What did you mean the other day when you said she had killed your baby?" Faith asked softly.

Chris curled up and rested her head against one of the jackets Faith had brought and that Chris had wedged behind her.

"I was very, very naïve. Girls were in those days, although my story is as old as the hills and probably still

276

going on. I thought it was true love. It was on my part. I adored him. He was a professor. Today they'd have him arrested, I suppose. Sexual harassment. I had never had much experience with boys, men. I spent my summers on my grandparents' farm, living in a kind of dream world—all very safe and secure—until my grandmother died, that is, and my grandfather developed Alzheimer's.

"Near the end of senior year when I found out I was pregnant, I was thrilled. See what I mean by naïve?" She gave a little laugh that really wasn't one, catching in the back of her throat. "Long story short. He wasn't thrilled—not at all—and he called in his longtime good buddy Prin, a fact I did not know, to handle the situation. I was so devastated by his reaction that I didn't even realize where Prin was taking me. I thought we were going to the city to spend the weekend in her family's apartment, an act of kindness on her part. I certainly couldn't have faced going back to campus. She took me to the city, all right, but not to that apartment. I still have nightmares about the ether cone descending over my face. Those hands, no gloves. A bright red ruby pinkie ring."

Faith put her arms around Chris. "It must have been terrible. You were so young."

"Maybe I would have chosen the same way out or had the baby and given it up for adoption. It was the not choosing! Prin chose. Sandy chose. I wasn't given the chance to say what *I* wanted. What *my* choice would have been."

Faith nodded.

"He, I'm sure he wasn't a doctor, didn't do a very good

job. I was quite ill for the next few days and it got so bad that I had to consult a real doctor. That's when I learned I would never be able to have children. They yelled at me, the doctor and his nurse. I was lucky to be alive. I was—so many didn't make it. Young women today have no idea . . .

"All I could think of was Prin. What she had done to me. How much I hated her." Chris sounded exhausted. "We all hated her. Every single one of us here. Even Elaine, I'm sure. I would see her look at her sister sometimes and there was a kind of fury that frightened me. Adolescents—that's what we were, not adults—feel things so intensely. And commit desperate acts out of real or imagined despair."

Faith didn't want to leave Chris and told her so.

"I'm all right. I feel safe here. Come get me when the boat arrives. Don't leave me on the island."

"I would never do that."

"I know, just my craziness. She made us crazy. That was Prin's gift to us all and why she had to die."

Reluctantly Faith retraced her steps. She'd left the smaller of the two flashlights she'd brought with Chris and wished she'd taken the time to pack her some food, but Chris had assured her she wouldn't be able to eat anything.

Faith could understand why.

It was still light. Back on the path, Faith decided to follow it a bit farther, and her hunch proved correct. Off to one side was a snug little cabin with the kind of vertical siding Faith associated with Scandinavian dwellings. A thatched roof completed the picture. The door was locked. Faith looked about for a key. There was no doormat, too obvious in any case, nor any flowerpots. A crushed stone path led to the door from the wooded path. Hostas, flattened by the storm, lined the way. Pobbles, those round rocks created by the crashing surf, were placed at intervals. The author had had various words inscribed on them: BELIEVE, DREAM, and HOPE, PERSEVERE. Rather trite, Faith thought judgmentally. Surely the writer could have come up with others, not these obvious sentiments. This thought led to another, and sure enough, the key was under SEEK.

Barbara Bailey Bishop's refuge was as Spartan as her handyman's, but then it was not her main abode. A woodstove, a large table stacked with yellow legal-sized pads, and a Dundee marmalade jar stuffed with sharpened pencils furnished the room. The only indication of the owner's wealth and status was an Aeron desk chair. The room had a closed-up feel, and Faith doubted anyone had been here since the author was here on Friday, the day of their arrival.

She looked at the pad in front of the chair. It was covered in Bailey's neat script, nothing crossed out. The dialogue was similar to that in the book Faith had brought to read, only this conversation involved an eighteenth-century married woman's rejection of her true love in order to remain faithful to her wedding vows, as opposed to the twentieth-century woman in the one Faith was reading.

If the room had secrets, it was keeping them. No sign of Brent, or anyone else. She had one more place to check and then she had to go back inside the main house. She hoped nothing of a gingham dog and calico cat nature had happened in her absence. The women were so tightly wound that it wouldn't take much to set them off, clawing at each other, or worse.

Soon she could make out the greenhouses and left the path, heading for them. Chris had been right about the damage. Faith circled them and shone her light through the glass. No one—dead or alive. From there she headed toward the house and the patio outside the pool room, backing against the door to the spot from which she'd looked out, trying to remember where the grass had been tamped down. She headed in that direction, but the storm had obliterated any traces of something or someone being dragged along. As she walked she was both afraid of what she might find and eager to do so. A few minutes' walk brought her to the end of the grass. There was a short drop to the water below and she was glad she had her flashlight trained steadily in front of her. At high tide, which it was now, stepping off would land you directly into the frigid water. Is that where Brent ended up? Dragged to this spot? Or was he hiding out, having constructed something like Chris's lean-to. Suddenly Faith wished she had forced Chris to come back with her. Safety in numbers. Rachel, too. As the night drew nigh, staying alone outside on the island seemed like a very, very bad idea.

The women must have turned on every light in the living room. The porch lights and outside lights were on, too. Through the mist, the house looked like a ghostly galleon, seeming to float above the ground. Faith walked up the front stairs and across the wide porch.

She didn't want to startle anyone, so she called out, "It's Faith Fairchild!" before knocking at the door and showing her face through the glass. Even so, as she walked in, she could tell that Phoebe, for one, had reacted. Her knitting was on the floor and she was standing up, poised for flight.

"Where have you been?" Maggie asked angrily. "We've been worried sick about you!"

Faith took the flag from beneath her jacket, where she had been protecting it from the damp, and said, "I told you I was going to try to find Brent Justice."

"Did you?" Maggie asked.

"No. No, there's no sign of him," Faith said.

"Rachel was right. You did send him away—with the only boat and whatever you use to communicate with the outside world. I never bought that, not for a moment," Lucy said, facing Elaine, who was seated in one of the large armchairs on either side of the fireplace. Someone had started a fire, but it was sputtering out now.

"What?" Elaine appeared to have been thinking of something else. "What are you talking about, Lucy?"

"Snap out of it! You sent your handyman off on the first day to trap us all here. Don't try to deny it."

Faith wondered whether Elaine had slipped some kind of pills into her pocket when she'd gone into her room. If she had, it had been adroitly done. Faith hadn't spotted it. But she appeared to be on something now. Almost in a trance.

"I have no idea where Brent is, Mrs. Fairchild. You were going to look for him. Did you find him?"

"She just said she didn't!" Lucy was enraged. "What's wrong with you!"

Elaine sat up in the chair. "Nothing's wrong with me; what's wrong with *you*?" She'd snapped out of it, whatever it was—at least for the moment.

Faith decided it was time to take charge, although Maggie had been doing a creditable job.

"I'm going to change out of these things, then make up a tray of soup and sandwiches. We all need to eat something. I'll start the coffee, too."

"Just don't leave the food unattended. Wait until you come downstairs to make the coffee," Phoebe said.

Faith raised an eyebrow, but the woman was making a good point.

"You didn't find Brent Justice, but how about Chris and Rachel?" Maggie asked.

Faith wasn't exactly sure why, but it seemed best to answer no, and in fact, she hadn't seen Rachel, only her guitar.

Before she went upstairs, she went into the pantry and checked the flour canister with the keys. They were all there in the Baggie, as she had left them. She shook the flour from the bundle, slipped it into her pocket, and replaced the canister. In her room, as she changed as rapidly as possible, Faith cast a longing look at the deep tub and promised herself both an undisturbed soak and undisturbed sleep when this was all over—back in Aleford. Then she walked quietly to Elaine's room at the end of the hall. She wanted to see what was on the piece of paper that Elaine had hidden when Faith had come in to tell her about Bobbi Dolan's death. It wasn't work. The author hadn't been writing on one of her legal pads. It had been a sheet of white paper, similar to the kind on which she'd written that initial arrival note to Faith.

Unlocking the door and closing it behind her, Faith went straight to the desk. There was nothing on the surface, save a blotter edged with Turkish marbleized paper. The same paper covered a pencil holder, the pencils themselves, and a small notepad. There was only one drawer, a large one that extended below the full length of the desk. It held various kinds of writing paper, an address book, stamps, but nothing revealing. There wasn't time to search the room further. Faith closed the drawer and started to leave, then went back to the desk and lifted the blotter. There were three sheets of paper beneath. Two were letters, one to her agent complaining about a delay in payment and instructing him to get onto the publisher immediately. The other was to someone named Kay Lyon thanking her for the expert help she had provided with some research. The tone of the letter was warm, even effusive, and it was clear that Kay was someone Elaine liked and admired very much. But it was the third sheet that drew Faith's attention. It was the third sheet she'd seen the other day—a list, as she had thought from her glimpse of it. Names, numbered from 1 to 9. All their names, even Brent's and Faith's own. What chilled her to the bone was the fact that Brent's, Bobbi's, and Gwen's all had a line drawn through them. They'd been eliminated. Three names, three vases shattered. What could be easier than to creep down your private staircase and tip over the roses, tip them over to spread fear among the survivors? And survivors for how long? Was this all a vendetta? Since Elaine didn't know who had killed her sister, was she going to kill *all* the suspects? Faith thought about the way she had seemed when Faith first entered the living room a short time ago. The author had been out of it. Was the woman truly insane?

She put the sheets of paper back and hastened out the door, locking it behind her. Just one night. Stay close to everyone and never be alone with Elaine. Joining Chris was a tempting notion, but Faith was afraid that would trigger Elaine's suspicions and she would track them down. A plot after the writer's own heart. She knew the island better than any of them and Faith had no doubt she would find them. Better to behave as if everything were normal. Normal! She almost laughed.

Why Brent Justice? Why had he been "crossed off"? He must have seen her when she'd killed Bobbi. If Elaine had sent him away, she wouldn't have had his name on the list. A list, Faith forced herself to remember, the writer had in hand before Faith told her about Bobbi Dolan's death.

"Soup anyone? It's piping hot. It's seafood chowder, but if anyone would prefer split pea, I have that, as well." Faith set the tray with mugs of the soup, warm breads, and some cheeses on a glass-topped table.

"I'm sure the chowder will be fine," Elaine said, yet she didn't move in the direction of the food. No one did.

"I'll get the coffee," Faith said. "I don't suppose anyone wants some of the cake I made earlier today. The Pelham Fudge Cake?"

"The cake that's been sitting on the counter all day," Phoebe said. "No, thank you."

"Oh, really," Maggie said. "What do you think? One of us is walking around with a hypodermic full of cyanide to squirt into some baked goods? I'd love a piece."

Faith gave her full marks for guts and went to fetch the food.

It was only eight o'clock, although it seemed like two o'clock in the morning. Faith had eaten some soup, bread, and cheese, although she wasn't hungry, and was now drinking her second cup of coffee. Phoebe had stuck to coffee and her knitting, which appeared to be a dog sweater. She, like everyone else, was saying almost nothing. Maggie had eaten some soup, then, rather defiantly, a large slice of cake that she declared to be a perfect duplicate of the college favorite. Elaine hadn't moved from her chair, or moved much at all. Faith had built the fire up and was keeping it going. There was a large supply of wood. One side of the fireplace had been fashioned to store wood, each log cut perfectly to size and stacked in an orderly fashion. Brent Justice's work, Faith supposed.

Lucy had gone to the bookshelves and was apparently absorbed in Nancy Mitford's *Love in a Cold Climate*. She'd had some soup and was nursing a cup of coffee.

"Well," said Maggie briskly. "How do you want to do this? When should we start our vigils?" She'd brought her voluminous briefcase from her room, along with a heavy sweater, and had been devoting herself to reading what were important papers relating to college business, judging from the serious expression on her face. Faith wondered about Elaine's beneficent gift. What would happen now?

"It's a little early," Lucy said, looking up from her book. "Why don't we start at ten and do two three-hour shifts, then one last two-hour one. If the fog clears, it should be light at six, maybe even earlier. Mrs. Fairchild should choose which one she wants, since she'll be alone."

Maggie nodded. Phoebe and Elaine appeared to be thinking of other things. In Phoebe's case, Faith was pretty sure it was the little doggie for which she was knitting. In Elaine's . . . ?

"Phoebe? Elaine? What do you think?" Maggie said sharply.

"Whatever you decide is fine with me," Phoebe said.

"I concur." Elaine's voice was unexpected. So was her next move. She got up and walked behind the chair to the door and started to ascend the stairs.

"Just a minute! We said no one was to leave the room!" Lucy called out.

Elaine turned around. "I'm just getting some Tylenol. You can all come with me if you want. I don't have a gun in my medicine cabinet, if that's what you think."

Syringes of cyanide, guns in medicine cabinets. Things were so far out of hand Faith couldn't think of a metaphor to describe them.

"I have some Tylenol in the kitchen," she said. "Extra Strength."

Elaine sat down again. "Good, then I won't need to get mine."

Faith brought the container and a glass of water. Tap water. If her employer wanted something else, she'd have to ask for it. She didn't, but swallowed the pill, leaned gracefully back in the chair, and closed her eyes.

"I guess we know who won't be doing the first shift," Phoebe said.

Elaine opened one eye. "Don't be so sure of that."

At ten o'clock, Phoebe and Lucy assumed the positions that Maggie had determined would be best for surveillance at either end of the room. Faith had cleared away the food and cleaned up the kitchen. She brought several insulated carafes of coffee back, along with some fruit, crackers, cheese, and cookies. Then she searched the shelves for something to read herself. She wasn't sleepy, just deadly tired. Earlier in the kitchen, before locking the door, she had stepped outside and been heartened by a small, clear patch studded with several bright stars in the night sky. Somewhere Tom, Ben, and Amy were slumbering under the same sky, or in Tom's case, perhaps gazing up into it. She wrapped her arms tightly around her own body, imagining that she was encircling those three, as well, and felt the strength of their love for each other. It would see her through this night, just as it had so many nights before.

Faith had chosen the last shift, planning to raise the flag as soon as there was a glimmer of daylight. But that was still many hours away.

"How can we get any sleep with all these lights on?" Maggie asked. "Surely we can turn some off, or at least dim them."

"No way," Phoebe said. "Tie something around your eyes. Mrs. Fairchild can get you a dish towel or something."

"We can turn a few out, Phoebe. Not many. Maggie's right," Lucy said.

A compromise was reached as Phoebe accompanied Lucy and Maggie to each fixture. Elaine was either asleep or providing a good imitation. She hadn't moved since Faith had given her the Tylenol.

With the room in semidarkness, Faith gave up her attempts to read *Pride and Prejudice,* a choice that had seemed inspired earlier. Jane Austen was her refuge in a storm—flu, insomnia, hospital waiting rooms.

At one o'clock, the shift changed. Maggie shook Elaine awake and asked Faith to give them both some coffee. Only Faith was allowed to dispense the liquid. Phoebe took Elaine's chair by the fire and Lucy stretched out on a long sofa that faced out toward the porch—as far away as she could get from all of them.

Faith had set her watch to go off at 3:30, even though her shift didn't officially begin until 4:00. She wanted to watch the watchers, just as she had kept an eye on Phoebe and Lucy until midnight before succumbing, allowing her eyes to close. Before that, neither woman had moved from her post, nor taken her eyes off the room's occupants. Now, awakened by the changing of the guard, Faith knew she had to get back to sleep, fitful though it would be. She had to be alert for her own watch and all this day might bring.

At 3:30, everything was as it had been earlier, except Phoebe was sound asleep, her breath making little whistling noises. The fire had almost gone out and Faith debated whether to keep it going or not. They would be leaving the island in a few hours—her desperate hope—better to let it die down.

She had stretched out on one of the sofas next to the kitchen door and could see the whole room. Except for Phoebe, there was total silence. No crackling fire, no whispered conversation. Nothing. Outside, the winds had stilled. The storm was over. It was too early for the birds, the chatter that she normally cursed for rousing her. Quiet. Total quiet. It was unnatural—and terrifying. She sat up and stretched.

"I'm awake," she whispered to Maggie. "I might as well take over now and you can get some sleep." Maggie nodded and relinquished her chair, trading it for the sofa Faith had occupied.

Faith went over to Elaine and said the same thing.

"I'm fine where I am, but thank you."

She looked like something carved from white jade, her exquisite features enhanced by the low light. She was wearing another caftan, a pale sage or, Faith thought, the color of tender celery.

Walking back to the opposite end of the room, Faith looked over the top of the high sofa where Lucy was sleeping, and before she could stop herself, gasped.

Lucy was gone.

"What is it?" Maggie's voice sounded as if she were speaking into a microphone, and everyone sat up.

"Lucy's not here. Perhaps she had to go to the bathroom?" There was a half bath off the living room, and a quick check revealed it was empty.

"Maggie, Elaine, you were on duty! You didn't see her go?" Phoebe was close to hysteria and Faith reached into her pocket for the paper bag she was glad she'd had the foresight to transfer when she'd changed clothes.

Elaine shook her head slowly. "No," Maggie said. "I didn't see or hear a thing."

It would have been easy to do, and a good plan, Faith thought. The sofa Lucy had chosen had a high back. Easy enough to slip onto the floor and roll toward the front door. Like everything in this exquisitely appointed house, the hinges were oiled and noiseless. Lucy would have been out in less than a minute. But why? What had she seen? What did she know?

"It's the two of you! You killed her in her sleep. While Faith and I were sleeping! And we're next!" Phoebe grabbed the bathrobe she'd been using as a blanket and dashed through the door into the kitchen. There was a crash. Faith went after her in time to watch her disappear out the back door into the darkness. What was left of the Pelham Fudge Cake was on the floor.

Back in the living room someone had turned on more lights.

"There doesn't seem to be much point to this anymore. I'm going to bed. My own bed," Elaine said, and disappeared up her private staircase, closing the door firmly behind her. Faith heard the one at the top close, then Maggie said, "I'm going to my room, as well. What are you going to do?"

"It won't be long until it's light. I'll stay here."

Maggie shrugged. "Please yourself, but I think you'd be more comfortable upstairs."

The woman was definitely a manager.

"I'll think about it," Faith said, determined not to be managed.

At 4:30, Faith walked out onto the porch. The sky was definitely getting lighter along the horizon. Through the early morning mist the sea was calm. She opened the door and sat down on the steps, filled with relief. It was almost over. She'd raise the flag and go find Chris first, then the others. If the island wasn't so far out, she would already be able to hear the fishermen's engines putt-putting from trap to trap. It might be several hours before they got this far, or they might start out here, working their way back. Whichever it was, she'd be ready. Everything was packed, even her kitchen equipment, and stood waiting by the door.

Someone was coming onto the porch behind her. It was Elaine Prince. She looked exhausted and had exchanged her flowing caftan for jeans and a sweatshirt. Her hair was pulled back and she looked her age, looked, Faith thought, like herself and not her sister.

"I hoped you would be able to figure it out. That's why I asked you to come. I'd heard from friends in New York about what you did for Emma Stanstead, found out who really murdered her father—and how discreet you had been. Someone else would have run straight to the tabloids."

Faith shuddered at the thought. As if.

Elaine continued. "I knew what Prin was like. Always had. At best you could say that she was easily bored, that she had to constantly create excitement for herself. At worst, well, she was amoral, treating human beings without any sense of decency or regard for right or wrong.

"I suppose we had a love/hate relationship. But she was my sister, and all these years I knew I'd have to find out what happened that night. Find out who killed her. Prin would never have killed herself."

"Why did you wait so long?" Faith asked, watching the dawn come up, a haze of pink and yellow.

"My parents either believed or were determined to believe that Prin's death was an accident. I couldn't do anything while they were still alive. My father died a year after Prin. He worshiped her. 'Prin' wasn't short for our last name, but his nickname for her, 'Princess.' He had a massive heart attack. A broken heart. Mother lived on alone, mostly in France. I think she was proud of me, but she didn't consider what I write 'real books.' She died last year and I was free—free to track down my sister's killer."

"Do you honestly believe that each of the women you invited here could have been guilty of such a crime?" Faith was incredulous.

"After what I've heard about the things you've seen over the years, haven't you come to believe that, given certain circumstances, anyone could commit murder? In the case of these women, some more likely than others, but each could have been driven to it by my sister."

Faith remembered what Chris had just said about the intensity of adolescent, late-adolescent, emotion— emotion that would cloud normal judgment and seem to justify even murder.

"I know about Rachel's brother, and Chris has told me about what happened to her during senior year."

"The abortion. You see, my sister told me everything. It was a kind of test. Would I still love her despite what she had done? And kept on doing. She was

292

very beautiful, as you've heard, but she also had an insatiable need to have that beauty recognized. She used it as a reward—and a weapon. One summer she carried on a torrid affair with Lucy's father and made sure Lucy found out. Then she stole Gwen's boyfriend. I'll admit that doesn't sound like much, but Gwen was totally besotted with him, and when you're that age, things seem more important than they do looking back."

"And Bobbi Dolan?"

"Bobbi was a thief, or rather she had a problem. She'd be treated by a psychiatrist now. Things disappeared from our rooms freshman year. Prin made her sign a confession."

"Blackmail?"

Elaine nodded. "But not for anything specific, just for the fun of watching Bobbi squirm. Prin couldn't stand what she called 'tacky people' and Bobbi fell into that category, a nonperson category. Then there was Phoebe. Prin lied to her about the severity of a car accident they'd been involved in. Phoebe was driving and kept going. Prin made her stop and went back. She told Phoebe she'd killed a dog. Of course she hadn't, but Prin got her senior thesis done."

Faith was reeling. Hélène Prince had been a monster. Not simply totally amoral, but evil.

"Which leaves Maggie."

"Yes, our president. Pills. Prin got her hooked on uppers and downers. Maggie was never a scholar and what with running everything on campus she needed some study aids."

"And everything came to a head at graduation?"

"I've never known what Prin planned to do exactly, but I imagine she was going to hand over any incriminating documents to the college, then sit back and watch various members of the group topple over like tenpins."

"You've figured out who killed your sister, haven't you?"

"Yes, and I imagine you have, too."

"I should have figured it out sooner. It might have saved three lives."

"But then you didn't know why I'd asked you here."

"No."

Elaine sighed heavily. "It's on my conscience. Especially Brent. I *should* have sent him away. I imagine he must have seen her kill Bobbi or come along just afterward."

"More likely that. There were traces of dirt from the garden on the tiles. He probably thought she could be saved and was struck from behind, much the way she must have been."

"And Gwen. She beat us to it and died because of it."

"I hope you realize, Mrs. Fairchild, that Elaine is crazy." Maggie's voice startled Faith. She had been so intent on what Elaine was saying that she hadn't heard Maggie come across the porch to the top of the stairs.

"She's been telling you fairy tales. Grim fairy tales." She smiled at her joke. "The only person in our group who wanted Prin dead was Elaine. I don't claim to be a psychologist, but I've been around young women long enough to be an acute observer of their particular style of human behavior."

She sounded as if she was lecturing.

"Elaine hated her sister from the moment her father's obvious preference became known to her. She slipped into the world in her sister's shadow and remained there biding her time. Do you think our famous author would be where she is now if her sister were alive? It would have been Prin in the limelight. Now why don't you gather all the others from their little hidey-holes and I'll raise the flag."

Faith looked at Elaine and they both stood up, backing down the stairs to stand on solid ground.

"No," Faith said. "It was you, not Elaine. You were the one who tipped over those vases with the roses. You were the one who *had* to kill. There's only one person here who had everything to lose—power, position, prestige, and Pelham—yourself. And only one person with everything to lose all those years ago. The same person. You."

Margaret Howard's face flushed angrily. "What do you mean, 'tipped over vases'? The ones with the roses. What vases? I don't recall any. The whole house is filled with flowers. Are you insane! Do you know to whom you're talking? I can sue you for an accusation like this. My husband is a very important lawyer in Washington. How dare you—"

"She's right, Maggie," Elaine said softly. "What was Prin going to do? She must have had some proof of your addiction. Was she going to present it to the dean or the president? Keep you from speaking at graduation? Keep you from graduating at all? You'd never be able to be Pelham's president after that, and we all knew that was your goal, your obsession. But poor Bobbi—and Brent Justice, you didn't even know him! And Gwen!"

"Stop it! Stop it!" Maggie screamed. She had her briefcase slung over her shoulder, hanging from its long strap close to her hip. She reached inside and pulled out a gun.

The sun had risen and it was going to be a beautiful day. The storm had washed everything clean. Even the air seemed crystal clear.

"You don't want to do this, Maggie," Elaine said.

"Charles got this for me. He was nervous about having me drive at night without some kind of protection. He taught me to use it, too. I'm actually an excellent shot. I always wondered if there was something he wasn't telling me. Some reason he had for wanting us both to keep guns in our cars, but I don't ask him to tell me everything and vice versa. I didn't want to leave it in the car back on the mainland. I was afraid someone might steal my little Mini—they're very desirable, you know—and then the gun might be used irresponsibly. It's registered, of course. All legal. Charles made sure of that," she prattled on.

It wasn't Elaine who was crazy, Faith thought in despair. It was Maggie.

"Now we're going to take a walk out to those cliffs where we had that lovely picnic when we came. Please move along. Afterward, I have to find all the others, tell them how you forced Mrs. Fairchild over the cliff, followed her in remorse, then get back here and hoist the flag."

It was quite a To Do list, Faith thought as she walked across the lawn and around to the back of the house where the cliff path started.

Maggie was still carrying her briefcase. Faith had the

wild notion that she would force Elaine to sign a document affirming her gift to the college before killing her. Elaine was directly in front of Maggie. Faith was in the lead, her mind racing through various scenarios. Unfortunately, the only ones so far involved at least Elaine, or herself, getting shot.

"Please listen, Maggie," Elaine said. "I'm sure these have all been accidents, nothing premeditated. Your husband is a lawyer and will get you a very good lawyer. What you're doing now will only make things worse. How will you explain the bullets from your gun in our bodies? It's low tide. From the cliff, we'll end up on the rocks, not in the water."

This was one of the scenarios Faith had been trying *not* to envision.

"I'm very good at thinking on my feet. Don't you worry," Maggie said smugly. "Now we've had enough talking. That was Bobbi's and Gwen's problem, too. Look where it got them. I wouldn't have been forced to do all this if you four had simply kept your mouths shut." Madam President was momentarily Madam Schoolmarm.

They continued on in silence, except for the occasional shriek of a gull overhead.

If only they had taken the path by Chris's lean-to, Faith thought. But then by the time Chris got to them with her trusty Swiss Army knife, it would be too late. But still, harder for Maggie to explain.

They were in the woods. The sun hadn't risen high enough to penetrate the pines and it was cold. It was harder going, too. The path was strewn with debris from the storm. Ahead Faith could see the opening that led to the field and high cliffs. Behind her Elaine stumbled and Maggie cried, "Watch it!" Over her shoulder, Faith saw Maggie move closer to Elaine. The gun must be squarely aimed at the writer's back.

The path ended and they emerged into the bright sunlight, the meadow stretching before them. There wasn't a cloud in the sky.

"Now!" screamed Faith, coming to a full stop and pushing Elaine to the ground out of the way as she herself dove for Maggie's feet. As she had hoped, her sudden exclamation, as well as action, had startled Maggie just enough for Faith to pull her down. Elaine immediately threw herself on top of Maggie, who was frantically trying to aim the gun at one or the other of her assailants. It was a wordless struggle, punctuated by grunts, as Faith tried to twist the gun from Maggie's grasp. Maggie pulled the trigger. The shot was so close that Faith was sure she had been winged. Exhibiting strength only a personal trainer could produce, Elaine had Maggie firmly pinned. She pulled the trigger again, and again the shot went off into the grass, well away from her intended target. Finally Faith leaped up and dashed the short distance to the path, seizing a rock she had spotted on their way out. It was the work of a moment to pound Maggie's wrist. She released the gun and Faith grabbed it, turning it on Maggie as she undid her belt and pulled it through the loops of her jeans.

"This will have to do for now. Let her up and tie her hands behind her back. I've got her covered."

Slowly Elaine moved off and Maggie stood up, but before Elaine could bind her, Maggie ran across the field to the edge of the cliff. They soon caught up with her at the edge. She was looking straight down.

"I can't do it; I've never been good with heights," she said sorrowfully.

Eleven

"Did Dad reach you?" It had taken Becky Stapleton enumerable tries to reach her younger sister in Nicaragua, and she doubted her father would have the same perseverance, especially in this case.

"No, what's wrong? Is it Mom? Has something happened to Mom?"

"She's fine, Callie. But, well, she's taken off."

"What do you mean 'taken off'? Taken off where?"

"You remember she was going to some kind of Pelham thing on somebody's island? Apparently she came home from that early and left a note for Dad on the kitchen table saying she was on her way to the airport to catch a plane for San Francisco and that she'd rented an apartment on Russian Hill for the rest of the summer and maybe longer. That she was going to write a book."

"A book? About what?"

"She didn't say. Dad read me the whole note. I don't think she wants a divorce, she signed it 'love.' He wants me to go up there and talk to her. Talk some sense into her was the way he put it."

"So, are you?"

"I don't know. I mean, maybe Mom just needs some space for a while."

"Yeah, but it's still a little strange. Going off like this. It doesn't sound like Mom."

"I'll tell you another strange thing. On top of the note, she left some flowers. Made into a circle, like the ones she used to make us when we were little, for our hair."

"I used to sit outside your door in the hall and listen to you play." Rachel and Chris were walking through Central Park. As soon as the police had given them permission, they had headed for the airport, and at the last moment before flying home, Chris had accepted Rachel's invitation to spend some time in Manhattan. There was an unspoken desire on both their parts to stay with each other a little longer, to try to process what they had been through in some way, even if just by strolling in the sunshine as they were now. They had spent that last night in the woods together. Trying to keep warm and scolding herself for grabbing her guitar and nothing else, Rachel had crisscrossed the island, staying well away from the house. She had literally stumbled into the lean-to where Chris was crouched terrified. Whoever the killer was, they knew instantly it wasn't either of them, and they had shed tears of relief—and fear—until dawn brought Faith's voice and, at long last, rescue.

"You should have come in," Rachel said.

"No, I was afraid you would stop, and I think I liked listening alone. Your room was at the end of the hall, where it turned, and no one could see me."

"I remember. That's why I chose it."

"Was there anything good about Pelham?" Chris asked.

Rachel smiled at her. "Yes, friends. A real friend. I could tell you were out there all those times."

"Because of the opening along the bottom of the door?"

"Possibly. Now let's walk over to the West Side; my mother's expecting us for dinner. She's making brisket, forget that it's summer and chicken salad is no kind of meal anyway, a direct quote. I keep a guitar at their apartment and you won't have to sit in the hall. Not unless you say the brisket is tough."

Phoebe James had also gone straight to the Portland airport after giving her statement to the police, and had booked the next flight to Colorado. The camp director had been resistant about releasing Josh until she added another check to the already hefty fee Wesley had paid them to keep Josh for the summer. When she finally was allowed to see her son, her heart almost broke. He was covered in bites and had lost ten or more pounds, making his skinny frame seem totally emaciated. His face was sunburned, but drawn. He stank of sweat and something else—something she had only smelled in hospitals in the rooms of her parents when death was close.

She opened her arms and he collapsed into them, both mother and son sobbing. Phoebe was tempted to demand her check back in lieu of suing the camp for negligence and God knows what else, but she just wanted to get her child out of that hellhole. Tough love? What had been the love part?

She drove the rental car to the first decent-looking motel she could find and they stayed there several days, lounging around the pool, eating—in Josh's case, whatever he wanted. Phoebe had started a strict diet. They flew back to New Jersey on the fourth day. When her husband returned from work he was shocked to find the dogs, his wife, and his son in what had become his private castle—the twins were a pleasant distraction the rare times they were home. He was even more shocked when Phoebe informed him that she had retained a lawyer and was filing for divorce. She was giving the children the choice of staying with her in the house or leaving with him wherever he decided to go.

"But Phebes, you must be out of your mind!"

"Don't call me that, and I've never been more sane in my life."

"But you don't have any grounds for divorce. You've always gotten everything you wanted! You bitch—"

"Please do not impugn my dogs, and I think you'll find I have grounds going quite far back. My lawyer dug up some interesting evidence after I found these." She held up the black lace thong and corded silk whip she'd found on the back of the master bathroom door. Definitely not hers.

Wes lunged for them, swearing at her and vowing to leave her penniless.

"You can have them. They've been photographed. Now I want you out of here before the kids come home. Josh has chosen to remain with me. He's going to help me do some landscaping this summer, then we may take a trip to see a friend of mine in San Francisco. I'll talk to the girls and either they or I will let you know what they decide. Your suitcases are in the garage. I'll be donating them and the contents to charity if you don't take them now."

The doorbell rang.

"That's my lawyer. She was afraid you might get ugly with me. I told her you were basically a coward—bullies usually are—but she thought she'd come by just in case."

Phoebe walked toward the door.

"Good-bye, Wes."

He pushed past her and the woman waiting outside without another word. A few minutes later they heard him burn rubber backing out onto the street.

If it all hadn't been so sad, Phoebe would have laughed.

"Don't worry, Aunt Hope, I'll only let his feet get wet." Amy Fairchild took her cousin's chubby hand in hers and patiently kept pace with him across the sand toward the water. She turned once and waved back at her mother and aunt, who were sitting under a large beach umbrella. Amy loved Sanpere Island in Maine, where her family went in the summer, but the Hamptons definitely had better beaches, and way warmer water.

"More iced tea?" Faith asked her sister, reaching for

the Thermos she'd brought filled with strong, sweet, very cold tea—the kind she liked to drink with barbecue, the kind she associated with the South.

"Love some." They'd eaten all the sandwiches Hope had made, egg salad with lots of chives on some kind of artisanal sourdough bread, the crusts trimmed off. Hope's culinary skills were limited to this specialty, although as she was quick to point out, she did vary the bread from time to time.

Elaine Prince had sent Faith to her sister's in a limo, and during the long trip when Faith wasn't napping she talked to Hope, trying to tell her everything that had happened. They were still talking this morning. Last night when Faith had arrived, it had been straight into a tub, and then into bed in one of Hope's comfy guest rooms with Amy curled up next to her. Faith's impulse had been to detour to Ben's camp and pick him up— she wanted all her chicks near—but she didn't yield to it, calling the director instead to say where she would be. In one of those serendipitous moments that can happen in life, Ben was right there, happy to hear from her and impatient to get on with that afternoon's capture the flag game in equal amounts.

"I feel so guilty for getting you into it all!" Hope had been saying this, or variations of the sentiment, since Faith had first called.

"That's ridiculous. How could you possibly have known?" Faith reassured her, as she had done each time. And it was true. A catering gig that would result in the discovery of two bodies, the certainty of a third, the denouement to a forty-year-plus mystery, and a close brush with death for oneself? The catering part had been virtually nil; she had done very little cooking. She thought of all those fabulous foods going to waste out on the island, the fantastic kitchen—and the exquisite joy she'd felt when she'd heard the approach of the first of what turned out to be many boats.

Boats. There had been boats on the island. Recalling Lucy's skills—and possibly that of some of the others—Elaine had had Brent remove the Zodiacs, canoes, and kayaks to a secluded beach accessible only by water at the base of the cliffs. The part about being cut off from the outside world was, however, true. Brent had some sort of marine radio, apparently, but it disappeared with the man himself.

Maggie had refused to say anything more as they had made their way back to the house, remaining stubbornly silent as they tied her up more securely once they reached it. She was being charged with Bobbi Dolan's and Gwen Mansfield's murders, but until Brent Justice's body washed up, she couldn't be charged with that. Nor with Prin's death.

"She'll crack," Faith said. "She seemed pretty close to it when she was telling us to shut up and when she marched off to the cliff."

"Don't be so sure." Hope had been struggling with the notion that the president of her beloved alma mater was not only a murderer, but mentally unbalanced. "You just want to know everything that happened." Recollecting what her sister had been through, she quickly amended her thought. "Not that you don't have a perfect right, and of course, we all want to know. But remember who her husband is. I'd be very surprised if counsel hasn't moved to suppress what she said to you already. Look at how the press is handling it."

This was true. There had been a brief article buried in the Portland paper and copied by the *Boston Globe* and the *New York Times* alluding to the "tragic accidents" and that President Howard of Pelham College was in custody for "observation and questioning."

I could get used to this, Faith thought, digging her toes into the warm sand. Moms and kids during the week hanging out at the beach. No worries. Dads, significant others, et cetera, arriving for the weekend. Quentin, Hope's husband, had stayed in the city in order to pick up Tom at Penn Station. She'd called her husband still in D.C. and given him a much-abbreviated version of the events that had occurred during her time on Indian—no, it was Bishop's, she reminded herself— Island. Depending on traffic, they'd be at the house in time for an unfashionably early or fashionably late dinner. Again she thought about the sumptuous supplies Elaine had stocked, but there was nothing shabby about the meal tonight. Chunks of fresh swordfish were marinating in lime juice, getting ready to be strung on skewers with cherry tomatoes, peppers, Vidalia onions, and summer squash. Besides the shish kebabs, Faith planned to grill additional vegetables: eggplant, more squash, and more onions. There was rice pilaf with wild mushrooms, and a Gorgonzola cheese soufflé in the fridge waiting for the oven. Hope had stopped her there and insisted on buying some scrumptious-looking fruit tarts for dessert, as well as all sorts of hors d'oeuvres, hot and cold. Both their husbands were proverbial "big hungry boys," who never showed the calories they put away with such gusto, much to their wives' delight—and envy.

She looked over at her sister; only one year separated them. They were almost twins, fraternal ones. For as long as she could remember, there had always been Hope, and for her sister, there had always been Faith.

One mystery would remain. Elaine had denied tampering with the three small vases on the mantel in the living room. She had assumed that the roses had wilted and that Faith had removed them. And Maggie's denial, unlike other of her statements, had had the ring of truth. So how had the contents spilled? Three roses, three people. If they had stayed on the island longer, would more flowers have fallen—until there were none?

Elaine Prince made good on her promise of a chair and money for Pelham's writing center. She also endowed two scholarships in Bobbi's and Gwen's names. She paid off the mortgage on Brent Justice's sister's house, his sole survivor, and promised to pay the high shore-frontage taxes for her lifetime. She'd sent checks to Rachel and Chris. When each sent them back, she'd called them and convinced them to take them. They were gifts, not hush money or compensation or anything else that might have crossed their minds. She told them she wanted to see them—in New York, not on the island. Faith Fairchild had accepted her fee, and when Elaine asked her if she would come to the city to cater small dinner parties occasionally—Elaine would send her plane—Faith agreed.

The reunion on Bishop's Island had oddly enough resulted in the renewal of old friendships, but the most important result, Elaine thought, as she sealed a letter to her assistant, Owen, was that at long last Hélène Prince was—dead.

Author's Note

I wrote the first author's note at the end of *The Body in the Cast*, the fifth in the series, to explain why I was including recipes for food mentioned in the book and why I hadn't done so earlier. Since that first note, I have enjoyed stepping from behind the curtain and speaking directly to readers. In the case of this particular book, I want to make it clear that, although some of my characters weren't happy at Pelham College, this in no way reflects my opinion of similar institutions of higher learning. I attended a women's college during roughly the same time period described here and have been forever grateful both for the education I received and the lasting friendships I made—and for all sorts of other experiences, which have provided such rich fodder for conversation over the years.

My class was a class on the cusp. When we arrived as freshmen, the rules were essentially unchanged from a time when young women were thought to need stringent regulations lest they wittingly or unwittingly run amok. By the time I graduated, sign-outs had been abolished, as well as many of the other carryovers (current students at my alma mater are the most shocked by the fact that we couldn't have cars on campus: "How did you get anywhere?"). The dress I wore for my admissions interview was demure—a Lanz navy blue cap-sleeved wool sheath with a white linen collar. It ended exactly in the middle of my knee. By senior year, we were all in microminis and bold Marimekko prints from Finland. We wore our hair as long and as straight as possible, forsaking the rigid rollers—the worst had brushes inside—that we slept on in our teens for ever more unusual techniques—some of us would ask a friend to iron her locks. And one girl had her fifteen minutes of fame as the inventor of a method that involved using your own head as a giant roller, swirling the wet hair close to the skull, securing it with clips until it dried, almost perfectly straight. We wanted to look—and sound—like Joni Mitchell and Joan Baez.

I loved those four years. My classroom experiences where every woman had a voice and used it empowered us. It was all right to be smart. We had wonderful mentors in both female and male professors. There was an extraordinary greenhouse, and yes, the century plant did bloom our freshman year, providing us with a symbol of both the transitory and enduring nature of life. We wouldn't be around for the next show of blossoms, but another group of young women, probably not unlike us, would.

The student body today is a diverse one in all ways—a vast improvement. Accents are not erased, nor are students assigned rooms on the basis of religion or ethnicity.

"Gracious Living" was stifling at times, but even then we treasured those sit-down dinners (most of us kept a "dinner skirt" within easy reach, one that could be donned quickly after shedding our jeans). We were forced to stop whatever we were doing, break bread, and talk to each other. Having been used to family dinners, I grew to treasure my new family, a family of friends. And over forty years later, the topics have changed, but not the act of conversing—especially the helpless laughter and, on occasion, the tears. When I applied to college, the mother of a friend of mine encouraged me to apply to a women's college, saying, "You will mostly be with women all your life, so you need to learn how wonderful and strong they are." I didn't really understand what she was getting at then, but I know it now, just as Faith does. I hope I've been able to convey how important her female friendships are to her, as well as the close tie she enjoys with her sister.

As I wrote this book, which depicts the way a group of friends is destroyed by the pathology of one member, I was concerned that readers might assume, incorrectly, that I think this is what happens when you isolate women in a college setting, or any other one, for that matter. This is why I made such a point at the end of the book of rekindling the friendships that were so horribly disrupted by Prin's actions. I like to imagine that Barbara

Bailey Bishop sells her island and finds someplace on the mainland where they all gather again in the future—with Faith in the kitchen, of course.

P.S. I hope you Christie fans have been having fun picking out all the *And Then There Were None* references!

ASIAN NOODLES WITH CRABMEAT

8 ounces rice stick or   8 ounces crabmeat,
    cellophane noodles   preferably fresh
¼ cup scallions,   ¼ cup dry white wine
    sliced thin   2 tablespoons sesame oil

Following the directions for amount on the noodle package, bring a pot of water to a good boil. When the water is close to the boil, sauté the scallions. Add the noodles to the now boiling water. They will cook very quickly. Be sure to stir with a pasta muddler or a wooden spoon. As soon as you have started the noodles, add the crab and white wine to the scallions. Be careful not to overcook any of the ingredients. This is extremely fast food.

Drain the noodles and place a portion on four heated plates. Divide the crab/scallion mixture among them, adding a few uncooked sliced scallions on top. Serve immediately. Faith likes to serve steamed sugar snap peas or peapods with this dish. Serves four.

BOEUF BOURGUIGNON (BEEF STEW)

2 pounds chuck beef cut
   into large cubes
Flour
3 tablespoons olive oil
2 tablespoons unsalted
   butter
Salt and freshly ground
   pepper
1/3 cup cognac (optional)
1/4 pound bacon, diced
2 cloves garlic, minced
3 carrots, sliced into
   approximately 1-inch
   pieces

1 leek, the white part,
   cleaned and sliced
1 small yellow onion,
   diced (approximately
   1 1/2 cups)
1/2 pound mushrooms,
   sliced
1 tablespoon minced
   parsley
1/2 teaspoon thyme
1/2 bottle Burgundy or
   similar red wine
Water

Dredge the beef cubes in flour (Faith does this the way her grandmother did by shaking the meat and flour in a brown paper bag). Melt the oil and butter in a large skillet and brown the meat. Sprinkle with salt and pepper. Pour the cognac, if being used, on top and carefully ignite. When the flames die down, transfer the meat to a casserole with a lid using a slotted spoon.

Preheat the oven to 350° F.

Add the bacon, garlic, carrots, leek, onion, mushrooms, and parsley to the skillet. Sauté until the bacon is slightly crisp and the onion, garlic, mushrooms, carrots, and leek are soft. You should stir the mixture frequently.

Add the contents of the skillet to the meat.

Add the thyme, Burgundy, and just enough water to cover the stew.

Cover and place the casserole in the center of the oven. Bake for 1–1½ hours. Serve with egg noodles and more parsley as a garnish. This dish tastes delicious the day it's made—let it rest for 10–15 minutes before serving—and even better if made a day ahead. Serves six.

FENNEL SOUP

1 large fennel bulb (about
   1 pound)
1 large potato, peeled
   and diced (Yukon
   Golds are good)
1/2 medium yellow onion,
   peeled and diced
1/4 teaspoon tarragon

4 cups chicken stock,
   preferably unsalted
1/2 cup light cream or
   half-and-half
Salt and 1/4 teaspoon
   freshly ground pepper
Seeds from half a
   pomegranate

Cut the tall stalks from the fennel bulb, saving some of the feathery fronds for a garnish, if desired. Cut the bulb into chunks.

Put the fennel, potato, onion, and tarragon into a heavy saucepan.

Add the chicken stock, bring the mixture to a boil, and simmer until the fennel, onion, and potato are soft.

Puree the mixture in a blender or food processor, return to the saucepan, and add the cream or half-and-half. Salt and pepper to taste.

This soup tastes best warm, not piping hot. The pomegranate seeds add flavor and texture. This is a good cold summer soup, too. Try shrimp instead of the pomegranate seeds. Serves six.

RHUBARB CRUMBLE

½ cup walnuts
1 cup flour
½ cup rolled oats
⅓ cup packed light
    brown sugar
½ teaspoon cinnamon

Pinch of salt
½ cup unsalted butter at
    room temperature
2 pounds of rhubarb
¾ to 1 cup white sugar
3 tablespoons flour

Preheat the oven to 375° F. Toast the walnuts in a baking pan until lightly browned and aromatic. Let cool and coarsely chop.

Combine the flour, oats, brown sugar, cinnamon, salt, and stir to mix. Working quickly with your hands or a pastry blender, add the butter until the mixture has a crumbly texture. Stir in the chopped walnuts and set aside.

Wash and trim the rhubarb and cut it into ½-inch slices (about 6 cups).

Put the rhubarb in a large bowl and add the sugar and flour. Toss until the rhubarb is well coated. Spread the rhubarb evenly in a 12-inch baking dish. Sprinkle the topping over the fruit and bake until the rhubarb is tender and bubbling, approximately 45 minutes to an hour. Serve warm with ice cream or whipped cream, if desired.

Faith also makes this with strawberries, both fruits happily in season at the same time. You simply replace half or more of the rhubarb with halved berries.

PELHAM FUDGE CAKE

4 squares unsweetened
    chocolate (Faith likes
    Scharffenberger)
1/2 cup water
2 cups sifted cake flour
1 1/2 teaspoons baking
    powder
1 teaspoon baking soda

A pinch of salt
1 cup sour cream
2/3 cup unsalted butter
1 2/3 cups firmly packed
    dark brown sugar
1 cup white sugar
3 large eggs
2 teaspoons vanilla

Melt the chocolate in the water over low heat, mix well. Let cool.

Sift the flour, baking powder, baking soda, and salt together and set aside. Preheat the oven to 350° F.

Add the sour cream to the thoroughly cooled chocolate.

Cream the butter and sugars together and then add the eggs one at a time, beating after each one. Beat the vanilla into the butter, sugar, egg mixture. Now add the flour mixture and chocolate mixture alternately.

Divide the batter between two round cake pans greased with butter or sprayed with a product like PAM.

Bake in the center of the oven for 30–40 minutes, until a broom straw or cake tester comes out clean.

Fill and frost when cool using your favorite chocolate frosting recipe, adding 3/4 cup finely chopped walnuts. Faith likes to use a traditional chocolate butter cream frosting and sprinkles more walnuts on top of the layer cake.

Turn the page for a glimpse at
THE BODY IN THE GALLERY,
the next delightful Faith Fairchild Mystery

Now Faith was sitting in her car waiting for Patsy. It was just 10 o'clock. Aleford's Yankee thrift extended to streetlights and aside from the outside light on her building, Faith was in the dark. Where was Patsy? A car slowed up. At last! Then it sped off. Faith suddenly felt very vulnerable. This wasn't a residential part of town and at this time of night, no one was around. Another car, but this time it pulled up next to Faith's.

It wasn't Patsy's.

For a moment, Faith felt a strong surge of fear. Then the car door opened and her friend got out. Faith joined her.

"Sorry," Patsy said. "You must have been startled. I should have told you I'd be driving this. It's a loaner. Mine is in the shop. Let's go."

Patsy was wearing what looked like a dark monk's

325

robe, but upon closer inspection it proved to be a long black cape, a black skirt and cowl neck sweater. The whole situation was beginning to seem like a scene from a movie Faith thought she might have seen or a book she might have read. Vaguely familiar and definitely bizarre.

"Love the cape, but Halloween isn't for a couple of weeks."

"I'll have you know this is vintage Oscar de la Renta and I wear it to Symphony."

They walked up a side street that dead-ended in the woods behind Aleford's Industrial Park—Faith's business, a small press, and a clipping service. The latter two were housed in one building. It wasn't exactly Silicon Valley. The woods were the start of the Ganley estate, now the museum and its sculpture park

"There's a path, actually a former service road left over from Theodore Ganley's day. It leads straight to the employee parking lot and the back entrance to the museum."

The path was easy to find. The dirt road was overgrown with alders and other invasive flora, but enough Aleford dog walkers and birders had kept the way open. The moon had risen and Faith could see the glistening orange bittersweet berries looped like necklaces in the surrounding brush.

They weren't talking much, which was why the noise Faith heard behind them was audible. The sound of branches being pushed aside, leaves rustling. She put her finger to her lips and motioned for Patsy to stop.

"What's up?" Patsy whispered.

The noise behind them had stopped. Faith stood still

for a moment. The whole escapade, including Patsy's cape, was spooking her out. The woods were filled with nocturnal creatures. Best not to think about them.

"Let's go. It's nothing."

She didn't hear the sound again and it wasn't long before they reached the museum. Patsy led the way up the hill straight to the large double door—wide enough and tall enough for all but the most gargantuan artwork—at the rear of the building. There was a loading dock next to the entrance and beyond that an overflowing dumpster. Unlike the rest of Aleford, which trekked to the Transfer Station, better known as the dump, each week, the Ganley had a trash collection service. This convenience meant that they missed out on the latest news, impromptu dinner invitations, and most important of all—the swap table, which could yield anything from a dog-eared copy of *Valley of the Dolls* to an only slightly nicked set of Spode dinner plates. Tom was addicted to the dump and Faith often had to surreptitiously return some of his "finds", a frayed leather belt, "still good for working outdoors" and clay flower pots, "do you know what these cost at the garden center!"

The moon was waxing and had risen sending its bright rays across the parking lot and the pond below. It would be full on Saturday. Faith wondered what stratagem Niki's mother would use to get her daughter to fast—and all the rest. Watching the battle of wills between these two equally stubborn women was endlessly fascinating. Now one was ahead; now the other. She looked over at her friend, another stubborn lady. Patsy was carrying a large pocketbook, one she'd had before the luggage-sized monsters had come into fashion last spring, bigger than ever this fall. Patsy's wasn't a Gucci or Fendi, but it would pass muster.

"Ready?" Patsy said softly, although their only company was a chorus of bullfrogs in the pond.

Faith nodded. She was as ready as she would ever be, and as doubtful. She took some comfort in the back-up plan, the one they'd put in place in case the alarm went off or they heard someone coming. Patsy would stand her ground and Faith would run like hell into the woods and go home, thus avoiding the inevitable "Local Minister's Wife B and E Suspect" headlines. Patsy wasn't sure what she would say, but as a trustee she figured she'd be able to bluff her way out of it.

Patsy punched in the code, opened the door and they slipped inside. They turned on their flashlights and Faith noted that they were in the long, wide sloping corridor with shelving on one side that she knew from catering events there. They soon emerged through another set of double doors into the museum proper. The gallery that had housed the recent exhibition was to their left. Patsy stopped at the entrance, set her bag on the floor, and began to rummage through it. From the light filtering down through the high windows, Faith could see the artwork, in brown cardboard boxes— some smaller pieces wrapped in brown paper— leaning against the walls, all ready to go into storage. Patsy had told her that the pieces were first wrapped in layers of bubble wrap before the final protective covering was added. Each work had a large label on the outside stating the artist's name, title of the work, and destination— Ganley's storage, back to the artist, owner, or another institution if a loan. Before any of it left the museum, the registrar would check it against the list that had been made upon arrival. A foolproof system—supposedly.

Patsy straightened up, leaving her bag open. "Take your jacket off," she instructed. Faith shrugged it off and put it on the floor next to Patsy's flashlight, a powerful lantern that any Scout would be proud to own. Patsy slid a roll of packing tape on Faith's wrist like a bracelet and handed her a box cutter.

"All you have to do is cut the tape on the top flap, remove the Bearden, and when we're finished, put it back, then tape it up—covering the place where you made the cut," she instructed as she bent down to get something else from her Mary Poppins-like bag.

Piece of cake so far as Patsy was concerned Faith thought, hoping her friend's assessment would prove correct. Cakes had a way of falling.

Patsy stood up again. She was also holding a can of hairspray—extra hold. Her dark hair was straight, a legacy from a Native American ancestor—"We *all* want to be part Indian you know, no nappy hair," she'd told Faith. "But not Condi Rice straight, no breeze would think of messing with that helmet." Patsy's hair swayed. Faith doubted she used any but the lightest spritz of spray. In any case, this did not seem an appropriate time for grooming.

"Watch carefully. You have to know how low the laser beam is."

"Wait a minute! It's invisible?"

"Don't worry. I saw this in a movie."

Before Faith could say anything more, Patsy sprayed

the entrance and sure enough, a thin red line of light was revealed. About two feet off the floor.

"Get down, quick, and slither under it. I don't know how long this lasts."

Faith crawled under, flattening herself as close to the ground as she could, although the knots in her stomach were raising her up several inches.

"You can stand up," Patsy said.

"But aren't there others?" Faith asked.

"Good point." Patsy rolled the canister along the floor and Faith picked it up, trying hard to remember she was in Aleford and not Istanbul.

"How are we going to know where the Bearden is?"

"I'm assuming they took them from the wall, wrapped them, and left them more or less in place, so start with the ones on the wall nearest you. That's where it was hung. The package third from the left looks about the right size."

Spraying the air in front of her, Faith cautiously made her way over to the artwork. Burdened with hairspray, tape, and box cutter, she'd left her flashlight behind, but Patsy was training her lantern's beam on the wall. The Bearden, clearly marked, *was* the third from the left and it only took a moment to slice through the tape and ease the collage out. She carefully unwrapped the protective bubble wrap layers. "Bingo," she said.

"Slide it over to me and I'll be right back," Patsy said.

"Where are you going?"

"To the restroom. I can turn on the light there. Don't worry. It won't take long."

Faith wished she could go with Patsy, but it would be

foolish to take the chance of setting off the alarm. She wanted to see what Patsy was talking about, the signature and the special mark. Even more, she had to pee. She shouldn't have had that second cup of coffee after dinner. She sat down on the floor. It *had* been a piece of cake so far and if it was for them, why not someone else? She looked around at all the tidy packages. Since it was a small museum, the Ganley didn't have a full-time crew to hang and pack up shows, but Patsy had told Faith the Museum had been using the same people from a company specializing in installations for many years. In addition, the curator and assistant curator were with them at all times. But, thought Faith looking around, during the hustle and bustle of packing up, it would be easy enough to slip a small piece under a jacket on the floor to carry out later, filling the empty container with bubble wrap and something slightly heavy. The label was on the outside. No one would find out for years if the artwork was on its way to the storage facility. Or the switch could be made in the truck. Or the truck robbed. Last year thieves had broken into a delivery truck parked overnight in a lot outside a Pennsylvania Howard Johnson Inn and scored a Goya on its way back to Ohio's Toledo Museum of Art from the Guggenheim in New York City. The Goya was apparently not what the thieves had in mind—flat screen HDTVs more likely—and deciding it was too hot to handle even for them, had a lawyer contact the FBI and arrange a pickup in New Jersey, no questions asked. The painting was unharmed and what happened in Jersey stayed in Jersey.

Then there was Boston's own, still unsolved, 1990

heist at the Gardner Museum. The treasures—a Vermeer, three Rembrandts and eight other paintings were still missing. The thieves had posed as police and gained entry at night where it was the work of a few minutes to grab what they wanted. Faith knew there were twisted collectors, whose pleasure would be increased, not lessened, by knowing they could never display a masterpiece. That it was for their eyes only.

Patsy was taking forever, but when she looked at her watch, Faith was surprised to see it was less than five minutes before her friend's return.

"I got some good pictures of the signature. I'm going to slide it back to you, then let's get out of here."

Faith quickly rewrapped the collage, put it back in the box, taped it shut, and placed it in what she thought was exactly the same spot, then made the return trip as fast as she could. Pulling on her coat, she followed Patsy out of the museum and waited until they were in the woods to speak.

"Well?"

"Without doubt a fake. Will didn't want to destroy the value of the piece by writing an inscription. It was an anniversary gift, but he wrote the date in pencil on the back. The numerals were so tiny they looked like dust spots. It was our secret." She paused. "They're not there."

"What now?"

"I'll send the photos to a couple of places I know that can tell me about the signature. Two very discreet dealers in contemporary African-American art. Once I hear from them, we'll go to Plan B."

"Plan B?"

"This being Plan A."

"I got that, but what's Plan B?"

"Plan B is you, sweetie."

A
Harlequin
Romance

OTHER
Harlequin Romances
by ANNE HAMPSON

Many of these titles are available at your local bookseller,
or through the Harlequin Reader Service.

For a free catalogue listing all available Harlequin Romances,
send your name and address to:

HARLEQUIN READER SERVICE,
M.P.O. Box 707, Niagara Falls, N.Y. 14302
Canadian address: Stratford, Ontario, Canada.

or use order coupon at back of book.

THE REBEL BRIDE

by

ANNE HAMPSON

HARLEQUIN BOOKS   TORONTO
WINNIPEG

Original hard cover edition published in 1971
by Mills & Boon Limited, 17-19 Foley Street,
London W1A 1DR, England

© Anne Hampson 1971

SBN 373-01672-7

Harlequin edition published March 1973

Printed in Canada

1672

CHAPTER ONE

From the verandah of her bedroom Judy looked over the narrow coastal plain to the lovely bay of Kyrenia. To the east the harbour was dominated by the castle, while in the distance, across a blue expanse of clear warm sea, rose the mountains of Turkey, snow-capped, and gleaming in the sun.

The lovely island of Cyprus had been Judy's home since she was five years old when, on the death of her parents within three months of each other, her maternal grandfather, a Greek Cypriot, had without hesitation accepted responsibility for her. He had given her love, a luxurious home and a good education. But he had brought her up in the way Cypriot girls were brought up, with a strictness amounting to severity and near imprisonment. However, when she was sixteen he had sent her to school in France; she had remained there for a year, and on her return two months ago he relaxed a little and she was allowed to go out on her own, visiting friends in Nicosia and on other parts of the island.

She turned into her bedroom, no longer interested in the scenic beauty outside. Picking up a comb, she tidied her hair and then, with a glance at the clock, she hurried downstairs. Her grandfather was sitting on the patio reading his newspaper and she watched him a moment in spite of the fact that she was catching a bus in less than a quarter of an hour. Wizened by a merciless sun, he looked much older than his sixty-two years. But there was a noble appearance about him which was emphasized by the firm jaw and mouth, the low forehead and fine dark eyes. His hair was jet-black still, his face burnt browner than an Arab's; he was slim and masculine, and very tall—far different from the average Cypriot, who was invariably stocky and overweight.

Christalis would be like him some day, she thought. Christalis to whom she was betrothed by her grandfather's choosing and design. The marriage had been arranged two years ago when Judy was fifteen and Chris twenty-six—arranged without Judy's ever having even set eyes on him, for she was sent into another room while the negotiations were going on. When at last she had seen him she had been struck with wonderment that he would consent to an arranged marriage. He was so distinguished and aristocratic, so haughty and self-confident, that she somehow thought he would have been more enlightened than to take part in one of the arranged marriages so common in Cyprus, and in Chris's own country of Greece. For Chris was not a Cypriot; he came from Athens but, like many wealthy ship-owners, he had a magnificent home on the island of Hydra, as well as a bungalow high above the mountain village of Karmi, in Cyprus. It was while staying there that he had seen Judy, when they had been attending church in Kyrenia. He had immediately offered for her and less than a week later the engagement party had taken place at the Corner Restaurant, one of the most magnificent and expensive places in Nicosia.

At the time of the engagement Judy had accepted that her grandfather's word was law and that she, like so many Cypriot girls, must face life with a man she did not love. But during the evening, as the gay party progressed, she began to feel a sudden fear of Chris, for he looked so formidable and aloof; and dwelling on the fact that two years must pass before the wedding was to take place, Judy subconsciously cherished the hope that something would happen to prevent its taking place at all.

But time was running out ... and to complicate matters Judy had met a young Englishman, Ronnie Tenant, one of the few foreigners allowed a work permit by the Cypriot government. Only technicians and people like Embassy officials were allowed to work on the island, for there were not enough jobs for the natives. Ronnie had been fortunate in landing a post with the television company in Nicosia, for he was an expert and, therefore, doing work that was extremely technical while at the same time teaching the young Cypriot who would eventually take his place. Judy had met him on the plane coming over from Athens where she had been visiting a friend and where Ronnie had changed planes on his flight from England.

They had been meeting in secret, but Judy knew a perpetual fear of discovery. In Cyprus girls did not go out with boys even if they were unattached ... and for an engaged girl to go out with someone else would be quite unthinkable. A dreadful scandal would follow discovery and the girl's name would be blackened for ever.

'Grandfather,' she said at last, moving towards him, 'I'm going to Nicosia. I want things for Manoula's wedding——'

'Manoula's wedding?' he frowned, lowering his newspaper. 'But you went into Nicosia twice last week. I thought you now had everything you need.'

She swallowed hard, her beautiful blue eyes fixed on her hands, which were clasped nervously in front of her.

'Not everything, Grandfather. I still want a sash for my dress and some—and some ribbons for my hair.' She glanced up. Was her grandfather looking at her

7

with suspicion, or was it merely her frightened imagination playing her tricks?

'I see. Well, you had better go, then.' He glanced at his watch. 'And you'll have to hurry if you're going to catch the convoy. What time does the bus go?'

'In ten minutes' time. I'll be back on the five-fifteen.'

'See that you are, Judy. You haven't forgotten your fiancé is coming to dinner this evening? He'll be here early, though, about six o'clock, he said in his letter.'

She nodded, and went for the bus. Chris coming. How many times had she seen him altogether? There was the day they became engaged, when she had been brought out of the lounge by her great-aunt, Astero, her grandfather's sister. Shyly and reluctantly she had entered the sitting-room and met the man who had offered for her and who had been accepted by her grandfather. He had looked at her without any sign of emotion—and there had not been even one kiss to seal the contract between them. The second time they had met was at the engagement party. Chris had given most of his time and attention to her grandfather—probably discussing the dowry, she thought—and the rest of his time was spent in chatting to his friends who had been invited to the party. But once or twice she had caught Chris glancing at her, and it was with the customary examination of her body, as if he were silently speculating on the degree of pleasure it would afford him when the time came for him to possess it. This was no more unusual than his indifference towards her, and Judy, having been brought up to accept such things, did not take offence or feel she was in any way being treated with disrespect. Nevertheless, she did blush, in much the same way a Cypriot girl would blush, and her fiancé's straight black brows were raised in a gesture of amusement.

The third time they met was at Margarita's wedding.

8

Chris happened to be over in Cyprus, taking a rest from business in his villa above Karmi, and he accepted the invitation to Margarita's wedding even though she was a total stranger to him, and so was her betrothed. But in Cyprus the whole village was invited to a wedding and it was traditional that if one received an invitation one must accept. On that occasion Chris had danced with Judy, and had talked with her for a little while, but the conversation was no more intimate than if they had been casual acquaintances who had met for the first time at the wedding.

And now Chris was coming again ... This time to arrange the wedding—no doubt about that. Judy ran as the bus was moving away and the driver stopped. They had been on their way only a few minutes when one of the passengers found he had no cigarettes; again the driver stopped, so that the man could go into a nearby shop and buy some. Within a short while they had joined the convoy; there was the usual checking by the Turkish officials and then the United Nations jeeps drove up, flags flying. Two speeded on ahead to the front of the convoy while the others prepared to follow on behind. A Turkish official boarded the bus and took the seat in front of Judy, smiling at her as he sat down. She smiled in response and they chatted for a space until the convoy began to move, snaking its way through the magnificent Kyrenia Range before reaching the arid, treeless Messaoria Plain in the centre of which was situated the beautiful capital of the island.

Three-quarters of an hour later she was hurrying to cover the distance from the bus to the gardens which now occupied the moat below the Venetian walls surrounding the old city of Nicosia. Down the steps she ran, to the café in the garden, where Ronnie was seated at a table right in the corner, under a swaying date palm. Over the weathered ochre wall close by, a bougainvillea tumbled down in a shower of purple bloom, gleaming in the sunshine.

'Darling, you made it!' Rising quickly, he held out a hand; Judy took it and held it and then put it to her cheek. 'I thought you weren't coming,' said Ronnie. 'I'll order and then we can talk. Sit down, sweetheart.' Clapping his hands for the waiter, he then ordered refreshments for them, frowning as she looked furtively about her.

'Ronnie ... Grandfather asked questions—oh, nothing serious, but I was frightened. I can't give the same excuse again.' Suddenly her eyes filled up. 'I don't think I can come again, Ronnie. And this evening Chris is dining with us; it's only so he can discuss our marriage; I'm sure of it.'

Ronnie's frown deepened.

'Judy, you must break this engagement——'

'Break it?' she cut in, her big eyes clouded with fear. 'I can't, Ronnie—no, that's not possible. An engagement's as binding as a marriage here, you must know that.'

'You're not one of these subjugated Cypriot girls! Your grandfather has no right to question you about your movements—much less has he the right to force you into marriage with someone you don't even know!' She was dumb, for this was not the response she had expected from Ronnie. And yet what did she expect? There was nothing he could do to help her. He had signed a two-year contract and could not leave the island until it expired. But she could not marry Chris, loving Ronnie as she did.

'What can we do?' she faltered. 'Ronnie, I'm so desolate at the idea of being married to Chris——'

'You can't be forced into it. All you have to do is break this engagement—flatly refuse to go on with the marriage. No one can force you. It's just that you lack courage,' he added. 'And that's because you've been brought up here and you feel bound by the customs—and they are only customs, you know, Judy. There's no law to say you must obey your grandfather in this.'

Quite true, she admitted, but custom was strong, just as it had been strong in England many years ago. In medieval times the 'laws' of the Manor were in reality only feudal customs, but no one ever thought of disregarding them.

'I can't, Ronnie,' she faltered. 'Oh, help me—take me away somewhere!'

'Somewhere? On a small island like this? Where could you hide?—and in any case you've just said you can't break the engagement.'

She looked at him, her eyes brimming. Did he love her, as he had said he did the last time they met?

'I can't break the engagement if I have to face them—my grandfather and Chris, I mean—but I could run away——' She stopped, because he was frowning heavily, but as he saw her expression his face cleared and he smiled at her. Grasping at this slight sign of encouragement, she went on to suggest, tentatively, that Ronnie might be able to find her an apartment in Nicosia where she could live in hiding until his contract expired, and then they could go to England together and be married. But Ronnie was frowning again, and shaking his head.

'You're under age,' he reminded her. 'And your grandfather is your legal guardian, after all. I should be in dreadful trouble were I to assist you to leave his care. No, Judy, there's only one solution; you must break the engagement. Then you can tell your grandfather you've met someone else and I can come and talk to him. If he'll accept me as your young man, and give his consent, we can be married here.'

'He won't let me break the engagement,' she cried,

11

her heart like a leaden weight inside her. 'I dare not mention it.' She fell silent as the waiter appeared with their drinks, and then she spoke again. 'He would want a reason.'

'Simply say you don't love this man.'

'That's not a good enough reason. People here don't marry for love. Besides, Grandfather would want to know why I hadn't objected before.'

He looked at her.

'You'd have gone into it willingly, and meekly, if you hadn't met me?'

She nodded.

'It's customary—and I was resigned.'

'Because you've been brought up to consider the male as all-important, whose wishes must be obeyed. This wouldn't have happened had you been brought up in England.'

'But I haven't been brought up in England and therefore I can't bring myself to disobey my grandfather.' A Cypriot girl would not even allow such a thought to enter her head. Her parents or guardian were held in supreme reverence; their word was law in everything. Judy felt like a Cypriot girl, which was natural, seeing that she had only the vaguest memory of her life in England before her parents were so tragically killed.

'You say you can't break this engagement without giving a reason,' Ronnie was saying. 'Then tell your grandfather the truth—that you've met me.'

She stared at him, appalled at that idea.

'I dare not,' she quivered. 'I dare not tell him I've been seeing you secretly!'

Ronnie sighed impatiently, and did not speak immediately. Judy watched him, and her heart ached because she could not be with him always, because she could not take him to her grandfather and introduce him as her young man—as they did in France, and in England. Yes, she'd learned a lot during that year in France—and she had seen English films and seen how she would have lived had not fate decreed that she should be brought up in this island where parental control remained so strong that even the young men were completely subdued. True, they were beginning to object, and when interviewed on television they expressed these objections quite strongly, but in the East change is slow and Judy felt it would be many years yet before the girls and boys of Cyprus were free to go about together before marriage and, therefore, able to find the one they could love.

'If you won't break the engagement,' said Ronnie at last, 'there's nothing we can do.'

'Nothing?' Her eyes filled up and she flicked away the tears with her fingers. 'But, Ronnie—if you love me . . .?'

'I love you—haven't I said that, Judy?' He made a gesture with his hands. 'Darling, what can I do to help you if you won't help yourself?'

'I suppose,' she whispered after a pause, 'I'm being quite unreasonable.'

He eyed her perceptively.

'In expecting me to do something?'

She swallowed hard.

'If—if p-people really love each other, they try t-to find a way.' Words were difficult because to Judy it seemed as if Ronnie had not been impressed very much by what she had said up till now. She knew from novels she read and films she had seen that trials often came the way of lovers, but they always strove to find a way out and of being happy together in the end.

'You consider I'm not trying hard enough and so I don't really love you, is that it?' She could not answer because he was looking so accusingly at her. His blue

13

eyes were narrowed, his brow creased beneath the lock of fair hair which had fallen on to it.

'I could say the same about you, Judy,' he said reprovingly. 'The whole solution is in your hands. No one can make you marry this Chris ... and if you're so weak-willed that you do go through with it, you'll regret it till the end of your days.'

Ronnie's words were with her as she sat at the table that evening with her grandfather and her fiancé. They were true, of course. If she did marry Chris she would regret it till the end of her days, but how was she to get out of it? Several times, while they were sitting on the patio, waiting for the servant to announce dinner, she had opened her mouth to tell them she did not want to marry Chris, but the words not only stuck in her throat; they actually choked her. It was so strange to know that had she been brought up in England, with her parents, she would now be a very modern miss with stacks of self-confidence and a will of her own which no one would be able to oppose. But she was now a little Cypriot girl, timid and meek and so afraid of these two men that she could not speak her mind, even though by her silence she was sentencing herself to a life of subjugation.

Chris was speaking to her grandfather and as always when men were in conversation Judy followed the normal pattern and remained silent, listening, and yet thinking all the time of Ronnie and the kiss he had given her when they parted. They had gone on to the car park, and sat in his car, waiting an unconscionable length of time before the park was deserted and Ronnie could take her in his arms. And she did not really enjoy his kiss because she was looking over his shoulder in case someone should come on the car park and see them. That was the trouble with a small island; you couldn't do anything without someone seeing you, and as everyone seemed to know everyone else gossip spread widely and swiftly. She looked across at Chris, sitting opposite to her. If he should ever learn that she had kissed someone else.... Her heart actually jumped at the thought and in her nervousness her knife clattered against her plate. Her fiancé's brows rose questioningly and she flushed. He smiled then, clearly amused. Funny, she thought, but he seemed so very Westernized ... and yet he had offered for her in the manner of his people, and was quite willing to take part in an arranged marriage. Judy did not know why, but right from the first he had struck her as a man who, if he married at all, it would be for love.

'I suppose I'm a romantic,' she said to herself. And added, 'But Lefki is too, because she has been to school in France, and she looks at the English films on television. I think I will go and see her tomorrow, because she had never seen Paul till the engagement, and yet she's deliriously happy with him.'

'Judy——' Her musings were brought to an abrupt halt by the voice of her grandfather. 'You're not eating, my dear. Come, what are you thinking about? Your forthcoming marriage?' he added, a twinkle in his eye. She frowned. Why did they always pretend it was all so romantic? For they did—even if some poor girl was dragging herself to church with tears in her eyes and a heart that was breaking the whole village pretended the couple were in love.

'No, I'm not thinking of my marriage,' she returned without any effort at tact, and again her fiancé's brows rose a fraction.

'You're not exactly enamoured with the prospect,' he commented drily.

She looked at him, her eyes clouded. What would he say if she told him she was in love with someone else?

'I think I'm a little young for marriage,' she returned

15

in quiet tones.

'You're seventeen and a half,' put in her grand-father. 'That is a nice ripe age. Girls are usually ready by then.'

Ready ... ripe. She felt a little sick. Ronnie would never use such expressions; he had more delicacy, but then sex was the beginning and end of marriage here. Rarely did one see a love match made, and even on the rare occasion when the couple did fall in love—which was in any case usually after marriage—the man still retained his own interests which were completely alien from those of his wife.

'If we could postpone it for another year,' began Judy, looking at Chris and wondering what would be the result should she get him on his own and plead with him. But her grandfather would not allow her to be alone with him—— Her meditations ceased abruptly. If Chris wanted to be alone with her she felt quite sure nothing would stop him. So firm and taut that chin, and those lines from nose to mouth ... they seemed to spell out the word 'domination'. And the arrogant superiority of him! He was even more dis-tinguished than her grandfather, she thought, and even more self-possessed and confident. Perhaps riches made one arrogant and superior like that, or perhaps it was merely his magnificent physique and height that made him so proud and haughty. With her, though, he adopted an air of rather bored tolerance; he seemed quiet and unemotional, but once or twice this evening he had regarded her with a sort of amused indulgence, almost as if he considered her a child.

'Another year,' her grandfather was saying. 'No, my dear, Chris here has come to discuss the marriage and we have decided it shall be next month——'

'Next month!' She stared at him, aghast. 'No, Grandfather, not so soon as that!'

16

Chris flicked her a glance.

'Diplomacy doesn't appear to be one of your virtues, my dear,' he remarked a little crisply. 'Why not next month?'

'It's t-too soon,' she faltered. She thought: it's like Christmas; you wait and wait and then suddenly it's upon you. 'I couldn't be ready.'

'Nonsense; you have about twenty maids of honour to do everything for you.' Her grandfather seemed a trifle embarrassed, and he gave her a stern and censorious glance. 'I must apologize for Judy,' he then said to Chris. 'Please make allowances—her father was English and she never forgets that.'

'She has been brought up to know her place, though,' returned Chris. 'At least I hope she has. I'm not expecting to have to deal with a rebellious wife.'

'No, oh, certainly not,' hurriedly put in the old man. 'Judy is most meek and obedient. She will not give you the slightest trouble.'

A short while later Judy was sent to bed, while her grandfather and her fiancé went into the sitting-room to discuss the wedding.

Lefki, Judy's married friend, lived in a luxury flat on the outskirts of Nicosia. She was twenty-one and had been married for four years; she had three little girls, but her husband employed a nanny for them, and in addition he had a maid living at the flat and a daily woman to come in and clean. Whenever Judy visited Lefki she was either reclining on the couch, looking elegant and fresh, or she was sitting at a table working on her most exquisite embroidery. She went to the hairdressers often and her black hair had been bleached and then dyed an attractive shade of auburn. Her nails were always immaculate, her clothes models of perfection. Twice a year her husband took her to London and she would return literally loaded with Georgian silver. This was elegantly displayed about the flat, mainly in cabinets in the massive sitting-room. The carpet had come from Persia, the furniture from France.

A uniformed maid opened the door, smiling instantly on seeing who it was.

'Miss Benson—how nice to see you! Mrs. Mavritis is in the sitting-room. She said you had rung earlier and she's been looking forward to seeing you.'

'Judy...' Lefki held out both her hands. 'I've been wondering when you'd come. But how well you look! I think you grow more beautiful every day, while I——' She shook her head in mock dejection. 'I am now past my prime.'

Judy laughed and sat down, looking round.

'You've been to London again since last I was here.'

'Do you like my trays, and my candlesticks? I spent three thousand pounds!'

'Three——?' Judy stared incredulously. 'No, Lefki, you surely couldn't have?'

'Certainly I did.' Lefki shrugged. 'Paul has plenty. Why shouldn't I spend money? He likes to give it me and I like to spend it, so we have a wonderful arrangement.' She sat down opposite to Judy and rang a little silver bell. 'Kyria, will you make some tea, please?' she said when the maid appeared.

Lefki and Judy chatted about everyday things until the tea came, then Lefki, the cool and elegant hostess, poured the tea from a silver pot and handed Judy hers, smiling affectionately at her as she did so.

'How long have you been home now?' she asked after a while.

'Almost three months.' A small silence and then, with a sort of frightened urgency, 'Tell me—truthfully —are you happy with Paul? Oh, I know you've said

18

many times that you are, but is it only the money you like, or do you ... love Paul, really love him, I mean?'

'But of course I love Paul, and he loves me.' Lefki's eyes opened wide. 'Why do you ask? I've always said we're deliriously happy.' And she certainly looked happy; her eyes were shining and there was a most contented expression on her face. 'I don't know why you should suddenly ask me this question, Judy.'

Judy glanced down at her hands and said quietly,

'Your marriage was arranged, as is usual, but I never asked you how long you'd known Paul before you married him?'

'Two months,' supplied Lefki, still puzzled. 'As you know, I'd never seen him until we were engaged, but he'd seen me. He liked me and his parents came to see my mother. I had just come home from school in France and Mother thought it was time I was married because I was seventeen. I wanted to be married, and I wanted a rich man. Paul was not only rich but handsome, and believe me I wouldn't have waited that long, only we got engaged at the end of November and, as you know, in Cyprus it's impossible to get married then.'

Judy nodded. No marriages took place during the forty days before Christmas; this was custom because during that time people's minds were supposed to be devoutly concerned with the festival of the birth of Christ.

'During that two months did you see each other often?'

'Every night. Mother was there, though.'

'Every night...?' Judy spoke musingly, almost to herself.

'You've known Chris much longer, haven't you? Is it about two years since you became engaged?'

'Yes, it's just over two years.' She put her cup down

on her saucer and looked straight at Lefki. 'I don't know him, though, and I'm—I'm frightened.' Should she confide in Lefki? She might tell Paul, and Paul might tell his cousin. His cousin knew several people in Karmi—and Chris was staying at his house just higher up the mountain.

'Frightened? What about?'

'I don't want to be married, Lefki!'

'But how silly. Marriage is wonderful.'

'For you, but you're lucky. In fact, you're the only one I know who's happy. Poor Manoula was crying bitterly last night. She doesn't want to marry Panos.'

'Well, who would want to marry Panos?' returned Lefki with a shudder. 'Your Chris isn't like that; he's wonderful—almost as good-looking as my Paul.'

All unknowing, Judy lifted her chin.

'He's even better-looking than Paul, and he's much taller.'

'I don't agree—oh, about the height, yes, but to me Paul's the handsomest man I've ever seen.'

'When did you see Chris?' asked Judy, puckering her brow in thought.

'At Margarita's wedding, don't you remember?'

Judy's face cleared.

'Of course. You said I was lucky.' Judy frowned as she said that, and Lefki noticed.

'What's wrong, Judy?' she inquired, eyeing her curiously. 'It's not usual for a girl to want to change her mind.'

'I'm not a Cypriot, Lefki. In England couples fall in love and then get married.'

'You've lived as a Cypriot,' Lefki reminded her matter-of-factly, 'and your grandfather will expect you to obey him. You'll probably fall in love after you're married—like Paul and me.' Judy said nothing; she was thinking of Ronnie and her heart was heavy.

Somehow she knew for sure that nothing could save her from Chris, and so she must spend the rest of her life loving someone else ... 'I should think you would be bound to fall in love with Chris, he's so handsome and rich. And he'll be sure to fall in love with you, because you're very beautiful, Judy.'

'I'm only ordinary,' Judy began, her face colouring at her friend's flattery. Lefki interrupted her before she could continue.

'You're far from ordinary. Just look at your hair, so soft and long and golden. I pay three pounds a week to my hairdresser and can't get mine like that.'

'You wouldn't want it so fair as mine,' put in Judy reasonably. 'It wouldn't suit your skin. I think you have your hair done beautifully.'

'Perhaps—but I have to watch the black roots,' laughed the older girl. 'However, we weren't talking about my assets, but yours. Those eyes are enough to cause any man's heart to quicken, and your mouth is just the sort men like to kiss, wide and full——'

'Lefki,' interrupted Judy, forced to laugh in spite of her dejection, 'do stop this nonsense!'

'All right. But I still think he'll fall in love with you, once you're married,' she said, and Judy became thoughtful.

Did she want him to fall in love with her? Since meeting Ronnie she had often felt she hated Chris, and the thought of either of them falling in love with one another had never even entered her mind.

'Tell me about France?' urged Judy after a small silence. 'You were in Paris a fortnight ago—oh, and thanks for the card. It brought back memories. I was happy at school.' Happy and carefree, learning how people of the West lived.

Lefki was eager to relate all that had happened on her visit to Paris with her husband; they had spent a fortune from all accounts, and Judy again wondered if it were only the money that made her friend happy. But surely money alone could not bring that glow to her face.

'I had some fun with a taxi-driver,' Lefki was saying. 'And Paul became very cross with me over it. You see, he took us a long way round, thinking we didn't know, so I told him off——'

'*You* told him off? Didn't Paul say anything?'

'No, he said we should have paid and said nothing, but I was angry at the idea of being made a fool of. Well, this taxi-driver began to curse me, thinking I wouldn't be able to retaliate—just having learned the nice, drawing-room sort of French. However, what he didn't know was that my nanny is half French and I've made her teach me all the *other* words——'

'You didn't!' Judy interrupted, shocked. Lefki looked far too elegant and ladylike to use the words, anyway.

'I did, because it's no use learning half a language. You should have seen that taxi-driver's face——' Lefki broke off, throwing back her head and laughing heartily. 'He just stood there, dumbstruck, while I let him have it. Then he looked at me in a sort of admiring way and asked me where I'd learned it all. But Paul was furious with me, and wouldn't speak to me for two whole hours. But then I said if he was going to sulk like that I was getting the next plane home. That brought him round!'

Judy looked curiously at her. There was no doubt at all that Lefki knew exactly how to handle her husband. There was no subjugation here, nothing different, in fact, from a marriage one would expect to see in England. How had Lefki done it? But there was only one answer. Paul was in love with her. Yes, Judy no longer had any doubts about her friend's marriage. It was perfect, because they had been lucky enough to have fallen in love with one another after marriage.

'I must be going,' said Judy reluctantly on glancing at the clock. 'Chris comes to dinner every evening now and I mustn't be late. I have to dress up for him, Grandfather says.'

'Don't you like dressing up for him?'

'Not really. I keep thinking that if he suddenly decides he doesn't like me he might break the engagement.'

'Break——?' Lefki stared at her in astonishment. 'You know very well that'll never happen.'

Judy stood up, sighing.

'Yes, I know. I suppose I'm just hoping for a miracle.'

'Is it really as bad as that?' Lefki rose from her chair and stood facing her friend. 'It'll be all right, Judy, I know it will. When is the wedding?—or haven't you fixed it yet?'

'We haven't fixed the date, but Grandfather says it has to be next month.'

'Well, you've waited two years, and that's a long while.'

'I was only fifteen, Lefki,' Judy reminded her with some indignation.

'You were, yes, of course. But poor Chris. He's had to wait all this time for you to grow up. How old is he?'

'Twenty-eight.'

'He must have liked you to offer when you were only fifteen. He knew he'd have to wait some considerable time for you.'

He must have liked her ... Judy thought about that as she rode home on the bus. Desired her, more like, and with a Greek desire once aroused is so strong that he would wait a good deal longer than two years for his desire to be fulfilled.

23

CHAPTER TWO

IT was in the cool of a summer evning, when they were sitting on the verandah, that her grandfather put the question. Over dinner, which this time they had taken alone, Chris having made a previous arrangement to dine out with friends, the old man had been silent, merely glancing at Judy now and then from under lowered brows. She knew something was wrong, but she was totally unprepared for what he had to say.

'Who is this man you've been meeting, Judy?'

She jumped, and her heart seemed to leap right up into her throat.

'M-man?'

'Don't prevaricate! It's all over Kyrenia that you've a boy-friend. You don't need me to tell you that your good name's ruined, that you've brought the direst disgrace on me and all my family. Who is he? Answer me at once!'

Her face was white; a terrible shudder passed through her. But in spite of her fear she experienced a tinge of relief. Her guilty secret was a burden which weighed her down and she was almost glad to be sharing it with someone as she said, though in a low and trembling voice,

'He's English, Grandfather, and—we love each other.'

He looked at her and she saw the grey lines about his mouth. She loved him dearly and the knowledge that he suffered hurt her exceedingly. Only now did she stop to think how deep his hurt would have gone had she run away and found a hiding-place in Nicosia as she would have done, had Ronnie been willing to help her.

'Where did you meet him?' he asked, pain and censure in his voice.

'On the plane—when I was coming home from that visit to Luciana in Athens.'

'So this is what happens when you're allowed a little freedom. This I did allow only because your father was English and I felt it was unfair, as you got older, to treat you entirely as a Cypriot.' He shook his head sadly. 'I should have known better, should have kept you under my eye. You realize, of course, that Chris will not marry you if this comes to his ears.'

Hope leapt; it was revealed in her eyes.

'I want to marry Ronnie, Grandfather. Please—please let me! I don't want to hurt you, but since I met Ronnie I've been so unhappy at the idea of marrying Chris.'

For a while the old man was silent, and Judy herself dared not speak while he was thus occupied in thought. Was he considering her plea? He loved her, she knew, and he would be greatly troubled were he to think she was unhappy. Perhaps, she thought breathlessly, she should have told him before, been frank with him and asked him to meet Ronnie.

Time passed; the fleeting twilight shades of gold and orange and rust melted into the deep purple of night. Stars appeared, hanging like diamonds suspended beneath a canopy of softest tulle. A wisp of cloud here and there, a floating moon, the calm dark sea, and carried on the breeze the scent of roses and jasmine. Sheep bells on the mountainside, a distant bray of a donkey.... This was Cyprus, island in the sun.

'This man,' said her grandfather at last, 'this Ronnie—he loves you, you say?'

'Yes.' Breathless again, she was—and wildly hopeful. 'And I love him.'

'You've known each other about nine weeks.'

She nodded, afraid to own that she knew Ronnie far better than she knew Chris, to whom she had been engaged for over two years.

'How often have you been seeing him?'

The question she dreaded, but she could not lie to her grandfather and she was forced to confess to seeing Ronnie every time she went to Nicosia.

'It's sometimes twice a week,' she added reluctantly, watching for any change in his expression that would tell her he was angry. But he remained oddly sad, although his mouth was tight.

'Your—er—shopping, then, was merely an excuse.' He looked straight at her and she lowered her head in contrition. 'That you could deceive me like this——' He shook his head as if quite unable to believe it. 'What has come over you, child, that you could act with such disregard for my feelings and my authority?'

'I'm sorry,' she said, tears on her lashes. 'I wouldn't hurt you, Grandfather, nor would I disregard your authority, but . . .'

'Yes?' he queried as she tailed off. 'But what?'

She raised her head, and he saw the sparkle of tears in her lovely blue eyes. His own eyes shadowed as he awaited her reply.

'It was love,' she said simply.

The old man gave a deep sigh.

'This young man knows you're betrothed?'

'Yes, Grandfather, he knows.'

'Do you consider it honourable of him to meet you when he knows you belong to someone else?'

'Belong?' She frowned at the word. Yet most Cypriot girls were possessions of their husbands. Judy's thoughts flashed to Lefki, who had learned so much from her year in France and from her frequent visits to England. Lefki was no possession, but a wife and an equal. 'We fell in love. No one can help that.' She met his gaze. 'Grandfather, will you let me bring Ronnie to see you?'

'You're betrothed, Judy,' was the sharp response. 'Chris is expecting to be married next month.'

Very slowly Judy was gaining confidence. Could it be the result of her visit to Lefki? she wondered.

'Ronnie says the engagement isn't binding, because —because I had no choice but to accept the man you had chosen for me.' Despite her slowly emerging courage she could not meet his eyes as she spoke those words.

'Not binding?' her grandfather suddenly snapped. 'Obviously the man has no idea what he's talking about! I should have thought you'd have corrected him.' He stopped and waited for her to lift her head, then gave her a stern and censorious look. 'You made no objection at the time of the engagement. Why not?'

'I hadn't met Ronnie. I accepted Chris because you had chosen him for me, and—and I felt I must obey you.'

He scowled at her.

'You were quite happy with my choice,' he began, when she interrupted him.

'Not happy, Grandfather, but resigned.'

'Well, you're engaged to Chris and there's nothing we can do about it——'

'You would, if you could?' she cut in eagerly.

'I hate to see you unhappy, child,' he admitted, his glance softening. 'Nevertheless, I am not in a position to make any changes at this stage. You know full well that the engagement's binding—so much so that in some villages it's really the marriage itself. You had the usual church service, just like anyone else, and as I've said there's nothing we can do at this stage.'

She bit her lip. Hope had soared for a moment, only to be dashed again. The engagement was binding and in those villages to which her grandfather referred, the engaged couple would immediately live together at the house of the bride's parents. And often the first child would be born before the marriage proper took place. There was nothing wrong in this arrangement because it was custom—but of course it applied only to a few villages, and Cypriots in general did not like to talk about it. Nevertheless, it demonstrated the strength and importance of the engagement. In all her years in Cyprus Judy had never heard of one being broken.

And yet she persevered, for so much was at stake— her whole life's happiness, in fact.

'If you would speak to Chris about Ronnie——'

'Speak to Chris! On the contrary, I must do my best to keep it from him——'

'But you said he won't want to marry me if he finds out. Please, Grandfather, help me! If Chris doesn't want me and I don't want him then surely we can break the engagement.'

But the old man was shaking his head.

'The disgrace is great enough already. We must contrive to get you married before he discovers what you've been up to—although I don't know how that will be possible, for it's more than likely that he knows already.'

And it so happened that he did. His face was a dark mask of fury when, the following evening, he came to dine with Judy and her grandfather. A swift glance passed between them as they noted Chris's expression and Judy was so terrified that she instantly made for the door, intent on escaping—for the time being, at any rate. But the voice of her fiancé, reaching her like the crack of a whip, brought her round to face him, her cheeks on fire.

'Judy! Come here!' She could not move and he pointed to a spot on the carpet in front of him. 'I said come here.' Soft the voice all of a sudden, but darkly imperious and commanding. Slowly, reluctantly, she obeyed, stopping a little way from the place he had indicated, and throwing her grandfather a desperate pleading glance. 'What is this I hear about your disgraceful conduct? Explain, if you please!'

She swallowed, but fear blocked her throat. Again she sent a pleading glance in her grandfather's direction. He came to her rescue, speaking for her.

'Judy's met an Englishman, Chris,' he informed him without preamble. 'She says they're in love and she wants to break her engagement to you.'

Judy held her breath. She had not expected her grandfather to be so obliging or so helpful. Would Chris also be obliging? she wondered, searching his face but soon dropping her eyes under the dark fury and contempt she saw there.

'I gathered she'd met an Englishman,' returned Chris gratingly. 'Her disgraceful escapades are the talk of Kyrenia—and every village for miles around! Do you realize,' he said, turning to look at Judy, 'that no one now believes you to be chaste?'

Miserably she nodded. 'She's had a boy-friend' people would say with a sort of brushing together of their hands—a gesture indicative of contempt and 'casting off' as it were. 'No good!' And on the very rare occasion that such an occurrence did take place, the girl concerned was scorned by everyone and her chances of marriage were nil.

'I—we only met,' faltered Judy at last, 'in a café in Nicosia—in—in the gardens. . . .'

If only she had the courage of Lefki. Why should she

keep on thinking of her friend? Perhaps it was because Lefki had been to school in France, just as Judy had ... and Lefki had learned to stick up for herself. Why can't I stick up for myself? Judy wondered, but even as she looked up at her fiancé's angry countenance deep terror assailed her again.

'How long have you been meeting in this café?' he demanded.

'Nine w-weeks.'

His face went taut, and white lines of wrath crept up under the tan. He looked ready to murder her, she thought, and took an involuntary step towards her grandfather. Her move was prevented, however, by the grip of a vice on her wrist. Viciously she was twisted round again, brought facing Chris, and her chin was jerked up by the pressure of a hand underneath it. Judy's legs felt so weak she could have dropped. In the happy sheltered environment provided by her grandfather fear had never been known to her, but she was now so frightened that her senses reeled. Chris was so big and tall above her, so overpowering and masterful ... and so very, very angry. And yet she really had nothing to fear because once over these next few moments she would be free. Chris would not want to marry her now. She should be glad that the truth was out, even though there would be the dreadful disgrace to endure. People would look the other way; young men would leer, and rake her body with their eyes— imagining things. ...

'Nine weeks!' rasped Chris, glowering at her before turning his attention to her grandfather. 'You ... have you no control over her?'

'I'm sorry, Chris, terribly sorry. Judy has deceived me just as she's deceived you. She owned to having kept company with this man when I tackled her earlier today.' He spread his hands. 'Because of her English nationality I've allowed her a little freedom, but she's abused it. I realize I should have been firmer, but the damage is done now. However, perhaps it's not as bad as it seems. You don't want her, obviously, and as she wants this young Englishman——'

'What do you mean, I don't want her?' Releasing her chin but not her wrist, Chris put the question slowly and quietly to her grandfather. 'Judy and I are engaged.'

Judy gave a little gasp; her grandfather stared at Chris in disbelief.

'You still want to marry her?' he exclaimed. 'Despite the scandal!'

'I still want to marry her.' The grip on her wrist slackened. 'Despite the scandal,' he added, although Judy heard the soft gritting of his teeth and knew that the quietness with which he spoke was only a cover for his fury and disgust.

Her body sagged. Hope, it seemed, was at last quite dead.

'But you've just said that no one now believes her to be chaste.' So her grandfather was actually trying, she concluded, but her hopes could not be re-born. Chris's expression told her all she needed to know.

'Judy and I shall be living in Greece,' he said shortly.

A most odd expression settled on the old man's face as he watched Chris. He said slowly,

'You, apparently, believe that Judy has done no real wrong?'

Chris looked down at his fiancée, noting the dullness of her eyes and the droop of hopelessness about her mouth.

'I'm quite sure she's done no real wrong, otherwise I shouldn't be marrying her.' He let go of her wrist; she glanced down at it and saw the vivid red mark he had made.

31

'Grandfather...' She looked beseechingly at him, but he shook his head.

'Let's have no more argument,' he almost snapped. 'I've given my consent to your marriage; you're engaged to Chris——'

'But I love Ronnie!' The cry came involuntarily and Chris's dark eyes glinted.

'You'll forget all about this Englishman, understand?'

Helplessly she looked from one to the other. She was trapped, just as all Cypriot girls were trapped. She had tried to tell herself she was not one of them, because her father was English, and her nationality British, but she was one of them, in reality, because she must conform to the customs of Cyprus, must obey her grandfather, and bow to the will of her fiancé.

It was to be a fashionable wedding, at the church in Nicosia, and the reception was to be held at the Hilton. Invitations were sent out by the hundred; presents poured in. Judy telephoned Ronnie, pleading with him to help her even while fully aware that she was asking the impossible. He, as a foreigner, dared not take her from her legal guardian. But he was just as unhappy as she, especially as they could not even see one another, Judy being guarded by her grandfather who no doubt feared she would attempt to run away.

'You needn't go through with the marriage,' Ronnie said over and over again. 'No one can force you to do so.'

But she hadn't the courage to fight. Her grandfather she could have persuaded eventually, she thought, but Chris had said emphatically that he would not release her from the engagement.

And so Judy was married to a man she did not love—a beautiful bride at whose appearance gasps of admiration were uttered from all sides of the church. The bearded priest looked enviously at her husband, so tall and distinguished as he stood at her side. There were photographs to be taken as they came out; there was the brilliant reception, the laughter, the pretence. Through it all Judy felt numbed, as if her heart were a stone. Chris too did not betray even a hint of emotion. What a sham! Judy gazed down the table and her eyes caught those of her friend. Paul was beside her, handing her things, smiling at her.... Their wedding had been as splendid as this, she remembered, although at that time Judy and Lefki were not close friends and Judy had been invited merely because Lefki's great-aunt was related to Judy's grandfather by marriage. Lefki had wanted to be married, so although she and Paul did not fall in love until afterwards, Lefki would not be feeling like this—dead inside and pining her heart out for someone else.

Lefki winked, but Judy did not smile. She had wanted to visit Lefki again, but from the moment of discovery she had not been allowed out on her own for one single moment.

'My child, do try to look a little more cheerful,' ordered her husband, his mouth close to her ear. 'Any-one would think it was a funeral you were attending.'

She flushed and her nerves went tight. She looked at Lefki again, Lefki who had somehow managed to shed the chains of bondage and to become an equal with her husband....

'How did you do it?' Judy asked the question much later when she found an opportunity of speaking to her friend alone. The conversation had been veered into these channels by Judy who, driven by some vague force she could not understand, wanted to know more about Lefki's personality and the strength of which she was endowed that had made it possible for her to reach, and hold, this position of equality with her husband.

'It's the way you start,' laughed the Cypriot girl. 'If you begin by being timid and allowing yourself to be downtrodden, then you're lost immediately. Men are all puffed up with a sense of their own superiority and women are resigned to being subjugated—in this part of the world, at least. Well, I learned a lot when I was in France, and during my stay there I made friends with English girls and visited their homes. No being mastered for me, I said to myself when I saw how things were with the women of the West. Oh, I did appear to be meek and tractable before the wedding because I did not want Paul to guess what I was about. Once we were married, however, I began to train him in the way I wanted him to develop. And now we're the happiest couple in Cyprus!'

Judy still had not formed a clear picture of what Lefki had done and she said,

'Do you mean that whenever Paul told you to do something you deliberately went against his wishes?'

'If I didn't want to do what he asked, yes. I just disobeyed him.'

'But ...' Judy tailed off as her eyes strayed to Chris. He was standing, hands in his pockets, talking and laughing with a small crowd of young men. He towered above them and Judy noted his jaw and mouth. Would Lefki have dared disobey a man like Chris? Judy wondered, looking round for Paul. There he was, by the bar, handsome and strong, and certainly possessing a commanding personality. 'Perhaps you succeeded because he was in love with you. You might not have done so otherwise.'

'He wasn't in love with me right away. But even had he never loved me I'd still have had a good try.' She looked sideways at Judy and laughed. 'What are you

34

up to? Are you intending to follow my example?'

Judy fell silent. Why had she asked these questions of her friend?

'When you disobeyed him—what was his reaction?'

'He was quite astounded at first, naturally, because I'd led him to believe I was a meek and mild little thing. Then he tried to master me and we did have some dreadful rows,' she admitted with a grimace. 'But I held firm and in the end he became so fed up he capitulated.'

'And now you're—well, I suppose you're the boss, really?'

To her surprise Lefki shook her head vigorously.

'Far from it. I know just how far to go with Paul, and I don't proceed one step farther.' She actually gave a little shiver. 'He *is* masterful, and as I've said I know how far to go. He tolerates a lot, but then he suddenly won't tolerate any more and it is then that I prudently cease to fight.'

Judy frowned.

'How do you know when to stop?'

'I know my husband.' Lefki looked curiously at her, her big eyes alight with amusement. 'You're picking my brains, Judy,' she accused.

'No, I'm not. But I am endeavouring to learn something from you about—about ...' She tailed off, scarcely able to frame her words and Lefki finished for her,

'About man-management?' Elegant hands were spread nonchalantly as Lefki's glance searched for her husband. 'It really isn't anything one can learn, Judy. It just comes. You've been in France, and you know what it's like in England. You surely kept your eyes open?'

'Yes, of course I did, but Chris—he's different.'

'Different?' Lefki raised her eyebrows. 'In some ways, perhaps, but all men are basically the same. Lie down and they'll trample on you; stand up to them and they'll usually see eye to eye simply because it's less wearing than being for ever in a tussle with you.'

'Does it always work?'

'Not always. For example, Kyria's husband beats her. She often comes in with her eyes all red from weeping. That makes me angry because she can't get on with her work and I have to help her.'

'Her husband beats her...' Again Judy sought out her own husband; he seemed aware of her scrutiny, for he turned and stared at her, questioningly but not with any particular sign of emotion. Judy flushed and looked away. 'So it doesn't always work.'

'That's what I've just said.' And then Lefki added, 'Of course, there's no affection at all between Kyria and her husband, whereas Paul and I love one another.'

'So it only works if your husband is in love with you? I did suggest that a short while back,' Judy reminded her friend.

'I think it would work better if your husband loves you,' admitted Lefki, and then she said, a twinkle in her eye, 'Do you remember I said Chris would fall in love with you, once you were married?' Judy shook her head and frowned but Lefki went on, 'He will, just you mark my words ... and then you'll be able to twist him right round your little finger——'

'Not Chris! No, it would be quite impossible! Besides, he'll never fall in love with me—and I don't want him to.'

Lefki's eyes flickered strangely.

'You wouldn't be in love with someone else, would you?' she softly inquired, and Judy looked up, startled.

'You've heard the rumour?'

'Everyone has,' came the frank reply. But then Lefki passed that off as if it were of no importance, which was another pointer to just how Westernized she had become. 'Getting back to Chris—when he does fall in love with you, and you get to work on him, be careful.' Lefki wagged a finger at her friend, her mouth curved with amusement. 'It's knowing when to stop that's the important thing. Chris will be like Paul,' she continued knowledgeably, 'He'll tolerate so much and no more, so take heed of what I've said and be careful!'

After the wedding reception Chris and Judy flew to Athens, where they stayed the night. The hotel was in Constitution Square and Chris had previously booked a magnificent suite of rooms.

They entered the lift, accompanied by a porter carrying most of their luggage, and only then did Judy seem to become really alive to the position she was in. This stranger was her husband, with rights over her; she must submit to the demands he would make on her, must respect him and obey him. She looked up; his eyes flickered and she knew he read her thoughts. Judy blushed and a smile of sardonic amusement touched his lips.

She tried to calculate how many hours she had spent in his company; not more than the twenty-four that make up a day and a night. She thought of Ronnie, whom she loved and from whom she had even been denied the bitter-sweet agony of a final goodbye. Judy felt she hated this man who had offered for her; she felt she hated her grandfather too. Tears sprang to her eyes as she dwelt on what she had been denied by the premature death of her parents. Her own life ... what was it worth?

They were suddenly in the bedroom; their suitcases had been put down and they were alone. Judy moved to the window and looked out. There were the familiar street traders—the little cart where one could buy *koulouria*, the rings of bread with those delicious seeds on top; the sponge-seller and the inevitable bootblack. The Greeks were always having their shoes cleaned— perhaps it was because there was so much dust about——

'What are you thinking?' Her husband's voice, close to her ear. Judy stiffened and would have moved away, but her shoulders were suddenly grasped and she was turned around so that she faced her husband. 'Those beautiful eyes are so dreamy and far away,' he said, looking deeply into them. She stood quite still, afraid to reveal her aversion in case she aroused his anger. How dark he was! And how inaccessible. If only she could talk to him and plead with him and be sure he would listen, and soften and understand.

'I wasn't thinking of anything in particular,' she faltered. 'The—the street-traders always—always fascinate me.'

He looked down into the square.

'You've been here often?'

'Only twice.' He was still holding her; his hands were warm and she didn't like them touching her. 'I have a friend who lives in Athens.'

'You might like to visit her some time.'

'I visited her several weeks ago...' She tailed off because his eyes were glinting like steel.

'Of course. Your frandfather told me you met this Englishman on the plane when you were returning to Cyprus.'

She nodded.

'Yes, I did.'

'And fell in love with him.' A statement, spoken in harsh and strangely bitter tones. 'It's a great pity you were allowed this freedom. Your life would be happier had you not met him.'

She put a hand to her throat, nodding again.

'I suppose it would.'

Suddenly he bent and kissed her on the lips. She closed her eyes and thought of Ronnie—and then burst into tears. Was it nerves? she vaguely wondered. She knew she was tensed and overwrought, afraid of the night and of the slow, agonizing hours before it came. Chris brought out a handkerchief and to her astonishment his voice held no hint of impatience as he said,

'Now what can these tears be for? Ronnie, I presume.' He sighed on answering his own question. 'Yes, it's a great pity you were allowed that freedom.' He dried her eyes, and she looked up at him wonderingly. He was no different—still cold and unapproachable, and yet there was an element of gentleness in the way he dried her eyes, and in the way he gazed down at her. Would he listen now—if she told him of her fears? She spoke his name falteringly,

'Chris . . .'

'Yes, Judy?'

She swallowed hard and then,

'I don't want—I don't want . . .' She felt the tears behind her eyes again and blinked rapidly to hold them back. Chris's patience would not stretch too far, she thought.

'Yes, Judy,' he said in tones suddenly crisp. 'What is it you don't want?'

'We're strangers,' she whispered, and all her fear was in her voice, mingling with her plea for understanding. 'If you would—would give me a little time to get to know you?'

Silence. Down below the lights were appearing as the brief twilight followed the rapid sinking of the sun. Chris moved away; she sensed the sudden tautness of him and wondered if this meant that she could hope.

'Why,' he asked in tight emphatic tones, 'do you think I married you?'

Judy sagged.

'So you won't wait a little while?'

'A bridegroom doesn't usually wait a little while.'

'No—but our marriage is different. I'm English.'

That appeared to amuse him. She was glad his manner had changed because that tautness only added to her fears, although she could not have said why.

'You're not English,' he corrected. 'Your mother was a Greek Cypriot. However, that's of no matter. What has nationality to do with it anyway?'

'English girls fall in love. What I mean is, they know their husbands well before the marriage——'

'So I believe,' he cut in dryly, and the colour flooded her face.

'I really mean,' Judy persevered after a while, 'that, to me, it doesn't seem right to—to——' She broke off, colouring up again, and he finished for her,

'To marry a stranger?'

She nodded.

'The marrying part is all right,' she said innocently. 'But it's the——' She glanced at the bed and quite unexpectedly he laughed. She was fascinated by the change in his face. Yes, she had been right when she asserted that he was more handsome than Paul.

'So it's the making love that troubles you, is it?'

She turned away, but for some strange reason her embarrassment was not as great as she would have expected it to be.

'You knew it was, right from the start, didn't you? And you've been enjoying my discomfiture.'

'You know, Judy,' he said, coming to her again and bringing her round to face him, 'it's going to be delightful being married to you. I'm sure we shall get along famously together.' His lips met hers and again she stood there, meek, unmoving, thinking of Ronnie. 'No response?' Amusement touched the hard outline of his mouth. 'What is it, my little Judy—shyness, or merely that you dislike having me near you?'

So he sensed her aversion. Perhaps he was remembering that she loved someone else. Judy wished she had the courage to mention this, for then perhaps he would not kiss her—or even...

She could not bear to think of the night and she switched her thoughts to Lefki instead, and to the way she had managed Paul. 'It's the way you start,' Lefki had said. 'If you begin by being timid and allowing yourself to be downtrodden then you're lost immediately.' No being mastered for Lefki. If she did not want to do what her husband asked she just disobeyed him, and although his reaction led to quarrels Lefki held firm and in the end Paul capitulated.

Judy looked up at Chris; he had asked her a question, but she made no attempt to answer it. She was so deeply engrossed in a recollection of that conversation with Lefki. One had to know how far to go, it appeared, and a pucker of bewilderment creased her brow. How did one estimate the distance one could go with safety? It worked better, too, if one's husband were in love—and of course Chris was not in love. He had seen Judy and, desiring her, had proceeded in the orthodox way and offered for her. Yes, it worked better if one's husband were in love, Lefki had admitted that. Nevertheless, it could still work if one's husband's only interest was desire, as was the case with Chris.

It was how you started.... If you did not want something you must openly disobey your husband.... Over and over again Lefki's words repeated themselves as Judy stood there, fear and courage battling for supremacy. To fight as Lefki had done took a great deal of initial courage, which Judy had not possessed at the time she was being forced into marriage, but now... If Lefki could do it, then why couldn't she? If you did

41

not want to do something ... Judy did not want Chris to stay with her tonight—not in fact until she knew him better. Her eyes still gazed into his. What could he do to her if she defied him? He could not murder her; nor could he beat her, as Kyria's husband beat her. No, not in the hotel, he couldn't, because she would scream and someone would come.

'I'm not letting you stay with me tonight,' she said—and blinked. Had she really uttered those words? It would seem like it, judging by her husband's expression.

'What did you say?' he asked unbelievingly.

Judy went white. But her determination was now strong. She was married to Chris and the marriage was permanent. Ronnie was not for her and she was resigned to the fact that she must try to forget him. Fate had sent her to Cyprus when she was young; by the customs of the island she had been forced to accept the husband her grandfather had chosen for her. But she was British, and in any case, even if she were a Cypriot she would still have learned from Lefki, who, herself a Cypriot, had found the courage to lift herself from the level of vassalage to that of her husband's equal. Judy decided she could do likewise; she also decided she must begin at once, and although her heart pulsated quite abnormally she managed to articulate her words with a clarity that amazed her.

'I said I'm not letting you stay with me tonight,' she repeated, but then she added, 'Later, when I know you better, I might change my mind.'

The silence of amazement filled the room. She had stunned him! Judy felt quite proud of herself in spite of her husband's dark incredulous face above her and the glowering expression in his eyes.

'You—might—change—your—mind?' Each word was pronounced with astounded precision. 'How very obliging of you. What am I supposed to do now? Express my humble thanks and bow myself out—backwards?'

Judy blinked uncertainly, rather at a loss. What would normally be the next move? How would Lefki deal with this situation? But Lefki had wanted Paul, so in her case a situation such as this would never have arisen. Judy's heartbeats were still racing, and no wonder, so darkly threatening was her husband's countenance. But she must not weaken. It was her fate to stay married to Chris and she intended to be his partner, not his possession. True, Chris did appear rather frightening, but hadn't Lefki firmly asserted that all men were basically the same? Lie down, she had said, and they would trample all over you; stand up to them and they'd usually see eye to eye simply because it was less wearing than being for ever in a tussle with you.

'It's only because I don't know you,' she began to explain. 'I don't think it ought to be yet. If we remain just friends, and—well, keep company, like they do in Western countries, and like I would have done had I been brought up in England, then we shall gradually get to know one another and everything will be—er—normal,' she ended vaguely.

He had moved away, but his eyes never left her face. She stood with her back to the window, a slender figure of nymph-like charm and captivating allure. In her innocence and determination to fight for emancipation she didn't stop to think what she was asking. And perhaps had she known just how tempting she appeared to this dark Greek she would not have been so sublimely confident of herself. Strangely, though, his features began to relax and Judy felt sure she detected a hint of amusement enter those dark metallic eyes. Perception was there too, and she had the odd conviction that he had guessed, quite suddenly, what she was about. What she did not know was that her own eyes still contained the shade of fear ... and that her husband had noticed this and realized she was very young and innocent.

'Tidy yourself up,' he said. 'We'll go somewhere and eat.'

She blinked at him. No argument or attempt at domination? How easy it all was! Why hadn't she asserted herself before? She could so easily have broken the engagement, she now decided. Had she stood firm Chris would have given her her way—and she would have been free to marry Ronnie. Somehow, though, it all seemed too good to be true and she was forced to say,

'But we haven't settled this matter.' She hoped she sounded businesslike and brisk and she searched his face to discover how he was taking this. All she saw was a kindling of his eyes as he said abruptly,

'We're going out!' And, remembering there was a point beyond which it was imprudent to go, Judy returned with sudden meekness,

'Yes, Chris, I'll get changed.'

This she did in the bathroom, putting on a tailored dress in white linen, and white sandals. A white Alice band round her hair made her look about fifteen, and Chris, emerging from the other bathroom, stood by the door for a moment, looking at her and shaking his head.

'Perhaps,' he said, giving a little sigh, 'I should have waited even longer.'

At this surprising comment her eyes opened very wide. But before she could think of anything to say in return he had picked up her coat from the bed and was holding it out for her to put on.

This little attention was unusual, and it set her wondering if perhaps she had made one big mistake in thinking he meant to subjugate her and treat her as a possession. But all Greek men treated their wives as possessions, as did Cypriots. No, she had not made a mistake. He was no different from the rest and she must never weaken in her efforts at 'man-management' as Lefki had described it.

They went out into the lighted square, and sauntered through the streets until Chris found the *taverna* he wanted. The meal was excellent, and after it was over they remained in the garden drinking wine and watching the Greek dancers leaping and twisting to the accompaniment of a *bouzouki* and a guitar. The gardens were a romantic setting, with coloured lights twinkling from the trees and a crescent moon poised in a purple sky from which a myriad stars looked down. Warm balmy air and a soft perfumed breeze; colour and music and the sort of gaiety and abandon found only in Greece.

To Judy's surprise she was reasonably happy—until her husband said it was time they were returning to the hotel.

'We have to be up early tomorrow in order to catch the ferry,' he added. They were going to his home on the island of Hydra, one of the 'Siren isles' of the Saronic Gulf. There they would live, on this small, almost barren island, one-time home of bold, buccaneering men but now the haunt of Greek millionaire ship-owners, and painters and writers. Practically the whole of the population lived close to the picturesque little harbour; only the mansions of the rich occupied magnificent sites on the hillsides to the west of the port.

In complete silence Judy and her husband walked back to the hotel. Had she really achieved anything? she wondered, looking up at him the moment they entered their sitting-room. His dark face was expressionless, and yet she sensed a sort of animal desire

45

which he was striving to suppress. Massive, he seemed against her, and powerful. How could she even contemplate engaging such a man in combat, let alone expect the spoils of victory to be hers? He could pick her up like a small toy, and her struggles would not only be futile but laughable. She was afraid, terribly afraid; her fear was seen by him again and, turning abruptly, he left her, only to return a few minutes later carrying a pillow and a blanket. She stared, speechless, as he placed the pillow on the couch and then spread out the blanket.

'Wh-what are you d-doing?' she stammered, quite unable to believe her eyes.

He straightened up, his mouth compressed and yet in his eyes the sort of expression that portrayed resigned amusement.

'Isn't this what you wanted?' and without waiting for an answer, 'I'd have booked another bedroom had I known. However, this will suffice for one night.' Taking her face in his hands, he bent his head and kissed her on the mouth. 'Good night, Judy, pleasant dreams.' She did not move and he gave her a little tap. 'Off you go before I change my mind,' he recommended, and she prudently did as she was told.

How perfectly simple it all had been, she thought as she slid down between the cool white sheets a short while later. So fortunate that she had questioned Lefki and learned about 'man-management'. Just to think, she had told him she was not letting him stay tonight and he had meekly taken himself into the sitting-room where he would sleep on the couch. It really was quite incredible, because his personality had always seemed so overpowering. Judy yawned and turned her face into the pillow. Lefki was so right when she said all men were basically the same. . . .

CHAPTER THREE

THE island of Hydra rose like some lovely jewel from a sea of dazzling blue. Above the spectacular harbour with its brightly coloured caïques and blue and white houses and shops rose the barren rocky mass of Mount Prophet Ilias, while gleaming in the sun were the impressive white mansions of the rich, rising one above another and standing on precipitous cliffs above the more humble houses of the village, which were arranged like an amphitheatre around the circular little harbour.

'It's beautiful!' exclaimed Judy impulsively, turning to look up at her husband, standing beside her at the rail of the ship. He merely allowed her a flicker of attention before returning his gaze to the island, which was coming so close now that the whitewashed cobbled streets could clearly be seen. Judy flushed, because of her husband's disinterest in her. She thought of the silent breakfast, the cool, impersonal remarks he had passed when they were in the taxi travelling to the Piræus to catch the ferry, and then silence again during the voyage to his island home. 'Can you see your house from here?' she asked perseveringly.

He turned a mild stare in her direction, and nodded.

'It's the highest one on the west of the harbour.' A negligent gesture of his hand indicated the gleaming white mansion whose marble fountains could be seen sparkling in the sunlight. 'It's called Salaris House.'

'That one?' She was used to luxury, her grandfather's house being one of the most outstanding in Kyrenia, but on seeing the imposing edifice reclining on the mountainside she opened her eyes wide. 'It looks wonderful!' she breathed, rather awed.

Her husband said nothing, but his detached stare remained upon her. She frowned inwardly. For some quite incomprehensible reason she was troubled by an uncomfortable little pang of guilt—nothing serious, but it was the sort of feeling she had experienced as a child when some misdemeanour had been committed and her grandfather was vexed with her.

They were very close now to the little old-world port and Judy picked out one or two grey-stone houses, tall and architecturally very different from the cluster of little cubic houses which seemed from this angle to be touching one another.

'Why are those houses so different—the grey ones, I mean?' she asked, still wanting him to hold a conversation with her, although she could not have said why.

'They were the homes of piratical traders who went in for lavish entertaining two hundred or so years ago. As a matter of fact mine is one, but it's had many alterations and additions over the years, some of which I've had done myself.'

'Were they Greek, these traders?'

'No, Albanians.' His eyes still lingered on her, their expression inscrutable. What was he thinking? It was impossible to guess, but she did wonder, a little fearfully, if he were regretting his calm acceptance of her decision last night. That he *had* accepted was a circumstance which to her surprise had kept her awake for hours pondering over it. He had married her for desire, that went without saying, and from the very first Judy had accepted that. So why, after having offered for her and married her for the sole purpose of possessing her, had he, on their very first night, meekly accepted her word as law? It just did not make sense, even though Judy had been firm and determined because, as Lefki had said, she must start right if she were to attain the status of her husband's equal. Chris was so confident and self-possessed, so obviously masterful even though as yet he had made no real attempt at mastery. On learning of her little affair with Ronnie he had fairly made her tremble in her shoes and it seemed so very odd that, simply because she herself had gained a little confidence and courage, Chris should instantly lose his. No, it certainly did not make sense, despite Lefki's assertion that men were all alike and would give in rather than become engaged in a tussle with their wives.

'Here we are.' Chris's voice broke into her reverie and she turned to him. 'Are you ready for a long climb?'

'We have to walk?'

'Naturally.'

'You haven't a car?'

'Not here. A car wouldn't be any use to get up there—even were there a road.'

Judy soon learned that the 'roads' were lanes so steep that they were stepped, and she seemed to have covered hundreds of these steps before she came at last to the great white house on the plateau cut into the side of the hill. It had thirty-eight rooms, Chris told her when on entering the massive hall she stared in bewilderment first at all the doors on the ground floor and then at the grand staircase leading to the upper apartments.

'Thirty-eight!' She stared at him, feeling smaller than ever. The hint of a smile curved his lips. He said with cool impersonality,

'My sister and her husband have a suite of rooms here, and so does my mother. They come during the summer for a long stay.'

His sister and mother.... Floria was nineteen and had been married a year. Judy had seen her only once, when she came to Cyprus with Chris for a holiday. Judy had not been able to attend her wedding, as she was at school at that time, in France. Chris's mother she had never met, nor his father. They were separated, a rare occurrence with Greeks. Judy had never learned the reason for the separation, for Chris had never offered one, and Judy, looking upon him as a stranger, had naturally refrained from broaching the subject.

Judy turned her head as two Greek youths entered the hall. They were bringing in the luggage, having picked it up at the quay.

'Down there.' Chris spoke abruptly and put his hand in his pocket. He paid them and they went out, thanking him with a smile that revealed a flash of white teeth. Chris clapped his hands imperiously and a man-servant appeared. 'My wife, Spiros,' he said briefly.

The man smiled and said,

'Welcome, Madam Voulis. *Isasthe poli haritomeni!*'

She blushed, unconsciously glancing up at her husband. His gaze was cool, sardonic, and her blush deepened.

'*Efharistó poli,*' she murmured even as Chris was telling Spiros to take their suitcases up to their rooms.

'So Spiros thinks you're pretty,' commented Chris in a rather bored voice when a few minutes later they were in Judy's room, having followed Spiros upstairs. 'I must admit your blush was quite charming, and you thanked him with the sort of smile you have never shown to me.'

They were standing in the middle of the room; vaguely, Judy was aware of a magnificent view of the town and the harbour and the great expanse of blue unmoving sea. Chris was regarding her critically now, as if Spiros's declaration that she was very pretty had given him something to think about. For her part, Judy just stared up at him, her lovely blue eyes very wide and innocent, her lips parted, and, although she did not know it, almost irresistibly inviting to this stranger husband of hers.

What was this odd note in his voice as he spoke of the smile she had given to Spiros? Was it pique? Undoubtedly ... and yet why should Chris be piqued? It certainly wasn't her smiles he wanted. ...

'Are your relatives here at present?' she inquired conversationally.

'Floria will be here in about a week's time and her husband will follow shortly afterwards. He has business to attend to in Athens and can't come just whenever he wants to. Mother will arrive in a couple of weeks or so. We all gather here for two or three months in the summer.'

'So we're on our own for a week?' The words broke automatically and his lips twisted with a hint of mockery.

'Quite alone, but for the servants.' Judy eyed him uncertainly. He seemed faintly amused, yet at the same time exasperated to a small degree. However, his voice was cool and unemotional as he added, 'Have no fear, Judy, you won't need to call upon them for help.'

Her face grew hotter even while elation swept over her. She fell to wondering why the girls of the East were so downtrodden when this man-management was so ridiculously easy. Of course, as Lefki said, it was the way one started. Because they had been indoctrinated for generations with the idea of male superiority the women of the East automatically offered no resistance. How foolish they were! Someone should give them lessons, she thought, just as Lefki had given Judy a lesson.

Chris turned away and her eyes followed him. The door between the two rooms was slightly ajar and he pushed it open and disappeared into his own room.

The door closed; Judy smiled to herself. She must write to Lefki and thank her.

As the days passed a small element of friendship developed between Judy and Chris, but otherwise theirs was an unimpassioned union of prosaic domesticity. During the mornings Chris would withdraw to his study, a vast and luxuriously furnished apartment with a terrace from where could be seen the colourful little harbour with its immaculate houses and shops and its congestion of little caïques and pleasure craft of all kinds. Judy would be consulted by the cook, Julia, a dark and stolid Greek woman who had been in the employ of Chris's father for many years, coming to Chris on the break-up of his father's marriage five years previously.

'What is the menu for lunch?' Julia would ask, a notebook held between her fingers and a businesslike expression on her face.

'Lunch?' Judy faltered on the first occasion. At home in Cyprus she had never been consulted about such things. 'Er—what do you suggest?'

The woman shrugged.

'It's for you to plan the menu, madam.'

'Yes. . . .' And Judy had then told Julia to leave it for a while so that she could give the matter some thought. But immediately on the cook's departure Judy had gone in to her husband.

'What would you like for lunch?' she inquired, glancing at the array of papers on his desk. One was a picture of a magnificent white pleasure cruiser and she wondered if it belonged to him.

Chris threw her a frowning glance.

'Meals, my dear, are entirely your department.' And he added crisply, 'I do draw the line somewhere.'

Draw the line? What a peculiar thing to say! A tiny

frown of perplexity settled on Judy's wide brow. There was no doubt about it, her husband did act in the strangest way, and say the strangest things. It occurred to Judy all at once that although she was succeeding in her fight for equality with her husband she was having much less success with her desire to understand his temperament.

During the afternoons she and Chris would swim in the flower-bordered pool in the garden, or sit on the lawn or terrace enjoying the sun. When doing this latter they would read, and sometimes, feeling her husband's concentrated gaze fixed upon her, Judy would raise her head to see him regarding her with an expression half frowning, half amused. What went on in that mind of his? With the passing of each day Judy found her curiosity increasing.

'We'll go for a walk,' he said one day after lunch. 'You haven't seen much of the island yet.'

Somehow, the idea of a walk with him was pleasant and it was with unusual eagerness that she sped upstairs and changed into a very short cotton skirt and a sleeveless, low-necked sun-top. Her hair was a glorious mass of gold falling in soft and tender abandon on to her shoulders, which were bare except for the narrowest of straps. She had bought this little outfit in Paris; there were shorts to match, but these she had not put on.

Lightly she ran down the stairs, hair flying, nymphlike and very lovely. Chris was standing in the hall waiting for her, his head bent as if he were endeavouring to unravel the pattern of the mosaic of black and white veined marbles with which the floor was elaborately paved. At the sound of her feet he looked up; something moved in his throat, but his glance appeared to be entirely lacking in interest. Therefore it came as a surprise when he said,

'Very charming. I believe I have the most beautiful wife in the whole of Greece.' Adorably she blushed, thinking that life with Chris might be pleasant in the extreme once she had established herself as his partner in the way Lefki had done with Paul. 'What have you got on underneath that skirt?' he calmly inquired, and Judy gave a start.

'Underneath...?' Unconsciously she touched a fold of the skirt, her cheeks hotter than ever. 'Nothing—— Oh, I mean——!' Mercifully he cut her short, his dark eyes kindling with amusement.

'Unless I'm mistaken, you have a very attractive pair of shorts to go with that top?' She just stared, endeavouring to regain her composure, and he added, 'No, you haven't worn them here, but you did when you were in France; your grandfather showed me some snapshots you sent him.'

'Oh...' she quivered as he paused for a space. 'Did he?' Judy had not known that her fiancé had seen the snapshots, but obviously he had. She would have expected him to be annoyed, or uninterested. But he was neither.

'Go and put them on,' he ordered quietly. 'I'll wait on the terrace for you.'

She looked doubtfully at him. Eastern he was, with the chiselled granite-like severity portrayed in the face of the average Greek aristocrat, but he appeared to have thrown aside the old-fashioned idea that a woman's body should be demurely covered. Every single day he gave her a surprise, she thought.

'Wear them, to go walking with you?' she queried, still a shade uncertain.

He nodded.

'And leave the skirt off.'

'Oh, but—when I wear the shorts for walking I just open the skirt——' She indicated the front. 'There are

54

buttons, you see.'

'Yes, I see.' He stifled a yawn. 'Leave it off,' he said again, and went out on to the terrace.

Judy ran back upstairs and it was not until she had emerged from the house on to the terrace, and noted the look of satisfaction on her husband's face, that she asked herself whether or not she should have obeyed him. Submission to his will must be avoided at all costs—but the trouble was that Judy had no idea at all about that point beyond which she must not go.

'That's better.' Chris's eyes roved over her, in the sort of appraising manner with which all Greek men examined women. Judy was used to it; she read his thoughts with accuracy—and somehow felt a tinge of desolation. Other men could look at her like that, but she wished her husband wouldn't. But how did she want him to look at her? A frown of bewilderment touched her brow because she could find no answer to her question. 'Why the dark look?' he suddenly asked, and her face cleared.

'I was thinking, but it's nothing important.'

'It must have been important to make you frown like that. Tell me.'

Judy did not want to reply, but Chris's mouth was set and his gaze demanding. She told the truth, saying that it was the way he looked at her.

'The way I look at you?' he repeated blankly. 'What exactly do you mean by that?'

She swallowed, wondering how to answer him without herself suffering embarrassment. Besides, she had a shrewd suspicion that he knew what she meant and that his puzzlement was feigned.

'It doesn't matter,' she said at last hastily.

He hesitated a moment in indecision and then, with an air of indifference,

'Come, we shall walk over to the other side of the

55

harbour and see a friend of mine.'

They went down, first, towards the harbour, traversing cobblestoned alleys the majority of which were stepped. The cobblestones were whitewashed almost every day, the houses were also white, with the traditional blue shutters found on practically every Greek house. The harbour was neat and clean and many graceful sailing craft stood moored, gently swayed by the prevailing north-west wind which could at times be troublesome to sailors, many of whom, when handling pleasure craft, preferred the safer port of Spetsai, an island some short distance away to the south-west. The whiteness and cleanness, combined with the masses of flowers—roses and jasmine, hibiscus and oleanders—gave the scene a gay and colourful aspect in spite of the immaculate air that seemed to typify this particular Greek island.

Judy trotted beside her husband in the sunshine, feeling far less unhappy than she had anticipated on her wedding day when, standing there beside Chris, before the smiling bearded priest, she had made her vows in faltering reluctant tones, her heart a leaden weight within her. At that time she had looked with overpowering dread to the time, only hours away, when her formidable bridegroom would demand and take from her what he had patiently waited over two years to attain. But, strengthened by her new-found courage and determination not to enter into that state of slavery to which all her friends but Lefki had resigned themselves, Judy had won the first vital round without receiving as much as a scratch. It was not that she meant to continue in this way; she intended 'keeping company' with her husband until some sort of affection entered into their relationship—love being quite out of the question because Ronnie had her heart, even though she sternly told herself she must forget him—and then, if in addition to the affection existing between them, Chris had also accepted her as his equal, she would, as she had half promised on her wedding night, 'change her mind'.

On reaching the shops in the harbour Chris bought her a box of chocolates. It was the first present he had bought her—she did not count the diamond bracelet he had given her for a wedding present because she had not liked it at all and it was now in its case in one of the drawers in her room—and she raised her lovely eyes as she thanked him in husky tones. He slipped the chocolates in her bag and they walked on, towards the white *taverna* with its blue shutters and tables set out on the pavement. Men idled on the chairs, drinking the inevitable Turkish coffee from minute cups which they filled up now and then from the glasses of water which in Greece always accompany the coffee. Fishermen had spread their nets to dry in the sun, and were sitting in little groups, gossiping and clicking their worry beads, but they all looked up with interest at seeing Chris with his new wife. Greetings were exchanged between them and Chris, and then the usual examination of Judy, from her sandal-clad feet to the top of her head. She was used to this and she did not blush; Chris turned his head to note her reaction and a hint of amusement touched his lips at her immunity to the stares of the men. He was not in the least jealous, she thought, remembering how angry Ronnie would become when the Cypriots allowed their eyes to rove over her in this way.

A little farther along the quay several youths were standing around two men who were pounding an octopus. She shuddered and again her husband appeared to be amused.

'You eat octopus, surely?' he asked.

She shook her head.

'I've never even tasted it.'

'They're delicious. You have the tentacles fried in butter.'

Judy said nothing. She was used to Greek food, naturally, because it was eaten all the time in Cyprus, but she had never been able to eat octopus. There was something revolting about those tentacles, and besides, she did not care for the way the octopus were tenderized—by banging them repeatedly on the rocks or stones, and then rubbing them until a great lather appeared.

A cruise ship was in and masses of tourists surged on to the quay; shopkeepers stood outside their doors, ready to do business, selling their souvenirs and postcards and of course the lovely sponges which the sponge-divers of the island brought from the rich fishing grounds of North Africa.

Judy and Chris left the port at last and began climbing one little flight of cobbled steps after another until they reached the house of Chris's friend.

'You walked?' he said after Chris had introduced him to Judy. 'I always use a donkey myself.' His house was not nearly so magnificent as that of Chris; nevertheless, it was on the scale of a mansion, with an immense drawing-room to which he led them after they had spent a few minutes chatting on the terrace. 'So this is Judy.' He looked her over once more, and appeared to like what he saw. 'Chris waited a long while for you. You should be flattered.' George Cozakis brought forward a chair for her and she sat down, her eyes remaining appreciatively on him. He was slight of build with laughing eyes and a ready smile. His hair was brown—not nearly so dark as that of Chris. His age, Judy estimated, was about the same as that of her husband—twenty-eight or nine. He was handsome in a softer, more gentle way than Chris, although there was a firmness to his features, nevertheless. He smiled often, unlike Chris, whose face was unmoving, reflecting the reserve which was an inherent part of him. George also talked a good deal, while Chris remained quiet, listening. George openly flattered Judy and Chris did not seem to mind; George informed her that she was the last in a long line of beautiful girls who had aspired to become the wife of the wealthy Chrisalis, but this time Chris did seem to mind.

'Don't exaggerate, George,' he interrupted with a frown. 'You'll have Judy thinking I'm a profligate.'

She looked at him and for the first time wondered about his past life. He would have girls, she felt sure, and as he also had a home in Athens that would not be difficult, for there life was freer than in the villages and islands of Greece; girls went about alone and could, therefore, find men-friends. A long line.... How many? She frowned then and recalled his fury on learning about Ronnie. How unfair it all was, she mused, her frown deepening. A man could do what he liked—have dozens of women before marriage—but a girl must keep herself for her husband, because if he discovered after marriage that she was not chaste he could divorce her immediately and she would never live down the disgrace and shame, which would not only affect the girl herself, but her family as well.

Chris's eyes were riveted on her; he was plainly endeavouring to read her thoughts. A small flush rose to highlight the lovely contours of her face and she saw a movement at the side of his neck. His gaze, however, took on a hint of mocking amusement and she guessed at once that her blush was responsible for his sudden humour.

'Exaggerate?' George's eyebrows rose a fraction. 'There was Stella and Maroula and Elli. Then you had the two English ones and the Swede—I'll bet she taught you a thing or two,' he laughed. 'Then the next thing I knew you were almost married to Corinne Moore—she's here, by the way——'

'My dear George,' interrupted Chris with a yawn, 'I'm quite sure Judy doesn't want to sit here listening to all this rubbish which flows so glibly from your tongue.' He looked at his wife. 'Take no heed, my dear. George just loves to hear himself talk.'

Judy remained silent. That George spoke the truth she did not for a moment doubt. She considered it in very bad taste for him to reel off the names of her husband's previous girl-friends, and yet she could not dislike George. On the contrary, it was Chris on whom her disgusted gaze came at last to rest. His brows rose then, arrogantly ... and could it be warningly? This idea brought a lift to Judy's chin. He must not adopt that manner with her, this gesture was meant to indicate, and Chris's eyes glinted darkly. At that Judy swallowed, realizing it was going to be most difficult to maintain her new-found courage—but maintain it she must if she were ever to attain the status she desired, the status which would automatically have been hers had she been brought up in England, and married one of her own people.

George was clapping his hands for the servant and this relieved the tension that was building up between Judy and Chris. George asked what they wanted to drink and the order was given on the appearance of the manservant.

The refreshments brought, the two men fell into a business conversation as they drank and Judy began to dwell on what George had said about Chris's having been almost married to someone called Corinne Moore. English, apparently ... and was he really almost married to her? If so, what had happened? She was here now, George had been saying when Chris had

60

interrupted him.

'I think I'll go to Venice to see the *Andromeda* set sail on her first trip,' George was saying, and Judy's thoughts were diverted from this unknown Corinne Moore to the conversation going on between the two men. 'It's all very ordinary to you, Chris, but this is the first ship built since I joined the firm. I'd like to take the cruise, even, but I'm far too busy.'

'You can take a cruise on her another time,' remarked Chris without much interest.

'But this is her maiden voyage, and that's why I'm so eager to take the trip.' But he shrugged then, and repeated that he was far too busy.

Later, on their way home, Judy said hesitantly,

'I gathered you have a new ship being built?'

'She's already built; takes her first voyage a month from now.'

'How many ships have you got?' she inquired curiously.

'I, personally, don't have any. It's a company.'

'But you're a ship-owner—Grandfather said you were.' It struck her as all wrong that her entire information about her husband had come from her grandfather. Chris should have talked to her, and told her about himself—about his childhood and his family and his business. But of course women from the East were treated as slaves, and one did not confide in a slave. Well, she was not from the East—and she would continue with the good work of bringing this home to her husband.

'I suppose I do own some ships,' he conceded. 'But, as I've said, it's a firm, so everything is shared, as it were.' He sounded bored, as if the explanation was a little wearing, because she was only a woman. Once more her pretty little chin lifted. She recalled that Lefki loved travel and that she also had no difficulty in getting her

61

husband to take her travelling.

'I think I would like to sail on the *Andromeda*,' she said and, as on another occasion, she blinked, amazed at her own daring.

They were climbing the last few steps before reaching the start of the terraced garden surrounding the house and in his surprise Chris almost stopped.

'Your place,' he said at last cuttingly, 'is with your husband, not gadding about all over the Mediterranean!'

'Oh, I didn't mean to go on my own——'

'You didn't? I'm relieved to hear it!'

'I thought we might go together,' she persisted, passing in front of him as they reached the gate. 'Where is the *Andromeda* going?'

'Her destination need not trouble you. You won't be on board.' He turned to close the gate because old Andonis would leave his donkey untethered and it wandered into the garden and ate the flowers.

'Lefki's husband takes her travelling all over the place.' Judy twisted round to gaze up at him with a sort of winsome expression in her beautiful blue eyes. 'I would very much like to travel, too.'

'Lefki? Who's she?'

'My great friend. She was at our wedding, but perhaps you didn't notice because there was such a crush. She married a rich man and he takes her everywhere she wants to go.'

'He does?' They were in the courtyard and Chris stopped. They were in a setting of marble fountains and ornate wrought iron, of exotic flowers whose perfume was scattered over the whole hillside by the soft warm breeze blowing in from the sea far down below. 'Tell me more about this Lefki,' he invited. 'Is her husband a Cypriot?'

'Yes; Paul. But he doesn't boss her about as they

usually do,' Judy informed him with adorable naïveté. 'He treats Lefki as an equal—just as if they were a couple from England or France. And whenever she wants to travel he takes her. Do you know,' she went on confidingly, yet with a touch of awe, 'Lefki spent three thousand pounds on Georgian silver the last time Paul took her to London!'

To her surprise Chris was not particularly impressed by her words. Nevertheless, he did say in dry and pointed tones,

'Well, don't you get any ideas of spending three thousand pounds on Georgian silver—or any ideas about going to London, even,' he added inflexibly.

She bit her lip. Her husband noted the action and an odd expression entered his eyes, an expression which brought back a fleeting vision of his face when, on their wedding night, she had looked at him in the hotel bedroom and felt instinctively that he knew what she was about.

'I don't particularly want to buy Georgian silver,' she told him accommodatingly, unaware that the conversation was entering into a humorous phase. 'You see, I don't know much about it, so I might be cheated.'

Chris regarded her inscrutably for a space and then, glancing round, he moved towards the wicker chairs which had been placed in the shade of the lemon trees growing on the fringe of garden adjoining the courtyard. He sat down, leaning back rather in the slouching manner of Greek men when they were idling their time away in the *tavernas* or by the waterfront. A very deep frown creased his brow and to her surprise his lips twitched. He straightened up and said,

'Again you need not worry. You won't be cheated because there's no possibility of my giving you three thousand pounds to run around London with.'

His sarcasm offended her and she set her mouth. At

this defiant little gesture his eyes opened very wide, and his dark head tilted in a way that spelled mastery and warning. Judy moistened her lips. Mastery was the one vital thing she meant to fight, but what move must she now make in order to avoid taking a downward step?

'I've just said I don't want to buy silver,' she returned at last, moving closer to him and looking straight at him. 'But I *do* want to travel.'

A small silence then and she sat down, waiting rather breathlessly for his reaction to her words. But he said nothing and she presently added, more to end the oppressive silence than anything else, 'If Lefki can travel, then I don't see why I can't as well.'

He emerged from his thoughtful silence and again she saw the humorous twitching of his lips.

'Lefki....' He repeated the name musingly. 'You should have introduced me to her at the wedding. I'm sure she must be a most unusual and interesting young woman.'

Judy glanced uncertainly at him. Was he teasing her? But no. Chris was always grave and detached. Today he was also a little disconcerting, and for the first time she wished he were like Ronnie—transparent and accommodating. They would get along fine then, she felt sure, and perhaps she would relent and allow him to be a proper husband to her.

'She is unusual,' agreed Judy at last as Chris sat there in an attitude of waiting. 'Unusual for a Cypriot girl, that is. You see, she has achieved this equal status with her husband.'

'So I gather,' was the dry comment from Chris. 'She's your great friend, you said?'

Judy nodded. Her gaze was concentrated on the glorious view across the terraced grounds of the house to the slopes below and the town and harbour lower down still. From the trees close by the sound of cicadas filled the air, which was fast becoming hot and sultry, for June was almost at an end.

'Lefki went to school in France, just as I did,' supplied Judy. 'So we have much in common.'

Chris lifted his eyes, allowed them to settle on his wife's face for a moment and then, in the same dry tones,

'So it would appear.'

The brief remark seemed to hold a wealth of hidden meaning and Judy blinked at him in an inquiring, puzzled sort of way. But he merely sat back in his chair, regarding her through narrowed eyes, and she suddenly felt at a loss for words. Certainly he was disconcerting today, and he seemed to be playing some sort of game with her, a game from which he derived a certain amount of pleasure not untinged with amusement. The silence threatened to become uncomfortable and she said with rather exaggerated carelessness,

'You've switched the conversation, Chris. I was talking about travel. I asked you where the *Andromeda* was going.'

He was not listening. His eyes were on a pink-clad figure climbing the steps up the hillside. Following the direction of his gaze, Judy took in the tall slim figure of a girl of about twenty-five years of age. Dark-haired and tanned to a deep golden brown, she was obviously not a holidaymaker from the gleaming white cruise ship resting at anchor in the calm blue waters of the gulf below, for she knew her way about and now and then she would glance up at the house, so there was no doubt as to her destination. Judy returned her gaze to her husband. He seemed totally absorbed in the figure approaching them and, frowning, Judy said with unaccustomed sharpness,

'I asked you where the *Andromeda* was going!'

Slowly he took his eyes off the girl in pink.

'The *Andromeda*?' he repeated absently. 'Oh ... to some of the islands, and to Egypt.'

'Egypt?' Her eyes glowed; she forgot the girl in her excitement. 'I've always wanted to go to Egypt. Can we go on the ship when she sails next month?'

'Together?' So soft the brief word ... and an odd expression in his eyes. Judy became guarded.

'Well, I could scarcely go on my own,' she evaded. 'It wouldn't be right, for one thing.' She was flushing and he smiled, but his manner of amused tolerance had vanished when he spoke.

'Whether it would be right or wrong is quite immaterial, Judy. The important thing is that I wouldn't allow you to go on your own.' He was all cool mastery, a husband whose word was law. Judy searched for something to say, but before any suitably impressive retort could be found Chris was speaking again, this time in affable, welcoming tones. 'Corinne, how nice to see you. You've been on the island some time?'

'A month.' Her brown eyes swept Judy an all-embracing glance. 'I sold four paintings, so I've used the money to come back. George was sweet; he rented me the room at the top of his house again.'

'Meet my wife, Judy. Judy dear, this is Corinne Moore, an artist friend of mine. She comes to Hydra to paint, then goes off somewhere to sell her work and returns just as soon as she can.'

Corinne ... the girl Chris had almost married! And if he had married her then she, Judy, would have been able to marry Ronnie.

'How do you do.' Corinne extended a hand and Judy took it. 'You didn't tell me you were engaged to a babe,' she laughingly said to Chris. 'How old is this child?'

Judy stiffened and her face went white. She hadn't

66

realized she had a temper until now. However, she restrained it with admirable calm as she said with feigned innocence,

'I shall be eighteen in two months' time—so I'm not really all that young....' A subtle pause and then, slowly, 'But I expect it seems young to you, Miss Moore, for you must be nearing thirty.'

No one was more amazed at her words than Judy herself. Strictly brought up, with a strong adherence to good manners, she had never before insulted anyone, either knowingly or unknowingly. But the girl had asked for it, she told herself, watching the colour flood Corinne's cheeks. A little fearfully, Judy stole a glance at her husband. He was staring at her in astonishment, but there was a most odd light in his eye too ... as if a sudden idea had just occurred to him. He said admonishingly,

'My dear, where are your manners? Corinne is an old friend of mine, and our guest.'

But an uninvited one, said Judy to herself, wondering why she should dislike the girl on sight. She did not want to apologize, but she felt ashamed of her lapse.

'I'm sorry,' she murmured with difficulty. 'I spoke without thinking.' Not exactly a gracious apology, but it was all the girl was going to receive.

Corinne looked at her through narrowed eyes. And she seemed to be endeavouring to convey the message that Judy would be well advised not to make an enemy of her. But Judy was fast gaining confidence in herself. She was no longer the little orphan who had fallen under her grandfather's stern control; she was a wife now, a wife whose intention it was to assert herself, whether it be with her husband, or her husband's ex-girl-friends.

CHAPTER FOUR

FLORIA arrived three days later and from the first there sprung up a friendship between the two girls. They swam together in the mornings when Chris was otherwise occupied; they strolled together down to the harbour or to the beach farther along where they would swim or just sit watching the glistening blue-green sea and talking. Judy had little to tell Floria because her life had been simple. She had been sent to a private school in Kyrenia which was run by an Englishwoman but where she had learned to speak the Greek language. From there she had gone to the *gymnasium*, the Greek name for a grammar school, and lastly she had been sent by her grandfather to the school in France. A few months later she was married, and at that time she thought her life was finished, for the bottom seemed to have dropped out of her world when she realized she would never set eyes on Ronnie again. But somehow she was not nearly so heartbroken as she expected to be, nor did she dislike her husband as she had expected to dislike him. Perhaps that was because he was so docile and easily managed. She had expected to be domineered and subdued, to be a slave to her husband's fancies and whims. She had resigned herself to her husband's indifference and to his eventual infidelity, for this was the lot of the majority of the girls she knew. But she had discovered she had courage; she had also been fortunate in having Lefki for a friend, and that had made all the diifference.

'Tell about yourself now,' she urged as she and Floria sat on the beach. 'I've told you my life story in less than five minutes,' she added, laughing.

'Mine can be told in less than that, even. Like you, I attended a private school. But I wasn't fortunate enough to go to France like you. My father's old-fashioned when it comes to girls being educated. Chris went to the university in Athens. It wasn't fair.'

'Are you glad you're married?' Judy was instantly sorry she had phrased the question, for a dark, brooding expression entered Floria's eyes.

'I don't know.... I suppose Vincent is, on the whole, a good man.'

A good man? Judy frowned. Was Floria unhappy? In saying Vincent was a good man she merely followed the pattern. A wife would refer to her husband as a good man, a husband would refer to his wife as a good woman. Never a reference to the vital quality of love. It was not expected by either side.

'Vincent's coming here soon—that's what Chris said.'

Floria nodded, her brooding gaze on the sea.

'In about a week.'

'What's he like?' Judy wanted to know, drawing her knees up under her chin. Both girls were in shorts and sun-tops, and both possessed a lovely golden tan which was the envy of the tourists who flocked from the cruise ships and ferries on to the island for a couple of hours or so before boarding the ship again and making for yet another Greek island.

'Vincent?' Floria brought her gaze from the sea and turned to look at Judy. 'Small, and stout and dark——' She shrugged. 'Nothing glamorous about him like Chris. You're lucky, Judy. My brother's the handsomest man I've ever seen.' Judy said nothing. You weren't lucky if you had to marry someone you did not love—whether he happened to be handsome or not. 'He offered for you two years ago, didn't he? You'd only be fifteen?'

69

She nodded.

'Yes, I was.'

'Weren't you flattered?' The hint of envy in Floria's voice was not lost on Judy and she felt somehow that her husband's sister would rather not be married.

'I wasn't flattered, no,' she replied truthfully. 'I didn't want to be engaged at that age. My grandfather made me, though, so I had no choice.'

'You're glad now, though?' Floria gave her a curious glance before turning her face to the sea again.

'I didn't want to marry Chris,' she owned after a moment's hesitation, and her sister-in-law gave a start of amazement.

'You didn't? But why?'

Judy shrugged. She could not tell Floria that she loved someone else, so she merely said she felt she was too young to marry.

'If men can wait until they're nearly thirty, then why can't women?' she went on to add.

'I wouldn't like to wait that long.' But a small sigh left Floria's lips and again Judy felt that she would prefer not to be married. For some reason Judy said,

'You're happy with Vincent?'

A long pause and then,

'I love someone else,' admitted Floria, her voice husky and low. 'And I think he would have come to love me if only my father had not forced me into marriage with Vincent.'

'He doesn't love you at present, then?'

Floria shook her head.

'If he had loved me he'd have offered, wouldn't he?'

Judy gave a helpless little gesture with her hands.

'They offer when they don't love you—so you don't really know where you are.'

Floria smiled then, in some amusement.

70

'You sound as if you don't care very much for men.'

She did care for one man.... What was Ronnie doing now? Perhaps already he had found someone else—a girl unhampered by custom, an English girl who could marry him. Pain caught at her heart for a moment, but it was gone before she could feel any degree of pity for herself. She was being remarkably brave, she told herself. To put Ronnie from her like this was a most praiseworthy achievement.

'I don't dislike men, not really,' said Judy at last. 'It's just that I think it most unfair that they get such a better deal than women.'

'In the East they do, but not in the West. I wish I'd been born in the West.'

'It didn't do me much good——' Appalled, Judy broke off. But it was too late. Floria brought her gaze from the sea to stare at Judy incredulously.

'You sound as if you actually hate being married to my brother!' she exclaimed on an incredulous note. 'Do you dislike him?'

'No, of course not,' Judy replied hastily. 'I only meant that, in my case, being British did not mean that I could choose my own husband, as would have been the case had my parents lived and I'd been brought up in my own country.' She felt disloyal to Chris, and guilty—but why? He had no right to offer for her when she was so young.

'I should have thought you would consider Cyprus as your own country. Also, you needn't have married Chris if you really hadn't wanted to. From things you've said your grandfather was kind, and he allowed for the fact that your father was English. I met him once, remember?—and I gained the impression then that he would always consider your happiness before anything else.' Floria paused, her eyes still on Judy. 'I think you really wanted to marry Chris, because if you

71

hadn't you'd have put up a fight—and you would have won.'

The protest that rose to Judy's lips was suddenly checked. She found herself reflecting on her sister-in-law's pronouncement that she, Judy, had really wanted to marry Chris. But she hadn't, Judy told herself emphatically. Of course she hadn't wanted to marry Chris. The very idea was ridiculous, simply because it was Ronnie she had loved. Judy's brow creased in a frown. Before she had met Ronnie ... what were her feelings towards the marriage? She had been resigned, she had asserted on her grandfather's bringing the matter up...., But was it resignation? Hadn't she told Lefki—not without a hint of pride—that Chris was far more handsome than Paul? And hadn't she rather enjoyed dancing with him at Margarita's wedding? Could these things possibly mean that she had subconsciously found Chris attractive, and that was why she had never put forward any protest until she eventually realized it was Ronnie she wanted to marry?

At this point in her musings Judy's thoughts became troublesome and bewildering. Had she really been in love with Ronnie? There was no doubt at all that she had put him out of her mind with more ease than she would ever have thought possible, and on the rare occasions when he did intrude, his features were somewhat blurred and elusive. Impatient with her inability either to admit or deny the truth of Floria's assertion, Judy dismissed the matter altogether and made to change the subject, intending to ask Floria about this man whom she loved, but then she checked her words, realizing that it was not quite the thing to do. In any case, Floria spoke, asking in the most matter-of-fact way if Judy had met Corinne Moore yet.

'She's staying up at George Cozakis's place,' Floria added. 'Has a studio in the roof—an odd sort of character she is.'

'I've met her once.' Judy's tones were stiff and cold.

'I suppose you know she's in love with Chris?' Floria's tones were still matter-of-fact. So many girls had been in love with her brother.

'George said they were nearly married,' began Judy when she was interrupted by her sister-in-law.

'He exaggerates.' She stopped, puzzling Judy by the sudden flush that tinged her cheeks. But a moment later she went on, 'They were—er—more than friends, but there never was any question of marriage. If Corinne had played her cards right I do believe there would have been a chance for her, but it developed into an affair, and Chris would never marry a girl like that.'

Judy swallowed. Why should she care that Chris and Corinne had had an affair?

'You mean . . . if Corinne had not let——? What I'm trying to say is . . .' Her voice trailed away into silence and a deep flush spread over her cheeks. To her surprise Floria laughed and said with complete lack of embarrassment,

'If Corinne had not let Chris have all he wanted she might have led him very nicely into marriage, for there's no doubt that she had an enormous attraction for him—none of the others were in his favour for so long.'

A soft breeze blew across the sea, and Judy was more than a little thankful for its cooling effect on her hot face.

'How long was she—er—in his favour?' she could not help asking.

'Now let me see. . . . It's about four years since he first met her. She came here to paint, and was looking for somewhere to live. Chris had a villa by the harbour and she came up here to see if he would let it to her,

73

but it was already let on a long lease to an American family who come every summer for three months. Chris did find her a flat, however, but of course she couldn't afford to live on the island all the time and she went off to England or somewhere to find a job. When she came back the following summer the flat was let to someone else and George let her have a room in his house. She's come here quite often since then because he doesn't charge her anything, her being a friend of Chris—and Chris being a friend of George, if you know what I mean?'

'So she and Chris have been friends for about four years—on and off?' Judy waited, all cold and stiff inside at the idea that Chris should be having an affair with Corinne while engaged to Judy herself. Men were horrid creatures, she thought, and wished her new-found courage had come to her earlier so that she could have thrown him over! How surprised he would have been! And there would never have occurred that scene over her friendship with Ronnie. Just to think, Chris had told her grandfather that, had he thought she had done any real wrong, he would not be wanting to marry her. And he himself had had scores of women— and one woman in particular ... Corinne Moore.

'Yes, it's at least four years.' A small pause and then, 'She was dreadfully upset when he told her he was engaged to you——'

'He told her right away?' Judy knew he must have informed Corinne that he was engaged, because she had mentioned it herself when asking her age, but somehow Judy would not have expected him to tell the girl until just before the marriage.

'Yes, he told her as soon as he came back from Cyprus. She didn't speak to him for weeks, but then she came round again and they used to go off to Athens for week-ends.'

Judy drew a deep breath, endeavouring to release the tightness in her throat. How utterly disgusting for him to go off for week-ends—— She checked her angry thoughts. After all, such behaviour was not by any means unusual. Chris had been forced to wait two years for her and she knew full well that he would find pleasure in the meantime.

Why had he married her? Judy then asked herself. Surely, as Corinne was so attractive to him, it would have been more enjoyable to continue in that sort of relationship indefinitely. Or he could have married Corinne, even though they had been lovers. But no, Floria was right when she said Chris would never marry a woman like that. Greeks very rarely did marry their lovers; they invariably chose an innocent young girl for a wife. And what of Chris's life now? Judy knew a moment of fear. Would he return to Corinne because she, Judy, would not allow him to make love to her?

'Oh dear,' she whispered fearfully. 'Perhaps I've made a mistake.' Should she tell him she had changed her mind? Judy blushed at the idea of that. Besides, they had been married little over a week; they were still strangers, with no affection between them yet. No, she must wait a little while until they knew each other better.

On the way back they met George, walking along the quay. He smiled at the two girls and fell into step beside them.

'Two lovely girls without their men,' he said teasingly. 'I'm certainly in luck!'

Floria looked down at her feet, avoiding his gaze. Judy's eyes flickered as she watched her. Could it be that she did not like George...? Suddenly Judy recalled that blush when she spoke about him a few minutes ago on the beach, and all at once she felt that

George was the man Floria loved. Her heart went out to her and a great sigh left her lips. How sad it all was! Floria married to Vincent, whom she did not love, while here was George, so handsome and charming and gay.... But he did not appear to be in any way attracted to Floria, and it did seem that Floria had been indulging in fanciful ideas when she had said he would have come to love her had her father not forced her into marriage with Vincent.

They came to the *taverna*, set back from the harbour and shaded by trees and an abundance of hibiscus and oleanders and other exotic flowering bushes. George suggested that they have something to drink, making his way to the *taverna* even as he spoke.

They sat in the shade drinking iced orange and watching the life going on around them. Men playing cards at a nearby table, a white donkey loaded with the luggage of a young couple who had just come off the ferry from Piræus. They were coming to the island for a lengthy stay, judging by the amount of luggage they had brought with them. They looked English, or American, Judy concluded, and drew George's attention to them.

'Mr. and Mrs. Palmer, from New York City. They come every year about this time. Mr. Palmer's the principal of a college there, and his wife's a private nurse. They must get devilish high salaries in America, because they come here for about ten weeks.'

'They'd have to live at home, though,' Judy pointed out. 'And it might be much cheaper to live here than in New York City.'

'The actual living undoubtedly is,' he readily agreed. 'But what about the fares? In any case, they don't stay on Hydra all the time; they'll be tripping off to Athens or Delphi or to one or other of the islands.' They had seen him and they told the man leading the donkey to wait. 'Back again already?' said George, standing up to give Mrs. Palmer his seat. 'It seems like a couple of months ago since you were here.'

'Time goes far too quickly. No, George, we won't sit down, but thanks all the same. We want to get settled in and then we can relax and do all the things one should do on holiday.'

'You must dine with me quite soon. I'll arrange a party.'

'Thanks a lot, George; we'll look forward to that.' Mr. Palmer looked at the two girls and George made the introductions.

'Chris's new wife!' exclaimed Mrs. Palmer. 'But how nice to meet you, dear. He told us he was engaged, but that you were too young. Lucky girl! He must have loved you to wait all this time—two years or more, I guess it must have been. Well, we'll be seeing you around. Goodbye for now.' And they went on their way, to the grey house on the hillside which had been let to them regularly each summer for the past seven years.

He must have loved you. What silly things some people did say! But then Mrs. Palmer was an American, and in America they married for love.

By the end of the following week both Chris's mother and Vincent had arrived at Salaris House. Madam Voulis greeted Judy with a smile and a kiss; she fully approved her son's choice and let both Chris and Judy see it.

'You look glowing, my dear,' she declared effusively. 'Marriage agrees with you, obviously.'

That startled Judy. With uneasy reluctance she cast a glance at her husband from under her lashes. He cocked an eyebrow, but it was his rather dry expression that disconcerted her and the colour leapt to her face.

'Marriage and this lovely island,' put in Vincent, relaxing in his chair. He was dark and stout and oily. Judy glanced across at Floria, sitting upright on a high-backed chair, small and dainty and wistful. Judy thought of George and a sadness crept over her. George and Floria would have made a well-matched pair.... But what was the use of dwelling on that? Floria was married to Vincent, and there could be no other future for her but that of his wife.

'You like it here?' Madam Voulis's eyes were fixed admiringly on her daughter-in-law, taking in every lovely curve of her face and neck and shoulders. For Judy was wearing a brief sun-suit—all too revealing, she had protested when Chris had told her to put it on. He himself had bought it in Athens, where he had been for two days last week, on business. There had been a tussle over the sun-suit, and Judy had been defeated, much to her consternation, because it seemed to prove that Chris was quite able to master her if he so desired. Deeply troubled by what appeared to be a set-back, Judy had written to her friend, tentatively asking Lefki what she would have done under the circumstances.

'Yes, I like it very much,' she said in reply to Madam Voulis's question.

'Better than Cyprus?' Vincent thrust his hands deeply into his pockets and stretched his legs out in front of him.

'Naturally I like Cyprus better,' said Judy with a frown. He was slothful, she thought, and wondered if he had money of his own or whether it was Floria's dowry that kept him in idleness. His eyes were roving lasciviously over her and Judy became aware of the swift compression of her husband's lips.

'If we're not doing any more sunbathing you can go and change,' he snapped, turning to his wife. Her chin lifted at his order; he himself had made her put the suit on and he must have known that any man who happened to see her would stare. But it appeared it was only Vincent to whom he objected, and Judy could not help wondering if Chris did not altogether trust his sister's husband.

'We might go out again shortly,' she began, feeling she must make a stand. 'I'll change later——'

'You'll change now.' Slow and deliberate the words; Judy flushed because all eyes were on her. She left the room without further argument, but as she passed her husband she lifted her head and glared at him. He set his lips again, but she was gone before he could speak.

Several days passed, lazily and pleasantly, for all of them were in a holiday mood. Judy and Floria visited the Palmers one morning and they all went down to the swimming pool. George had arranged his dinner party and they were all invited, so on parting just before lunch time they said they would be meeting again that evening.

'So long, girls,' said Mrs. Palmer gaily when, on reaching a fork in the narrow twisting lane going up into the hillside, they went their separate ways. 'Be good!'

'Be good,' repeated Floria disgustedly. 'How can a girl be anything else here!'

Turning, Judy stared.

'Do you want to be anything else?' she asked with a half laugh.

'I think it would be fun to have an affair.'

'You don't!' Judy declared emphatically, shocked.

'Men have affairs, so why can't we?'

For a moment Judy said nothing. Like Floria she considered it most unfair that men could enjoy total freedom while women must carry discretion to ridiculous limits. Nevertheless, she herself had no desire to

79

indulge in an affair—no, not even with Ronnie, whom she had dearly loved.

'With women, it isn't the done thing,' answered Judy unnecessarily. 'We'd be disgraced for ever.'

'I sometimes think I wouldn't care.' They were climbing steeply, taking step after step up the lane. Houses on both sides gleamed, white and blue, while on the steps leading up to the front doors were pots of gay flowers—modest roses and carnations. And there was the more flamboyant hibiscus with its huge scarlet trumpets. These bushes grew up the sides of the houses, contrasting vividly with the brilliant whiteness of the walls. Bougainvillea sprayed the cobblestones with violet petals that came drifting down incessantly, carried by the breeze sweeping gently down from the high places. Exotic perfumes filled the air. Paradise Isle, this rock had been called, and Judy felt its romance as one would feel the romance of a promised land. Some magical power seemed suddenly to hold her poised in space, in timeless space, vast and bewildering and enticing. Something within this vast eternity of space seemed to beckon, but from what direction she did not know. She was entranced and floundering, spellbound and excited, groping and sinking all at once.

Swiftly she turned, her spine tingling.

'Chris!' she exclaimed. 'How long have you been following us?'

Falling into step beside her, he regarded her searchingly from his superior height.

'You're not overjoyed at my appearance,' he commented dryly, taking the next couple of steps in one languid stride. 'Do I intrude into maidens' secrets?'

'We were talking,' put in Floria unexpectedly, 'about the unfairness of men being able to indulge in affairs while women can't.'

Judy held her breath, peeping up at Chris in a

rather horrified sort of way. To her surprise he asked calmly,

'Does one of you desire to indulge in an affair?'

'Oh no, Chris,' returned his wife hastily. 'We were only talking about the unfairness, as Floria has just remarked.' Why was she so breathless at the sight of her husband? He had said she was not overjoyed at his appearance, and of course that was true ... and yet how must she account for the sudden jerking of her heart as she turned to find him walking there? More important, how must she account for the prior knowledge that he was near? For she did know he was near....

'Tell me honestly, Chris,' said his sister as they turned in preparation to take the last flight of steps up to the house, 'do you consider it unfair?'

'Unfair?' He transferred his gaze from his wife to his sister, giving her a mild stare. 'I don't know what you're talking about, Floria.'

'You do!' She actually stamped her foot. 'Why can't women have affairs?'

The deceptive cool disinterest vanished. Chris's dark eyes glinted.

'You talk like a baggage,' he snapped, then added, 'If the matter is so vital, then I suggest you discuss it with your husband.'

Floria bent her head, but not before Judy had noted the swiftly rising colour and the sharp catching of her lips between her teeth. It was George with whom she desired to have an affair, obviously, but it was also obvious that Floria was exceedingly afraid of her husband, for at the very mention of him just now she had seemed to tremble. She had of course started all wrong, decided Judy knowledgeably. Pity she hadn't had a friend like Lefki who would have taught her a thing or two. But of course there wasn't another like Lefki—she was unique among women in this part of the world.

On their arrival at the house Floria went inside while Chris and Judy stayed on the verandah for a few minutes while waiting for lunch to be served.

'What's all this nonsense about affairs?' Chris asked abruptly the moment they sat down. 'It's disgusting talk for two young married women!'

He sounded angry, she thought, recalling that she had seen him angry only once before—when he had tackled her about meeting Ronnie. That was more than anger, she mused, feeling again that grip on her wrist and seeing the dark fury in his eyes. He had reduced her to a jelly, so afraid of him she had been. That was before she gained courage, though. He would not be able to terrify her so easily now.

'The conversation just drifted in that direction,' she murmured after a little hesitation.

'There must have been some reason for this "drifting" as you term it.'

Was it a question? Her husband's mouth was set, his eyes narrowed and coldly metallic. This was somehow like an entirely new man, someone she did not know. She had become used to his mild tolerance alternating with indifference. He had asked her questions before, but evasion on her part had resulted in a bored dismissal of the topic and Judy had been left with the impression that he had not really been interested in receiving answers to his questions at all.

But now his attitude was demanding and stern.

'I can't think how it all began,' she said at last. 'Perhaps it was because of what Mrs. Palmer said.'

'Jean Palmer? What did she say?'

Judy gave a little shrug, feeling foolish as she answered,

'She said "be good".'

Chris stared at her, as well he might.

82

'Be more explicit,' he ordered at last. 'Why were you and Floria talking about women having affairs?'

Unable to repeat what Floria had said about thinking it would be fun to have an affair, Judy said with a tinge of apprehension,

'I don't know how to answer you, Chris. It was a—a private conversation——'

'And an incriminating one,' he broke in swiftly. 'Obviously Floria is discontented with her life——'

'Anyone would be discontented with Vincent,' Judy had flashed before she could check herself.

An arrogant gleam entered her husband's eyes. His voice was steel as he said,

'A woman should be satisfied with her husband, no matter what he's like. Has she been speaking to you about Vincent in disparaging terms?' he wanted to know after a small pause.

Vigorously she shook her head.

'No, honestly.' But although she had not lied Judy knew she had left the important thing unsaid and she felt the colour rise in her cheeks. Chris kept his gaze upon her, his unmoving countenance causing her a tinge of fear in spite of her good resolutions and firm decision not to allow him to frighten her again.

'Is Floria in love with someone?' inquired Chris at last, and Judy's eyes flew to his. This was all he required, but even as she saw perception dawn the other aspect of his words impressed itself on her mind. 'Is Floria in love with someone?' . . . not someone *else*.

'So you know she's not in love with Vincent?' she said, half hoping to divert him until the gong should call them to lunch, bringing an end to this most uncomfortable conversation.

'Of course she's not in love with Vincent. It was an arranged marriage like that of everyone else. Who is this man with whom she desires to have an affair?' he

83

demanded to know, but Judy shook her head, looking him directly in the eye this time.

'I don't know, Chris——'

'So she does want to have an affair?' he broke in, and Judy put a nervous hand to her head.

'You're tying me up in knots,' she complained. 'I shouldn't have said that. Floria's affairs are her own and she'll be so angry at my slip. Please don't tell her, or be angry with her,' she pleaded, looking at him with a troubled gaze. 'I don't know if she does want to have an affair.' She stopped, reluctant to say more because her suspicions were strong within her and should her husband persist in questioning her about this man with whom Floria was in love she might inadvertently reveal those suspicions. And that would be disastrous, for George was not only a friend of Chris but also a close business associate. 'You won't say anything to Floria?' she asked again, drawing a deep breath as the gong sounded at last.

He stood up, and with an unexpected gesture reached down and pulled Judy up beside him.

'It's not my business,' he said at length. 'Let her husband deal with the problem. He'll probably beat her——'

'Oh no!' cut in Judy, appalled at the idea. 'He wouldn't do that, surely?' She was looking up at Chris, her blue eyes scared and her lips quivering. After regarding her in silence for a moment Chris suddenly took her chin in his hand and, before she could grasp his intention, he had kissed her full on the mouth.

'Certainly he would,' he answered unemotionally, and paused a little while, again looking into her face. Could he sense the queer little rhythm of her heartbeats? she wondered, profoundly stirred because the warmth of his kiss still remained on her lips. 'Certainly he would,' repeated Chris, and then, deliberately, and very softly, 'So would any husband worth his salt ... even if his wife only looked at another man, let alone harboured thoughts of having an affair with him.' He kissed her again, possessively. She would have liked to draw away because the kiss was not at all like Ronnie's, and it scared her a little. But a warning voice told her not to draw away ... and just as Chris stopped kissing her she made the disturbing and quite incredible discovery that she would have liked to respond to his kiss, and that she felt somewhat flat because it was now too late. Her beautiful eyes were raised to his; he smiled down at her, but his eyes were metal. 'So take care,' he warned, and strode briskly away in the direction of the house.

CHAPTER FIVE

THAT evening they all set out together to go to George's party. Vincent, declaring that he could not walk so great a distance, rode on a white donkey, much to Judy's disgust, for one could never get the smell of the animal off one's clothes. Vincent did not appear to care; in any case, he had not troubled to acquire the immaculate appearance of Chris, although his pretty wife had taken great care to look her best. Judy was in lilac, with a matching ribbon in her hair; it made her look younger than her age, she knew, and when Chris shook his head, after allowing his eyes to flicker over her from head to foot, she was well aware that he was once again seeing her as a child.

To Judy's dismay Corinne Moore was invited to the dinner party—and Judy did wonder how she could have forgotten she was staying in George's house and, therefore, would naturally be his guest this evening. She looked dazzling in blue, the neck of her dress so low it left nothing to the imagination. Her dark hair shone, and it flowed in waves on to her shoulders ... the sort of hair a man would want to bury his face in, Judy admitted grudgingly. Long dark lashes threw shadows on to sun-tanned cheeks; the brown eyes were liquid and alive. No doubt about it, Corinne Moore was devastatingly attractive. And she had the assurance of a woman of the world in addition to possessing the ability to use the charms nature had so lavishly bestowed upon her.

Judy felt like a tiny star outshone by a glowing silver moon.

Corinne sat opposite to Chris at the table, which was lit with candles, the electric lights in the room having been switched off. It was a romantic atmosphere, with the soft lights and music in the background. Corinne monopolized Chris, and once or twice Judy caught George looking strangely at them and then transferring his gaze to herself. Two things Judy learned even before the meal was over: Corinne Moore was in love with Chris, and Floria definitely was in love with George. What of George's feelings for Floria? He spoke to her often, but impersonally. This was not a pointer to his feelings, decided Judy. He could scarcely be anything other than impersonal in the presence of both Floria's husband and her brother. Another thing Judy learned that night: Chris had no idea that George was the man Floria loved.

Vincent talked a good deal to Judy, and always she was uncomfortably aware of what could only be described as a leering gaze fixed on her the whole time. And when, the meal over, they all went out on to the softly lighted patio, Vincent somehow managed to seat himself beside his sister-in-law. His arms slid across the top of her chair and then dropped on to her shoulder. She looked round for her husband and discovered that he was missing. And so was Corinne ... they were at the far end of the patio, she presently discovered, practically hidden by the vines and the oleander bushes. The temper Judy had discovered she possessed suddenly flared, but she had of course to control it, there being no one on whom she could vent it. But wait until she was home again ... and alone with her husband!

'What are you drinking, Judy?' George's voice cut into her angry musings and she managed to smile. She told him what she wanted and he poured it for her, clinking his own glass against hers a moment later and sitting down at the other side of her. The night was warm and sultry, the air filled with heady perfumes and the sound of crickets and the occasional sheep bell or bray of a donkey on the lonely hillside. 'Just look at the lights of that ship out there——' George pointed seawards to where the lights of a pleasure cruiser gleamed above the horizon. 'It's probably one of ours.'

'Will it be?' Judy edged forward on her seat, trying to free herself from the clammy touch of Vincent's hand on her shoulder.

George nodded.

'Could be; we have a fleet of pleasure ships all over the seas round here at present.'

'There's a new one being launched, I heard you telling Chris?'

'That's right. She's a beauty——' He broke off, and then, as if making a decision, 'Would you like to see the plan of the *Andromeda*?' he asked eagerly. 'I don't suppose Chris has shown it to you; he isn't that interested, but I am. You see, I've not been with the firm that long. Do you want to see the plan?' he asked again.

She did, if only to get away from Vincent.

'Now where are you off to?' asked Jean Palmer as Judy and George rose from their chairs. Jean spoke banteringly, but she was a loud-voiced woman and her words carried to the two at the far end of the patio. Judy was conscious of her husband's attention being diverted from his glamorous companion to herself, but she was unable to read his expression owing to the distance and the foliage. 'This place is far too romantic,' Jean was saying, while her husband laughed loudly. 'You'll be getting up to something out there in the moonlit garden.'

George laughed; Floria, who had been deep in conversation with her mother, glanced up quickly on hearing Jean's question and her eyes rested first on George and then on Judy.

'We're not going into the garden,' George informed Jean. 'We're going into the house to see——'

'That's worse,' put in Keith Palmer. 'George, I know you of old. You want watching! Chris, what are you doing allowing your new wife to go off in the dark with your best friend?' It was all very lighthearted, but suddenly a tenseness enveloped them all except the Palmers, who sat there laughing and uttering further teasing remarks to no one in particular.

'Come on,' said George, rather sharply. 'Take no notice of these two!' And when they had entered the house and he had switched on the light in his study he added, 'That was in extremely bad taste.'

'They were only joking.'

'Obviously—but talk like that can cause trouble.'

'Trouble?' She went over to the massive desk and stood looking across the room at him. 'What do you mean, George?'

Colour had entered his face; he seemed unable to supply an answer, but Judy wanted one and she repeated her question.

'Remarks like that put odd thoughts into people's minds,' he said after a long and silent pause.

'What kind of odd thoughts? And who are the people to whom you refer?'

'Oh ... let it drop,' he returned, again with a sharp edge to his voice. And then he added, on noting Judy's expression, 'I'm sorry. That was downright rude of me.' His nerves seemed to be on edge and her eyes glinted perceptively. He had been thinking of Floria.... And that could only mean that he cared for her.

What a damnable situation. George and Floria in love—and Floria married to that horrid Vincent, married to him by the order of her father. Her father.... What was he like? No one ever mentioned him, and all

89

at once it struck Judy that this unknown man was her father-in-law. Did he know he had a new relative? It was unlikely—unless Chris had written to him. He lived in Sparta, that much Judy did know, for her grandfather had mentioned it once.

'Is that the plan?' asked Judy, pointing to the wall, and anxious to put George at his ease because at the moment he was looking extremely apologetic and uncomfortable.

'No, I have it here.' Opening a drawer in his desk, he withdrew the rolled-up plan. Together they spread it out on the desk and leant over it. The various decks were described to Judy, and George pointed out the two swimming pools and the sports deck.

'There are two night clubs, a theatre—that's here,' he added, pointing to it. 'There's a nursery, and a playroom for the children. And the cabins are just marvellous. I must go to Venice and see it set sail on its first voyage,' he said with ever-increasing enthusiasm. 'I only wish I could take the cruise.'

'It's certainly a beautiful ship.' Judy spent some silent minutes looking at the plan. The *Andromeda* must surely be one of the most luxurious cruise ships sailing the Mediterranean. 'I asked Chris to take me on the cruise,' she told George. 'It calls at Egypt—at Alexandria—and I've always wanted to go there. I want to see the Pyramids and the Sphinx. But Chris didn't reach any decision,' she added.

'You mean he was considering going?' asked George in surprise.

'Not really. I was asking Chris about the cruise, but before we could discuss it properly Corinne came and interrupted us. I mentioned it again a few days later, but Chris was busy and wouldn't listen. I never mentioned it again because I thought it would be too late. It sails next week, doesn't it?'

'That's right—on Sunday from Venice, as I said.' He paused in thought. 'It would be a wonderful trip for you, Judy.' He smiled at her and added, 'You haven't had a honeymoon, have you? There might be a cabin vacant—I could find out—and if so Chris might take you.'

A cabin.... Softly the colour fused her cheeks. On asking Chris to take her she had concluded that they would have separate cabins. But then Chris had murmured that one subtle word 'together' and she had suddenly become guarded. However, even then she had not been unduly worried. She had told him right at the start that they must keep company and get to know each other better before she allowed him to be her real husband. Her word was still law about that and Chris was apparently fully resigned to this fact.

George was poring over the plan again, pointing out things he had missed, but Judy's thoughts were now entirely on her husband. Were they getting to know one another better? Chris was so aloof and more often than not quite unapproachable. Sometimes it would seem that he did not have the least desire to know her better, and this was most odd indeed, seeing that he had married her for desire alone and the sooner they did get to know one another the sooner his desire would be fulfilled. Judy reached the conclusion that there was something inexplicable about the whole aspect of their relationship and wondered why it had not struck her before now.

It would almost seem that, having married her, he had then decided he did not really want her after all. Could that be the reason why Chris had appeared to bow so meekly to her will? Could it be that she had been giving herself a pat on the back for nothing?— that she was not being clever at man-management at all, but that she had appeared to succeed simply because Chris no longer desired her? Certainly she had many times pondered over this meekness of his, for undoubtedly he was a man of strong personality, and she was sure that had he the mind he could bend her to his will, no matter what Lefki said about all men being the same.

A tight little lump gathered in Judy's throat and she suddenly wanted to cry. If all her plans had gone wrong—and she now felt sure they had—then how could their marriage succeed? She had certainly wanted it to succeed, stoically making herself forget Ronnie, whom she had loved to desperation, and waiting for the time when some affection would grow up between Chris and herself so that they could be happy together, like Lefki and Paul. Yes, that was what Judy had been aiming for—a marriage as successful as her friend's, where she herself would be her husband's equal and mutual respect would play its all-important part in their relationship. Anger against her husband rose up to take the place of her desolation. He had no right to marry her and then not want her! That she was being somewhat illogical did not strike her as she continued silently to condemn him. He should have left her alone to marry the man she loved; he should have stayed with Corinne—— Corinne! So *that* was why he did not want his wife. Judy had already wondered if he would return to Corinne.

'Oh . . .' she breathed. 'I hate him!'

'What did you say?' George looked up from his concentrated perusal of the plan. Judy flushed a deep rosy red. She had forgotten all about George.

'Nothing,' she answered, feeling extremely foolish even though it was plain from her companion's expression that he had not heard her exact words. 'I was thinking aloud.'

'Obviously you were thinking aloud.' He straightened up and stared at her flushed face; Judy lowered her lashes because of the brightness of her eyes. But the tears were pricking her lids and she failed to hold them back. George just stood there, consternation spreading over his handsome face as she wept as if her heart would break. And then he came to life and took her gently in his arms so that she had the comfort of a shoulder to weep upon.

'Judy, whatever is the matter?' he asked perturbedly. 'Why are you crying like this?' His tones were gruff and hesitant; he was disconcerted, not knowing how to deal with the situation.

And Judy did not know how to answer, because she was not sure as to the real reason for her tears. Perhaps it was because of Ronnie, or simply that she was a little tired.... Judy would never own even to herself that her unhappiness stemmed from the discovery she had just made—that her husband no longer wanted her, but chose to find pleasure with Corinne instead.

George was giving her his handkerchief, and holding her away from him, gazing interrogatingly at her. What must she say to him? Her eyes fell on the plan....

'It's because I want to go on the cruise,' she said, grabbing the handkerchief and pressing it to her eyes, more to hide their expression than to dry her tears. 'And—and Chris won't take me.'

'He's a busy man, Judy——'

'He's on holiday now, and will be for the whole of the summer. He could take me.'

'Yes ... I suppose so, but——'

'What,' rasped a voice from the doorway, 'is going on here?'

'Chris!' Judy leapt away from George and pushed the handkerchief into her eyes again. 'We—we were looking at the plan of the *Andromeda*.'

His level gaze rested on her tear-stained face; she

93

noted the slight movement of a muscle in his neck and wondered fearfully if anger had caused it.

'Looking at a plan of the ship, were you?' He directed the question at George, from whom he appeared to expect an explanation.

'That was the reason we came in here,' returned George, looking at Chris with an odd expression. 'I wanted to show the plan to Judy.'

'I see. And do you have to hold her in your arms in order to show her the plan?' A knife edge to his voice, dark fury glinting in his eyes. Judy looked apprehensively at him and then swiftly lowered her head.

'Chris,' said George, still eyeing his friend with that odd expression, 'don't get anything wrong. Judy was suddenly unhappy and I comforted her. It was an automatic gesture, I assure you.' The sincerity of his manner and the frankness of his gaze as he spoke to Chris, these were sufficiently impressive and Judy was relieved to see her husband's face begin to clear. But the movement in his throat continued and she watched it, fascinated and puzzled.

'I think,' said Chris abruptly, 'that I'd better take you home.' He turned to George. 'You'll excuse us?'

'Certainly.' A small pause and then, 'You know why Judy's unhappy? You heard?'

'I heard. Judy, go and collect your handbag, and everything else you left out there.' His curt order was obeyed without hesitation. Chris requested his friend to make their apologies, saying his wife was unwell, and very soon he and Judy were walking home in silence, each lost in thought.

Why had he left Corinne and come to find her? Judy asked herself. The feasible explanation was that he was annoyed at the remarks of the Palmers and this had led to pique that his wife should have gone off with George. But if Chris could occupy himself with

Corinne why shouldn't she, Judy, have similar freedom to occupy herself with George? This equality was what she was fighting for—and she was still determined to fight for equality even though all her plans for a happy marriage had crashed about her ears during those past few moments of enlightenment.

However, the more Judy dwelt on this feasible explanation the less it satisfied her, simply because it did not include the reason for Chris's decision to leave the party and take her home. She had been distressed and the natural thing for any husband would be to suggest that she go home, and that he accompany her—but that would be the situation only where a husband was concerned for his wife, and Chris was by no means concerned for his wife. In fact, for most of the evening he had been concerned with Corinne, and his action in deserting her, as it were, did not fit into Judy's neat little pattern at all, and once again she felt there was something inexplicable about Chris's attitude towards herself.

What were his own thoughts? she wondered, for he was so quiet—and sort of brooding. Was he thinking about the scene he had recently interrupted? Why hadn't he been angry about that? He had certainly been angry over Ronnie, she recalled with a slight shudder. Yet he had not believed her guilty of any real wrong—and he obviously did not take any great exception to the fact of her being in George's arms. Yes, .there was indeed something inexplicable in her husband's attitude towards her, and suddenly she felt full, and choking inside, and a warmth spread through her because he trusted her.

She cast him an upward slanting look which brought a cool inscrutable response as Chris took his eyes off the bare rocky mass ahead, Mount Prophet Ilias, silhouetted against the dark mysterious reaches of an Eastern sky. She frowned, disliking intensely the look he gave her. It took him out of her world and placed him in some remote domain of his own, some lofty celestial realm where mere mortals such as she dare not tread. She had to break the silence, and a hint of irascibility edged her voice because there was something tantalizing about him ... and something profoundly disturbing.

'I'm sorry you had to come away from George's.' She didn't mean George, of course; she meant Corinne. Moreover, she wasn't sorry at all, on the contrary, she was glad that Corinne was now forced to make do with less attentive company, having been deprived of that of her lover.

'I didn't have to come away from George's,' was his mild rejoinder. He began walking more quickly, his long strides taking each step with ease as it came along. Judy had to trot; he must be aware of this, she thought, but it troubled him not at all.

'You had to take me home.' Her voice was sharp. She desired more than anything to lose her temper with him, but she was a trifle scared. He had treated that little scene all too calmly, she decided on recalling his barbed threat of what would happen to her if she only so much as looked at another man.

Dark frown lines creased her brow. Why should she allow herself to be scared? If Lefki had allowed herself to be scared she would never have won her fight for equality.

'I didn't have to take you home. I chose to do so.'

'Why?'

He subjected her to a frowning stare and said,

'What do you mean, why?'

She remembered her earlier anger at the attention he was extending to Corinne. She had determined to have it out with him about that and now she knew a sense of elation as her temper rose above her fear.

'Surely you would have preferred to stay with Corinne!'

To her surprise his lips twitched; he glanced perceptively at her. He appeared to be extraordinarily satisfied about something.

'So that troubled you, did it?' he commented with a dawning smile. 'Corinne is an old friend of mine, as you already know. I haven't seen her for a couple of months or so and therefore we were each catching up on the other's news.' His words were not an apology, but they *were* an explanation. She found it odd that he should take the trouble to offer her one and quite suddenly perceived that it was done deliberately.

He wanted to talk about Corinne! He might almost be trying to make her jealous, she thought, then dismissed the idea as ridiculous.

'I wasn't in the least troubled that you sat so long with Corinne,' she denied, but tartly. And with a daring born of her newly acquired courage she added, 'For my part, I was perfectly happy with George.'

Again that glance of perception, and accompanied by a deepening of his smile. What an enigma he was! She had expected anger, and another threat.... Another threat? Judy gasped, stunned by the revelation that she was thoroughly disappointed at not being threatened. What did it mean? She shook her head, bewildered. She had no wish to be threatened, she told herself crossly. She was striving for freedom, for equality—so how could she possibly want to be threatened?

'Happy, were you?' Amusement fringed his voice. 'Do you normally weep when you're happy?'

Her mouth compressed.

'I wanted to go on that cruise,' she said peevishly.

'So I believe,' yawned Chris. 'But why were you crying?'

'Because I wanted to go on the cruise. Why else should I be crying?' she added defiantly.

'That is what I'm trying to discover.'

Judy fell silent, disconcerted. She should have known he would not accept that as a reason for her tears; it was totally unconvincing. But to her surprise and relief he did not press her for a more likely explanation and they continued on their way to the house without another word passing between them. It was still early. The air was inexpressibly soft and clear, drenched with the timeless fragrance of oleanders growing along the dry river bed high on the hillside. On reaching the house Chris sat down in a low armchair on the patio. Automatically taking possession of the chair opposite to him, Judy picked up a magazine from the table and began idly to flick the pages, acutely aware of her husband's dark eyes fixed interestedly upon her.

'Do you really want to go on that cruise?' Reaching up, he snapped on the light. It was a soft amber, subdued and flattering to his wife's colouring and the burnished gold of her hair. She looked up; the pages of the book fluttered from her fingers as she stared at him, startled and disbelieving.

'You'll take me?' she quivered, conscious of the wild beating of her heart. Was it elation, because Chris was weakening and allowing her to have her own way? He was even willing to leave Corinne, it seemed, a circumstance which was puzzling in the extreme. 'Yes, indeed. I do want to go.'

Thoughtfully Chris watched her, leaning back in his chair, and Judy waited a little breathlessly for his decision.

'I'll find out tomorrow if there's any accommodation. There might not be, so don't built up your hopes.'

She wondered about the accommodation. But hadn't

she made her sentiments absolutely clear? And had not Chris meekly bowed to her will? Nevertheless, recalling again his subtle, softly spoken word 'together?' she found herself saying,

'Suppose they don't have enough cabins?'

'Enough?' He quirked an eyebrow and she blushed at the action. 'Do you mean two?' She could only nod and he said mockingly, 'So I must turn it down if there happens to be only one?'

She hesitated. From a small girl she had craved to visit Egypt.

'Perhaps—perhaps——' Judy coughed to clear her throat. 'What I mean to say is, it would be a shame if we had to miss the opportunity of going to Egypt simply because there was only one cabin.' Again she cleared her throat, disconcerted by his quizzical gaze. 'There might be two bunks in the cabin—if there happens to be only one cabin available, that is.' There were private bathrooms with many of the cabins, she recalled. The bathroom could serve as a dressing-room. She visualized no problems should they have to share a cabin.

Chris was leaning back in his chair, his long lean fingers tapping the arms as he watched Judy, his gaze still quizzical, yet narrowed with a degree of impatience.

'Your desire for a glimpse of Egypt is stronger than your fear of your husband, apparently,' was his sardonic comment at last.

Her chin lifted.

'Fear? I'm not afraid of you,' she swiftly let him know, wondering how he had managed to get an idea like that. She was standing up to him very well, and he knew it. To her surprise he laughed as if at some private joke of his own.

'Aren't you, Judy?' he inquired, rather gently, and her eyes flew to his.

'You know very well I'm not,' she returned with magnificent bravado, and then, with the uncomfortable conviction that he was enjoying himself at her expense, she changed the subject, reverting to the possibility of their taking the cruise. 'Do you think there will be some accommodation available?'

'I've just said, my dear, that I'll find out tomorrow.' Rising from his chair, he reached out and also brought Judy to her feet, his hold gentle on her wrist. 'I said it was going to be delightful being married to you—and I'm still of the same mind.' He was towering above her; she wondered why she trembled so and why she liked the nearness of him and the look in his eye and the way his hair came low on his forehead to form the 'V' of a widow's peak. And she did wonder too if he were aware of how profoundly she was affected by these things. All around them stillness hung in the perfumed air; they were enveloped in that magical, mothy darkness of a Grecian night. From the black mysterious hillside floated the tinkling sweetness of the sheep bells, and across the purple vault of the sky a star raced towards the dim horizon and was lost. Judy stirred beside her husband, caught in a web of timeless unreality, and completely detached from the world. There was no one in all this vast realm except her husband and herself. In the sweet intimacy of the moment he bent his head and kissed her, with gentle possessiveness and then with ardour, unfanned, restrained, but requiring little to coax it into an all-consuming flame. Of this Judy was sublimely unaware as she accepted his kiss, too shy and unsure of herself to respond. But she was warmed by his declaration that it was going to be delightful being married to her, for it revealed the fact that whatever he felt for Corinne it was not love. Judy's hopes for the future had been crushed earlier in the evening, but now they rose again. If she and Chris could go on that cruise together then they would surely get to know one another better, and that friendly relationship would develop into the affection which Judy desired to be established before she agreed to becoming a real wife to Chris.

And if affection did come to exist between Judy and her husband what price Corinne's designs then? A pleasant feeling of elation swept over Judy as, in thought, she had already ousted Corinne and taken her place in Chris's affections.

Chris had his cheek against Judy's hair, and then she felt the hardness of his lips on her temple. But when they found her mouth again they were soft and tender —and persuasive. She responded and felt a quiver run through him. Was it desire—or triumph? She drew away with more haste than diplomacy and half expected a quality of anger to replace the softness that had touched his face. Instead, he merely shook his head with the smallest hint of asperity and murmured across the space now dividing them,

'You're a tantalizing creature, Judy, and I only hope my patience lasts out.' He shook his head, as if he doubted that it would, and with a sudden frown Judy asked him what he meant. His eyes opened wide at this naïveté, but he saw at once that it was genuine and a softness marked his features again. 'Forget it, child. Just carry on as you are—you're doing very well,' he added with a smile of amusement not untinged with resignation.

Swiftly she glanced across at him, for in a flash of memory she recalled her slight suspicion that Chris had guessed what she was about. She said, taking a step towards him,

'Chris, why are you taking me to Egypt? Is it because

I wanted to go?'

His lips twitched, but his expression was wooden and his voice toneless as he answered,

'But of course. Why else?'

'You mean—that you've let me have my own way?'

'Isn't it apparent that I've let you have your own way?'

She frowned suspiciously at him. His dark face was still wooden.

'In England women have their own way. They're equals with their husbands.' That seemed irrelevant once it had been uttered, but Chris did not appear to notice.

'So I understand,' he returned with dry amusement.

Her suspicions remained. She wished she could understand this husband of hers. In appearance he was so superior and arrogant, and he was so muscular and strong. Surely he was aware that he could master her if he chose ... and yet he meekly accepted her decision over their marriage, and he had by his own admission let her have her own way regarding the projected cruise. It must be as Lefki said, men would capitulate rather than argue—if they were handled correctly, that was.

To her delight Chris managed to get two luxury cabins on the *Andromeda*, and there followed a flurry of preparation on Judy's part because the ship was sailing in five days' time. Floria's face took on an animated expression when Judy informed her that she and Chris were going on the cruise, and Judy regarded her with extreme puzzlement.

The reason for Floria's excitement was conveyed to Judy the same evening when, after dinner, when the family were sitting out as usual on the patio, Floria said to her brother,

'Can I come and see you off? I've always wanted to

see Venice.'

Chris frowned and directed his gaze to Floria's husband, slouched in a chair with a cigarette dangling between his lips and a string of worry beads clicking between his fingers. Vincent was going to Athens for a week, ostensibly on business, but Floria had recently confided to Judy that he had a woman friend there, an Englishwoman with whom he had been keeping company long before his marriage to Floria.

'I don't mind,' said Vincent in reply to his brother-in-law's unspoken question. 'I shan't be here anyway.'

'But she can't come back on her own.' Chris shook his head. 'No, Floria, it's impossible.'

Floria moistened her lips.

'George said something about going to see the *Andromeda* launched,' she remarked with a casualness that brought a tiny gasp of admiration from Judy, who by this time had the complete picture before her eyes. Floria could not have gone to Venice with George, but she could go with her brother and his wife. And as George would be returning there was no reason why Floria should not return with him.

'So he did.' Chris was thoughtful, considering, and Judy held her breath, saying a little prayer for her sister-in-law, yet wondering if the trip would eventually bring Floria more pain than pleasure. The Greek girl waited, tensed and pale, for her brother's verdict. Madam Voulis was also waiting, a slight frown between her eyes. Clearly she did not like the idea of Floria's going to Venice without her husband, but she voiced no protest, leaving the matter entirely to her son who, after what both to Judy and Floria seemed an eternity, said he would make up his mind after discussing the matter with George.

Judy, watching Floria, saw her face become even more pale and tensed. She was afraid her brother, after this consultation with George, would suspect the truth. But Judy had more faith in George than did Floria. She knew instinctively that he would successfully hide the truth from his friend. And he did. The following day Chris consented to Floria's accompanying Judy and himself to Venice, and later, when George dropped in for a drink, it was decided that the four of them should go to Venice on the day prior to the sailing.

'Seems a pity to go all that way and not even see the place,' commented George. 'I know you've been there, many times,' he went on to add, looking at Chris. 'But Judy hasn't and neither has Floria. If we go the day before we'll have a full twenty-four hours there, because embarkation isn't till five in the evening.'

'You're absolutely sure there's a flight back to Athens on the evening we sail?' inquired Chris of George.

He nodded.

'Yes, I'm quite sure, but, as I said, we'll have to stay overnight in Athens.'

'With your parents, you said? They can accommodate Floria?'

'Of course. Mother will be delighted to have the company.' He looked straight at Chris, and Judy glanced at Floria. The Greek girl was inexpressibly happy as she gazed back at her sister-in-law. Happy and innocent. In spite of what she had said about desiring to have an affair she *was* staying with George's parents.

CHAPTER SIX

THEY arrived in Venice at six in the evening and as they expected they had difficulty in obtaining rooms, it being the height of the season. No mention had previously been made between Judy and Chris regarding their accommodation in Venice, but Judy had somehow felt Chris would arrange for them to have separate rooms without the other two being aware of this.

However, when finally they did get fixed up, at one of the luxury hotels close to the Piazza San Marco, two rooms only were procurable. Chris came from the reception desk and glanced at his wife with a hint of mocking amusement as he said,

'Two rooms only, so you and Floria will have to share one, and George and I the other.'

'Oh,' said George, his eyes twinkling as he glanced from Chris to Judy and back again, 'what a shame. Only just married and separated so soon. Shall we try somewhere else?'

Judy flushed and lowered her head. Chris merely remarked that it was not important for one night and they were then shown up to their rooms. After dining at the hotel they went out into the *piazza*—the famous St. Mark's Square—and sat over cups of Venetian coffee and listened to the orchestra playing nostalgic, haunting music, while through the world's most glittering square sauntered a cosmopolitan crowd of tourists and natives. Cameras clicked at San Marco—surely the most photographed cathedral church in the world. Necks were craned as bedazzled eyes took in the spectacle of golden domes and crosses and the incredible campanile over three hundred feet high. The pavement of the square was of marble and trachyte; there were glittering mosaics and benches of pink marble. Over the whole magnificent square there was an atmosphere of gaiety and abandon; Judy was enthralled, her eyes shining like stars, her mouth slightly open as if she were breathing one long uninterrupted 'oh' of wonder and disbelief. Floria too was equally impressed. She had led an even more sheltered life than Judy, for she had never been out of her own country until now. Her pretty face glowed and, glancing at her, Judy surmised that this was the happiest occasion in the whole of Floria's life.

She and George were very discreet and Chris, sharp as he was, had no inkling of what went on beneath the surface. But Judy sensed the deep love which existed between these two and her heart ached for them. Her sadness clouded her eyes momentarily and, seeing this, her husband frowned and demanded to know what was wrong.

'Wrong?' Judy blinked at him uncomprehendingly.

'A moment ago you looked as if you were on top of the world, but now you appear to be in the depths of despair. What are you thinking about?'

Inadvertently she glanced from Floria to George and then with the swiftness of fear lest she had given something away she dropped her eyes.

'Nothing in particular,' she replied, and then added, in order to change the subject, 'This is a wonderful city, and I think I'm very lucky indeed to be here. It was kind of you to agree to take me on the cruise.'

'Kind?' He raised his brows. 'Did I have any option but to agree to take you on the cruise?'

Both George and Floria looked sharply at him. Their action set Judy thinking, for it clearly betrayed astonishment that Chris should make such an admission as that.

'Surely you're not saying Judy bullied you into taking her?' George spoke at last, his words accompanied by a half laugh of disbelief.

Chris answered without much expression,

'That, George, is exactly what I am saying.'

Floria actually gasped, then treated her sister-in-law to a look of profound admiration. For her part, Judy remained thoughtful, one half of her jubilant at her success, while the other half warned her that all was not as it appeared on the surface. She looked at Chris; he was intent on the music, tapping his fingers rhythmically on the table, apparently oblivious of anything but the melody, which was a waltz, romantic and slow. Suddenly aware of her gaze fixed upon him, he turned his head; a smile hovered on his lips for a space before he lost interest in her again.

'Well,' said George on recovering from the shock his friend's words had given him, 'I must congratulate you, Judy. Chris is the last man from whom I'd have expected an admission like that. Aren't you proud of yourself?'

Judy glanced uncertainly at Chris. He appeared not to have heard George's comments, because he was now humming the tune to himself.

'Yes,' she answered, but rather hesitantly, one eye still on her husband. 'I s-suppose I am proud of—of myself.' But she frowned in thought. She had certainly not bullied her husband—but she had been a trifle peevish and defiant, she recollected, insisting her tears were shed solely because she wanted so desperately to go on the cruise. But then Chris had expressed his disbelief, not in so many words, it was true, but his doubts were evident for all that. Still, in the end he had told her quite frankly that they were going on the cruise simply because he was letting her have her own way.

And suddenly Judy was swelling with triumph—quite forgetting that other half of her that had only moments ago warned that all was not as it appeared on the surface.

A short while later they left the café and sauntered along the arcades where the shops displayed fascinating glassware from Murano and beautiful lace from Burano and of course the lovely knitwear that always seemed to surpass any other in design, if not always in quality.

The romance of the famous city was impossible to ignore and as they strolled along the sides of the square Judy experienced a sense of nearness to her husband and it seemed quite natural that he should slip an arm round her shoulders and keep it there. Window-gazing, they stopped now and then to stare, and Judy would twist round, in her enthusiasm drawing Chris's attention to something, and she would find herself close against him, with her fair head touching his shoulder. Once, he kissed the hairline on her temple and she blushed rosily and her lips quivered in an adorable smile as she looked up into his dark face.

Meanwhile, George and Floria had wandered on ahead, alone for a few precious moments, avidly grasping what fate so grudgingly doled out, and storing these treasures in the place lovers keep for such things. Judy watched them, walking with a space between them while yearning to be close.

The next day they all left the hotel together to explore the city and it was natural that they should begin with St. Mark's, the fantastically beautiful church with its different styles of architecture and its fabulous treasures, many of which were taken as loot from Constantinople, while its marbles and golden mosaics often dated from as far back as the thirteenth century.

The exploration of the church took two hours, but

they could have stayed all day and not seen everything as they would have liked to see it. When they came out into the brilliant sunshine again Floria said she wanted to see the Doge's Palace, and then it was that the idea suddenly came to Judy. George had mentioned that Chris had been to Venice many times, so it was reasonable to assume he had been into the Doge's Palace.

'I feel like being outside,' she said, smiling at them in turn before her eyes settled on Chris's face. 'Do you mind very much if we don't go? Floria and George can go, of course,' she added, hoping she sounded as casual as she intended to do.

Floria looked at the ground; George did not bat an eyelid as he said,

'Are you sure, Judy? Aren't you keen to go into the Palace?'

She shook her head.

'We've been in the church all this time and I would prefer to be outside for a while. Do you mind?' she inquired again of her husband.

'As a matter of fact I also prefer to be outside, but——' He glanced apologetically at George. 'It's not very sociable of us to leave you and Floria——'

'Nonsense. We'll wander round on our own and then meet you somewhere for lunch—if that's all right with you?' His ready smile appeared; Judy smiled in response and assured him the arrangements suited her admirably, but glanced again at Chris. He nodded and they went their separate ways, George and Floria to the Palace and Judy and Chris to wander at random down the back streets, along some of the smaller canals, before finding themselves once more in the vicinity of the Piazza San Marco. They stood on a bridge and looked along the canal to the famous Bridge of Sighs; they were two among hundreds of holidaymakers and yet

Judy experienced again that sense of detachment from the world, of being alone with her husband. It was a magical, exciting sensation; she was gripped by a force she could neither understand nor control, yet a moment later she was floating through some heady atmosphere where, touched by the gentle breath of dawn, she stirred ... and awoke. Bewildered and unsure of herself, she turned, looking up at Chris as if she were seeing him for the first time. He smiled at her, but then, noting her expression, his smile faded and he looked questioningly at her.

'Little one, what is it?' She just shook her head, continuing to stare at him. A soft laugh broke from his lips. 'If you look at me like that another second, I shall be forced to kiss you.'

Colour rushed to her cheeks as she glanced away, down the canal again to the famous bridge. On the canal, boats were passing to and fro, carrying goods, not people.

'I'd like to—to sail in a gondola,' she stammered. 'On the—on the Grand Canal.'

He frowned at her, half in perplexity, half in amusement.

'Whatever you wish,' he returned obligingly, but went on to add, 'We'll have to leave it until after lunch, though, because we haven't time now. We're meeting Floria and George in just over half an hour.'

'Yes, of course we are. Can we go later, then?'

He nodded.

'We can all go together.'

'I expect you've been before—many times?'

'Not many times. Once in a gondola is usually enough.' They were standing very close, hemmed in by people. 'It's a novelty; once you've done it you're satisfied.'

'Perhaps you'd be bored, then?'

'Not at all. Besides, I'm here to oblige you, my dear.'

Her eyes gleamed suspiciously, but Chris was smiling at her and the idea that his voice was tinged with amusement was swiftly dispelled.

'Shall we go?' she suggested after a while. 'It's becoming rather a crush here.' She still knew the stirrings of an emotion that had hitherto lain dormant; she quivered as Chris took her arm and tucked it into his. They strolled on to the Rialto Bridge and Chris had to draw her attention to the glittering shops along the roadway, for she was in a world outside such mundane things.

They stopped under a central high arch and gazed along the world's most splendid highway, the Grand Canal, to the Palladian palaces and Gothic mansions, one-time homes of wealthy merchants but now used for other purposes like municipal offices and art galleries.

The bridge led to the Rialto markets. Chris stopped at a fruit stall and bought some enormous peaches.

'For you to eat on the gondola,' he laughed, swing the bag in one hand and taking Judy's arm with the other.

Floria and George were awaiting them when they arrived at the appointed meeting place and after finding a suitable restaurant they went in and had lunch. Several times during the meal Judy cast Floria a glance from under her lashes, but nothing was to be read in the Greek girl's face. George was his customary jovial self and Judy could not help admiring them both for their excellent acting.

Chris told them of Judy's suggestion that they hire a gondola and take a trip along the Grand Canal; the others were quite agreeable, and after leaving the gondola station near the Piazza San Marco they were soon travelling along an incredible waterway strewn on both sides with some of the most magnificent Renaissance architecture in the world. Palace after palace glided away behind them as even more magnificent residences took their place.

Judy brought her eyes from the splendour around her as she felt her husband's amused gaze fixed upon her.

'I'm so confused,' she laughed. 'I don't know which side to look.'

'That's how I am,' Floria put in. 'I'm so afraid of missing something.'

'You're bound to miss something,' said George. 'One could travel along here a hundred times and still miss something.'

They had passed under the Rialto Bridge by this time. The Canal pulsated with life; gondolas glided by carrying their wide-eyed tourists and rather bored gondoliers; *vaporetti* and *motoscafi* chugged along at a less leisurely pace, stopping at every station to allow their passengers to surge out, jamming one another with total disregard for etiquette, and with a haste that could be likened to a crowd fleeing from a burning building.

'What about that for magnificence?' exclaimed George all at once. 'The builders of these palaces must have been millionaires!'

They were passing the Ca' d'Oro, or House of Gold, a perfect example of the way in which the wealthy merchants of Venice displayed their opulent and extravagant tastes. Originally, gold decorations had been lavishly splashed all over the peerless façade. Colour was also used unsparingly, but although the building was Gothic in character it possessed a sumptuousness which seemed to brand it oriental.

Both girls gasped in wonderment as the architectural pageant unfolded before them. There was the more simple Renaissance Palazzo Fontana, and the Palazzo Corner del Regina; there was the magnificent Palazzo Pesara and the elaborate white baroque façade of the Church of San Stae.

'It wasn't long enough,' sighed Floria as the trip came to an end. 'I wish I could come here for a holiday.' A swift glance at George and then a lowering of her eyes. Not difficult to read her thoughts, Judy decided. Venice would be a wonderful place to come to with George. . . .

A sigh escaped Judy and she wondered again what Floria's father was like. No one had yet mentioned him; he appeared to be an outcast whom not one of his family had the least desire to see. He had made Floria marry Vincent, though, so he still maintained certain rights and authority.

'You might come for a holiday some time in the future,' George was saying in a rather gentle tone. Chris looked at him and said,

'It's most unlikely; Vincent isn't the man to take his wife travelling.'

Floria's lashes came down and something made Judy say,

'Chris and I might come one day, and then you can come with us, Floria.'

Judy received a mild stare from her husband, who made no comment on what she had just said.

'Have we time for some tea?' George wanted to know, breaking into the tense little silence that had for some reason descended on them all.

Chris glanced at his watch and nodded. They made their way to a café in one of the arcades in the Piazza where they had afternoon tea and listened to the lilting strains of the orchestra. People were milling about in their hundreds; it was a fantastic scene of colour and splendour and gaiety enacted under the dazzling blue of a cloudless Venetian sky.

And then it was time for them to return to the hotel to collect the luggage. Floria and George were going aboard with Judy and Chris, but on reaching the quay they all stood looking up at the graceful *Andromeda*, all white and gleaming and festooned with bunting because it was her maiden voyage.

'Oh,' breathed Floria, tilting her head right back, 'I wish I were coming with you!' So wistful her voice, and tinged with longing and envy. A slight frown gathered between her brother's eyes and noticing this Judy gave a sudden intake of her breath. Hitherto Chris had never revealed any interest in Floria and Judy had somehow gained the impression that he had little or no affection for her. This had seemed strange, because in Cyprus men were devoted to their sisters, protecting them and always showing concern for their happiness. Judy continued to stare at Chris, and she saw his mouth tighten as if he were angry about something all at once.

'So do I wish I were coming with you,' George was saying enviously, but he added, 'I'll make an effort next year to take a trip on her, probably at Easter.'

Floria looked at him and then she lowered her head. If he took the trip it would have to be on his own, they were both thinking, and a terrible bleakness had entered Floria's eyes when a moment later she looked up as Chris suggested they go on board.

'Can I see your cabin?' asked Floria, throwing off her unhappiness as she eagerly asked the question. Judy's expression became veiled; Chris threw her a smile of sardonic amusement before he turned to Floria and shook his head.

'You three stay on deck here while I see the luggage is safely taken away. I'll be with you in a few minutes.'

There was time to explore the ship and on Chris's

114

return they wandered around. George and Floria uttered more envious exclamations as they entered the ballroom and then the restaurant. There were the two night clubs, the sun decks and sports deck and the swimming pools. Eventually they found a quiet place to sit on the top deck, away from the bustling crowds and the noise. Judy, looking at Chris, wondered a little apprehensively if he would be bored with the trip. He preferred peace and quietness, she knew, and that was why he had a house on Hydra, high in the hills, and a house in the mountain village of Karmi in Cyprus. He would not have much peace and quietness on a trip of this nature, she thought, wondering if she had made a mistake in forcing him to take her on the cruise.

The voice of one of the hostesses over the air informed them that it was time for the visitors to leave the ship, and after kissing her brother and sister-in-law Floria followed George down the gangway and on to the quay where they stood until the ship moved slowly away. Judy and Chris stood by the rail, Judy waving all the time while Chris merely gazed down, appearing to be bored. Several times Judy stole a glance at him, and when at last George and Floria turned and walked away that tiny frown appeared between his eyes again. But that was all, Judy noticed with some considerable relief. Chris was concerned about Floria's not being too happy with her husband, but he had not the slightest inkling that she and George were in love.

Chris glanced down at Judy and said,

'Well, do you want to see your cabin?'

'Yes, please,' she replied demurely, and he laughed.

He allowed her to have her pick, but she would not at first agree to that.

'You should have the first choice,' she told him, looking round the second cabin to which he had taken her. 'Do you want this one? It has a verandah.'

'The choice is yours, my dear. Haven't I said I'm here to oblige you?'

She blinked at him uncertainly and said,

'I think it's only fair for you to have the best cabin, Chris. This one has the verandah, but the other's larger....' She tailed off because of the amusement in his eyes. He seemed always to be laughing at some secret of his own, she thought, subjecting him to a little frown of censure.

'Don't fuss, little one,' he begged. 'Is this the one you prefer?'

She nodded then, and as all the luggage had been put in the other cabin Chris went and brought hers along for her.

'Dinner's at half past eight,' he told her on turning to go.

'Half past eight? Won't I see you before then?'

'I've some writing to do. Have a walk round the ship for an hour, and then it'll be time to get yourself changed.'

Judy stared at the closed door; it seemed an eternity till half past eight....

A week later they were in Alexandria, having called at several Greek islands on the way, and also at Piræus, from where they went by taxi to Athens and spent a few hours in Judy's favourite place—the Acropolis. They then bathed in the sea at Cape Sounion, returning to the ship in time for dinner, and sailing away from Piræus later in the evening.

The ship was to remain in Alexandria for two days; passengers could either stay in that city, returning to the ship for meals and for sleeping, or they could go to Cairo by coach or taxi and from there they would be taken to the Pyramids.

'I don't think we'll join in with the organized trip.'

Chris had decided earlier, and Judy knew that by this time he was becoming tired of the crowds and the noisy activity that went on until the early hours of the morning. Also, it had leaked out that Chris was a member of the company owning the shipping line and for a couple of days or so everyone on the *Andromeda* seemed intent on meeting him and shaking hands with him. That he was annoyed was evident, although he managed to display a courteous enough front to his 'customers'. Judy, however, received the brunt of his annoyance and on one occasion he was so sharp with her that she almost wished she had not asserted herself and made him come on the trip.

'You mean we'll go by ourselves, by taxi?' she asked, recalling that the Naughtons, the middle-aged couple sharing their table in the restaurant, were also loath to go on the organized trip to Cairo. They had been looking round for someone to share a taxi in order to cut the cost of the fare, it being over a hundred and thirty miles from Alexandria to Cairo.

'Yes,' replied Chris. 'I couldn't face a coachload of chattering women and squealing children.'

She had to smile. The men, it would appear, would do nothing to aggravate him!

'Shall we share a taxi with the Naughtons, then?'

'No, my dear, we shall not.' Firm and deliberate was his decision. Judy would have liked the company of the Naughtons, but she did not think she would insist. No, on this occasion she would allow him his own way because she rather thought any argument on her part would lead to unpleasantness between them. This she would deeply have regretted because she meant her first visit to this most fascinating and mysterious city of the East to be a happy and memorable occasion. Often in the past she had dreamed about it, mentally sailing down the Nile in a *felucca*, standing in awed silence

117

before the treasures of Tutankhamen in the museum in Liberation Square, entering barefoot into the great mosque of Ahmed Ibn Tulun. She had visualized eating *kebabs* in a houseboat café on the banks of the sacred river, of watching the sun go down behind the Pyramids and seeing it rise again at dawn. She had wandered through the streets of Cairo buying flowers and souvenirs; she had gazed up into the sky to look into the face of a Nubian—for she had been told by her grandfather that the Nubians were *enormous*!

When the time came for them to leave the ship and step on to Egyptian soil Judy was so excited that she trembled visibly. Chris noted this and a faint smile touched the corners of his mouth; he made no comment, however, and within less than ten minutes they were in a taxi, the road taking them through the Nile Delta where thick marshy vegetation covered the swamps and where men kept appearing, up to their waists in water, fishing for something.

'What are they trying to catch?' she asked Chris, who was also interested in the men.

'I don't know—— Look, that one's caught something. It's wriggling, can you see? It looks like an eel.'

Judy looked, and swallowed. The thing was wriggling, as Chris said, and it seemed from this distance to be covered in mud and slime.

'Do they eat them?' she asked, feeling quite sick.

'I don't expect they go to all this trouble just for amusement,' he returned with a touch of humour.

The desert was more to Judy's liking, although it soon became monotonous as mile after mile was covered and there was at times absolutely nothing to see. Then there would appear a camel train on the horizon or a few stunted trees growing, no higher than bushes and warped by the wind. Sometimes they would pass a hovel made of sacks fastened to sticks plunged into the sand; sometimes they would see an Arab family—parents and several ragged children—far away from anywhere.

'There isn't any water!' exclaimed Judy. 'Why are they there, wandering about when there isn't even water to drink? And what do they live on? How can the goats find food when there's nothing but sand?'

Chris laughed at her expression, asking which question she would like answered first.

'I don't understand why they're here.' She threw out her hands, indicating the solitary road running through miles and miles of desert with absolutely nothing to see except this family, wandering along a few yards from the road, the woman carrying a baby on her back and the man walking beside three other children, and his two goats bending their heads to the barren ground. 'Where are they *going*?'

Again he laughed.

'Shall I stop the taxi and get out and ask them?' he inquired, and Judy blushed. Nevertheless, she said insistently,

'There isn't anything, anywhere—so where can they be going?'

'They're nomads. They just wander about.'

She allowed the matter to drop, feeling rather foolish, but she still wondered how these people lived—existed was a more fitting word, she thought, twisting her head to take a last look at the bedraggled family whose two goats of skin and bone appeared to be the total sum of their worldly goods.

The sun was beating down and a shimmering heat haze spread like elusive tulle across the parched and barren land. Nomads appeared again, this time on the other side of the road. The man carried a filthy bag on his back, the woman trudged along, like the other, a brown-faced baby on her back. The man stopped to watch the taxi; his lips parted to reveal a few stumpy black teeth as he grinned at the occupants. Judy waved and the man raised his hand. The tears pricked Judy's eyes. What was wrong in the world that human beings had to live like this—without homes, without proper food and clothing, tortured by the merciless sun during the day and by the intense cold at night? She suddenly felt ashamed that she had all the comforts money could buy, but her one deep emotion was pity, pity she could not control, and the tears streamed down her face.

'Judy ... little one!' Chris had turned his head and as he saw her tears he uttered the exclamation. 'What's wrong?'

She shook her head and wept all the more—and then she was in her husband's arms, her head against his breast, ashamed of her emotions and yet unable to stem her tears.

'It's so—so awful! Why don't people do something for them?'

'Hush, you silly child. They're used to this life; they were born to it. They don't know anything else.'

'What has that to do with it? Why isn't something being done!'

'Something is being done,' he assured her patiently. 'Wait until we reach the irrigated part, then you'll see a difference. These nomads wouldn't thank you for putting them into houses and making them go out to work every morning.' He drew a clean white handkerchief from his pocket and, gingerly taking the soaked little scrap from her fingers, he dried her eyes. 'Come now, I shall begin to wish I hadn't brought you if you go on like this. You're on holiday, child. You've come here to enjoy yourself.'

'I feel so guilty.'

He had to laugh, even though he knew he would

receive a plaintive and censorious glance from his wife.

'You're a very silly child to feel guilty. Have you contributed to any—er—discomfort these people may be suffering?'

'No, but neither have I contributed to any cause which might relieve their suffering.'

He gave an amused but faintly exasperated little sigh and took his arm from around her. She leant back against the upholstery and gazed out of the window. A few flatroofed houses now and some other buildings. Electric wires overhead ... she had always considered them ugly, wondering why they could not be taken underground, but now their appearance brought her an odd, ridiculous sort of comfort.

More miles of desert, flat and monotonous, and then trees! Here was where irrigation had begun, Chris told her. The desert was becoming productive, but these things took time. He spoke softly and soothingly, and she became calm; the dry sobs which were the after-math of her tears ceased abruptly and she turned to give Chris a sheepish smile as she said,

'I'm silly, aren't I?'

'Yes, dear, you are.' But there was no amusement now in his attitude towards her, and no impatience. In fact, there was a new tenderness about him which moved her profoundly, stirring her memory to bring a fleeting recurrence of that magical, heady sensation she had experienced when standing beside her husband on the bridge in Venice. What was this feeling? She could have believed it to be the beginnings of love had her heart not already been given to Ronnie. Ronnie.... She had not thought of him for a long while ... but hadn't she made a determined effort to be brave and put him out of her mind? Her musings were checked by Chris's drawing her attention to the camel train on the skyline, far away across the wide desert.

'Three young ones; can you see them?' The quivering haze hung over the sand, but Judy could make out the young camels quite clearly.

'Yes; oh, I wish they were nearer! They look so sweet, and sort of helpless, walking so slowly beside their mothers.' She then added unconsciously, 'Will there be any water over there for them?'

'Not again, Judy, please. Camels can manage without water for ages. You know that.'

'The big ones, yes, but what about the little ones?'

'Apparently they manage to survive, otherwise the species would die out.'

She nodded absently, still watching the camels. There was something unreal about the silhouettes across the sand. The scene ought to be on a Christmas card, she thought.

'Are we nearly there?' she asked after a while. The vegetation was becoming more lush and healthy-looking. There were buildings all the time now, and vehicles.

'There are still a few miles to go; you'll see the buildings thickening up very soon now.'

At last they were in the city, an oasis in the wilderness—Cairo, largest of all desert cities. Excitement caught Judy again; she forgot everything but the thrill of reaching the city she had longed to enter since the time when she became old enough to read about it.

She also knew where she wanted to stay, and she spoke before Chris could mention Shepheard's or the Hilton.

'Can we stay at the Semiramis?'

'Do you know it?' he asked, puzzled.

'I've read about it. It's massive, and was once very splendid—when the English used to have lots of servants with them and needed many rooms. Can we stay there?'

'You're an old-fashioned little puss, aren't you? Are you sure you don't want the Hilton?'

She shook her head vigorously.

'No, it's the Semiramis I want.'

'Then the Semiramis it is.' Leaning forward, he gave instructions to the driver and soon they were there, at the hotel overlooking the Nile, with Shepheard's to one side of them and the Hilton a short distance away on the other.

'Oh!' she breathed on entering her room. 'I knew it would be like this!' The room was indeed massive. She moved swiftly to the window and stepped out on to the balcony. It looked west over the water. She turned into the room again, aware that Chris was standing there, regarding her quizzically. The Arab porter stood by him, holding his suitcase, but Judy continued to explore. The bathroom was also massive, and splendid. There was a dressing-room and inside this was the largest wardrobe Judy had ever seen. 'They must have had hundreds of dresses!' she exclaimed on emerging from the dressing-room.

'Or suits,' commented Chris and, turning, he went off with the porter to his own room next door.

But after a very quick wash and brush-up Judy went out on to the landing, intending to go to Chris. An unsmiling Arab appeared as if by magic and she stepped back into her room and pushed the door to. After waiting a few moments she went out again. The same Arab appeared—out of thin air, it seemed to Judy. Again she stepped back, frowning. A few more minutes passed and then, cautiously and soundlessly, she pulled the door inwards. Peeping out, she saw the great wide landing was empty and on tiptoe she made for Chris's door. The Arab appeared and she gave one final leap, almost crashing against the door.

'What on earth——?' Chris turned from the mirror,

a comb in his hand. Judy, rather breathless, and very white, was by the door, her hands behind her back, pushing against it as if she anticipated imminent invasion. 'You look as if you've seen a ghost. What's wrong?'

Fear had lodged in her throat and she swallowed hard to remove it.

'That man——' Vaguely she pointed over her shoulder. 'He kept coming out every time I came from my room. Wh-what d-does he want?'

A broad grin replaced the frown on Chris's face. But he did not answer her question immediately.

'Every time you came from your room? What were you leaving your room for?'

'I was coming to you—because I was ready and didn't want to waste any time.'

'Away from me, you mean?' was his swift inquiry, accompanied by a flicker of amusement in his eye.

She flushed.

'I want to start seeing things right away,' she said, and his face fell with mock disappointment.

'The man out there merely wanted a tip,' he then informed her.

'A tip?' She blinked at him. 'What for?'

The grin reappeared on Chris's face.

'Not for anything in particular. These men dart out from some mysterious hiding-place and, for some reason I can never understand, expect you to give them a tip.'

'For doing nothing?'

'They ring for the lift for you or, in the case of the ladies, offer to carry their handbags downstairs for them.' He looked at her with an odd expression as she came farther into the room. 'What did you think he wanted?' The shrewd inflection in his tone caused an increase in her colour again.

'I couldn't make out what he wanted,' she replied evasively.

He made no comment on that, although his brow lifted sceptically. But there was only amusement in his voice as he said, turning to the mirror again and applying the comb to his hair,

'If you decide you require male protection during the night just thump on the wall. I'll rather enjoy rescuing a damsel in distress.' His eyes met hers through the mirror; she noticed the sudden light of mockery in them and lowered her head. Yet she was dwelling on the careless way in which he spoke those words—with no sign of anger or a darkling look—and she thought again how westernized he was, and enlightened. On her marriage she had taken it for granted he would be no different from the average Greek or Cypriot husband: he would treat her as a possession and, therefore, regard every other man who came near her in the light of a trespasser. But Chris was not like that at all; the first time she had noticed this difference was when he made her wear those brief shorts. It was as if he didn't mind at all if other men looked at her so long as she was attractive for *him*. Perhaps, mused Judy as she glanced up again and saw him making the final draw of the comb through his hair, she should not have adopted that determined attitude of man-management, for she had a shrewd suspicion that had she taken the trouble to investigate his character she would soon have made the discovery that he did not require 'managing' at all.

CHAPTER SEVEN

CHRIS insisted on their having lunch in the hotel before going off on their sightseeing expedition. Judy had no time for food and she told him so.

'We'll eat, nevertheless,' he said firmly, and they went into the restaurant. On their way out again Judy stopped in the foyer and stared at the massive figure of the commissionaire standing there.

'He must be at least seven feet tall,' she whispered to her husband.

'Every inch of seven feet.' Chris, at well over six feet, had also to look up at the handsome Nubian. The man smiled at Judy and she thought she had never seen a more attractive man—other than Chris, of course, who for some unfathomable reason was in Judy's eyes becoming more attractive every day. 'Your manners, child!' Whispered words, but admonishing; she gave the man another smile and followed her husband who was already making for the street.

The Nile, sacred river of the Egyptians through aeons of time, shimmered in the sun which blazed down on the bustling city. The water was blue-green and docile; even when it swelled in late summer it could be subdued—not like that other great Arab river, the Greek name for which was Tiger. The Tigris of Iraq was a violently rapacious river, flooding inconveniently in the spring when water was not required. But the gentle Nile had always flooded in the summer, bringing life to the thirsty land. Nowadays the waters were controlled by dams, and at the Barrage above Cairo they were held back against the thirsty

months of drought. And the Nile was also an accommodating waterway, its northward-flowing movement
taking boats to the Mediterranean, while the prevailing wind coming from that sea assisted the boats on
their return journey.

'Can we go on a *felucca*?' asked Judy excitedly as
they crossed the road and stood looking at the river. A
tawny-skinned boatman was waiting expectantly for
more customers to fill his partly-laden vessel. The next
moment Judy was walking gingerly across a rickety
plank, Chris's firm hand under her arm. They sat together in the boat; the sails flapped as the *felucca*
skimmed the water, heading for Al-Gamia, the University Bridge.

Their sail lasted an hour; Judy was flushed and excited, avidly taking in the scene of bustling activity
along the bank, the lovely buildings and mosques and
minarets, the palm trees on the water's edge and the
lovely bougainvillea with their floral bracts of glowing
red or purple. Dusky figures moved like extras on a
crowded stage, some in white flowing cotton robes and
others in stripes, their feet shod in leather slippers and
on their heads white caps or turbans. It was an oriental
scene, alive and vital, yet mysterious and bewildering.

In bygone days when the August floods were expected from the interior of Africa the whole of Cairo
would turn out to celebrate the event of *wafaa al-
Nil*—the faithfulness of the Nile. The Nile, however,
was on occasions a little dilatory and then the long
procession would be entreating, not thanking. The
Sultan in his jewelled robes would lead the priests of
Islam in a united evocation to the Nile to be generous.
In very ancient times an added incentive would be the
pagan rite of casting alive into the river a beautiful
maiden—'the bride of the Nile'—as a sacrifice. In the

days of the Pharaohs the life-giving flood waters of this mighty river were believed to be the tears of Isis, goddess of the earth's fruits, mourning for Osiris. In more recent times the Nile, like the Bosphorus, was a dungeon of abandoned hope into which wrongdoers would be thrown, trussed and still breathing.

'Did you enjoy it?' Chris asked the question as they left the boat and began strolling along the waterfront again.

'It was marvellous!' She looked up at him and added impulsively, 'Thank you for bringing me, Chris. I'm sure I'd never have come to Egypt if I hadn't been married to you. . . .' Her voice trailed away and a hint of colour touched the lovely contours of her face as her husband's brows rose a fraction.

'So marriage does have some compensations,' he commented drily, apparently determined to see that she was even more put out than at present.

'I don't think my grandfather would ever have brought me here,' she admitted willingly after an evasive hesitancy which she was unable to maintain owing to the persistent glances cast at her by Chris. 'Being married makes me . . . freer than I was before.'

'You feel freer with me than you did with your grandfather?' he asked curiously.

'In one way,' she owned. 'As I've just said, I'd never have seen Egypt had I not been married to you.'

'Tell me,' he said glancing down at her, 'are you glad or sorry that you consented to marry me?'

'Consented?' Judy left his question unanswered for a moment as she politely reminded him that she did not consent; she had not been consulted. Both he and her grandfather had forgotten she was British. She had been treated as a Cypriot girl obliged to obey her guardian, accepting the man he chose for her and not offering one word of protest. 'I was only fifteen, too,'

128

she went on to add. 'That was very young for me to be forced into an engagement.'

A cold little silence followed, and as they walked along, making for nowhere in particular, Judy began to regret her outspokenness. She had never complained before—and indeed she wasn't really meaning to complain now—but had resignedly settled down to the life which fate had mapped out for her. Now, it seemed, she had vexed him and a coolness was surely going to mar their holiday ... unless she could repair the damage she had quite inadvertently done to the rather pleasant relationship which had begun to develop between them.

'I understand, then, that you're telling me you wouldn't have been forced into the engagement had you been older?' Judy did not answer because an answer was too difficult. All her thoughts were contradictory these days. Sometimes she would reflect on what marriage to Ronnie would have been like, but the picture seemed to have entirely lost its charm, for she was daily growing closer to Chris, experiencing pleasant sensations when they drifted into moments of intimacy like those on the bridge in Venice—and those when Chris took it into his head to kiss her. She told herself one minute that he had married her for desire, while in the next bewildering moment she would wonder why, if his desire had been so strong, he was able to resist coming to her. True, she had laid down the law to him regarding that, but her idea that he was docile and meek had already undergone some modification even before she witnessed George's astonished disbelief when Chris baldly admitted that he'd been bullied by his wife into taking her on the cruise. Floria too had been amazed by her brother's admission, so it was reasonable to assume Chris had always been regarded by Floria as a strong-willed man whose wife would be kept well and truly under his domination. In addition, Judy had herself owned more than once that her husband could master her if he chose, although it was true that each time she acknowledged this she found herself back to the argument Lefki had made: men were basically all the same, 'stand up to them and they'll usually see eye to eye because it's less wearing than being forever in a tussle with you'.

Judy drew a deep breath, wishing she could sort out this untidy muddle of her thoughts. There was the gnawing little suspicion that Chris was often deriving some sort of amusement from their relationship, that he was enjoying himself at her expense; there was also the question of Corinne, who had been much more than a friend and who was still in love with Chris. Judy was sure Chris was not in love with Corinne, but she felt equally sure he was human enough to continue accepting any favours that Corinne proved willing to give. 'I've asked you a question, Judy.' Her husband's soft voice put an end to her musings and she was again filled with a desire to repair the damage she had done by her unnecessary reference to the injustice she had suffered in being forced into her engagement to Chris. But she had to be truthful, and this meant frankly admitting that had she been older she would most certainly have put forward some sort of protest. But after that she added, in answer to his first question,

'Nevertheless, I cannot truthfully say now that I'm sorry I married you, Chris.' The simple confession, softly and sincerely spoken, was more eloquent than anything else she could have said, and it was also more touching. Chris slipped an arm about her shoulders, then his hand found her waist and stayed there, caressingly.

'Fifteen was young, my dear,' he said gently. 'As you've remarked, it was very young for you to be forced into an engagement.'

His words naturally surprised her and she glanced up swiftly. He was staring at the road ahead and she was unable to read his expression. But there was an air of sadness about him, she thought—or could it be regret? At the idea that it might be regret dismay out of all proportion flooded over her and she faltered, automatically placing her hand over the back of his as it gently gripped her waist.

'Can I ask you the same question you asked me?' and when he looked inquiringly at her, 'Are you glad—or—or sorry you married me?' Her sweet young face was pale; her lips quivered. These he noticed and a wondering light filled his eyes.

'I knew, the moment I saw you, that I wanted to marry you—and I haven't changed my mind, Judy. I'm not that sort of person.' Gravely he spoke, in English as always, his tones rich and deep. She was far from satisfied with the answer he had given her, although she could not have produced a reason for this.

'What made you offer for me—when I was so young, as you have just admitted?'

The hint of a smile, the almost imperceptible lift of a brow.... These seemed to give Judy her answer even before he spoke.

'I was afraid that if I left you to grow up I'd be too late—that someone else would offer for you.'

Her heart sank and a long trembling sigh left her lips. She had always known why he offered for her, had been fully aware desire was all that had been in his mind. And only seconds ago this stark truth had been revealed in those two small but meaningful gestures. So why should her heart sink at his words? For what other answer had she yearned?

Judy knew, without any doubts at all, what answer she had desired. And yet how stupid she was. Had she, in all the years she had lived in Cyprus, known of any man who had offered because he loved the girl? A man saw, then desired, then assessed, and finally he went into the matter of a dowry. How much had her grandfather given Chris? she wondered. The matter had been so humiliating, because she was British, that Judy had cast it away, and the question of a dowry had never once been mentioned between her grandfather and herself.

Her sudden revelation filled her whole being. She had never for one moment visualized falling in love with this dark Greek, this man whom she had at first regarded with no small sense of fear. She recalled his fury on hearing about her meetings with Ronnie. How possessive he had been! And how he had frightened her. Perhaps he would be like that again, she thought, should a similar occasion arise. But no similar occasion could arise—unless she saw Ronnie again, which was most unlikely.

'Little one,' said Chris at last. 'What are you thinking?'

She awoke from her reverie and looked up. He was smiling in a way that set her heart racing and she determinedly put up a guard. But she would not be cool with him, because she was here in this wonderful city, where she had always wanted to be, and nothing was going to detract from the pleasure she had for so long anticipated. Besides, nothing had really changed; Chris did not love her, but she had known and accepted this. Affection could still enter her marriage, as she had intended it to when she suggested they 'keep company'.

'I was thinking of all sorts of things,' she frankly replied, returning his smile. 'But right now I am thinking about where I want to go next.'

'And where do you want to go next?'

'To the old city to buy some presents, and to the mosque of Ahmed Ibn Tulun, because everyone goes there. It will be time to go back to the hotel for dinner then, but——' She hesitated, then went on diffidently, 'Can we go to a night club?' She had heard of the belly-dancers and wanted to see them, for in Cyprus the girls did not dance in night clubs. This was done by foreign women—French and English and other nationalities.

Chris might have read her thoughts and, westernized as he was, he had no intention of relaxing to that extent. In Greece or Cyprus he would not have taken his wife to a night club of that kind, and he would not do so here.

'No, Judy, we can't.'

Silence. Should she insist? Lefki would have insisted....

'But I want to go. I've never been to one——'

'And you're not likely ever to do so,' he cut in softly. 'We'll be taking quite a long while over dinner, and then, after a little stroll we'll be ready for bed. If we're going to have a full day's sightseeing tomorrow we'll have to be up early.' The two major items for the following day were the Pyramids and Sphinx at Giza, and the Pharaonic museum in Liberation Square.

'We needn't stay long,' began Judy when she stopped, warned by one quelling glance.

'Careful, Judy,' he advised, and added cryptically, 'Don't go too far or you'll spoil everything. You've told me of your plans for the rest of today and I'm quite willing to do what *you* want to do.' He paused a moment and withdrew his arm from around her. 'This evening we shall do what *I* want to do, and that won't be visiting a night club.'

Judy remained silent, her head lowered. This, she surmised, was the point beyond which it was imprudent to go.

She missed his arm, warm and gentle, on her back, and his hand on her waist. It was her own fault, but she felt miserable all the same. She inquired at length if they were anywhere near the mosque.

'We'll take a taxi,' was the rather abrupt reply, and after they had been in the taxi a few minutes she said meekly,

'I'm sorry, Chris.' She had not meant to be meek and apologetic, for that meant a retrograde step in her aim for equality, but her heart dragged abominably and she would have done anything to ease the tension that had dropped like a barrier between them. He shot a glance at her profile; her head was bent and she did not raise it. She was gazing fixedly at her hands, clasped on her lap. She looked the picture of misery and a relenting smile broke over her husband's dark and handsome face. He reached out and patted her hand. Her spirits rose. 'I didn't mean to be disagreeable.' She looked at his hand resting on hers and had an almost irresistible urge to raise it to her cheek.

'I know quite well you did not mean to be disagreeable,' he returned surprisingly. There was a dry edge to his tone, though, and she knew instinctively that he was fully aware that her intention had been to assert herself, aiming as always at having her own way.

Yes, she definitely decided, Chris knew what she was about—had done so from the first. Why, then, had he not resisted? His behaviour was incomprehensible and Judy thrust the matter from her, turning her thoughts to the pleasures in store.

The massive solemn square in which stood the ablution fountain of the Ibn Tulun Mosque was silent and awe-inspiring. It was an oasis of peace and serenity amid the turbulence and ugliness of crowded streets. The ugliness pressed right up to its gates, but once inside these gates there descended upon Judy an atmosphere that was outside time. Here her feet were on the soil of Islamic Cairo; nomads in ancient times had pitched their tents here—and here they had lived and died, free from the shackles of the modern civilization that was to come.

'Isn't it ... peaceful?' Judy whispered the words because that seemed the thing to do. Chris merely nodded, his concentrated gaze fixed on the oddly shaped, unconventional minaret.

'What happened there, I wonder?' he remarked at last. Used as he was to the elegant, slender minarets of the Turkish mosques in Cyprus, Chris regarded this contraption with acute dislike.

Judy looked up, and gave a little gasp.

'That's not a minaret?'

'Certainly it is, but it's more like a debased *ziggurat*. This Ibn Tulun must have been an eccentric.' At that moment a coach load of tourists filed through the gates and Chris and Judy exchanged glances of resignation.

'Never mind,' said Judy comfortingly. 'The guide will be useful.'

'We haven't paid,' began Chris, when he was interrupted.

'What does that matter? We'll shuffle along at the back and make ourselves small.'

'You make me feel quite old,' he said, taking her arm and proceeding towards the crowd gathered around the guide.

'Old? Why should I make you feel old?'

'Because you yourself are so young—and so uninhibited——' He broke off there and laughed. 'Uninhibited in *some* ways,' he qualified, and a swift rise of colour told him the malicious barb had found its mark.

'I said we must get to know one another better.' Her natural defensive instinct had been put into words before she could restrain it, and the rosy colour spread right up to her temples at the look her husband gave her.

'Darling,' he laughed, 'there is a time and place for the discussion of such things! Come, we're missing something.'

Darling.... It didn't mean a thing, of course. Men often called someone darling, as did women. No, it had no special significance—why should it?

The guide, round and dark-skinned and wearing a turban, was in a spotless white *galabiya* which, when Judy happened to get near him as they all entered the mosque, gave off the fresh clean smell of a garment newly laundered. She knew instinctively that whenever such a smell assailed her nostrils again she would think of Ali Baba. For that was what he asked the tourists to call him, although there were laughing protests that Ali Baba could not possibly be his name. With a grave countenance and unmoving eyes he assured them that it was, so everyone was left guessing. However, with the typical friendliness of guides all over the world Ali Baba had very soon created a happy carefree atmosphere and everyone joined in the laughter whenever he told a joke or related some humorous incident that had happened when he had been taking tourists around.

The oddly shaped minaret, he had already told them, came into existence because Ibn Tulun, noted for his impatience with idlers, was once seen amusing himself by folding a piece of paper into all sorts of odd shapes. Ashamed of being caught in this idle pastime, he made a swift recovery by saying that this was how he wished the minaret to look. The great mosque was at that time in the course of construction and the limestone minaret, looking very odd indeed because the base was square and the upper part circular, was duly erected in obedience to the great man's wishes. However, as the present minaret was dated much later than the ninth century—when the mosque was first built—the story could not very well be true.

The inside of the mosque was characterised by that coolness and air of spiritual and meditative restfulness which is found in any mosque, wherever it might be. Ali Baba sat down on one of the beautiful carpets covering the floor and his audience gathered around, entering into the spirit of this adventure in emulating his posture by squatting, cross-legged, on the carpet.

The history of the mosque was related, Ali Baba's audience learning how Ibn Tulun, coming to Egypt from a great city of Samarra, in Iraq, built a new city, with the magnificent mosque, a palace for himself and of course a hippodrome for polo, because all Turks and Arabs loved horses.

On emerging from the dim cool interior of the mosque everybody put on their shoes again and after the tourists had wandered around the courtyard taking snapshots, Ali Baba politely informed them that it was time to go. Chris had a few minutes previously managed to get him alone and offered to pay him, saying that he and his wife were not of the party, but Ali Baba would not hear of accepting money.

'You're staying at the Semiramis,' he said, as if this were sufficient reason why they should make use of his services.

'We are—but what has that to do with it?' Chris regarded Ali Baba in some puzzlement. 'And how did you know we're staying there?'

'I saw you arrive. I was waiting for these tourists; they'll be staying at the Semiramis.' He paused a moment. 'I don't know what plans you've made, of course, but I shall be escorting these same people to the Pyramids of Giza in the morning and you and your wife are very welcome—if you would care to join us, that is?'

'Yes,' intervened Judy, her voice bright and eager. 'Can we, Chris?'

Ali Baba's dark eyes rested on her face and before Chris could reply to her question he was speaking, softly, and with that timeless wisdom and insight known only to the people of the East.

'This combination of English and Greek ... what beauty it creates.' He transferred his gaze to Chris, having to look up even though he himself was by no means small. 'Your exquisitely fashioned wife *is* partly Greek, I think?'

'Her mother was a Greek Cypriot.' Chris smiled at his wife, searching her face.

'I knew. And you, sir? You are from Greece, not Cyprus.' A statement, and Chris nodded. 'You're a lucky man indeed.' He paused and then with the outspokenness that was also characteristic of the East he added twinklingly, his eyes roving over Judy's slender figure, 'It's easy to see why you chose her....' Chubby fingers were suddenly pressed to his mouth and then flicked away, while Ali Baba's eyes took on a dreamy, faraway expression. 'What pleasure she must give you! What ecstasy to be mated to such a divine creature!'

The blood rushed to Judy's cheeks and she dared not venture a glance at her husband. But she could picture the mocking amusement she would have encountered in his face; she could almost see the wry curve of his lips as he produced the smooth reply which would be expected from the eager man before them.

'How right you are, Ali Baba. The pleasure my wife gives me is indescribable.'

Judy did look up then—to glare at him. His eyes widened in a sort of warning gesture, but they held a kindling of humour as well, and suddenly both he and Judy burst out laughing.

'Now I wonder why you laugh?' murmured Ali Baba strangely. 'I wonder...' He fell silent a moment and then, 'Shall you be accompanying us in the morning?'

'Most certainly—and thank you very much for asking us.'

'You,' pronounced Judy with heat as the last of the tourists disappeared through the gate, 'were absolutely horrid!'

'A guilty conscience, eh? Serve you right!'

'Why do you let me have my own way?' she asked, quite out of the blue. He started but instantly recovered, obviously realizing she had spoken on impulse.

'I must bow to your will,' he replied woodenly, and Judy's lips pursed. 'What say do I have in the matter?'

I must bow to your will.... Judy's eyes narrowed. Those were almost the exact words she had written to Lefki.... 'Thank you for telling me what to do. It certainly works...Chris bows to my will in most things....'

And Judy had left that letter around in her bedroom for days before putting it in an envelope and posting it....

'I shouldn't have imagined you to be so—so—er—cooperative.'

'Co-operative?' he laughed. 'That wasn't the word you intended to use.'

No, she had intended using the word 'meek', but some inner voice warned her this would be unwise.

'That first night,' she murmured, unable to comment on his latest remark, 'you didn't seem willing then to—to bow to my will, as you term it.'

'The first night?' He frowned in thought and she looked severely at him. He knew very well to what she referred and she felt tempted to inform him of her awareness that his questioning manner was feigned. However, she decided against it, unwilling to say any-

139

thing which might bring about a recurrence of that coolness which had come between them only an hour or so ago.

'You were very sarcastic, asking me if you should bow yourself out—er—backwards.'

They were standing by the domed ablution fountain which was both functional as well as decorative, for here it was that those entering the mosque must first wash themselves. Visitors did not wash, of course, but men could often be seen using these ablution fountains. The sun blazed down and the air was humid and oppressive. Judy yawned behind a small brown hand and fleetingly there appeared an almost tender light in her husband's eyes. Yet his voice was crisp and faintly arrogant when at last he said,

'I expect it was shock at the decision you had reached. It isn't usual for a bridegroom to be shown the door on his wedding night.'

'I didn't show you the door!' she denied indignantly, quite oblivious of the fact that her words were irrelevant. They were also amusing, apparently, for a sudden gleam of laughter entered her husband's eyes. 'I would like to know, Chris, what is so funny?' She had meant to be coolly inquiring and faintly bored, stealing some of the dignity her husband often portrayed, but somehow her intention went awry. Chris threw back his head and laughed, at the same time taking both her hands in his and drawing her close to him.

'*You* are so funny!' He stopped laughing and gazed down into her face. 'Do you remember my saying it was going to be delightful being married to you?' She nodded vaguely, her eyes wide, her young lips softly parted, invitingly. 'Well, Judy, it *is*—quite soon, I think.' And on that rather obscure statement he slid his arms around her and kissed her gently on the lips. They were the sole occupants of the square. Silence reigned; the peace and the calm entered into them both. Shyly Judy responded to her husband's kiss. 'Ali Baba was right in one thing,' he whispered close to her ear. 'You're beautiful ... and you're exquisitely fashioned.'

The vibrancy in his voice, the shadowed expression that could have been tenderness, the caress of his hands on her arms and the small pulsation of a vein in his neck ... Judy noted these things and bewilderedly endeavoured to translate them into a language she could understand, but this was impossible. Chris was holding her away from him, his handsome face serious, and very dark in the shadow cast by the domed building by which they stood. At last he shook his head, as if trying to clear it after partaking of some heady draught.

'Come, my dear,' he said matter-of-factly, 'we'll have to be getting a move on if you want to do this shopping you mentioned.'

The shops were fascinating to Judy. Typical of the East, they were literally bulging with merchandise. Displays, if they appeared at all, were muddled and unattractive. On the other hand, there was something exciting about having to look carefully and concentrate because there was such a vast array of goods to see.

'I want that.' Judy pointed to a silver medallion on a chain. It was in a glass case and Chris indicated to the white-robed assistant that he wished to see it. 'Do you like it?' Judy looked questioningly at her husband and after a careful examination of the object he nodded.

'Very pretty. Yes, we'll have that,' he told the assistant, who eagerly began wrapping it up in tissue paper. The medallion was beautifully worked by hand. Trees in filigree and animals in solid silver were surrounded by a fluted frame of silver, and a decorative loop attached it to the silver chain.

'How much was it?' Judy wanted to know as they moved on to the next counter.

'Mind your own business.'

Judy laughed and allowed the matter to drop. At the next counter they bought a bronze inlaid plaque of Nefertiti, and another of Tutankhamen and his queen.

'One of these is for Floria,' she explained when Chris pointed out the similarity of these two plaques, suggesting that she buy the one in wood carving which the smiling assistant was persistently thrusting before her eye. 'I like these better than the wooden ones.'

'What would you like me to buy you?' he asked when they were out in the street again, looking at other shops. There were masses of people about, many wearing the long cotton robes but many also wearing trousers and shirts. Stalls occupied the centre of the road and tourists were bargaining good-naturedly with their owners. The sun was still hot even though its rays were beginning to slant; the air was still sultry and perspiration could often be seen pouring down the faces of the tourists who were not used to the heat. Judy and Chris were used to such heat and it did not affect them as they strolled among the crowds, or stopped now and then to examine some object which caught Judy's eye.

'You've bought me the medallion,' she reminded Chris. 'That's all I want.' She had been searching for something for Chris, but had no idea what he would like.

'I heard you saying something to Floria about an Alexandrite ring.'

'Oh yes, I almost forgot! Lefki has one and it's beautiful. It changes colour—did you know that?'

He nodded.

'Alexandrite does change colour. Sometimes it's red and sometimes it's purple.'

'Yes, and all the shades in between,' she added. 'Do

you think we can buy one here?' She glanced round vaguely. 'I expect there were some in that first shop, but I suppose it's too far to go back?'

'It is, rather. We'll find some along here, though.'

It was almost seven o'clock when they returned to the hotel, Judy twisting the pretty ring on her finger and carrying a small ivory Buddha, exquisitely carved and very old. She had found it quite by accident in a small shop in a back street and had bought it for Chris. He had been so delighted with it that he pressed his lips to her temple, right there and then, and thanked her in a faintly husky voice.

'I'll keep it on my desk, where I can see it every day,' he promised gravely, and Judy felt a warmth spread through her because of the way he looked, and the way he smiled, as he said those words.

They had taken a taxi after finishing their shopping, and had travelled for miles round the back streets of Cairo. They had seen all kinds of houses, from the tenements of the *baladi* to the more spacious abodes of the middle-class, or *frangi*, as they were called. Their gardens boasted flowers which were familiar to both Chris and Judy—hibiscus and bougainvillea and poinsettia, and other exotic blooms whose perfume hung in the soft still air. They had visited another mosque, then stopped to watch the river traffic for a while. Then Judy had felt sorry for a street vendor because all the tourists were passing him by and patronizing another man a few yards away. Amused but resigned, Chris ordered the taxi driver to pull into the side of the road. Judy got out, and on returning a few minutes later she had two handfuls of trinkets—necklaces, brooches, earrings and bracelets.

'Only fifty piastres!' she exclaimed. 'How about that for a bargain?'

'Fifty? And you consider you've obtained a bargain?'

Dropping the trinkets into her lap, Judy then proceeded to examine them separately.

'Two scarab rings, four necklaces in silver——'

'In what!'

'Silver-coloured metal,' she conceded, looking at Chris in a half-amused, half-deprecating way. 'One ... two ... three—— Seven brooches with pretty stones——' She darted him a sideways glance, her eyes twinkling. 'Stones the colour of rubies. Then I have two pairs of earrings. Yes, of course I consider I've obtained a bargain!'

'It's all rubbish,' he returned mildly, taking up one of the brooches and frowning at it.

'Costume jewellery,' she insisted. But then she added, 'I can give it away when we get home. The little girls of the village will love these things.'

'What made you buy them, if you're only going to give them away?'

She blushed faintly, and spread her hands.

'The man had nothing else to sell.'

'So you just had to buy something?' With a totally unexpected movement he took her hand and gave it an affectionate squeeze. 'Yes, little one,' he murmured gently, almost tenderly, 'you're going to be delightful to live with.'

CHAPTER EIGHT

THE sun was up and the city bustling with life, but Judy lay in bed, stretched out luxuriously, and gave herself over to a pleasant reflective mood, there being plenty of time before she must take her bath and proceed downstairs to meet her husband at the breakfast table.

She had been awakened by the call to prayer from Cairo's minarets. This call to the faithful took place five times a day; men would leave what they were doing and proceed to the mosque of their preference and there they would pray, devout barefooted suppliants, their faces turned towards sacred Mecca, the city of Mohammed's birth, and to which all Cairo's mosques were orientated.

This summoning to prayer was no novelty to Judy, as it was to most tourists, because there were Muslims in Cyprus and, therefore, mosques in plenty. And from the minarets of these mosques the Turkish Cypriots would be called to prayer in exactly the same way as the Muslim inhabitants of Cairo, this desert city of Africa.

She dwelt on her activities of yesterday, and knew she was fortunate in being married to Chris. Her grandfather could have given her to someone else ... someone like Vincent, for example. Judy shivered. Vincent was oily and stout; he always seemed as if he required a shave and a shampoo. His clothes were never immaculate like those of Chris; his shirts were not changed even once a day. Chris on the other hand would change his several times if the weather were particularly hot. Judy changed several times too. This changing was necessary if one desired to keep fresh in a hot country.

Yes, her grandfather had really chosen well, Judy conceded as she lay there, gazing up at the high ceiling and the ornamental cornices portraying the splendour of this hotel in the days of the British administrators and businessmen. How different would have been her life had she been married to another Vincent, a man who would nauseate her and who would also imprison her. She would not have been allowed her own way with Vincent, or one of his kind, she felt sure. And her heart went out to Floria, and all the girls like her who were forced into marriages with men they could never respect, let alone love.

Yesterday.... Never had she packed so much into a few short hours. For after dinner they had walked for miles, although they had set out to take a short stroll along the waterfront. Chris had taken her hand immediately they left the hotel and had retained it for the whole of the time. He had kissed her cheek on one occasion and her head on another. Judy supposed it was the romance of this mysterious city, set in the desert yet with the life-giving aorta of the Nile running through it, making it unique in that it never knew thirst. There was a saying that 'who drinks the water of the Nile often can hardly bear to leave it'. If one did leave it, travelling a few miles east or west, one could die of thirst.

Judy yawned; she felt sleepy again, but she must not sleep. Today was the day for which she had waited almost all her life. Today she would see the Pyramids and the Sphinx!

A deep sigh of contentment left her lips. It seemed incredible that there ever was a time when she did not want to marry Chris ... and yet that time was less than two months ago!

146

At last she had to think of getting up. Her door was locked and she smiled to herself. The last thing Chris did was to remind her to bang on the wall if she required help. He had laughed with her when she had shown him the very adequate lock, with its large key ready to be turned the moment he left her. But his laugh had died away after a second or two and the most odd expression had settled on his face. Judy had experienced a certain degree of discomfort, brought on by an aggravating little devil of guilt that would not leave her alone. She had in the end felt she could have let her husband stay—but try as she would no suitable words, eloquent or otherwise, obliging appeared to fill the gap in her vocabulary which she now saw as a chasm which was going to prove exceedingly difficult to bridge. It was hardly the thing to say, 'We know each other better now, so therefore you may stay.' In fact, she had the extraordinary conviction that should she say something of that nature her husband would don an armour of pride and tell her where to go!

Ali Baba was waiting when they came from breakfast into the entrance hall; gradually the other tourists assembled and then the coach arrived and they all made their way towards it.

From the heart of Cairo they drove along a broad modern highway with views of the open countryside beyond its edges. With the gradual thinning of the buildings the vista became one of low-lying fields and a few scattered houses, with occasionally a cluster of mud huts fringed by a circle of palms. And then, across the fields, there they were—the great mountains of stone, the Pyramids of Giza, built on a high desert plateau above Cairo.

'Oh,' breathed Judy, staring towards the great bulk of the Pyramid of Cheops. 'Chris, isn't that a magnificent scene!' The sun reflected back, leaving a tawny-gold translucence on the gigantic side of the Pyramid. 'What must they have been like when they were covered with alabaster, all glittering like mother-of-pearl? And can you imagine the Sphinx—her head hanging with priceless ornaments and her face painted a brilliant crimson?'

Chris merely smiled, for now a loud murmur ran through the coach as excitement began to mount and increase. The journey had taken less than half an hour, but the latter part had to be taken either by camel or pony and trap.

'Are we riding camels?' asked Judy as they left the bus. She looked up rather doubtfully at Chris, and was not at all surprised when he shook his head and declared emphatically,

'No camel for me, thank you, Judy. You can please yourself, of course.'

At that moment a driver brought his camel close. Precariously perched on its back was a giggling woman, urging the animal on in some way of her own, anxious to catch up with her friends who were leaving her behind. The smell of the camel was by no means pleasant and Judy decided that although she would have liked to boast of having ridden a camel she preferred to go with Chris in the trap.

Other tourists had arrived before them and there was a short wait for Chris and Judy until a trap was available. The place was rather crowded, and noisy. Cameras were snapping at laughing people standing beside camels or sitting on their backs. White-robed Arabs were hawking their wares—models of the Pyramids and Sphinx, leather goods and picture postcards and numerous other souvenirs which the tourists were eager to add to their collections.

At last the trap arrived and the couple it had brought down alighted. Judy and Chris took their places; at the pony's head a smiling Arab walked slowly, carrying a stick which he never used. Progress was slow, but there was no necessity for speed. Ali Baba was already there when they reached the Great Pyramid, talking to those of the party who had arrived at the same time as he.

Enthralled and speechless, Judy desired nothing more than to stand and stare, which she did, oblivious even of her husband. Her hands were clasped in front of her, her big eyes were wide and incredulous.

'I never believed I'd stand here,' she breathed rapturously at last. 'Oh, Chris—*thank* you for bringing me!'

A faint smile twisted his mouth; today he was the cool sardonic husband again and the tenderness of yesterday might have been a dream, elusive, fleeting— something that could not be recaptured, ever.

Ali Baba was speaking, talking about the Pharaohs of ancient Egypt and their deep concern with the afterlife. He quoted Herodotus who estimated that one hundred thousand men had slaved for more than twenty years to build the Great Pyramid of Cheops. The stone was quarried from the Mokattam Hills and after being accurately shaped and dressed it was put into place, layer upon layer, until the Pyramid was completed. As he spoke Judy tipped back her head and stared upwards to the indescribable immensity of the man-made mountain soaring above her.

'It makes you feel like an ant,' she whispered to her husband. He nodded in agreement, glancing up himself but absorbed in what Ali Baba was saying.

'Monge, a mathematician employed by Napoleon, calculated that the masonry of the three largest Pyramids at Giza would make a wall, one foot thick, and ten feet high, long enough to surround the whole of France.'

Gasps were heard, but no one doubted this calcula-

149

tion. What did amaze people was the gullibility of the slaves of ancient Egypt. They would toil in this way for half a lifetime or more simply because they fully believed their ruler to be a god.

'Those who wish can now enter the grave,' Ali Baba was saying, and again Judy looked doubtfully at Chris. But he nodded and they made their way to the other side of the Pyramid. 'You'll have to bend, ladies and gentlemen,' said Ali Baba. 'And please hold on to the handrail.'

The passage was steep and long ... and certainly eerie, thought Judy, reaching out her other hand in an automatic gesture. Chris felt its warmth through his shirt and took it in his.

'All right?' he asked, half turning his head.

Judy nodded and smiled.

'It's creepy, though,' she said. 'How many years is it since Cheops was buried?'

'Five thousand; didn't you hear Ali Baba mention that?'

'I was looking—not listening,' she admitted. 'I must have missed a lot of what he said.'

They continued along a passage, lit by electricity, but no more than three feet high; Judy dared not think about the weight above, for to do so made her feel quite terrified. The Pharaoh's burial chamber was of black volcanic rock, his sarcophagus of red granite.

'It's ... weird,' quivered Judy, longing to be out in the sunlight again. It seemed almost like sacrilege for all these people to be in Cheops' funerary chamber.

A great sigh of relief left her lips when at last they were out in the light again.

One of the other Pyramids was built by Cheops' son, Chephren, and some of the people went into that too. But Chris and Judy wandered about among great granite blocks and slabs, the remains of temples which had been excavated after long centuries of being buried in the sand. And then they were gazing up at the Sphinx, which was close to the Chephren Pyramid. In Cheops' day the Sphinx was almost buried by sand; only its head gazed out over the vast desert, serene and inscrutable.

'You know,' murmured Judy smiling at Chris, 'I felt exactly like this the first time I stood on the Acropolis in Athens and looked at the Parthenon. You see the pictures of these famous places over and over again, and deep inside you there comes a longing that is really an ache, and it hurts awfully. Every time you see another picture the pain comes back and you say to yourself "I must see it—I *must*!" and then you start to—sort of—of—heave——'

'Good God, Judy,' broke in Chris, revolted. 'Spare me those sort of details, please!'

A tinkling laugh echoed through the clear warm air.

'I didn't mean I felt sick in the real sense of the word,' she began, when he again interrupted her.

'I'm relieved. Can we change the subject?'

Her laugh rang out again.

'I don't think I'm very good at describing my feelings, am I?'

'It just depends what your feelings were. I gained the impression you were suffering from some sort of malady.'

She stole a glance at him from under her lashes, sure he was teasing her. His face was set in unreadable lines. He appeared to be totally absorbed in the Sphinx. She fell silent, sharing his interest, taking her fill of the wonder of this colossal sandstone figure standing there on the plateau of Giza, where the Pharoahs who built these pyramids hoped to rest in peace. Strangely, though, scarcely any of them, no matter how great their ingenuity, had managed to beat the grave-robbers.

Ali Baba was talking again to those who had just come out of the Pyramid. There were English, Americans, French and Germans in the party and Ali Baba used the three languages in turn. He was an extremely highly educated man, and a philosopher. Chris and Judy joined the party and were in time to hear him talking about his wife. Someone asked if he ever took her out and he shook his head.

'She prefers to stay in,' he replied, and impulsively Judy said, not meaning her voice to carry to Ali Baba,

'They all say that! Ask a Cypriot why he doesn't take his wife out and he'll instantly say she prefers to stay in.'

Several heads turned, including Ali Baba's. His dark intelligent eyes moved slowly from Judy's flushed face to that of her husband.

'Often when I'm out with people like this,' he said, turning back to his audience, 'I talk about my wife and about the relationship we have. This leads always to a discussion in which all take part. And during this discussion I always ask the same question of the ladies. The response always interests me even though it never varies. Yes, I've asked the question to every nationality in the world, I think, and the response is always the same.'

Everyone was interested, especially the ladies, who were watching Ali Baba expectantly, waiting for the question. After a sidelong glance at Judy he smiled enigmatically and said, 'Ladies, if you are of the opinion that a husband should be the master then please raise your hands.'

The men were clearly amused, and curious, looking around, some with reluctant grins on their faces. Chris regarded his wife with an odd expression; Ali Baba sent her another glance as one hesitant hand was slowly raised. It had only required someone to make the first move and now every feminine hand except Judy's was raised. Judy bent her head, conscious of many eyes upon her, but more acutely aware that she most certainly was causing Chris embarrassment by not raising her hand. She seemed to be placing him in a position inferior to that of the other husbands present. Much as she regretted this she could not bring herself to raise her hand, and when she eventually looked up she was overwhelmingly relieved to see that all hands had now been lowered.

'Yes, ladies, that is the response I invariably receive. Of course, there are always the odd one or two who will not admit that they enjoy being mastered, and I noticed that today is no exception.' That was all, and Ali Baba did not look at Judy again.

What was Chris thinking? she wondered, unable to derive any information from his impassive countenance. She felt a surge of anger against Ali Baba, aware that his question was prompted by her retaliation to his assertion that his wife did not wish to go out with him.

But it was impossible to remain angry with him and when, a short while later he sought them out as they were wandering round the ruins of what had been massive buildings, Judy found herself unable to resist his smile.

'I was only teasing,' he assured her. But then he added, amusement in his eyes, 'You weren't honest, little lady—— No, do not interrupt, but listen to a wise old man for a moment. You are trying to deceive yourself, as many women do. You walk in the shadows because the fierce sunlight frightens you a little ... but don't remain in the shadows too long, my dear. The sun goes down, you know, and then there is complete darkness.' He reached out and patted her bare arm

153

with a chubby, spotlessly clean hand. 'Go out to meet the sun, for assuredly if you don't it will move on ... to shed its warmth somewhere else.'

This rhetorical little speech stunned Judy for a moment. The man was omniscient! She glanced up at Chris; his unmoving countenance revealed nothing of his thoughts and yet all at once Judy saw him with Corinne, sitting at the far end of George's patio, and screened partly by the oleander bushes so that there was an intimacy in the scene which, Judy recalled, had made her furiously angry at the time. The sun would move on, Ali Baba had said ... 'to shed its warmth somewhere else'.

Fear touched Judy's heart. Was it already too late? Had she remained in the shadows too long? Ali Baba had wandered off, and urged by some magnetic force she stepped swiftly to her husband's side and took hold of his hand. Fear dropped from her like a cloak as his fingers curled round hers.

'What is it, little one?' He smiled down at her, but shook his head. 'Don't take Ali Baba too seriously; the sun always comes round again.'

Her face glowed.

'Chris....'

'My dear?'

She moistened her lips.

'What I'm trying to say is—is...' Again her voice trailed away and his mouth curved in amusement.

'What is it that you find so difficult to say?' He had begun to walk on, over the hot sand towards the place where the ponies and traps were waiting to take them back to the coach. 'Can I be of any assistance?'

She laughed then ... but the moment was lost and she merely said,

'You're kind, Chris—and understanding.'

A small sigh and then,

'Kind, am I? And understanding. . . .' He released her hand, increasing his pace at the same time so that she had to skip now and then to keep up with him.

They sat side by side in the trap, neither speaking a word. Chris's face was set and his chin thrust forward. He had drifted from her and she felt chilled. But with the resilience of youth she rallied, turning her head to look back at the picture postcard scene of the Pyramids and Sphinx, standing as they had stood for centuries and centuries, under a blue electric sky from which the sun blazed down on to the arid, burning desert.

The pony began to trot and Judy twisted round again. The coach was there, the driver in his seat, waiting. There were other coaches, too, with people pouring from them. Camels waited, often emitting the weirdest sounds, to carry the more venturesome sightseers up to the Pyramids. There were the ponies and traps, with dusky Arabs at the ponies' heads; there were the Arab hawkers, and the obiquitous dragomen who would —for a fee, of course—recite parrot-fashion the historical narrative that had been passed down from father to son for generations. There were the places where refreshments could be bought, there were eager children talking to the smiling camel-drivers. It was exciting, although rather overcrowded. For Judy it was the fulfilment of a dream and she sighed contentedly when, a little while later, they were in the coach and driving back to the hotel for lunch.

The afternoon was spent in the museum, the major attraction naturally being the Tutankhamen Gallery. On either side of the entrance stood a man-sized figure carved in ebony. Skirts of gold encircled their loins, golden sandals were on their feet and on their foreheads they wore magnificent gold headdresses. They had guarded Tutankhamen's tomb, standing erect and holding staffs on the top of which were golden balls.

Facing the entrance was an ebony figure of the ancient Egyptian deity, the god Anubis, conductor of the dead, the ears of his jackal's head cocked and alert.

The fantastic grave furniture included golden chariots, chairs, beds, chests and divans. The jewellery of the Pharaoh filled case after case and in one room stood the magnificent golden casket in which the body of the king lay when it was found in the tomb in the famous Valley of the Kings. And of course there was the incredibly beautiful mask of the king in gold and lapis lazuli which had covered the head of Tutankhamen's embalmed body.

'I feel completely dazzled,' exclaimed Judy as they came out of the museum. 'Have you ever experienced anything like it in all your life?'

'Never. It was a good idea of yours to suggest coming to Egypt.'

'You're glad?' His admission had made her happy. She was glad he had used the word 'suggest'. It had begun to trouble her that he had come simply in order to pander to her wishes.

'Yes, Judy, I'm glad.'

On the way back to the hotel his manner of cool disinterest fell from him and he drew Judy's arm through his as they sat close together in the coach.

'Oh, look!' exclaimed Judy as they passed a mud-brick village some distance from the road. 'They use buffaloes here where in Cyprus they use donkeys.'

The blindfold water buffalo was tethered to a primitive water-wheel, sadly treading an endless circle. In Cyprus donkeys were used in this way, but only in the very remote villages.

'Poor thing!' cried the woman behind. 'What a life!'

But the animals were well fed and appeared to be healthy. True, the camels in their train often grumbled and a donkey would occasionally send out a cry of complaint.

Farther along they passed three gaily clad women with earthenware pitchers balanced gracefully on their heads, going to draw water. There were flashes of white teeth in dusky faces as the women smiled and waved to the occupants of the coach.

'How do they do it?' someone asked incredulously. 'Just look at that one. The pitcher's enormous!'

'And it isn't even upright. How they can balance them in a sideways position like that beats me!'

'It beats me how they can balance them at all!'

Yet to the women it was no trouble. They learned from being small children and balancing these heavy vessels on their heads was almost part of their education.

On arrival at the hotel there was the rather sad parting between Ali Baba and his group of tourists. Although typical of the kind of man who escorted parties of tourists on their various trips in and around Cairo, Ali Baba possessed something more than the mere ability to share his knowledge. He was more than a guide; many of the tourists felt that had they known him just a few more days he would have become a friend. He was a deep thinker, and yet he could joke himself and laugh at the jokes of others. To both Judy and Chris the memory of Cairo would always be the memory of Ali Baba, and they suspected this would be the case with hundreds of other tourists whose good fortune it was to meet this wonderful man.

'Remember what I said about the sun,' he twinkled as he shook hands with Judy. And then, to Chris, 'I declared that you were a lucky man, sir, and I repeat that. Take care of this delectable child!'

'That is my intention,' smiled Chris, and held out his hand. 'Goodbye, Ali Baba, I sincerely hope we shall meet again some day.'

CHAPTER NINE

WITHIN a fortnight of returning from the cruise Judy
was having her birthday party. Chris had been away in
Athens—on business, he said—for the past week, but
he had promised to be back for her birthday. The
Palmers were invited to the party, as also was George.
To Judy's disgust Chris told her to invite Corinne
Moore. This request placed Judy in a quandary. If she
refused to invite Corinne, Chris might conclude that
her refusal stemmed from jealousy. If she did invite the
girl then the evening would assuredly be ruined for
Judy because Corinne would repeat her performance
and monopolize Chris for most of the time.

'I don't care for Corinne very much,' she ventured,
hoping that might just be sufficient to make her husband drop the matter. But he frowned and said,

'She's an old friend of mine. It would be the height
of bad manners to exclude her. Besides, George is coming and they're living in the same house. It would
embarrass him to have to come without her.'

A determined light entered Judy's eyes. She forgot
everything except her original intention of attaining
equality with Chris.

'It's my party and I can invite whom I like. I'm not
inviting Corinne.'

A metallic glint in his eyes, a compression of his
mouth. He stared down at her with fine arrogance from
his superior height.

'You appear to have misunderstood me,' came his
soft words after a silence which robbed Judy of much

of her confidence. 'I said—Corinne is an old friend of mine.'

A quarrel could have ensued, had Judy persisted in her refusal, but a coldness would have remained between her and Chris and this she could not bear. In any case, she had a shrewd suspicion that, no matter how prolonged her stand, she would in the end have been forced to submit to her husband's will.

Judy saw that George and Floria sat together at the table. By the same planning she saw that Corinne was as far away from Chris as possible. In fact, with a sudden little surge of spite she put the English girl next to Vincent. If Chris noticed this last deliberate move he gave nothing away. He talked to his mother for a good deal of the time; Judy noticed that there was a seriousness about their faces and a certain gravity in their tones, although she could not catch a word of what was being said, no matter how she strained her ears.

The meal over, they strayed out in twos and threes to the verandah where Spiros served the coffee. Chris was with his mother and after they had walked along to a shadowed spot, sheltered by vines growing along a trellis and encroaching on to the roof, they both sat down. Judy frowned in puzzlement and curiosity. There was some mystery, she felt sure, especially as on one occasion as she caught the older woman's eyes she had seen an unnatural brightness there.

Judy and Corinne had not met since she and Chris had returned from the cruise and on finding a place next to Judy Corinne asked how she had enjoyed herself.

'It was most pleasant, thank you,' coldly came the reply. Judy reached for her coffee cup and raised it to her lips. Corinne smiled faintly, musing a while before she spoke again.

'It was the idea of visiting Egypt that attracted you,

159

George told me.'

Judy listened to the night sounds—the crickets and sheep bells, the distant barking of a dog and the familiar cry of a donkey on the lonely moonlit hillside. The north-west wind blew up from the sea, warmed by the heat which the water had stolen from the sun. Carried on this breeze was the exotic perfume gathered from the flowers blooming in profusion in the hillside gardens.

'I've always wanted to visit Egypt, yes.' Still quite cool was her voice, but Judy turned now, to look at her companion. 'It more than came up to my expectations,' she added with a touch of well-aimed malice, for Judy was caught by a desire to make the girl jealous, if that were at all possible. Perhaps, though, this type of woman was never jealous. Floria had hinted that had Corinne played her cards right Chris would have married her. But Corinne had not played her cards right; she had succumbed to Chris's persuasions ... and that had put an end to any chance she might have had regarding marriage. So now Corinne was probably resigned, knowing she could still make good use of that 'enormous attraction' which she had for Chris.

'I should find it a dead bore myself,' frowned Corinne. 'Tombs and ruins and museums are not in my line. I expect poor old Chris was bored, but of course he'd hide that fact. There's one thing more than any other which I adore about Chris—his manners are impeccable.'

Judy reddened with disgust. The girl had neither tact nor sensibility. She spoke in the manner of one whose intimacy with Chris was common knowledge. In view of this Judy saw no reason for holding her own thrust and she said in cutting tones,

'You did not learn from him, apparently.'

An astounded silence followed, cut through at length

by the rather strident voice of Jean Palmer, talking to Vincent, whose obese body reclined ungracefully in a low wicker armchair.

'Are you insinuating,' muttered Corinne between her teeth, 'that *my* manners are *not* impeccable?'

Judy measured her with a scathing glance.

'They're far from impeccable. In fact, you appear to have forgotten you're talking to Chris's wife.'

Another moment of silence, and then, in a voice tinged with the soft guttural threat from an animal's throat,

'Be careful, Judy. I'm all for freedom in marriage and I think it's good for husband and wife to have a change now and then. But Chris might not be of the same mind....' Corinne sent Judy a narrowed, significant glance which was designed to convey more than words but which, on the contrary, only succeeded in bringing a blank expression to Judy's face. 'Make an enemy of me, Judy, and you'll regret it for a very long while.' Corinne broke into a smile, but there was no humour on her face as she added, 'You know what I'm talking about, so there's no need for that dazed and uncomprehending look.'

'I haven't the faintest idea what you're talking about.' A husband and wife should have a change now and then.... The girl spoke in riddles.

A short laugh fell from Corinne's lips. It attracted the attention of both Jean and Keith Palmer, but for the moment neither Judy nor Corinne noticed.

'Your little escapade when Chris was away in Athens——'

'My——?' Judy gaped at her. 'What did you say?'

'Such well-feigned innocence,' sneered Corinne, all efforts at politeness dropped. 'I happened to see you and George—oh no, don't look so startled; I haven't said a word either to him or to Chris. But be careful how you treat me, or I might choose to tell Chris of this little affair going on between you and George——'

'Corinne, I must apologize for neglecting you.' Chris's deep rich voice broke in on the conversation; he smiled charmingly at Corinne and sat down close to her. But as his glance strayed to his wife's face he said sharply,

'What is it, Judy? Are you unwell?'

She swallowed the little ball of fear that had lodged in her throat. Floria and George.... Corinne must have seen them together somewhere, and it must have been dark, otherwise Corinne would not have thought it was Judy she had seen.

'No—I'm f-fine. If you'll excuse me——' And without any further explanation Judy rose and left them, going over to Floria and sitting down beside her. Yet having made this determined move Judy was at a loss as to how she should handle the situation. But there was only one course open to her, she decided after the minimum of thought. There was neither the time nor the need for diplomacy and she came straight to the point.

'I've just been talking to Corinne——'

'I saw you.' Floria's eyes were on the wide doorway leading from the patio to the sitting-room. George was standing in the aperture, talking to Madam Voulis. 'I thought you didn't like her.'

'I detest her. Floria, she's seen you and George somewere together——'

'She's——!' The colour drained from Floria's face. But she recovered somewhat almost immediately and said, 'She couldn't have. We've only met at night...' And then her voice faded as she realized what she had admitted.

'Floria ... have you been seeing George regularly?' The Greek girl nodded unhappily.

162

'Yes, Judy. After having those two days together we both knew we really loved one another—we knew before then,' she told Judy. 'But those two days really brought us together.' She stopped, her eyes filling up, and Judy said, her voice choked and husky,

'Where have you been meeting?'

'In the arbour.'

'The arbour?' frowned Judy. 'You don't mean here—in our garden?' and when Floria again nodded, 'Are you crazy? In the garden—*this* garden!—with Vincent in the house? Are you crazy?' she repeated, staring at Floria in amazement.

'He never goes to bed early, but he thought I did. Instead, I went to meet George in the garden.'

Judy shook her head, unable to take in this utter lack of care.

'George . . . couldn't he see the danger?'

'There wasn't any danger. Vincent never walks in the garden. He's too busy with the bottle. George came up each night and I met him in the arbour. There's a gap in the hedge, as you know, and he entered the garden that way. It's a great distance from the house.' She stopped and frowned. 'Did Corinne see us in the arbour?' she asked, forgetting she had just asserted that Corinne had not seen them together.

'She must have done,' returned Judy reflectively. 'That's why she concluded that it was me.'

'You?' Floria knitted her brows questioningly.

'Corinne thinks it's George and I who are having an affair.'

'She said so? She tackled you with it?' For the moment Floria was diverted from the more serious matter of her own position. 'She wouldn't do that, surely?'

'Corinne will say whatever she's a mind to say. She threatened to tell Chris of my—affair if I didn't treat her with civility.' Judy paused thoughtfully. 'How did she come to be in our garden, I wonder?'

'That's what I've been pondering. She's a great walker and often strolls about the lanes at night. And one evening I did think I'd heard someone, because it frightened me. I couldn't speak for fear, but George was so kind and—soothing. He just held me and we sat there, very quietly, but we concluded that I'd been mistaken because we didn't hear anyone wandering about either in the garden or in the lane outside.'

Judy became thoughtful again.

'I think I can see it all,' she murmured at last. 'She must have been walking along the lane and heard George's voice on the other side of the hedge. Naturally she'd be curious, and she must have entered the garden through the gap, just as George was accustomed to doing. That was what you heard. She would then stand still and quiet, listening. You say you didn't speak?' Judy stopped, waiting for a response and the Greek girl nodded. 'George spoke, though, so you said. So she would naturally conclude that he was speaking to me.' Judy looked at her sister-in-law. 'There were only two girls who could be there in George's arms— you or I. As she would instantly conclude that it couldn't be you, because your husband was in the house, she decided it was I who was having an affair with George.'

'What will she do?' asked Floria, her face still very white. 'You said she threatened to tell Chris?'

'No——' Judy shook her head. 'She said she'd tell him if I wasn't careful how I treated her. You see, I'd just been rather uncivil to her—only in retaliation for something she had said, though. However, it aroused her anger and she then went on to inform me that she knew of the "little affair" I was having with George.' It would be amusing were it not so serious from Floria's point of view, thought Judy, smiling faintly to herself. 'Can you remember what George said to you that night—when you were scared by this sound, I mean?'

'He just said "Hush, darling. Don't tremble so. I'm here, and I love you." ' Floria's colour rose as she spoke, but she seemed to feel she owed it to Judy to offer an adequate answer to her question. 'What was the outcome?' added Floria. 'You didn't tell her it was I, obviously.'

'Chris came up and interrupted us. I realized that Corinne had seen you and George together, so I wasted no time in coming to you.'

Floria looked at Judy, scared and trembling.

'You're going to tell her it wasn't you?'

Judy shook her head.

'For the present, no. I'll try to get her into conversation again and see what else I can learn. But I don't think she intends mentioning the matter to Chris——'

'Why, I wonder? She's a spiteful cat and I could rather imagine her running straight to Chris and giving you away, especially as she's so crazy about him herself. I should have thought she'd seize upon such a wonderful opportunity to blacken your name.' Floria's voice was edged with fear. 'If she does, you'll have to tell Chris the truth, in order to clear your own name, and he'll tell Vincent...' Her voice quivered away to nothing and tears started to her eyes. 'I wish I were dead,' she whispered distractedly. 'Oh, Judy, what is to become of me?'

'Don't cry, Floria,' pleaded Judy. 'And don't worry too much. I'll not give you away, I promise.'

'But you'll have to!'

'Corinne didn't seem at all inclined to put Chris in possession of the facts—no, like you, I don't know the reason, and, like you, I'm puzzled. However, for the present you're safe and so am I.' Judy looked straight at her. 'But don't take any more risks, Floria. Please promise me, for I don't want to see you in trouble.'

'I promise——' Floria burst into tears. 'I don't know h-how we can go b-back to being acquaintances, b-but we m-must.' A handkerchief was dragged from her pocket and she hastily dried her eyes, casting a swift look round to see if anyone had noticed her breakdown. 'I wanted to have an affair with George—but it isn't possible, is it?'

Judy shook her head, fingering away her own tears. 'No, Floria, it isn't possible.' It would also be fruitless, and would in time become unsatisfying, but naturally Judy saw no necessity for mentioning this.

'You can't let Corinne go on thinking an awful thing like that about you,' cried Floria as the thought registered at last. 'No, you can't! Judy, I'm—I'm in dreadful trouble, aren't I?'

'Of course you're not. I'm willing to leave things as they are, so stop worrying.'

'You're so kind. I don't know how to thank you——' Floria shook her head. 'No, I can't think of words to express my gratitude.'

'Then don't try,' returned Judy, wishing only to end this dismal conversation.

'You've saved me from——' Floria's eyes wandered to the table farther along where her husband sprawled inelegantly on a chair, his short legs stretched out in front of him. 'Who can say what you've saved me from?'

'Forget all about it,' advised Judy in soothing tones. 'It's all over and done with and we should be thankful that Corinne has got us mixed up.' At that moment George came out and joined them. Madam Voulis had gone over to join the Palmers and Floria said, speaking to George,

'Has Mother been talking about Father?'

George looked puzzled.

'Your father? No, why should she?'

'He wants to come back to her.'

Judy stared, wondering again what her father-in-law was like.

'Is she intending taking him back?'

'I think she'll let Chris advise her. They've been talking the matter over this evening; I watched them. I think Mother will have Father back.'

'Does your mother care for him?' The words came hesitantly, for Judy was disinclined to intrude into personal affairs. Yet at the same time she felt she should exhibit some degree of interest.

'She loves him. Theirs wasn't an arranged marriage. They met at the house of a mutual friend and fell in love.' Floria's voice contained a hint of anger; it was not difficult to guess that she was condemning her father for arranging her own marriage when he and her mother had chosen their own partners.

'Will he come here—if she takes him back?'

'I expect so. We all spend the whole of the summer here with Chris—always have.'

Vincent came out and sat close to Judy. His hand moved unnecessarily on to the arm of her chair, then she felt his hot fingers on her wrist. Swiftly she removed her hand, but with the persistence of his type Vincent then moved his leg so that it touched hers.

'Will you all excuse me?' Judy rose as she spoke, hoping her tones were not too unpleasant. 'I'm neglecting the Palmers. . . .'

Both Jean and Keith gave her odd glances as she joined them, and only then did Judy begin to wonder if they had heard anything Corinne said. Obviously they had, because Jean baldly asked Judy about the 'little escapade' Corinne had mentioned. There was a teasing light in Jean's eye, but to Judy's relief there was nothing else and Judy managed effectively to pass over the matter, saying it was a joke of Corinne's.

But Judy felt a surge of anger against the English girl; she also felt the strain of the past few minutes and a desire for solitude assailed her. After talking politely to the Palmers for a few minutes she went off on her own into the garden. The night-scents were heady, the air soft and still. A moon hung in the sky, but it was cut into by a wedge of the mountain which detracted from its light. She sat down under a tree and allowed her mind to dwell on Floria's plight. There seemed no future for her—just a long unhappy trek with the shadow of George in the unreachable distance and the very real figure of Vincent walking beside her.

A sudden check was put upon Judy's musings as a slim dark figure approached. Corinne. . . . She saw Judy and sat down on the bench beside her.

'What's this?—a desire for solitude?'

'What do you want?' asked Judy sharply, ignoring the sneering accents in which the question was put.

'I saw you come out and thought you might like to continue our interesting conversation. You see, just before Chris interrupted us I gained the impression that you were intending to bluff.' No comment from Judy and Corinne went on, 'It would be quite useless, because I saw the pair of you with my own eyes.'

'In the arbour?' Judy was curious to know whether or not her deductions were correct.

'In the arbour.' A small pause and then, 'Obviously you're used to meeting George in the arbour?'

Judy allowed that question to pass unanswered.

'You're very sure it was me you saw.'

'Certainly I'm sure.' Corinne's voice was slightly raised; Judy could almost see the accompanying lift of her delicately pencilled brows. 'Who else would be allowing George to make love to her? And it wasn't the first time, was it, not by any means?'

'You saw me on more than one occasion?' queried Judy. Floria had heard a sound only on one occasion—or so she said.

'I didn't see you on more than one occasion, no. But what about the night you stole away from the rest of us and went into the house with George?' Judy remained silent, for a tingling of fear assailed her. Supposing Corinne were not intending to keep quiet? Judy would be faced with a terrible decision. Either she must expose Floria, who would then be in the most dire trouble, or she herself must be in trouble with Chris. And recalling that terrifying scene when Chris had discovered she had been meeting Ronnie, Judy shivered in her shoes, all her ideas of 'man-management' rapidly disappearing.

'Did you come into the garden?' inquired Judy at last, again desirous of learning if her deductions had been correct.

'Naturally I was curious when on taking a walk along the lane I heard George's voice uttering the most amorous love phrases. There was a gap in the hedge, so I stepped through——'

'So you were intent on prying,' cut in Judy, her tones vibrant with disgust.

'I've just said it was interest, but you can call it what you like,' added Corinne with a laugh. 'Here was George, in Chris's garden, and with Chris away in Athens ...' Corinne's voice tailed off. She seemed to be chuckling inwardly now, as if the whole thing were one huge joke. 'I must admit I admire your courage, for Chris can be a nasty piece of work—but perhaps you've not met up with that side of him yet. However, as I was saying, I stepped through the hedge, and there you were, all cosily in the shadows, your head romantically nestling into his broad shoulder, and George declaring his love, with you a rapt listener, not saying one single word.' Corinne's laugh rang out again and Judy flushed as if the guilt had actually been hers and not her sister-in-law's.

'So I was right in everything,' murmured Judy to herself.

'What did you say?'

'Nothing that would interest you.' The words were curtly spoken and Corinne's sudden anger could be sensed. Judy turned her head, but the shadows hid her companion's expression. 'You—you gave me to understand you—didn't intend telling my husband....' Judy spoke with difficulty, almost unable to articulate words which pronounced her own guilt.

'I'm no spoilsport,' returned Corinne with a chuckle. 'I know you dislike me intensely, and I don't particularly like you, but as I said earlier, I consider it is good for a husband and wife to have a change.' Something indefinable in her words troubled Judy and presently she said,

'Are there ... conditions?'

'Obviously. And that's the real reason why I sought you out here, in the garden.' The flow of Corinne's tongue was smooth now ... but again that soft guttural noise could be detected. 'You will be left free to indulge in your affair with George so long as you leave me free to conduct mine with Chris.' Corinne crossed her shapely legs in the dark; the movement was neither swift nor sudden and yet Judy jumped. Her nerves must be pretty frayed, she concluded, beginning to feel quite drained by what she had been through during the past half hour or so. She knew her face was white, and her heart was heavy, because it seemed that Chris was indeed having an affair with Corinne, even though he was now married, and Judy was overwhelmed with the tragic conviction that it was all her fault. Chris was a Greek and Greek men were virile and passionate. She had known this, and yet had persisted in her endeavours to bring some affection into her relationship with Chris before agreeing to put their marriage on a normal footing. Chris had not waited—could not wait....

Tears pricked Judy's eyes. She had lost him, she concluded despairingly, and all through her own silly efforts to manage him and her striving for equality. She had stayed in the shadows too long, and now the sun had moved round to shed its warmth elsewhere. If only she had taken more notice of Ali Baba—but she had tried, she recalled. It had been shyness on her part, not any longer an insistence on getting to know Chris better, which in the end had kept them apart. And, with the inconsistency of woman, Judy experienced a surge of anger against her husband. He should have known she was shy, should have been firmer and more manly; he should have asserted himself right from the start, insisting on his rights. And then he would not have been forced to go back to Corinne.

The tears fell, tears of anger and hopelessness; and disappointment that her husband was a weakling, and not masterful as she now knew she wanted him to be. Ali Baba was right when he said she had not been honest. But what was the use wanting to be mastered when she had a husband like Chris? Judy frowned suddenly. He had been masterful on occasions, though, now she came to think of it. What about that scene over Ronnie? That had been rather too dramatic, really. She didn't want to be terrified ... no, just made to feel a little apprehensive of her husband, as she had on the one or two other occasions when he had decided to assert his authority.

Judy's frown deepened. What a contradictory character he was! Would she ever understand him? But why ask that, when she had now lost him altogether?

Her tragic reflections were interrupted by Corinne's soft and silky accents inquiring the reason for this long silence.

'The matter doesn't require thought,' Corinne added. 'Promise to be a little helpful, and in turn I shall keep silent about you and George.'

'Helpful?'

A small silence, broken only by the soft echo of laughter coming from the great drawing-room of Salaris House. The windows were wide open, for the night was warm and balmy and intoxicatingly perfumed.

'You'll not be possessive where Chris is concerned. You'll turn a blind eye when he goes off for a week-end. And you yourself could on occasions take yourself off to Cyprus. I'm sure you miss your grandfather—as he must miss you.'

Judy felt quite sick.

'You're disgusting!' she cried. 'Have you no sense of decency?'

An incredulous little laugh reminded Judy of something she had quite forgotten: she herself was supposed to be having an affair with George.

'I like that! Who are you to adopt the righteously indignant manner? You really are the limit, Judy!' exclaimed Corinne with another incredulous little laugh. 'Mind you, it does puzzle me that you can so shamelessly indulge in an affair after the strictness with which you've been brought up——' she stopped. 'Did you hear anything?' she inquired after a moment.

Judy shook her head in the darkness.

'No—did you?'

'I was probably mistaken. However, I'm going back —but remember what I've said. No possessiveness where Chris is concerned. He was mine before he was yours, always remember that. And,' added Corinne with emphasis, 'see that you treat me with respect. No icy disdain from now on. I'm just as good as you are, and you'll keep that in mind or else...' That was all. Judy stemmed the rising fury within her for, far from treating Corinne with respect, she could at this moment have turned around and soundly slapped her face.

CHAPTER TEN

On returning to the patio the two girls found it deserted except for Floria, who was still sitting in the chair, tapping one hand absently on the table in front of her.

'Is everyone inside?' Corinne glanced towards the open doorway of the drawing-room. 'All drinking,' she laughed. 'I must join them!'

'You've been crying,' observed Floria anxiously as Judy sat down on the opposite side of the table. 'What's wrong?' Her glance flickered to Corinne's quickly disappearing figure. 'Has she been upsetting you?'

Judy hesitated. How long could she allow Corinne to go on thinking she was unfaithful to Chris? The girl would snigger each time they met; she would broach the subject often, Judy felt sure ... she might even want to discuss it, as, no doubt, she would discuss her affair with Chris. Floria was waiting breathlessly for her reply and Judy's heart sank within her. She could not ask Floria to confess.

'No—it's nothing——' She broke off, giving a sigh of relief as Madam Voulis joined them, a smile on her face which Judy had never seen before. She spoke at once, to them both, as she glanced from one to the other in turn.

'Father and I are going to live together again. He has asked me to forgive him and to try again. I'm taking Chris's advice and taking him back.'

Judy did not know what to say; Floria on the other hand smiled at her mother and said she was glad.

Madam Voulis then glanced questioningly at her daughter-in-law and Judy felt she had to say something, although she fumbled for words and even when she did manage to speak she felt shy and embarrassed.

'I'm glad, Mother—if it will make you happy, that is.'

'It will make me happy. Both Michalis and I have been stubborn, but we're older now and, I hope, wiser. I don't know if Chris has told you, but we've been parted for over five years.'

Judy nodded.

'He did tell me, yes.'

A silence fell between them and eventually Madam Voulis said good night and went inside. She could be heard saying her good nights all around and a short while later her bedroom light was switched on, throwing its amber glow on to the lawn.

'Mother was generous when she said they both were stubborn,' commented Floria after a while. 'Father's very much like Chris—haughty and superior and very domineering—or at least he was. Mother's travelled around and seen how women should live, how they should be treated by their husbands. From the first she tried to—well, to mould Father, I suppose is how one might put it. But he was stubborn, insisting on adhering to the customs of the East. A husband should be like a god, was his idea, and even though, when we were small, Mother threatened to go when we were older, he still remained arrogant and domineering. Mother did not have a happy life because she couldn't be content with that sort of subjugation which Greek women normally accept. The marriage was really on the rocks from the beginning...' Her voice trailed away as a strange light entered her eyes. She looked across at Judy and as the full truth hit her she gave a little gasp. 'I see it all now! I've been puzzled by

175

Chris's attitude with you; I couldn't understand why he should be so—soft, and so obliging, allowing you all your own way—but it's as plain as can be; he doesn't intend letting his marriage go the same way——' Floria broke off and then added, 'I always thought he loved you, waiting all that time, and I'm sure of it now.' She gave a smothered little laugh. 'Just listen to *me* telling *you* that my brother loves you. You know, of course—always have done.'

Love.... Judy realized she was trembling all over. Chris loved her? And yet wasn't it feasible? Two years he had waited—over two years. And how could it be desire, she asked herself again, when he had never attempted to take her? How could she have been so blind? And to think—— Ashamedly Judy checked her thoughts, but they were insistently clamouring for attention. To think she had assumed he had gone back to Corinne, because he now no longer desired the girl he had chosen for his wife. Judy tugged at the little lace collar of her dress, which seemed to be choking her. She had suspected him of all that was bad when in reality he was wonderful. She had only a short while ago branded him a weakling, because he had not asserted his rights. He had been treading warily, she saw that now, and Judy spoke her thoughts aloud when presently she said, shades of contrition in her voice,

'He intended learning a lesson from the break-up of his parents' marriage....'

'Yes; that's obvious. Women today are fighting for equality and if men are wise they accept that women are in fact equals in all but physical strength. Only where a wife is a partner can real happiness dominate the marriage. My father wouldn't have this, but he must have promised to reform or Mother wouldn't be taking him back.' Floria paused broodingly. 'His last act of true domination was in coercing me into marriage with Vincent. Mother and he had a dreadful quarrel over that.'

Judy looked at Floria in some puzzlement.

'You were living with your mother at the time?'

Floria nodded.

'You're going to say that I needn't have married Vincent?'

'Yes, that's what I was going to say. You were with your mother and you could have remained with her.'

'Father said if I didn't obey him he would cut all of us off without a penny; he would also stop Mother's allowance.'

'I still don't understand. Surely Chris would have looked after you both?'

A long silence ensued, for the Greek girl seemed reluctant to speak. However, eventually she did, to say that, at the time, Chris possessed all his father's arrogant belief in the inferiority of women, and he agreed entirely with the system of arranged marriages. He had been a party to the coercion, but Floria firmly believed he was now sorry and that had he his time to come over again he would certainly not listen to the offer of a man Floria did not love.

Judy thought a long while about this. She herself had gained the impression that Chris was sorry for his sister in spite of his once having said, with what appeared to be heartless unconcern,

'A woman should be satisfied with her husband, no matter what he's like.' And later on he had appeared even more heartless when he had observed that Floria's husband would most likely beat her.

Chris probably felt that the damage was done and as it could not be undone Floria must endeavour to resign herself to her fate.

As the slow minutes passed and Judy continued to muse on what Floria had said she remembered a remark Chris had made to her grandfather. Chris had said he hoped Judy had been brought up to know her place as he wasn't expecting to have to deal with a rebellious wife. At that time, then, he had not intended allowing his wife much of her own way, evidently. And yet he had loved her—if Floria's deductions were correct, and Judy was now quite sure they were. Yes, he had offered because he loved her, but at that time he was still imbued with the idea of male superiority. But it would appear that his love had been so great that he was not taking the slightest risk. He wanted Judy for ever, and so he was willing to let her 'manage' him, and he was also willing to wait until she herself had decided that management was complete. Would he always be so obliging? A wry smile hovered on Judy's lips and unconsciously she shook her head from side to side....

She could not find him anywhere. Impatiently she inquired of George where he was.

'He was going off down the garden the last time I saw him,' smiled George, all unaware of what Floria would eventually tell him when an opportunity came for them to be alone. 'He's an excellent host, but he gets tired of the babble and goes off now and then for a moment of peace and quiet. Always was like that, but we understand him. Should be back directly.' George had not been looking at Judy and when, on finishing speaking, he did glance at her his eyes opened wide in consternation. 'You're as white as a sheet. Is anything wrong?'

'No—no, of course not.' But Judy's heart thumped. Chris was in the garden.... 'When did he go?' she eventually quivered.

George frowned in puzzlement.

'He's been gone about fifteen minutes. Is it important what time he went?'

Judy shook her head, mumbled an almost inaudible, 'Excuse me,' and left George standing there in the drawing-room, staring after her before turning to speak a friendly but impersonal few words to the lovely girl standing some little distance away from him.

Corinne had stopped speaking, to ask Judy if she had heard anything.... This incident occupied Judy's mind to the exclusion of all else as she stepped out on to the patio. Fifteen minutes. Yes, Chris would certainly have been in the garden when Corinne was asking that question. Had he heard anything? 'I must look for him—even i-if he h-has heard....' She must know at once. It was as if she were being drawn out to the garden. But she *must know*—immediately!

And she did, without going in search of Chris. He appeared at the end of the patio and began to cover its long length, slowly, his eyes never leaving Judy's face. Stark savagery burned in those dark eyes and his lips were drawn back almost in a snarl. He and Judy were alone on the patio, he advancing towards her and she automatically taking backward steps, vaguely aware that someone had pushed the big doors to, so that the people in the drawing-room were now quite separate from the two outside. Still Chris came towards her and Judy continued to move away, with a sort of strategic panic, towards the vine-covered trellis at the far end, while her brain worked furiously in an endeavour to find words with which to answer him when he should at last decide to break this terrifying silence. What must she do? she asked herself feverishly. She could not expose Floria ... but ... was he intending to murder her? wondered Judy, choking with fear. Fleetingly she lived again through that scene over Ronnie; she had thought she would collapse with fright, but what she had experienced then was a mere fluttering of nerves in comparison to this. If only her heart wouldn't thump so; it made her feel quite sick and for one wild moment she thought she must blurt out the truth. But she managed to check the impulse at the same time as coming to a physical halt as the backs of her legs touched the vines.

'Chris...' She just had to speak, even though she knew she could find little to add to that huskily-spoken word. 'You were in the—in the g-garden?'

He made no answer to that as he came to a halt, very close, so that he towered above her, threatening and pale with fury.

'So you're trembling, are you?' he said through gritting teeth. 'But, by God, that's nothing to what you will be when I've finished with you. Affair with George, eh——?' He broke off, unable, it seemed, to speak for the smouldering wrath in which he was totally enveloped. Judy put a shaking hand to her heart; her own lips moved, but soundlessly. 'I'll strangle you! I'll break every bone in your body! Get into the house—up to your room—at once!' He swallowed thickly as if endeavouring to free his throat from the ball of fire that was lodging there. 'Ten minutes from now you'll wish you were dead!' He meant it, too, she had no doubt of that, and Judy knew she could not continue shielding Floria. Yet the words that would save her and condemn her sister-in-law would not come. No, she couldn't expose Floria—not until she had spoken to her.

'I w-want to sp-speak to Floria,' she began, but was immediately interrupted.

'I ordered you into the house! Do you go or do I drag you there?'

But Judy was unable to take one single step. Sheer terror possessed her even as her husband was possessed by a white-hot fury. His eyes burned into her like an all-consuming flame and she wished only for some sort of merciful oblivion to descend upon her. Vaguely through the paralysing fear of her mind emerged the conclusions she had formed so short a time ago. Chris loved her and had pandered to her only as a sort of insurance for a happy life with her. He had allowed her to believe she was managing him and attaining equality. Yes, he had always known what she was about and yet he had observed it with amused indulgence. All this suggested softness and understanding ... but ... Looking at him now, with murder in his eyes, she could not believe he possessed one atom of softness—or of mercy.

'Chris,' she faltered, extending a hand towards him. 'If you will call your sister——' She broke off, feeling she must surely collapse with relief as the doors to the drawing-room were flung wide and Keith Palmer and George came rushing out, followed by everyone else.

'Chris!' It was Keith who spoke, for the others seemed completely dazed. 'Chris—it's Vincent. He's—he's...' He could not continue, but George managed to explain that Vincent had suddenly slumped in his chair, uttered just one little groan of pain, and when Keith ran to him he was dead.

'Dead?' Chris stared. 'Dead?' he repeated, unable to take it in.

'I couldn't believe it at first,' Keith was saying, but Judy went to Floria and, putting her arm around her, led her away from the chatter and consternation, and into a small sitting-room which Judy and Chris favoured when they were alone.

Floria was dry-eyed and dazed and for a long while they both sat there, each trying not to dwell on what this sudden death would mean. At last Floria's unnatural restraint broke and she sobbed uncontrollably on Judy's breast.

'I wanted him to die ... oh, Judy, I'm wicked—wicked!'

'Darling, you have no control over such things——'

'I wanted him dead!' interrupted Floria wildly. 'You're not listening, Judy. I wished him dead—I prayed for it!'

'Nothing you did could have caused this—this disaster.' Judy spoke softly and soothingly, her hand automatically stroking Floria's hair. 'These things are not in our hands,' she went on practically. 'And you mustn't blame yourself for anything—hush, Floria, don't sob like this! You mustn't feel guilty—you must not!' A slight sharpness touched Judy's voice; she experienced an unreasoning anger that Floria should be troubled by conscience. She had suffered at Vincent's hands when he was alive and now, it seemed, she was to be plagued by a guilt that was going to mar her chances of happiness later, when she and George were able to marry. 'You were never unfaithful to Vincent——'

'I was, in my mind—oh, many times!' Sobs shook Floria's body again and Judy just held her close, thinking that Vincent had been unfaithful many times too —and not merely in his mind.

Chris entered the room, accompanied by his mother —clad in a dressing-gown and followed by George. Without any hesitation George sat down on the couch and put his arm around Floria. Judy rose and, still rather fearful, she looked up at her husband. His face was a little grey, which was to be expected when someone had dropped dead in his house, but a smile touched his mouth and, reaching out, he took hold of Judy's hand and gave it a reassuring little squeeze.

It was two o'clock in the morning before Judy found herself alone with Chris. She had gone up to her room much earlier, for Chris had told both her and Floria to go to bed.

He himself had to see the doctor, who pronounced death to be caused from heart failure.

'Carried too much weight,' he had said in rather heartless tones. 'A young man like that should take more exercise. I make a practice of walking for at least an hour every day,' he went on, speaking to no one in particular. 'That's why I'm so fit at sixty-three years of age.'

Vincent had been taken to a little chapel of rest behind the harbour; George had at last gone, after having had a long talk with Chris when eventually they were alone. He had informed Chris earlier of his meetings with Floria, but later he told Chris that when a reasonably decent period of time had elapsed, he and Floria were to be married.

Chris repeated this to Judy when, having retired to his room, he realized the light was still on in hers. He tapped gently on the door and then opened it. Judy, in a pretty little frilly thing, was sitting on the bed, having just been in to Floria to see if she was all right. The girl couldn't sleep and Judy had suggested she either come in to her or go to her mother.

'I'll go to Mother,' Floria had said. 'I don't want to keep you awake all night, Judy.'

Judy did not mind in the least, but she felt that Floria would be better with her mother.

'You knew what was going on.' Chris made the statement after telling Judy about the conversation he had had with George. 'Why didn't you tell me?'

'One doesn't, Chris,' she returned simply. She knew there wouldn't be much to explain, for obviously George had left nothing unsaid, but Judy lifted her eyes, searching Chris's face, and then ventured hesitantly, 'How much did you overhear?'

'In the garden? Everything, I presume,' came the grim rejoinder. 'Although Corinne had obviously been speaking to you before you talked together in the garden.' Judy nodded and told him what Corinne had said about seeing her and George together, adding,

'She was talking about the "little escapade" as she called it, when you came up and interrupted. It's a wonder you didn't hear her.'

Chris did not seem to be taking that in, for after a preoccupied silence he said wrathfully,

'Why did you let me scare you like that?'

Her eyes opened very wide indeed.

'Scare?' she echoed, diverted. 'If that isn't an understatement I don't know what is! You had me petrified! I thought I'd have fainted, I was so terror-stricken!' Much to her disgust her husband's sole reaction to that was an amused curve of his lips. However, there was no amusement in his tones when he spoke. In fact they were both stern and censorious as he asked her why she hadn't defended herself.

'I know you were shielding Floria,' he added, 'but your position was desperate.'

So he did have the grace to admit that!

'I tried to get you to let me speak to Floria, if you remember,' she told him patiently, 'but you were in such a fury you wouldn't listen.' And, because she was now so sure of him, 'I don't know how you could believe such a thing of me! You ought to be ashamed of yourself!'

'I should——?' He stared down at her from a great height. 'Perhaps you'll tell me what the devil I was supposed to think after what I'd overheard!'

Judy thought about this and a rueful smile curved her mouth.

'I suppose it did sound damning,' she admitted. 'Yes, perhaps there's an excuse for your anger.'

'I saw red; jealousy blinded me to everything—to the obvious flaw in the whole thing, to the logic and to the trust, even.'

'Certainly you didn't trust me,' Judy was quick to agree, her eyes flashing indignantly.

'You can drop the self-righteous air,' was his cutting rejoinder. 'You didn't trust me, either.' Judy swallowed; she had forgotten he'd heard everything. Corinne had talked openly of her affair with Chris, saying Judy must turn a blind eye when he went away for week-ends. By her lack of response Judy had accepted the fact that an affair was going on.

'You'd been having an affair with Corinne,' she said in self-defence. 'So—so I did have an excuse for mistrusting you.' Watching him, Judy saw a movement at the side of his jaw; he said, meeting her gaze,

'You speak in the past tense, Judy.' And he paused a moment before he added, 'Do you believe I'm having an affair now?'

She flinched, but shook her head.

'No, I believe it's finished now.' He did not speak. She wished he would deny ever having had an affair with Corinne even while she knew he could not do so with truth. And she knew also that he would not lie to her. But as she searched his face she was satisfied. Corinne had never meant anything to him since his marriage, and she would never do so from now on. 'You,' she said at length, 'you didn't really believe that of me, Chris, did you?'

He moved close and took hold of both her hands.

'As I've said, darling, it was jealousy—and temper, of course. I was inflamed, but I should have stopped to think.' He smiled tenderly and tilted her face with a gentle hand under her chin. 'No, darling, I didn't think that of you—not deep down inside.'

Darling.... Her heart swelled as happiness flooded

over her. How could she have been so stupid as to think she had lost him?

'You called me that once before,' she murmured shyly, and Chris bent his head and kissed her, but he did not comment on her hesitantly uttered words and she went on to relate what Floria had said about her father's arrogance and his dominating attitude. 'I soon decided you'd been allowing me my own way because you had learned a lesson from the break-up of your parents' marriage.' Her words were a question and when he had explained she knew that once again her deductions had proved to be correct.

'I loved you on sight,' he then told her, drawing her close into his arms. 'But I must admit I meant to keep you in your place. However, I do possess my share of intelligence and the moment you began your little battles I remembered Mother. Then it was that I realized I could lose you, when you were older. And as I wanted you for always I began to tread warily.' He held her to him and kissed her passionately. 'I also knew I wanted you for my partner and my equal and not as a pretty little plaything.' He drew away, looked deeply into her eyes, and she saw that his own eyes held a hint of amusement. He was laughing at her again and she said,

'My little battles as you call them weren't really necessary—not after a while, were they?'

'They weren't, Judy, but it was a pleasant game and I thoroughly enjoyed it.'

She looked severely at him for a moment and then, not without a hint of puzzlement,

'Didn't you want me?' It was strange, but she did not feel at all shy—not even in the scanty attire she wore.

'Want you!' he ejaculated. 'My lovely wife—of course I wanted you!'

'Well, then...?' Judy *was* shy now, and she lowered

186

her head and then buried it in his coat. Chris laughed softly, raised her head and kissed one burning cheek, tenderly and lovingly.

'That first night, sweetheart, you were so scared and so young. I'd waited so long already—of necessity, of course—and I suddenly realized I could very easily create in you a revulsion for me, so I decided to wait a little while longer, especially as at that time there was the added complication of this Ronnie whom you thought you loved.'

'Thought?' She glanced up quickly. 'I did love him once——'

'Nonsense!' he interrupted, amused. 'Had you really loved him you'd have flatly refused to marry me. Neither I nor your grandfather could have forced you to marry me——' He broke off and a slight tremor passed through him. 'I might have seemed inflexible and overbearing, my dear, but I was afraid—terribly afraid I might lose you.'

Judy trembled then and clung to him tightly.

'I'm glad you were inflexible and overbearing—— Oh, Chris, wouldn't it have been awful if I'd married Ronnie!'

'I don't believe you would have married him. You'd have discovered your true feelings in time, discovered you didn't love him at all.'

'But I'd have lost you——' A kiss prevented her saying more, a kiss that was ardent and long. 'I'm sure now that I was beginning to like you,' she continued when he had released her and she had managed to get back her breath. 'That's why I made no protest. It must have been a subconscious thing.' She went up on tiptoe and kissed him, her eyes shining with love, and with something akin to adoration. 'Chris....'

'Darling?'

'Did you think I would fall in love with you?'

'I hoped to make you love me, dearest; that's why I was so patient and why I regarded your struggles with such tolerance.'

'You exaggerated when you said I bullied you!' Chris laughed.

'So I did; I felt like pandering to your ego. You were obviously so delighted with your progress——'

'That was horrid of you!' she protested and again he laughed. But he said with mock severity,

'Stop looking like a termagant! I threatened once to beat you, so take care.' Despite this he pressed his lips to hers in a kiss that was both reverent and passionate, both gentle and possessive. 'Did you really want me to be a weak and submissive type of man—or was Ali Baba right when he said you weren't honest?' He held her away from him, his eyes alight with humour. Judy laughed and blushed and shook her head.

'Ali Baba was right,' she admitted, but went on to say with feigned anger and indignation that Chris was downright mean to enjoy himself at her expense.

'I knew you were laughing at me,' she ended, pouting.

'I couldn't help laughing, sweetheart. It was so diverting watching you fighting for freedom when in fact you were already free.'

'But you said yourself you meant to keep me in my place,' she reminded him, 'so I must have achieved something.' It was too much altogether to confess, even to herself, that all her struggles had been unnecessary.

'All right, darling, you did,' he admitted frankly. 'You brought back the memory of Mother's struggles, and of what resulted because of Father's obstinacy.'

A small silence followed and then, because she just had to know, Judy asked if Chris had accepted a dowry from her grandfather. But instantly she wished she hadn't, for a cold metallic gleam entered his eyes and his lips compressed.

'I had no need of a dowry,' he almost snapped.

Judy's lip quivered.

'I'm sorry, Chris, but I just had to ask.'

He became gentle, much to her relief.

'I've said I married you for love—that I loved you from the first moment of setting eyes on you. I also told you once that I offered for you because I didn't want anyone else to have the opportunity of doing so.' He spoke softly, a wealth of love and tenderness in his voice, and Judy wondered why she should have jumped to the conclusion that he had offered simply because of desire.

'Your phrasing was wrong,' she murmured, unaware that she spoke aloud until Chris asked her what she meant. 'When you said you offered because you were afraid someone else would do so I thought it was just—just...' She tailed off, her blushes telling him the rest.

'Just desire for your body?' He shook his head, rather sadly. 'You're a silly, puss, Judy,' he admonished. 'Why did you jump to all those stupid conclusions?' She merely nestled close, her head on his shoulder. But after a little while she voiced a question that had been puzzling her of late.

'Corinne ... were you trying to make me jealous?'

'I was,' he owned freely. 'It was becoming so hard to wait and I'm afraid I resorted to making an endeavour to arouse your jealousy in order to help you to see the light—to make you realize you loved me and desired me just as much as I desired you.'

Judy's head remained on his shoulder, for she would not let him see her expression, and after a few moments he told her that Corinne was leaving the island very soon. Judy did not pursue this subject, having a shrewd suspicion that Chris had tackled Corinne about what he had overheard in the garden, and then had given her a piece of his mind. However, Judy did look up after a while and her expression revealed all the relief she felt at the knowledge that his ex-girl-friend was leaving Hydra. She felt sure Corinne would never return.

'My dear, dear love.' Chris spoke softly, yet with a vibrancy that thrilled and excited her, and she lifted her face for his kiss. He was infinitely tender and gentle, yet there was a possessive quality in the warmth and strength of his body, so very close to hers. She quivered under the touch of his hands, feeling their warmth through the thinness of her attire, and as the silent moments passed she became profoundly aware of his rising ardour and the heavy uneven thudding of his heart above her own. Judy could not speak ... but her response to his kiss told him all he wanted to know.

A Treasury of Harlequin Romances!

Many of the all time favorite Harlequin Romance Novels have not been available, until now, since the original printing. But on this special introductory offer, they are yours in an exquisitely bound, rich gold hardcover with royal blue imprint. Three complete unabridged novels in each volume. And the cost is so very low you'll be amazed!

Handsome, Hardcover Library Editions at Paperback Prices! ONLY $1.95 each volume.

This very special collection of classic Harlequin Romances would be a distinctive addition to your library. And imagine what a delightful gift they'd make for any Harlequin reader!

Start your collection now. See reverse of this page for **SPECIAL INTRODUCTORY OFFER!**

v